Disco Evil:
Dead Man's Stand

I0667417

Author
Rod Marsden

Publisher
Night to Dawn

Publisher Night to Dawn
www.bloodredshadows.com
ISBN: 978-0-578-02093-8

Copyright by Rod Marsden
First edition 2009

http://www.bloodredshadows.com
Printed in the United States of America

Editors: Barbara Custer and Lyn McConchie
Back cover illustration by Marge Simon
Front cover illustration by Dreamstime Images

Names, characters and incidents depicted in this book are products of the author's imagination or are used fictitiously. Any resemblance to actual events, locations, organizations, or persons, living or dead are entirely coincidental, and are not to be construed as truth or fact.

All rights reserved:
It is illegal for you to copy or distribute copies of this or any copyright written work in print or electronic form without expressed written consent from the publisher. Please do not purchase unauthorized copies. For information: Barbara Custer, c/o Night to Dawn, P. O. Box 643, Abington, PA 19001.

This book is dedicated to Ari, Not-the-Daniel, the Uni Grad who walks like an Egyptian and the All-that-Jazz girl. It is dedicated to my mother, May Marsden, who is a star nowadays brightly shinning down upon my family and friends with her love.

It is also dedicated to Star Trek fans everywhere, God bless our pointy ears, and to the Maclean Secret Compass who gallantly continue to keep parts of Scotland, Canada, the USA as well as the North Coast of New South Wales, Australia safe from the undead.

Last but not least it is dedicated to my dad, Charles Marsden, who taught me how to fish and valiantly tried, over the years, to imbue me with a kindly sense of humor.

Acknowledgements

I wish to thank Barbara Custer for her help from tossing around what the title should be to keeping the writing jogging along nicely for the reader.

I wish to thank the writers and artists of Night to Dawn magazine for their insights into the undead and especially the artists who have put time and effort into making this book look good.

I wish to thank the people of the great North Coast of New South Wales for being an inspiration for many years and, in particular, Wayne and Kim Bush of Maclean on the mighty Clarence. Then there's Shoe-Shoe, Belle and She-Hulk.

When it comes to technical advice concerning computers, Debra Perala has been a good sport.

I have been inspired by the fiction of British writers Bram Stoker, Lewis Carroll, William Morris and Captain W. E. Johns. I have always been inspired by the Marvel bullpen of the 1960s and 1970s as well as by American television shows such as *Buffy, Twilight Zone, Outer Limits* (the 1960s version), *Star Trek* (the lot), *Smallville,* and *Flash Gordon* (the 21st Century version).

Australian writers Don Boyd, Steve Carter, Antoinette Rydyr and Peter Ryall have provided advice, feedback and inspiration over the years. Also I have received good advice and encouragement for this project from Lyn McConchie of Norsewood, New Zealand.

The Secret Compass came together, in its present form, through my reading of *Born in Blood, The Lost Secrets of Freemasonry* by John J.

Robinson, UK, 1989, and *Restless Bones, the Story of Relics* by James Bentley, Great Britain, 1985. It also came together via numerous documentaries on Scotland, Ireland, England and Wales produced for and by the BBC over the past two decades. Then there is my friendship with Scottish surrealist writer, Neil K. Henderson, who lives in Knightswood, Scotland.

For insights into the Egyptian dead and how the Egyptian dead have been handled and, in some instances, mishandled over the centuries, I give a hearty salute to *The Mummy Congress, Science, Obsession, and the Everlasting Dead* by Heather Pringle, New York, 2001.

My insights into Catholicism have come from Catholic friends, news reports on television and the newspapers (Including the *Illawarra Mercury*), documentaries shown on the ABC television program, *Compass* and numerous other sources.

My insights into the American Civil War and General George Armstrong Custer have come from *Favor the Bold, Custer: The Civil War Years* by D.A Kinsley, 1967, USA (Given to me as a present by Barbara Custer some years ago), Ken Burns' superb documentary series *The Civil War* and other sources such as American monthly magazines on the subject.

The disco known as *The Blue* is fictional but based on a real Sydney disco of the 1970s that did help to destroy the promises to and the hopes of a generation. Both name and location have been changed to protect both the guilty and the innocent.

Introduction

The menace of the vampire has been with us for a very long time. Over the centuries people in various societies have developed their own methods of dealing with it. The Japanese in the 17th Century, for example, created the *Rising Sun Group* of specialist ninjas and samurai. In the West the *Secret Compass*, an offshoot of Freemasonry, came to the fore. In the USA there was the *Pinkerton Detective Agency* out of Chicago followed by the FBI and the CIA. Over time such organizations have come to share information, resources and even personnel in the continuing fight.

Rod Marsden 2009

PART I

THE BEGINNING...

Fury said to a mouse that he met in the house,
"Let us both go to law: I will prosecute you,
Come, I'll take no denial; we must have a trial:
For really this morning I've nothing to do."

Said the mouse to the cur, "Such a trial, dear sir,
With no jury or judge would be wasting our breath."

"I'll be judge, I'll be jury," said cunning old Fury:
"I'll try the whole cause and condemn you to death."

"The Mouse's Tale", Chapter Three
Alice's Adventures in Wonderland by Lewis Carroll, 1865

Prelude

Lizzy was far from new to the disco scene. At age twenty she was already a veteran. Slinky and sexy, she had a long way to go to middle age and responsibilities without number. She had a long way to go before she became her mother. Her favorite place was *The Blue* and she would go there at least once every two weeks with her friends. It was just a hole in the ground with lights and sound but the barmen were friendly, she liked the alcohol they served, and she loved to dance. It was that complicated. There wasn't much else to her and she liked to keep it that way. She felt there was little point in cluttering up one's mind with too much junk.

On her lunch break at the diner, where she flipped burgers, she would get into the latest Zen book to make it onto the shelf at the local newsagents. And there was no big deal in that. Everyone was doing it. Christianity had failed quite miserably and anyone who was anyone was looking to the East or maybe India for a solution. She might have done well to have looked at karma, especially her own, but she didn't. Being young, she figured cosmic balance had more to do with other people and their actions. She couldn't have been more wrong.

"I'm free and I'm into Zen when I dance," she once told Kassie, her best friend, over coffee.

"God help anyone who breaks your divine concentration," Kassie had replied.

"Yes. When I'm in my church and praying in my own way, I don't want to be disturbed by anyone unless, of course, the guy is super hot. Even then he'd better think twice about doing it."

"But what if...," Kassie began.

"What?" snapped Lizzy.

"Never mind," Kassie breathed. She felt it was dangerous to continually attack people, even guys at discos, even if only verbally. Someday one of them might take her all too serious and react in a physical way and, though he might well get into trouble for his actions; she would be worst for it. Kassie knew nothing about the bad points in the realm of karma Lizzy was accumulating by continually hurting those who have meant her no harm. What she did know was that Lizzy might be heading for a fall. What's more, she wasn't in a listening mood to have common sense presented to her.

There was a moment's pause while Lizzy looked sternly at her friend. In this way Lizzy was telling Kassie to back off.

"Cigarette?" offered Kassie, showing Lizzy the packet.

Lizzy shook her head. She wasn't into smoking but it didn't matter. She was part of the in-crowd at dance-spots where she could meditate away with her feet. That, for her, was what counted.

While Kassie lit up and puffed away, Lizzy examined the salt shaker on the table in front of her. It was square and a heavy grayish-brown. It reminded her of her uncle, Miles, the big, important Freemason, who was square as they come and tended to wear heavy grayish-brown suits loaded with God knows what. There was a time when she thought he was a spy for the Australian government.

What he wanted most was for her to come back to what he called the true faith. He was convinced there were dark forces she would do well to be on guard against and the best protection she could have was to be part of a good congregation. She thought he was old-fashioned, but she knew he meant well so she was never quick with her tongue or her temper. She'd even gone to Easter Mass a few times over the years to keep him and her parents happy. When it came to religion, though, no one was going to make up her mind for her, least of all her mother's overly protective brother.

Smoke drifted across the diner and Lizzy found herself remembering the time she'd gone to Cronulla near the sea and, as a lark, had paid a fortune teller to tell her fortune. Well, the crystal ball jazz was what she expected. Stuff like meeting a tall, dark stranger and becoming really good at her job being typical fare for any young woman and therefore a yawn. But when the old hag read her palm there was something in her eyes which showed an inkling of fear. She was pushed away with: "A short life. Best make plans for eternity" if that made much sense. The hag wouldn't go on. Strangely enough, Lizzy had the feeling for a moment

3

that the hag was afraid to say more. How did anyone plan for eternity anyway? All she got as a reply was a shrug of bony shoulders and the words: "Bad karma, best address the issue while you may." She asked what was meant by bad karma and two words emerged from the old woman: men and manners. What the hell did that mean? The hag didn't seem to know except to say it was written in the stars but there was still time to change. Change what? If she had been told more maybe she could have planned better but that remains doubtful.

As a cigarette butt was dashed out in a glass ashtray, Lizzy accidentally spilled the sugar bowl. She had been reaching for a napkin. The spill reminded her of the men and the boys of the disco scene and how their nights usually came out. Still, no matter how much verbal abuse she and others slammed them with they always came back. If things were in reverse, she wasn't sure she could take abuse in such a philosophical way. Then again she was a girl and far more sensitive by nature or so she told herself. In any event, she didn't care.

Anyone who got between her and her Zen state was asking for it and she was more than willing to give it to them. In her mind's eye she could even see guys lining up to offer up themselves as a kind of sacrifice to her for, say, a bad day or week she'd just had. She saw it as their contribution to making her feel better and what was it to her if they didn't get much out of it? Hey! They got to see her in a mini-skirt and she had good legs. Surely that was enough, and if it wasn't then tough. No one made them ask her dumb questions and, once they did, she was free to rip forth with whatever she liked.

Occasionally she would hear things whispered such as "She'll get hers" and "What comes around goes around" (karma) but she couldn't make anything out of any of that. It would have been good if she could have.

The afternoon rolled around and Lizzy found herself powdering her nose in the ladies' room of the place where she worked. She was powdering and thinking at the same time of what a long and difficult day she'd just had. She'd been yelled at by her boss and the customers and felt more than ever like yelling back at someone, anyone. She knew her boss liked to yell and would find any excuse to do so. Last time it was over a dropped cup that had coffee in it. The coffee spilled over a patron's foot, making him get mad at her too. Before that it had been a plate she hadn't properly washed because she had sore feet and had also been daydreaming. She felt bad and now wanted to take this feeling out on somebody, anybody.

She had plans to have a meal with friends before heading off to *The Blue*. She felt like going straight home instead. There her parents might offer a sympathetic ear. But the hole in the ground with its dance floor beckoned and she felt she really needed her Friday night out. It might also make up, in some small way, for the day she had just had.

It was going to happen at *The Blue*. Nothing and no one was going to keep Lizzy from her destiny or even, in the end, offer an explanation to her and her loved ones as to why her fate was going to be what it was going to be. Strangely enough, *in the lap of the gods* would be her last coherent thought for the night. It was almost a prayer outside Zen, outside her own internal workings. It was almost a proper reaching out but it had come far, far too late to count for much.

Despite her youth, there would be a crossing over. Despite her youth, a tally would be made of her minor misdeeds and what little good she had done and a conclusion would be reached. She would be found wanting. Despite her lack of belief in her accountability, there would indeed be an accounting.

Some nights earlier in another part of the city, a young man also had thoughts concerning *The Blue* and what went on there. He was about to emerge from his cocoon. He would be fresh born and ready for a new life when he did. He would shrug off the old and step forward into his future. It would not be a future without risk, he knew, but he would no longer be anyone's fall guy. The people who had once used him as a doormat would now be his meat.

The covering over him provided no warmth because he no longer required warmth. But it did provide a place to emerge from and that was good enough. He needed to emerge, but there was a lot to assimilate, including black deeds to be done and wrongs to be avenged. Did he really want to be involved in black deeds? Did he want to avenge wrongs, even minor ones?

There was a time when just getting ahead would have been enough. There was a lot to be said about just getting ahead. Who cares, for instance, about past slights and indignities when you're ahead? A hero gets ahead and − glory to behold - all is right with the accumulated goings on of the universe. After many trials, the hero triumphs and the crowd cheers. Then some reader somewhere applauds and wishes he was that hero toppling that evil and making the world a better place.

All up, he was never going to meet that hero and see him shine let alone be that hero. What's more, the world didn't deserve such champions and would not get one in him. Why this was so was something to contemplate at some later date. Right now all he had to do was accept it as a fact and move on. No hero, sure, but there were other ways. There was now an avenger.

With this new life he was going to be that avenger and balance out the earth if not the universe in his favor. He had the strength to do it too. He just needed the courage. He was going to be more active in combating the wicked, but he would be doing it as a dark angel rather than a creature of light. He was going to strike balances in his own favor and then tilt the scale to teach the world at large a lesson. Those that do wrong, even minor wrong, were about to be wronged; they were about to be wronged many times over. Life was going to be very different for certain individuals who thought they ruled their planet, very different indeed. And *The Blue* would never, ever be the same again.

They had created a monster and he was that monster. Now they would have to, God help them, deal with him in his fresh new guise with his fresh new abilities. He could hardly wait to have them try and fail. He could hardly wait for his first victory. He could almost taste it on his lips as a wine critic might a fine burgundy. Yes, a fine burgundy, the red of reds. He would savor it and take more and more until the vessel was empty and it was time to call for another.

Is this madness? He wondered as he was getting ready to throw aside the covering. If it was, then it had to be of the divine variety. There was a large glitter ball he was going to destroy figuratively if not literally, and before that he would destroy as many of those who had wronged him as possible. Perhaps, instead, he would leave it as a sort of tombstone to those whose vitality he would claim. If indeed he did see to its destruction then he was going to tear it apart and watch all the false sparkle drift down like snow in summer time, all untrue in its plastic and glass nature but marking an end to such representational falsehoods. *The truth will out*, he said inside his head, his hand moving the cover aside, his eyes opening to greet the night. His time for complete rebirth had come.

Chapter 1

Sydney, the Rocks, the First Friday in November, 1976

The dock rats were around but in fewer numbers than before. The smart ones had already staked their claim to the Hyde Park area and to the railroad tunnel system between Town Hall and Circular Quay. There people dumped plenty of food in quarter, even half-filled packets. Also, there were many dark, safe places to get some sleep during the day.

The Rocks area of the docks, however, had retained some nocturnal life. It had built upon certain beliefs in humans and had flourished. Strangely enough, like the rats of yore, certain comings and goings were not only of the night but also took place beneath the pavement where life could be chilly in winter and muggy in summer. There was even the mating dance, not dissimilar to the one performed by the rodent, only crueler in its promises and in too many of its outcomes.

For Western style humanity the summer of love had died, killed by a number of movements including disco, a less than amiable bowel movement. Even so, young men still went along to the underground venues of false light and loud music for the remnants of the hippy dream. They wanted to howl at the distant moon like lycanthropes or maybe at the giant ball that rotated in all such places as a cold, rotund ice goddess. It was all so similar to the North American ghost dance and the hope of turning back the world to a better time that one could choke on the tears it invariably elicited. Yet dance cannot turn back the clock or the calendar. Dance can neither bring back the buffalo to the American prairie nor can it take us to that oh, so special summer in which the best of emotions reigned. So what, in the end, is the use of it?

The young men at the disco were told that how you danced no longer mattered and were then judged on how they danced. The scotch served early in the night was of a cheap brand no matter what was on the label of the bottle it came in. It got weaker from being watered down as the night progressed. It was a rip-off from start to finish but, hey! Where else did you go to meet girls? And they were girls and you were not quite a man but, oh so anxious to become one, God help you!

Listening to the recorded music was like having two gallons of corn syrup from the States or forest honey locally produced dumped on you. The senses became blocked with all the phony sweetness. A hole to breathe through could be cut with a glass or two of scotch or bourbon but the ensuing alcoholic haze carried its own falsehoods. The liquor in the gut, in the end, held best the lies one tells one's self when things are not going well. Only one usually has the common sense to keep those lies to one's self. It was amazing what one might say while in that haze and to whom. It could be downright tragic or, if not tragic, then comical in an executioner's joke book sort of way. And who needs a laugh more than the guy about to get it in the neck?

Sure, I'm Bogart looking at some tall, luscious babe. Sure, I'm Sean Connery going after some hot dame who knows something. Sure, I'm Errol Flynn with a drink in my hands. And all in one night folks! All in one single night and without strings. All happening right here, right now, this night folks.

Here there was a nasty cycle of unrealistic promise followed by despair followed by more unrealistic promise. Only the elite got anywhere but few participants understood this. Plenty of fools thought they could make their dreams come true and their money was as good as anyone else's. Others knew from night one the odds against them were ridiculously high but gambled anyway because there was nothing else they could see themselves doing. Besides, didn't the Phantom beat the odds? Didn't Batman fly home a winner to the bat cave? Was it then so impossible to meet a nice girl you could have a good time with? Did the success stories all have to be about supermen with their Lois Lanes?

The Blue was once part of a warehouse. It was the below ground part where coal used to be stored. Since becoming *The Blue,* there had been a glittering sign on the street pointing downwards to the action. From there stairs descended into what appeared at first to be a dark pit lined with old, cheap carpet. The carpet was red and the stairs always smelled. Sometimes they reeked of vomit but more often than not of cleaning alcohol or industrial strength antiseptic. No one commented going down and once down it was hard to communicate with anyone except whoever was serving the drinks. The management liked it that way. There wasn't a cover charge. Watering the drink at the appropriate hour was enough.

Paul Priestly had taken the stairs a dozen or more times. On the last night he would truly be himself he said to that inner voice, his subconscious, he would never, ever do it again but that would not be entirely true. The truth was that if he ever did return it would be as a new, possibly improved Paul Priestly. The Taoists believe that a person cannot cross the same stream twice because, with each crossing, both the person and the stream are different. Possibly an extra leaf here and there for the stream, possibly an extra wrinkle here or there for the person. The differences might be so minor they are impossible to detect or so huge they cannot be ignored.

He was on his own. He was a small, skinny guy always alone and he wanted to change that. He had come to realize that this was not the right venue for him. Maybe it wasn't the right venue for anyone with a soul. Maybe this realization at last made him smarter than some of the other people who tried their luck there; but he was still dumb enough to turn up one last time just in case he was wrong. It was pathetic. Hope burned and the intensity of the flame meant he had to have at least one more throw of the dice he knew had to be loaded against him.

The only thing he could think of to make himself feel better about where he was and what he was doing were the bizarre murders he'd read about in the paper. They had taken place less than two blocks away and involved a jock football player who had had his right arm broken in three places before being siphoned of blood. A female tennis player had had her neck broken before being emptied the same way. Paul didn't see himself as the type this killer or killers were after, but that could change. At present, they seemed to be after people he had no reason to like and that suited him fine.

From the bottom of the stairs it was two hundred of Paul's own paces to the bar and another hundred to the nearest table. From the tables it was virtually no distance at all to the polished wood dance floor that would make or break him. Beyond the dance floor was the stand bands sometimes used. Songs were launched from this platform but generally didn't fly very high or very far. For the most part they were easily forgotten. Why they existed at all was no mystery. It wasn't just the guys on the dance floor with hope for lost causes.

Looking at the platform, Paul remembered there had been a drummer and champion weightlifter named Mike O'Dea who had disappeared after playing there. Someone had heard a lot of yelling after the last set for the night and then he was gone. The cops were still looking. Could his vanishing act have something to do with the murders? They had all happened about a month apart.

It was laughable that none of the local talent the management got in could play disco music. If they could play at all it was mostly pop or rock or heavy metal. No singer could sing without swallowing the mike and then regurgitating it before the audience. It was like watching a pelican feed its young. One night Paul wondered if someone came along the following morning and sprayed it with mouth wash or detergent or something. He thought it would otherwise stink badly and then no one would be game to do the swallowing and the regurgitating. He knew the female singers liked to treat the mike like a phallic object but he had no idea what the male singers were thinking and he didn't want to know. It was all a bit seedy, stupid and unprofessional. Still he wasn't there for the bands or the singers; maybe no one was or ever had been.

The girls that drifted in ranged in age from their late teens to their mid-twenties. Sometimes an older woman walked in but she wouldn't stay long. The same could be said for the guys. They were more likely to be loners, most of them shot out of a cannon and flying solo without a net, hoping for the best but expecting a rough landing.

On Friday nights the place was packed. Not even the two recent killings, having taken place not far away, made much of a difference. It did a good business Saturday too. Paul had mostly come on a Friday after work and this, the last night for him as he presently stood, was a Friday.

Paul sauntered up to the bar pretending to be as casual as he looked in his designer jeans and black, long-sleeved shirt. He wanted to project an image somewhere between that of a man-about-town and a Spanish matador. He wasn't sure what he ended up with but, whatever it was, it belonged to him and he wasn't sure if that was a good thing. Maybe it should have belonged to somebody else. In any event, he was happy to settle for whatever worked on at least one girl.

He had to raise his voice to get his first scotch and coke which was not cool – the raising of the voice, not the drink. He didn't consider it his fault but that didn't matter. It was a sign of weakness in a place where to show weakness could prove disastrous.

There was a smiling blonde bombshell who merely whispered in the bartender's ear to get what she wanted. Now that was cool. She gave Paul a stern who-do-you-think-you-are look and that would have been enough to have deflated his moustache if he had one. It was his first put down for the evening and nobody had said a word. No one needed to.

A flock of peacocks disguised as women nodded at the blonde and invited her over to their table. She went but not without first giving Paul a final blast with her eyes. They were arctic blue and they sent a cold shiver up and down his spine. He needed the drink he had in hand. He needed something to keep him from shaking.

There were cat-like leather girls eyeing him as if he were a pigeon about to be plucked, leaving him to wonder if that was a good thing or not. It was a shame that cat-like leather girls didn't come with sub-titles. He remembered reading about one of them turning up stark white and dead a few stations away on some Saturday night a year ago but he wasn't sure if that had anything to do with *The Blue* or his current situation. Just what was one less cat-like leather girl in the world supposed to signify anyway?

The dance floor was half empty but it wouldn't be that way for long. Paul enjoyed looking at the space between dancers as much as he did the dancers themselves. Actually, the space could be much better. It might shrink or it might expand but it wasn't going to give him grief. The same could be said for the overhead ball with its many tiny glass segments that reacted to the various lights shone on its many surfaces.

He knew some of the history of the bedazzling sphere. It dated back to at least the 1920s Jazz era when the music was better and not out to fool anyone. Or, if the music did lie back then, they were different lies for a different generation. No doubt no one could remember the untruths going back so far. No one to Paul's knowledge was around at that juncture and still around who might remember.

It seemed to him that everything grand had come to an end once the Vietnam conflict was over. There had been a precious moment when young people were out to create a shiny new future based on pretty dreams and exotic whimsy. What eventuated was not little diamonds for all, or even paste masquerading as diamond, but plain ordinary glass on a ball, with strobe lights occasionally hitting it at just the right angle to make miniature rainbows that looked lovely, but meant nothing. But what were you supposed to think, what were you supposed to do to build a better world when you were drunk and there was emptiness around you and just the ball for company? Maybe you were best off not thinking. Maybe you just became a vegetable. He was nowhere near being in that state, not with the first drink, but he could easily get there.

It was seven-thirty and already there were clusters of tank top girls in their mini-skirts and white leggings talking furiously at each other in secret little smoke-filled corners like so many hornets around secret little smoke filled nests. No doubt they were planning their next collective move against mankind. God knows they had the ammunition. Some were seated at smoke-filled tables in perpetual shadow while others showed a preference for standing behind pillars made wispy by what they exhaled, or near walls but close enough to the dance floor to see what was going on.

Paul had planned on making three moves before going home. They would either be bold or skittish. Chances stood they weren't likely to work because he'd never had a success and wouldn't know one if it came up and shook his hand and introduced itself.

Time to face facts, he told himself. *You can't win here, but you can get drunk watching other people fail if that's any consolation.*

It seemed that, in the early hours of any night, all that the eager guys did was fail. Part of him wished them good luck but part of him wished they'd just go away and take all the bad vibes with them. He also wanted to see the offending girls punished in some way.

Two scotch and cokes in him and Paul was ready to make that first move. It was half past eight and he was feeling a little better about the whole thing. The scotch was working. They couldn't hurt him as much as they could have even half an hour ago. He felt a comforting dullness ease over him heralding a blissful semi-not-caring. Three more drinks and he'd be floating and no use to anyone, not even himself. It was thus that he had to act before those three drinks eventuated or forfeit the night. And he had forfeited too many nights already.

He was about to go forth when someone did the going forth in his stead. A woman – not a silly girl around his age but a woman – was making her way to him. He was taken aback. Some time ago it would have been a dream come true. Now he didn't know what it was and suspicion that it could only be something bad was taking hold. Girls, certainly, didn't do this sort of thing. Why then was this woman doing it and what could it mean?

Immediately he found himself taken with her as if he didn't have much choice in the matter. Once her hazel eyes had locked onto his, he was gone. Even before she opened her strawberry lips and said, "Shall we dance?" he belonged to her. At the time, however, he still had the concept of free will swimming around in his head but it was becoming more and more illusory.

If he had a real choice, Paul would have been torn between what he felt must be true about his current situation and what he hoped was true. He was afraid of a set-up. *Women like her don't have anything to do with guys like me*, he tried to tell himself, *unless she plans on making some sort of example, unless she has something awful in mind for me*. He also found himself afraid it wasn't a set-up at all but his one big chance to get somewhere. If he blew it he might as well go to the tallest building he could find, climb to the top floor and jump off. It was thus that the second, more tantalizing fear won over the first. Thus, with one of his fears in the lead plus her own mesmerizing influence, she took him onto the dance floor.

To say she walked onto the polished timber would have been wrong. She drifted. Paul was amazed and, at the same time, surprised no one else noticed. But maybe everyone else was used to her or could think of her weird talent for moving, but without the usual propulsion, as too much drink on their part. Also, the air was cold, almost frozen around her and it was high summer. How could that be?

He noticed that, in absolute contrast to her dress, her skin was pale in a condensed-milk-out-of-a-tube sort of way. There was a touch of yellow in the white but not a hard yellow. She looked European but he couldn't figure out from where and something within him, possibly an ancestral memory, told him not to ask. What's more, what told him not to ask wanted him to bolt for the stairs and not look back. This, of course, he could not do and probably wouldn't have even if he was in full charge of his own faculties. Ultimately, she was too good to be true and he knew it but what he knew didn't make one iota of difference.

He danced to the overly sweet sounds of the band Sherbet as it was being played over the disco system. For once he didn't feel foolish doing so. He was beginning not to feel at all. Her eyes were more and more a prison holding him. Her silken black hair touched his hand, sending a thrill up his spin. She kept him on the floor for a couple of songs then took him to a darkened pillar where things went strange. Daddy Cool's Eagle Rock replaced Sherbet. Daddy Cool in more ways than one was superseded by a cold embrace where the woman's icy hands roamed everywhere.

"What?" he began, unsure of what was happening.

"Shhh!" she admonished. Her fangs then sank deep into his flesh.

He tottered for quite some time against the concrete, unsure of his role in events unfolding. Wasn't this, or something similar, what he had been wanting for ages? Of course he had always imagined himself the instigator but did that really matter?

Briefly he wondered about his flagging strength. Where was it going? He was beginning to feel like an orange that had been left out in the sun too long. His lips trembled as they shriveled. Still, her smile assured him everything was all right; nothing was amiss.

No one watched them leave. No one cared that he was going early or that the woman he was with was virtually carrying him up the stairs. The fresh air of the street revitalized him and he struggled all too briefly to get away. She held on so tightly she bruised his arm. What's more, it didn't take any effort on her part to do so and he knew it. Her fangs plunged once more and, moments later, he tasted something sour on his tongue that could only have come from her. The night was crowding in. What's more, it was the night of forever — or was it?

Chapter 2

A Time without Place and a Place without Time

Lightning bolts lit up the sky and there was the harsh sound of thunder. The sky was in various shades of red as if it had been bruised, even horribly beaten by the lightning. Only the moans coming from the ground drew Paul away from this spectacle. When he did look down, what he saw was even more disturbing.

There were heads on pikes. They were left-over from a great battle. The question now was: had they fallen in their ranks or had there been a grand sweep of the surrounding villages after the dust had settled? A wolf sniffed at one of the heads and moved on. It stopped at another to pee. They were female, these heads.

A wind got up blowing gravel everywhere until the red sky was dark with grey debris. Then the clouds of filth parted and the moon in its yellow fullness shone down on the carnage below with its muted, non-judgmental light.

There was an appropriate frigidity to the barren landscape. Some war had obviously ended and of the victors only Paul could be seen. But what had he won? Where were the other victors? Surely he could not have slaughtered so many all by himself. There were at least a thousand heads on spiky poles gathered around his position and none of their bodies were lying about. The heads were in neat clusters. Some dripped blood while others were past that sort of thing and turning blue.

"Forgive me!" cried a blond head with long flowing hair. He suspected the woman it had once belonged to had been tall, elegant and arrogant. Of course, now with fortune having gone so badly against her, she was anything but tall or elegant and even her arrogance was gone.

It was then Paul realized he had a shovel in his hands and there was no one with a complete body in shouting distance to say what he could or could not do with it. There was no one to stop him from smashing the talking head.

Then another head cried out: "Save me!" It was followed by a chorus of heads wanting the same thing. Their eyes followed him. It was a novel idea what they wanted but how do you save someone who is minus things like hands, arms, stomach, legs, and feet?

He moved on past the grim clusters without so much as a single word to them. Every once in a while his own eyes rested upon a particular face but he didn't feel much like either hurting them more than they'd been hurt or, for that matter, rescuing them from a condition of fate they'd probably brought on themselves. He threw away the shovel.

The land was red but darker than the sky. There were patches of gray. It was without vegetation. Not a single tree stood. Yet in the distance there was something. It looked like more than just another collection of rotting skulls. Whatever it was it moved and he was attracted to the movement. The general stillness was making him uneasy.

He went down into a deep valley where there was a pool of brackish blood and up onto a gray knoll where the object that had caught his attention from afar was made clear under the rosy glow of nearby torch light.

It was a crucified woman decked out in white flowing robes. Like so many paintings that got it wrong, the nails went through her palms and into the wood. Miraculously, she was not able to free herself no matter how she struggled and her weight would not simply remove her from the overhead beam as gravity dictated. The nails in her feet completed the picture.

Her crimson hair rippled in the warm breeze as did what passed for her clothing. She had small breasts and long legs like a dancer. There was a spear up against her cross; she was trying to point to it with one of her fingers. Her breathing was labored. It was obvious she'd been crying.

"Please help me!" she begged. "Please!"

She wanted him to run her through with the spear to end her agony. He was tempted but could not comply. She was there for a reason and until he knew the reason he wasn't about to act. For all he knew she was a criminal who was getting what she deserved.

"Ask whoever put you there," he told her and left.

He wondered why he hadn't done something for her the way he would have when he was a kid. Then it came to him that he liked her helplessness and her misery. Such helplessness and misery reflected his own or at least it reflected the way he had felt at various discos. For once someone else – *one of them!* – would not be saved. For once someone else who could have been brought back into the bosom of humanity wasn't going to be and he was glad.

Paul came to a blacksmith's establishment where a big man was pounding down on the skull of a rather stressed-out woman in her late teens. He was using a hammer made for making horseshoes. She was pleading for him to stop but with a pleasant smile he continued. Then he saw his audience and stopped to wipe sweat from his brow.

"Top o' the morning to you," he said to Paul as if he had been busy making footwear for horses and could do with a bit of a rest.

"What are you doing?" asked Paul.

"Don't fret son," said the man. "She's secure. She won't be getting away until I get my chance at civilizing her."

"Civilizing?" cried Paul. "But you're hurting her!"

The man examined the straps and the head vice in which his victim was trapped with a critical eye. All was secure. He'd even broken a few of her fingers to make escape even more difficult.

Sweat mixed with blood and bits of bone and hair glided down the poor female's face like a sewer pipe that had been broken by inclement weather. Her eyes were bloodshot. Her mouth and tongue moved continuously as if they alone had a chance to somehow remove themselves from what was happening to the rest of her. Paul didn't know if she was a blond, a brunette or a redhead because of all the matted hair as well as flowing blood. There might have been dandruff but, if so, it was hidden among the flakes of cranium that shouldn't have been visible.

"Just an experiment," said the man cheerfully. "I am trying to locate the on switch she should have here somewhere. I haven't had any luck so far but you never know."

"The on switch?"

"Yes. The poor dear grew up with her good manners switch in the off position."

As if to prove a point, the man swung mightily and a cracking sound echoed well into the distance. The woman's skull was now split in two and the man was able to peel the bone way from the brain. Paul witnessed the sight of clear goo of some kind leaving her head as the pulsating grey mass he took to be her brain throbbed riotously like a caged tiger released into the wild.

"I don't think this will do any good," said Paul.

"Probably not," the man admitted, "but it is fun trying. And you never know. Do be a good fellow and hand me the probe on the bench. It's the thin, metallic object."

Paul did as he was told and then left the man to his task. There seemed little reason in staying though he did not blame the man for what he was doing. *Who knows?* Paul thought. *Maybe, just maybe, the man will find that on switch then glue her back together and send her on her way.*

He suspected there was a gravesite somewhere of the man's previous attempts at finding other such on switches but it really didn't matter. Paul's heart was growing cold and, where once he might have had sympathy for the laid-low creature being tormented, much of that had gone the way of the disco. With the loss of his hippy innocence much of his sense of mercy had also fled and there seemed little chance of getting either back.

In a dead field not far away, Paul came across a group of cheer-leaders bouncing up and down before a group of football players playing football. Unbeknown to both the cheerleaders and players, a group of men in khaki and full battle gear were sneaking up on them. Then an order was given and bullets from semi-automatics began to pummel the cheerleaders and the footballers. Paul couldn't help but watch the cheer-leaders dance their dance like the skeletons on the sides of medieval Italian and French homes. But these weren't the victims of plague doing such a familiar tango but victims of their own barbaric nature come back to see them transformed into moving pulp. It was a grim business but only for the jockettes and the jocks. Paul found it quite entertaining.

"We can keep them rising and falling with our ammo but a short while," said an army officer coming up beside Paul for a talk. "Still, it is a sight, isn't it?"

"Yes," Paul agreed. He'd never seen such a wonderful ballet. *If the cheerleader and the football player didn't want peace and love and all that hippy jive then why not make them cannon fodder? No war for them to be decent cannon fodder in, you say? Well, why not blast them to hell and back anyway? If cheerleaders preferred footballers to regular Joes and therefore the world of violence over the world of peace then why shouldn't they get a proper belly full of it? At least this lot was not going to mate and beget warriors for the next war.*

Paul looked down and saw how his heart was now encased in a block of ice. If he touched it, he would have burnt his fingers on the almost complete lack of warmth. *Time to move on,* he thought.

He came to a cliff and some caves. A short, buxom female with short black hair stood outside a particularly deep cavern. She had a winning smile despite the sack cloth and ashes she was wearing. She was carrying a baseball bat which she offered to him and which he took off her hands. He then clubbed her with it. With a soft crunch, she went down and he watched her fall. Instinctively, he knew what he was supposed to do next and got on with it. Grabbing two hands worth of short black hair, he dragged her into the cave and propped her up against the far wall. *Primitive*, he thought, *ugly and primitive. Take away love and understanding and the rest of the hippy shit and what have you got but primitive and ugly? I can learn to live with primitive. I can learn to care for it and nurture it if that's what they really want. I can even be a good sport about such ugliness.*

He waved the bat around once then twice more before throwing it away. The woman groaned. A lump was forming where she was bleeding. He looked at his hands and saw blood mixed with strands of her hair making two delicate patterns like a double *Blue Poles* painting only in red.

"Who are you?" he asked his semi-conscious victim. "And what do you want from me? What do any of you want?"

From high school onwards Paul wanted to get along better with the opposite sex. From high school onwards they'd given him nothing but grief, no matter how nice he was. Now it was all changing. Now he was no longer as nice. But what did it all mean? Why here? Why now?

It had begun to rain, light at first but then heavier. The water was crimson and smelled of iron and trace elements of calcium and fish oil. It gave him a thirst but a thirst for what? Was it coffee? No. Was it tea? No. It was raspberry colored and the seat of most if not all life.

He left the cave and became drenched. Up so close the rain had a bitter sweetness he recognized from the time he'd fallen off his push bike at age ten and had skinned his knee. He'd tasted his own blood back then and it was just as salty and just as strong, like the building blocks of the universe melting down and being served up as a kind of heavenly soup.

It pushed him down, the rain. It threatened to drown him but he knew that wouldn't be. It was a baptism, that's what it was, a baptism summoning him to a new existence.

He was wet, sticky, and gummy and, oh so marvelous. He wanted to laugh and might well do so in a future so fresh, so savage he could hardly wait to experience it.

Chapter 3

Redfern, Sydney, the Second Monday in November, 1976

The crimson downpour stopped and Paul, after some moments spent gathering his thoughts, opened his eyes. He pulled away the sheet covering him. He was alive, that much was certain. What was also certain was the fact that he was not alone.

A round faced woman with a knot for a nose, generous lips and deep green eyes was staring down at him. Her curly yellow hair was almost touching his face. She looked like someone who had just stepped out of some 1930's film only she was in color.

"I'm Sapphire," she told him. "He's coming around," she told the others.

"Yes," said a tall man in black.

It was then Paul came to realize there were five of them and they were all in black. He looked at his own clothing and saw that he too was wearing black. There was a small pouch he suspected was filled with earth on a chain around his neck.

"Who are you?" he asked. "And who dressed me?"

"I did," said a woman with long black hair and a lethal looking chin. He recalled her from the disco. Hadn't they been intimate in some sort of way?

"And my clothes?" he asked.

"Disposed of," she told him. "Don't worry; your wallet is safe in your new pants – the ones you are wearing. Nothing of real importance has been taken from you. Nothing you were using or going to make much use of. The pouch around your neck is important though. If you wish to remain vigorous, if you wish to remain healthy you must wear it when you sleep. It is a good idea to have it on you always. We all have such pouches around our necks and, you may have guessed, under our clothes where they can't be seen by those who do not need to know they are there."

Paul felt around for his wallet and found it. *At least on that score you're telling the truth*, he thought. He looked and, finding the pouch, felt the earth move inside it, that part was also true. *But where am I and what's going on? Why dress me like this? Why destroy my old clothes?*

He tried to sit up and was greeted by a rush of dizziness. He lay back on what he now saw was an antique divan. It was flush red and felt silken. He thought it might be from the set of some old silent movie, the sort shot in and around Sydney in the 1920s. The other furnishings also reflected earlier times from the grated fireplace with its burning log that could have come from a railway Inn, circa 1910, to the paintings that looked as if they'd been done by the Dutch masters of the 17th Century, to the oil lamps that harkened back to the days when New South Wales was a mere colony of the British Empire.

The room was small and as far from disco in quality as one was likely to get. Everything smacked of an age when people actually cared about what they made and how they made it. There was even a musty bee's wax perfume coming from some lit candles, reminiscent of when elegance wasn't simply part of an ad campaign but a real presence, a product of true craftsmanship.

"Where am I?" asked Paul, slowly shaking his head to clear his thoughts. If he shook too hard, he had the feeling it might fall off. The sheet that had previously covered him fell from the divan to the carpet.

"Elizabeth Street," said a large, middle aged man with glasses. "You were transported here because Lilith thought it suitable for your awakening."

"My awakening?"

"Yes. You're one of us now."

"One of you?!"

Paul had the sinking feeling he'd been drugged, manhandled and was now expected to join a religious cult. This was the last thing he wanted. Religion hadn't done much for him in the past and he had a feeling it was going to do a lot less for him in the future if, indeed, he had a future.

"We're not a religious body," said the heavy jawed woman. "Far from it, in fact. I am Lilith and you are one of us and, being one of us, you are without any religious concerns whatsoever."

"Who are you? What have I joined?"

"First you drink," said a small, mouse-like woman with brown hair and glasses who came up to him with a silver goblet filled with something thick and tangy on the nose. It was then that Paul became aware of his raging thirst. But should he drink? Perhaps it contained poison or a drug to make him docile and pliable. He wanted to refuse but his growing need for something liquid and Lilith's gaze got the better of him. He drank and found himself smacking his lips for more. His dizziness had now gone.

"What was that stuff?" he asked.

"We'll tell you in good time," said Lilith. "Right now you need to put your skepticism to one side and open up your mind to new possibilities."

"We have something extraordinary to tell you," said the large man.

"Your new condition may be hard to accept at first," said the tall man.

"Very hard," agreed Lilith.

It was then the world went mad. There was a ghastly scream in another room followed by an explosion and the stench of burning flesh. Someone from the outside kicked the door in and several men in gray suits advanced in Paul's direction. They had silver crosses raised and wooden knives at the ready.

"I knew that small woman I saw feeding would lead us to the rest," said one of the intruders.

"We've got them at last," cried another, menace in his eyes.

"Trapped!" cried Lilith, raising her hand to her face to ward off the horrible glare coming from the crosses.

The others in black hissed at those in gray though why Paul joined in he didn't know. It was reflex to something teasing at the edges of his brain and causing him one hell of a migraine.

"Secret Compass," snarled the tall man before being stabbed through the heart. What followed was a lot of smoke and some flame resulting in a pile of ash and a burn mark on the carpet.

"What the hell?" Paul cried, getting to his feet.

A man in gray came at him with sharpened wood and it was all he could do to get out of the maniac's way. Then he tripped on a Persian rug and the window loomed large. Before he knew it, he was through the breaking glass and heading for the concrete pathway four stories below. *I'm dead*, he thought on the way down. *No more migraine, no more anything.*

As he met the pavement he was right at least on one score but not the important one.

Broken bones were new to Paul. One thing about them is they hurt a lot. Being dragged and then carried off increased the pain and also interfered with his concentration. Objects blurred. The person carrying him blurred. Was it Lilith? He thought he caught a glimpse of long black hair. If so how could she propel him so swiftly, so effortlessly through the night? Yes, eyes clearing a little, it was her. Who could mistake that chin?

She spoke to him but her words were indistinct, chopped up by the bleating of his snapped ankle, broken ribs and shattered arm. Was she taking him to a hospital? No, not a hospital. Before long he found himself in a dark cellar. There was the smell of brandy. It was so strong it was almost overpowering. As he slipped into unconsciousness, he heard her say among words he couldn't quite grasp: "Safe from the Compass."

For two days and two nights he battled his injuries. Lilith helped with mugs of warm blood and comforting words. She also told him of his new role in the world and how he was neither truly alive nor truly dead. She also told him about the vampire hunters and how best to avoid their company. Belief came when he began to rapidly recover. On the third night since his fall, he was completely healed and ready for his first hunt.

Why she had rescued him and not one of the others from the attack of the Secret Compass he wasn't to know straight away. The black thoughts, dreams, illusions, delusions of his death and of his becoming undead made him wary of her. He felt shame but also justification in all that had obviously gone on in his head during his transition. Revenge was likely to become the cornerstone of his new way of being and it wouldn't be revenge against men. She must have known this even before she made him or at least had some inkling. Yet she had made him and then, when he was badly injured, looked after him.

"Why?" he asked her at last, knowing that asking might not be a good idea. "Why have you done so much for me?"

"I see promise in you," she said. "Your deep anger piqued my interest from the start. You have purpose. You want to get the bimbos, ya? I have purpose, too. I want to get the bozos, what you call the jocks. So, you hunt bimbos, I hunt jocks. We are alike, nein?"

"When you put it that way, I guess you are right. But what if I refuse?"

Lilith laughed the husky laugh of the undead. Then, wiping away a tear, she said: "You don't eat, you starve, your choice. I think you will eat and I think you will feast on bimbos."

"Yes," smiled Paul. "On bimbos I will feast."

"Now go! Hunt! Come back when you have sated your thirst and tell me all about it. Ah! But I see a great beginning in you and in this night."

Outside the cellar, existence was rich in shadows and in possibilities. Paul didn't have much time to get what he needed before the sun intruded upon his fun. And so, after an hour of wandering around and before returning to Lilith, he pounced upon a blond who had just left a pub. He didn't say anything to her. He just took her life. This somehow seemed wrong. Was he justified in giving her oblivion? Was she truly a bimbo? Next time he would make sure. Looks were not enough. He had to be certain his next meal and the one after that were truly what he thought they were before he acted upon his own needs.

Chapter 4

The Rocks, Sydney, the Second Friday in November, 1976

Paul glided down the stairs and into *The Blue*. He didn't bother with the bar; instead he fast-paced past some John Travolta wannabes that shivered in his wake. He moved on past a bunch of leather jackets that pulled their namesakes closer to their bodies as if experien-cing a sudden chill. He was ignoring them because he was after the Barbie-doll wannabes and, in particular, the jockettes/bimbos sub-branch. He felt for a pulse on his wrist and found none. *Perfect,* he thought. *I have no heart. And here, somewhere, is a beauty deserving of a man with no heart.*

It seemed that eons had gone by since he'd passed this way but not much had really changed. The recorded music was still syrupy enough to give you diabetes of the brain and the live stuff was enough to make your ears bleed. It was a great combination to make the patrons drink more and, in too many instances, hope more. Even the liquor was dishonest. It started out at full strength but, as the night progressed, got more and more watery.

It was said the place was owned by gangsters out to launder dirty money and, at the same time, make easy money. It was also said to be a fire trap with not enough ventilation for the amount of traffic going through every Friday and Saturday night. This last one made sense. Why worry about people's safety when the main aim was to get rich?

Paul's sense of smell had greatly improved. Not only could he pick out the various perfumes and colognes; he could distinguish between the various types of perspiration among the dancers and onlookers. Through sweat he could read fear, anxiety, desire – even love and hate. What's more, he felt immune to all that he could read, and in the reading he felt his power base of knowledge of the human experience grow. It was strange but people who had, in appearance, all the confidence in the world smelled as if they had no confidence at all. And those who did radiate true confidence were, for the most part, dumb as bricks, too stupid to be any other way. They acted as if they had nothing to lose because they were too dim to realize what they could, in fact, lose. *And God tends to look after such fools*, Paul told himself, *but not tonight. I am here tonight.*

Since there was such a fine selection of jockettes around, it took Paul some time to pick his target. She had to be beautiful and preening in her beauty. She also had to speak to him in the fashion that would seal her doom. She had to be a firm part of what was to happen so that, in essence, his chance to feed would also come down to her doing and not his alone.

That night he put the question: "Would you like to dance with me?" to three girls who turned out to be proper women. One danced with him. The others politely refused. A fourth, however, was more typical of the place and what he had come to expect.

The arrogant one was tall and slender and in colors befitting a bird of paradise. In his head he heard the word Lizzy over and over again. Was that her name? Regardless, she was a natural on the dance floor and didn't seem to have time for anyone, especially him. The "Fuck off!" which had emanated from her lips meant he would make contact with her a second time only he would be using the newly acquired powers of his mind and eye to bring her down. It would be justice as well as revenge.

No one knew, as he escorted the female he now thought of as Lizzy out of *The Blue*, that he'd thrown an invisible blanket over her thought processes and that he was controlling the very muscles in her arms and legs. Inside, she fought to regain control and, despite it being an unfair contest, he relished the minor battle he was having with her. As they climbed the stairs, he decided he didn't want her to go with him without at least having a clue as to how she had contributed to her own downfall.

"Your choice," he told her. "Of all the girls here I could have chosen, you were the one who chose me. I thought you might like to know."

A block away from the disco, he propped her up against a wall. She tried to speak but couldn't. Then, as his fangs entered her flesh, he released his control allowing her to cry out in pain. Taking from her in such a way filled him with both nourishment and delight. And once the practical side of this slaying was over, she was nothing but an empty husk, no good to anyone. He let her go.

The night had been wondrous. It had started off slow with too many good women around but had come right in the end. Now it was time to go back to his lodgings for a full day's rest, satisfied that if he'd taken a life it had at least been the right one. He had been as fair and as reasonable about the whole business as he could have been. Surely fate could not ask for more.

Chapter 5

Mitchell Library, Sydney, the Second Saturday in November, 1976

Miles Henry's hands were shaking. His niece, Elizabeth, better known as Lizzy, had been delivered to him. Despite the choice of having someone else do the deed, he was the one who wielded the stake and hammer. He was the one who made sure she would never rise again though it was almost a certainty she wasn't about to anyway. He was the one who had been covered in her blood. The body was then burnt and the ashes interred at the local cemetery. What remained of her body was safe and sound in a wall. What remained of her soul and whether it was safe and sound he could only guess at. Theology was best left to those with a stronger understanding of the subject. All he and his sister, Patricia knew for sure was that she had been lost to them and was not coming back.

He remembered buying Lizzy ice-cream when she was a little girl. He remembered helping her with her math homework when she reached the age of thirteen and really needed his help. He also remembered their endless arguments over the Church and the safety he knew it would provide for her. Now all that remained of any consequence were the memories and they were not enough.

"Silly child," he told his assistant, Frank Long, but not with any real conviction. "I tried to reach her but I couldn't. Now she's gone." He tried to pick up his coffee cup but couldn't. The tremors, caused by what he had to do so early in the morning and in the lowest level of the complex he was in, persisted.

Miles could say he was used to death in its many forms, but not this untimely death that touched his own family. Even so, he was too tough for tears. He was bulldog tough like his father and brothers and knew it. But the shakes were something else. It had been over an hour since he'd showered and got the remains of Lizzy off him. So why wouldn't the shakes go away?

"What was she like?" ventured Long, his skeletal face pressed against his own coffee mug.

"Flighty, young," said Miles. "She had the world in the palm of her hand and she didn't know what to do with it."

"Typical teen."

"A few years older than a teen but, yes. She was typical. Dancing was her passion. She wanted to make it her life."

"Next thing to do is hunt down her killer. Any clues?"

"Apart from being a vampire you mean?"

"Yes."

"There's a strong possibility he is young and not terribly clever. He just dumped her without any attempt at hiding the body. Also, someone new to this as he is probably has a mentor. Possibly one of the vampires we cornered the other night, possibly one of the ones that got away."

"Yes, there were two of them, a female and a younger male. The male could be the one we're after and the female could be mentoring him. It makes sense."

"But where are they hiding?"

"Not far away I'll wager but not forever. If I were them I'd be getting out in a hurry."

"Let's just hope, whoever the female is, she's not that smart."

Miles rose from his chair, shook his head sadly and left the little kitchenette he was in for the nearby elevator. Long followed him. As they got in, Miles reflected upon the age of the machine. As he pressed the button for the surface, he wondered what the designers and builders of the 1920s were thinking when they had designed and built it. No doubt they wanted it to last and, if that was their prime concern, then they had won out over more modern designers and builders whose work could no longer be appreciated. The journey upward didn't take long. Soon they were back in the world of ordinary people with ordinary outlooks and ordinary problems.

"Don't worry," Long said as he opened the elevator cage to let them out. "We'll get them."

"No matter how long it takes," stated Miles firmly.

"No matter how long it takes," Long agreed.

They adjusted their minds to face the public. The library foyer was empty but Macquarie Street was teeming with people, almost all oblivious to the menace that lurked at night. *If only they knew*, thought Miles, adjusting his tie out of habit, *But there's no point in them knowing, no point at all.*

The sun would set in another eight hours but the city would not sleep. It was the weekend and her people loved to play after dark almost as much as their unwelcome visitors from the grave. He'd already organized a search of basements in the local area where Lizzy's corpse had been found and had arranged for patrols to be on hand once the streetlights came on and until the streetlights went out. Apart from making sure he was in one of the patrols, there was little more he could do and he knew it. He had never felt so helpless and didn't like the feeling one bit.

"I'm a man of action," he told Long as they parted. "Put the word out that if anything breaks, I want to be there. Got it?"

"Will do."

Miles' sister Patricia was with her husband, Tom, at a coffee shop in Surry Hills. They had their only surviving daughter, Anne, with them. Miles said he would meet them there in half an hour and he aimed to keep his promise. Looking at his watch, he realized he had twenty minutes to make the meeting. He would have to hurry.

He knew he would have to tell them about vampires and about how their daughter, Lizzy, had really died. The police he sometimes worked with had told them a hit and run driver was responsible. He could let them believe that, but they deserved the truth. He had to get special permission from his section head so that he could tell them. It was going to be tough. It was going to be the hardest thing he'd ever done and he was an agent with a good record for bringing down the undead. Still, this was so personal and also so wrong. Why couldn't he have saved his own niece?

His sister had wondered how he could work in a library without getting bored. Now she would know. Now she would be brought into the circle of people who weren't Secret Compass operatives but knew about the Secret Compass. He wouldn't tell them in the coffee shop, rather in their car on the way to their place at Menai, but he would tell them.

A few nights later, on a visit to Rookwood Cemetery, which was in New South Wales but quite a distance from where Lizzy was cremated, Helen Kiln, one of the Secret Compass psychics, thought she saw the ghost of Miles' niece. It was blue like the others and was wandering about asking other ghosts questions as if it were lost. The dead without bodies and who weren't going anywhere fast were, for some reason, mostly blue. Helen tried to go up to it but it wandered off as if it would have nothing to do with the living. Maybe it was still having a tough time acknowledging its own death.

Other ghosts were happy to speak to her about the Lizzy look-alike but none of them could say where she'd come from or how she got there. One of the spirits thought Helen might be a wingless angel testing them for the great beyond. The others knew better. Concerning Lizzy, the consensus was that if she didn't own up to her sins and communicate better with her fellow spirits, she was going to be alone a very long time. For some reason, the Lizzy look-alike saw Helen as a real ghost and the ghosts, herself included, as actual living beings. It was some time since the psychic had come across such a case but she knew that such a view did not bode well for the spirit involved.

There was a Zen Buddhist monk who spoke English and had been dead for half a century. He was trying to get through to the pseudo Lizzy but only having minimal success. This Lizzy would dance around him expressing her interest in meditation that way. When he suggested there might be other, equally valid ways to meditate, she would rush off in confusion claiming he couldn't be a real monk with that attitude.

Helen asked the monk why he was among those yet to depart. He told her he saw the others as his flock just as some of the Christian spirit-priests did. His job, as he saw it, was to get them all away to a better, healthier place. He had had only a handful of successes but he was far from discouraged. He didn't have immediate, high hopes for the ghost girl Helen was interested in but he was determined to do his best for her as he was determined to do what he could for the rest of the spirit people around him.

If this was indeed Lizzy, it was not looking good for her. It was a known fact that the longer a soul took to accept their new plane of existence the harder it was to depart. The best time to go was within minutes of death. At Rookwood some souls had been there since the arrival of their remains from what is now Central Station. Some were still discussing the virtues of buying a plot for so-called eternal rest only to be uprooted fifty or forty or even ten years later and shipped elsewhere because your being there was getting in the way of somebody else's progress. Some knew ghost people who, for whatever reason, couldn't have their bodies shipped and were still drifting around where the cemetery at Central Station had been. It was enough to incense the dead into playing what tricks they could upon the living.

Helen had learned from experience not to trust spirits that tended to carry on about their rights and about being unceremoniously uprooted and shipped off to the middle of nowhere when they had, or their wives or husbands or who ever had paid good money to have them be where they were expected to be forever. Some of the dead took the "forever" bit, when it comes to graves, very seriously. They would even lie to get this point across. It was a case of, if you lie to me about my eternal rest, then by Jupiter I'll tell you such falsehoods your head will spin. It never occurred to such spirits that Helen didn't have the power to reverse what had happened to their coffins or ashes or whatever more than a century ago or, if she had the power, what she could do with the trains and the platforms that were now at Central.

Helen left Rookwood, had coffee at a nearby restaurant and took the train back to the city. As she travelled, she became aware that some of the ghosts had chosen to go with her at least as far as Central.

The following morning at her desk underneath the Mitchell library and two elevator stops below where Miles had his desk, she made a phone call. She hung up though before the other party could answer. *What is the point of letting an uncle still in shock know that I might have seen his niece?* Helen asked herself. *Would letting him know she probably hasn't gone from our plane but has remained, in spirit form, do him any good? No. Would he even understand what is happening to her if indeed it was her? No. Would he hate me for this useless gobbledygook of an interruption to his grief? Probably. Would he ever trust me again for useful information? Who can say?*

Helen made a note of what she thought she knew and passed it on to her superior. If her superior wanted to pass the information on to Miles, she would do so; otherwise the matter was settled. One of the major dictates of practicing medicine is first to do no harm. Right now she felt like a doctor who might do a lot of harm if she were to open her mouth and let the wrong words out. She thought Miles was a little gruff, but she liked him anyway. They had worked together on a couple of cases and no doubt would do so again. They even had a good rapport. The last thing she wanted was to mess that up for nothing. Sometimes it was best to let the dead rest as best they could, especially when there was nothing much else you could do for the moment to set things right. Getting Lizzy's killer, of course, would help. *You're growing up, Helen*, she told herself. *You're doing just fine. Now let's see what we can do about getting that God damned murderer!*

One night later, she went back to Rookwood and, though the spirit monk was still there, the Lizzy look-alike had moved on. She hadn't ascended, or so the monk told her, just drifted off to another place where spirits congregate. Helen tried Central Station and then the wall that housed Lizzy's ashes but she wasn't at either locale. She had been hoping that, with a little coaxing, she might get Lizzy – if it was Lizzy – to give her a description of her killer she could then take to Miles.

Chapter 6

The Rocks, Sydney, the Second Friday in November, 1976

Paul returned to *The Blue* not to show remorse for Lizzy or to feed but to gloat. He wondered if his first disco victim, that obnoxious dancer, had truly been missed by her friends. He hoped she had been and that taking her out had made an impact on the place.

It was then, to his disappointment, that he found she either hadn't been missed or people simply weren't willing to talk. Some of the guys told him that dumb blondes were plentiful and that it didn't do to fixate on any particular one. "Plenty out there, man," said a fellow with greasy hair and a greasy looking coat. One of the cat-girls said that, now she was gone, there was more room on the dance floor for the super cool people. Others didn't like him asking questions and told him as much.

"Not cool to hassle people about the dead, man," a bouncer in a leather jacket told Paul.

The disc jockey put on "Ben," a Michael Jackson song, and half the cat-girls and some tank-toppers got onto the floor to dance to it.

"Just cool it, man," said another bouncer who also had a leather jacket. "We don't want trouble."

Paul looked at the tank top fraternity that was still seated around their tables. They were a little twittery like brightly colored parrots who knew something was wrong but didn't quite know what. They could scatter at any moment and that was fine with him. One he noticed was from his old neighborhood. Her name was Betty Sail. She wore her lovely red hair in pig tails this evening as if she were back in high school. *What shall I do about her?* He wondered. He wanted to do something.

He hadn't spoken to Betty since high school and counted it a blessing. Destroying her would be a pleasure. It would mean a better life for her father who would then only have one noisy, irritating female, not worth the expensive shoes she walked in, to contend with. Destroying her might even be considered by some a public service.

If I decide to feast upon Betty, Paul reasoned, *I won't have to put the question to her.* He couldn't remember a single day in high school when she wasn't being rude to somebody. She had a mouth the size of South Australia but not as dry and, too often from her mouth, dripped the most horrible venom. She was and, no doubt had remained, the type of nasty girl he knew should end up in some garbage heap on a garbage dump for everyone's benefit. The question was whether this was a good time to do anything about her.

Paul was about to make a move against Betty when he sensed someone who could be a lot of trouble. It was someone non-vampiric who could read minds or at least touch them in a way that made him wary. Her name was Helen and she had come into *The Blue* hoping to get a clue to who had murdered Lizzy and why. She wasn't a fully fledged field agent but she wanted so much to catch the killer to help out some friend of hers that she had gone out of her way to discover what she could. She worked for the PSI division of some organization. He could read that much before she shut him off from her thoughts. She was a psychic and he had to get away before she knew too much about him. He didn't think she was from the police but she might be from the Secret Compass. The Secret Compass was likely to have a PSI division.

He glimpsed Helen, the psychic. She was a medium built brown-haired woman dressed in a lightweight power suit as if she'd just come from the office. She was probably on her own time. She probably didn't have back-up but Paul didn't want to take that chance. As a psychic she might be able to call for help with her mind and thus put him into a difficult situation. The glimpse he had taken of her plus what little he knew about people with her talent was enough for him to realize the possible danger she presented. He could not bolt for the exit without giving himself away but he did move briskly. When she went to look at him he was sure all she could see was the back of his head. Then there was the smoke from the smokers making it even more difficult for her to get a handle on his features when he turned to take the stairs. He felt like a spy in some British spy thriller or television series. He wasn't James Bond or The Saint. If anything he was the enemy spy making his getaway.

Paul had stayed only an hour at *The Blue* before leaving. Apart from his oh, so brief encounter with Helen, it wouldn't have done to remain longer or to have picked up another one there so soon, even someone like Betty. Already he could sense people, aside from Helen, asking questions about him. Questions like who he was and what he was really up to. Even if the regular police got involved, it would be bad. Then there were the disco bouncers to consider. They hadn't done anything physical so far but they were suspicious of him. With his strength he could take them out easily but in doing so he would give himself away to others who were better equipped to bring him down. Besides, there were plenty of other discos around where no one would suspect his motives, plenty of places to get takeaway where the risk was lighter. He would meet up with Betty Sail some other night and then have her. What's more, in two hours, Lilith would meet him at the Opera House. She had told him so. She had also told him she had business with "blue bloods" there and he had no reason to disbelieve her.

It was a nice night to be out and so Paul wandered for a while. His wandering took him to the entrance to *Stacks* in Hunter Street not far from Wynyard Station. Outside the swinging glass doors were two bouncers on guard collecting an entrance fee of ten dollars but he didn't have to bother with them. A young woman was but a few feet away leaning against a shop wall, bawling her eyes out. Obviously someone inside the disco had upset her. One of the bouncers seemed to want to say something to her, but he couldn't leave his post.

"She's be fine, mate," said the second bouncer to the concerned one.

Less than a month before he met Lilith, Paul remembered getting off the train drunk from a night at *The Blue* and walking past one of the churches in his neighborhood. Two hundred yards later, the alcohol and his dismay at being alone got to him and he picked up a rock. He headed back to the church to smash a window but changed his mind. He knew the colored glass windows were all donations from either widowers or widows with little metal inscriptions below the glass to their departed spouse. Remembering this fact, he couldn't smash one no matter how mad he was at the Church and himself for not having a girlfriend. He could not smash someone's gravestone or something very much like it. He put the rock down but cursed the place anyway before heading home. When he sobered up, he was glad he didn't throw the rock for a second reason. No way did he want to get into trouble with the law.

Thus, understanding how heavy drinking can make one belligerent, Paul felt bad about putting the question to this particular girl, but he did it anyway. He got the result he needed to put his extended teeth to good use. Then he used mesmerism to have her walk contentedly away with him, down the street to her death. It wasn't his proudest moment but sustenance was required and she was there to provide it. Maybe under other circumstance, she would still have failed the test.

When he met up with Lilith, he told her about his latest conquest. He was surprised to discover she was only slightly annoyed. She was more upset when he told her about his return to *The Blue*.

"Careful," she told him. "Remember the companions I have recently lost? One was careless and now they are gone forever. You could have been among them, nein? I could have been among them. We could still be among them if you do not tread carefully."

Chapter 7

Redfern, Sydney, the Second Saturday in November, 1976

It was time to prepare for the future. Thus Paul was intently observing Lilith, trying to learn all he could from her.

Word had reached them from vampires unliving in the Cross that the Secret Compass Freemasons were up to something and, whatever they had planned, was not good for those of their kind still inhabiting the city. Even those in the Cross were in danger. Paul and Lilith had strong recollections about how they had been chased out of one nearby apartment and almost destroyed. Soon they would have to leave the city.

The transformation from man to flying rodent was essential to being a member of the undead. Paul tried to get it right but it wasn't easy. It had to be the hardest thing he had ever attempted to do. First, as explained by Lilith, there was the absolute knowing that it was indeed possible. Here she could help. It took her no more than a minute to demonstrate that woman into bat was not only workable but, for certain entities, a somewhat mundane exercise. Even so, it was difficult for Paul to not only translate seeing into believing, but also translate it in his mind into something he could actually do. Over the decades she'd been undead, Lilith had become an expert and it took some effort, on her part, to think back to when she was a beginner so that she could bring him along.

"Done well, it is elegant and graceful," she told him. "It is high art, ya? Yet even done in a very ordinary, tiresome way it can be useful."

For his twentieth try, Paul was able to make the change in a rather clumsy but functional manner, giving Lilith some hope for his survival. He did manage to fly out of their apartment window with her, ready to take on the city with all its hidden terrors. His first great feat was avoiding smacking his head into the brickwork of the building across the street. After that he slowed down and tried to glide, using his newly formed wings to do so.

You're doing fine, a voice came from inside his head. It was Lilith. *I'm speaking to you through my thoughts. I am able to do this when we are both in this form. Clever, nein?*

Marvelous, said Paul in his head wondering if she picked it up. *You can hear all thoughts?*

Only the ones you want to broadcast.

Good.

Did the bat form really make a difference? Paul had had some success touching living minds, especially if they had psychic potential. He had tried touching Lilith's mind, when she was in human form, without getting anywhere. He was beginning to wonder, bat form or not, whether he might be able to read a fellow vampire's mind anywhere, and in any form it might be in, with a lot of practice and determination.

On his maiden flight, they flew toward Centennial Park where they met up with a flight of living bats out for their evening feed. When some veered off toward Hyde Park, the vampires followed them.

Camouflage, nein? thought Lilith.

Yes, thought Paul. *But it won't fool anyone for long. We're much bigger than the fruit eaters.*

Even so, a half a minute, or even a few seconds might make a world of difference.

Paul wanted to laugh but he no longer had the equipment to do so. Still he could laugh on the inside if nowhere else. Once he'd worked out the rudiments so that he wouldn't fall to his second death, there was a joy to flying, the sort of joy he'd never known before. It was good being out and seeing and hearing much of what he'd known for years but with new eyes and ears.

Down below, humans could be marked out by their ethereal glows amongst the distant buildings and streets. There were lots of oranges and reds in the healthy men and women and yellows, even greens in the not so healthy. Also, deep blues glowed around the town hall building at Town Hall and around Central Station at Central. Paul wondered what that was all about. Surely they couldn't be human but the shapes were human. What were they? Was he mistaken or had he seen an image of Lizzy, his first disco victim among those at Central?

Unbeknown to Paul, because he was so new at it, he broadcasted his thoughts about the blue entities to Lilith. She picked them up with some amusement.

They're specters of the dead, she beamed back. *Old cemeteries may disappear, be built upon and replaced to fulfill the new needs of a new generation, but the spirits may remain to wander the old grounds, especially at night, wondering what has happened to their gravestones if not their very lives. Others, who are simply confused and frightened, might join them just to be somewhere and with someone.*

Why?

I used to ask that question. I asked it in Budapest. I asked it in London and Manchester. I have asked it of humans and of vampires. I have even asked it of the specters and, yes, you can communicate with them. Some are lost and afraid. Others are determined to do something but can't remember what. There are those who wish to remain a part of their family, their town, their city though their time for such connections was up long ago. Some will lie to you. Others will tell the truth. All should be elsewhere but many are locked into their place of so-called eternal rest though not always this time period.

Are they dangerous?

They are dangerous only if you allow the corrupt among them to lead you astray. They don't have bodies so they rely on the foolish or the corrupt among the humans and our kind for their present and future accomplishments.

Are there vampires among them?

Nein. We are trapped on this mortal plane in a very different fashion. Do they envy us? Some would like to hunt the way we do. Some hunger greatly for even a few seconds of warmth among the living which make them desperate and capable of trying anything, even the dislodgement of a living soul from its body, to get what they want. But dislodging one soul from a body so that you can take its place is no easy feat.

Straight blue for the dead, thought Paul. *And cemeteries where I thought none existed.*

Cities are much like living creatures. They change, they evolve, or they die. Even a city as young as Sydney has been built upon and rebuilt upon many times.

And life and death go on.

Hunter and hunted, yes. And, while we are here, we are an un-living part of it all.

Paul and Lilith landed in the park across the road from Central to sate their hunger. Lilith swiftly changed form. Paul took his time but eventually got there.

A short distance away from the destitute there was a couple on a lone park bench. For all appearances, they were jock and jockette. Paul asked the jockette, who was wearing a watch, for the time, expecting and receiving a savage rebuff.

"Get lost, creep," she told him.

"How rude you are," he said.

It was thus finding her wanting as a human that he was happy to feed. Lilith, believing that only a true jock could be with a jockette, didn't bother addressing her meal before digging in.

After supper, they transformed into bats, this time Paul making a smoother and quicker transition, and so headed back to Redfern. Both were full, sleepy and had a need to rest. Paul wondered if seeing what might have been Lizzy as a specter would keep him awake. It did no such thing.

Chapter 8

George Street, between Central and the Town Hall, Sydney, Third Monday in November, 1976

Fred Mills, a Secret Compass operative, was nursing a scotch in a pub when he noticed a conversation turning nasty. It was a conversation between a twerp, a jock and a cheerleader type girl. Fred thought the poor twerp was in real trouble, but he was wrong.

"Nobody insults Polly like that!" the jock was bellowing over his beer. He seemed to be a man who was used to making a lot of noise and getting his own way. His girlfriend didn't seem to be much better. Certainly she looked miffed and quite happy with the idea of her hunk defending her.

"Fine," said the twerp. "How would she like to be insulted? I could draw up a list. I must warn you, though, it could be rather lengthy. Mind you, it would be a fun exercise and I'm all for fun. The question is whether she could read it or not. There, I must confess, I do have my doubts but someone could always read it for her, I suppose."

"That's it!" snarled the jock, turning red in the face. "I don't give a damn if you are half my size. On your feet! Now! Let's take it outside."

The twerp got to his feet all right, no question about that, but then he did something extraordinary. He lifted the jock by the throat and hurled him across the room to bounce onto an old cigarette machine. After that there was the smell of blood in the air even a human could detect and it made the twerp twitchy. Fred imagined there was some moral imperative that meant the twerp wouldn't taste it, but the signs of vampirism were definitely there. This twerp was a member of the undead and most likely the one Miles, his boss, was after.

Slowly putting down his drink so as not to arouse suspicion, Fred reached into his coat pocket for his crucifix and vial of holy water. The twerp turned, however, in time to see the move for the coat. Before Fred could bring his weapons to the fore, the vampire had snapped the neck of the shocked jockette and was already halfway out the door.

"Better luck next time," Fred was told by the killer as he made his getaway.

On the broken cigarette machine the jock moaned. He looked pitiful but no one had any pity for him. He'd been a bully. Even Fred, who'd been a half-back in his younger days, could see that by the way all, save his girlfriend, regarded him. He'd no doubt terrified anyone who wasn't a jock who came into the establishment. It was a good thing he'd got his comeuppance.

The bar staff was well aware that potentially paying customers had, over the years, gone elsewhere because of him and that was hardly fair. Now someone had either gotten him back for past ills or for possible future trouble and that was fine with them. Whatever the case, the bar staff was glad to lose an old machine just to see the tyrant brought low. No one liked to pour drinks for the creep. No one wanted to hear his talk about past glory on the football field. Now maybe they could opt for a better class of customer. Even jocks and jockettes that were friendly to everyone would be preferable. The dead jockette was a worry but not their fault. They would have thought more of her demise if she hadn't had such a detestable companion.

"Maybe now we can pull in that University crowd," said one of the barmen as he phoned for the police.

"Yes," agreed a barmaid. "Happy days."

"Help!" groaned the jock. "Back broken!"

"We can only hope," said one of the barmen.

"Happy days," repeated the barmaid.

Fred didn't have time to care about a jock and a jockette no one would miss. He wouldn't even stay for the police. The chase was on and, before the bar staff could register his disappearance, he was lumbering forth into the gloom after a creature that obviously despised jocks and no doubt thrived on all manner of darkness. He wondered, as he moved, how Miles' niece, Lizzy, had fitted into this being's destructive urges or if she had at all.

Fred's means of attack were out now and ready but his quarry was nowhere to be seen. He heard the flap of wings but it was no good.

He couldn't work out the direction. With nothing else to go on, he called to Long on the walkie-talkie he kept in the glove compartment of his old Morris he'd parked a short distance away.

"Fred here," he said. "Spotted black pigeon but he got away. Pigeon in the George Street area either heading toward Town Hall or Central Station, over. Close net. I am heading for town hall building. Meet me there but make sure Central's also covered. Inform Miles. He'll want to know."

"Will do," Long replied, "over and out."

As quick as he could, Long reached Miles with the information and then the others. If this was the vampire who had killed Lizzy, his old friend would want to be involved in its demise. He realized, however, as he made his way toward the town hall, that this might not be possible. He might have to settle for knowing the fiend had been destroyed. Still, he would do what he could to get some justice for Miles, for Lizzy, and her parents.

Later that night, there was a report from two Secret Compass members that there had been vampire activity at Hyde Park involving the loss of life of a late night jogger. Soon after the kill, a woman with long black hair had been seen changing into a bat and flying off in the direction of Centennial Park. Around the same time, near Wynyard Station, a street bum minus all the blood in his veins had been found in a gutter by two other Secret Compass operatives.

Before Fred Mills could get back to Macquarie Street to give a detailed description of the vampire he reckoned was Lizzy's murderer, he was attacked and had his throat ripped out. It occurred outside a second-hand bookshop near the Woolworth's building at Town Hall. There was blood splatter to prove it. His body was found the next morning lying up against the wall of a bank on George Street, very white and very dead.

Chapter 9

Pitt Street near Central, Sydney, Third Tuesday in November, 1976

Lilith had told Paul he was better off hunting on his own until she was able to get them safe passage on a ship or a plane out of Australia. He didn't know if this was true or not but felt he couldn't at this stage go against her wishes. Even so, things were heating up for him and it seemed as if there were enemies at every turn.

As he was about to put a question to a young woman coming out of a wine bar, he noticed movement in a nearby alley. The woman fled and then he felt his arms being grabbed by men he'd taken to be simple, of no interest to him, pedestrians.

Paul knocked down what turned out to be two burly Secret Compass men. In the process he burnt his hand on a crucifix dangling from a chain. If he'd been slower, more contemplative, they would have had him. From an upper story window in a nearby building, someone threw a net that reeked of garlic, barely missing him. A wooden bolt fired from a crossbow sliced into his jacket, grazing the skin of his left arm but, fortunately, doing no other damage.

Paul ran. They chased him into a dead end street. Only the open back door of a Chinese restaurant offered a way out and he took it. A waiter had opened it to take out the garbage. Paul pushed past him, speeding into the restaurant's kitchen. There he knocked plates, pans and woks onto the floor to hinder the progress of his attackers. Bursting out onto the dining area, he grabbed a young waitress, dragging her out the front door into the night. He then hit her hard on the top of the head to keep her quiet, hailed down a cab and, inside the vehicle, feasted on his captive. Her blood tasted of almonds, rice and pine nuts. She was delicious. She was also most probably the second truly innocent person he'd murdered. The name tag on her waitress outfit read: "Lotus". He didn't kill the cabbie but, via mesmerism, arranged for the fellow to dump the body miles from the scene of what he definitely considered was a crime.

Paul got out of the cab not far from Redfern and walked the rest of the way to the place he shared with Lilith. He felt satisfied with what he'd taken from the Chinese-Australian but sad by the fact that he had been reduced to taking it from someone whose guilt had not been, even in terms of clothing, established.

Before morning, Long was driving around Newtown, chasing down a possible vampire bat sighting, when he came upon the latest corpse. He drove a stake through its heart. He felt it an unnecessary act, but he had been told to take no chances. He informed Miles and then the Rising Sun Group of what he had done and why. Both Long and Miles had wanted to strengthen ties with the Asian vampire hunters. This seemed like a good way of doing it. The corpse was Chinese Australian and so he knew the Rising Sun people would be interested. He just didn't know how interested.

Chapter 10

The Rocks, Sydney, Third Thursday in November, 1976

Paul was visiting *The Blue* for what he believed would be the last time and he was only doing so because he was starving. The Secret Compass had chased him out of all the other discos. He was hoping they wouldn't chase him out of this one. Here, where his dark journey had begun, he hoped would be a place where those after him would not be expecting him to go back to so soon.

At the bar the bar staff eyed him darkly. Some time ago they'd seen him order one drink, sit on it for an hour, and then leave with a girl. The girl was later reported dead, killed by some fiend. Then he came in a bit later to find out who had actually cared about the girl. Was this fellow, in some way, responsible for her death, or was he a nut with some other, less harmful agenda? The bar staff thought it most likely Paul knew something the police ought to know but a barman served him anyway. It was his job and there was no proof the creep they suspected was guilty of any real crime. None of them were cops and they weren't paid to mind other people's business unless upper management said so. Even then, it was more likely to be the bouncers who would be called upon to do the rough stuff.

"Scotch on the rocks," said Paul, handing over dead women's money to pay for it. When he was alive, he wouldn't have ordered such a pain-deadener without something sweet like coke to go with it. Now it didn't matter. He wasn't going to gulp it down because he couldn't and no one could make him do it, either. His stomach no longer handled alcohol. If he wanted to get drunk, he had to partake of a drunk. Still, he felt nursing a drink made him look normal to at least some people. He needed to look normal as he sized up his next victim. Hungry though he was, he had better not rush things or he would get into more trouble.

The music seemed extra loud this night as if attempting to quell the fear on the air even a young vampire could sense. Half the people were not aware of the growing sense of anxiety around them. They were happily getting drunk. The other half knew, to varying degrees, something was up but only those working at *The Blue* had any real idea of what that something might be.

There is a system of mental scales and balances women, even girls becoming women, use to judge the men who approach them. As an unliving creature, Paul could burn through all of that with his mind and just have the female walk out with him. It wasn't his way, however, for he always wanted his victims to be victimizers in their own right. They had to be of the so-called gentler sex since there were already vampires such as Lilith out after the male offenders. It would be best if some kind of balance could be struck, some kind of equilibrium maintained.

Paul had thought about siring someone. Lilith had told him how he could do so. Again, it would be a female. She would have to be someone he could bring into the cause and would do her part in eradicating jocks as he was doing with jockettes. When he wasn't so harassed by Secret Compass operatives, he would seek out the right woman. Surely there were such women out there in need of an undead existence and the chance for revenge upon their persecutors. In the meantime, he would continue to hunt, feed, and escape destruction. As with every other being walking the earth, he needed to thrive as well as survive, but survival had to come first.

It had come to his attention that the Secret Compass had no idea he was working, in his own way, for the betterment of humankind. If they did, maybe they would ease up a little. Even he wondered how much good he could do just taking out a jockette here and there. Some night, he would find a way to take out a lot of jockettes all at once and pass on the secret to Lilith so she could do the same with the jocks. Then maybe he would really do some good in the world and the hippy promise of a world of love and joy might be fulfilled.

A song from Sherbet came on over the speakers and, half way through it, he saw his prey. He'd seen her in the place before, back when he was fully human. There was no point in putting the question to her since he had already done so a month ago and had been told to "fuck off." Should he put it to her again just to show good form? No. It was dangerous to tarry.

Paul knew he was about to be sworn at again when he nailed her with his gaze. His eyes met hers and she was, in an instant, transported into that world where his word was all she could care about. Since he was still new at it, the trick took concentration. It didn't last long, this form of hypnosis, especially when engineered by someone who had only done it a few times, but the connection he had established between himself and his intended victim would last long enough for him to get her to a place where he could make a quick snack out of her.

She was a voluptuous blond. Her shoulders were broad like those of a swimmer. Bits and pieces of her past were beginning to flow from her into his brain. All it did was make him want her blood more. He could see the earlier contempt she had for the earlier, less assertive version of his person. Also how she regarded this latest version with less contempt. She didn't admire him and never would but somehow he had become less contemptible. *How is this possible?* He wondered. But hunger gnawed at his insides. He had to take her away as quickly as possible.

Her name was Ann Rivers. It appeared to anyone looking in their direction that she went with him freely but she was under his mental control. On the stoop of a nearby building society edifice, they sat. She imagined herself drowning where in reality it was her life draining away. Somehow the ebb and flow was getting mixed up in her head. It didn't matter though for when she died, her mixed up thoughts stopped. Paul was flush with her energy, her strength.

As he left her, and was about to change to bat, the feeling he could take on anybody was in him. The next instant, he found he had to prove it.

Out of a nearby two-story window whizzed what might have been a miniature buzz-saw, only smaller and made out of some kind of hard wood. He ducked in time to have it miss his face. It smashed against brick. Two more took its place and, though he was able to escape permanent harm, one managed to scrape his left cheek causing it to bleed. To avoid more such missiles, he threw himself into the shadows and then behind some garbage bins.

It would be too ironic, thought Paul, *to die the second and final time outside a society building.* He'd been a teller before he'd died and had regretted not being able to pick up his last pay packet. Unfortunately, dead men don't have pay packets owing to them. They don't have bank accounts worth squat from their previous existence. His parents and his sisters had what they cheerfully called his personal effects. That was fine with him. He was officially still missing, not dead but he wasn't planning a return any time soon.

More missiles came Paul's way. These were stainless steel so they glinted in the semi-darkness. They also had sharp oak edges especially made for his kind. One skated across the top of the bin he was hiding behind, hitting him in the shoulder. The thing bit deep. He couldn't help but cry out. Then it dawned on him that his attacker wasn't advancing. Others who were part of this would-be vampire slayer's team were doing so. What's more, he was being pinned down and denied the sky.

Why are they after me? What do they think I've done? He tried to pull the sharp object out of his shoulder. It wouldn't budge. It wasn't just in the flesh; it was buried in the bone. However it was going to come out, it would be bad and quite painful. He was dripping life essence down the front of his shirt onto the pavement.

Is this the end? Paul wondered as two men in black with swords appeared in front of him. The swords were made from a polished timber. Apart from not being metallic, they were shaped in the Samurai tradition. There was also a woman in black with a spear. She was emerging from a doorway. Another fellow in black with a battle axe was getting out of a car parked across the street. *Who are these people?*

He prepared to defend himself.

Paul dodged the swords coming for him but not the spear thrust. It dug deep causing him to grunt. It was painful. The withdrawal was worse. It missed his heart by barely an inch, which was fortunate, but what was not so fortunate was the way it opened up the hole in his shoulder, letting out more of his blood. He was feeling sick and dizzy. Then, when it stopped throbbing, he was numb and spots, connected to one another via grey, wispy veins, appeared before his eyes. *This really is it,* Paul thought.

He grabbed the spear and broke it in two, using half of it to fend off the swordsmen. This bought him two seconds, the time it took for them to turn his new weapon into kindling. Someone said something in an Asian language. Then, as the world around him became blurry, he felt someone push him into a nearby doorway he'd thought had been, a moment ago, closed. What followed was more Asian talk coupled with the sounds of combat. An oriental face was clipped by a high kick and another oriental face was rearranged by a powerful fist. It was a woman doing the fighting for him but why would she want to do that? Was she a vampire? Was it Lilith? When his vision cleared, he would know.

With surprising speed, one of the swordsmen came crashing through a window near where Paul lay, still feeling more than halfway out of things. The second swordsman followed the first looking very much, as he sailed across the room, as if he'd ever-so-recently been beaten about the head. Then Paul's vision did clear and Lilith appeared. If she'd been human, she would have been all sweaty from her exertions. As things stood, she was alert and anxious to get Paul as far away from where they were as possible.

It took some effort but she managed to wrench the star knife out of his shoulder and toss it to the floor. She cleaned and dressed the wound with napkins she took from nearby tables.

"There," she said, finishing up. "Can you walk?"

Paul stumbled to his feet. He looked down at the stunned swordsmen. He wondered if they needed killing.

"No time to bother with them," said Lilith, half-dragging him out the main room and finally to the street beyond. It was a bookstore. There were people in the book buying area, but they kept their distance as did the people on the footpath. The blood seeping through the dressing and the desperate look on Paul's stark white face kept them at bay.

"Have you eaten?" asked Lilith.

"Yes," said Paul almost hissing the word out.

"Good. Can you change form?"

"Don't know."

"Try."

While Paul concentrated, Lilith removed her left shoe and threw it at the roof of a nearby building, knocking a man with a bow to the pavement below. She did the same with her right shoe with similar results.

"Hurry!" cried Lilith. "There'll be reinforcements."

With his wound numbing his arm plus his lack of experience, it took just about every iota of his will to even get the process started. Then he found that burst of energy desperate people sometimes come up with to complete it. Thus Paul was able to fly away. Lilith made the transformation and followed. Moments before three new adversaries with swords came forth to challenge them, they were airborne and gathering height.

They zigzagged across the city twice to shake off any pursuers before swooping into their Redfern refuge. Paul moved slowly, even drunkenly because of the injury which appeared as a long cut on his wing. Thanks to the wind, he must have spread his blood across half of Sydney before Lilith deemed it safe to rest and become once more human.

"What was that all about?" asked Lilith after taking on her usual appearance. Mind talk between them had been difficult with Paul being in such a weakened condition.

"Don't know," gasped Paul, clutching his arm and looking in the medicine cabinet in the kitchen for bandages. He was finding the very lack of feeling in one of his joints plus the substantial amount of blood he'd already lost frightening. If he'd been truly human he might very well be in a state where recovery would not be possible.

"Supped on any Chinese lately?" asked Lilith pointedly.

"One. Her name tag said she was Lotus. She was a waitress at a Chinese restaurant. I didn't want to attack her, but I was very hungry and I had been chased to distraction by the Secret Compass. Besides, I was careful with her remains. I deposited them at Newtown, some distance from where I had attacked her. Why?"

"Why?" cried Lilith. "Do you know what you've done? Do you know who they are and why they're after you and, because of you, now after us both? Do you have any idea?"

"No."

"They're from the Rising Sun Group."

"Rising Sun?"

"They were once Japanese ninja and samurai dedicated to the eradication of the vampire. Now they can be Chinese, even Caucasian and it doesn't matter. Whatever they are they have one major concern and that is our destruction. Killing a Chinese woman is a brilliant way of getting their attention."

"And now we have them after us as well?"

"Yes, that's right. Now we not only have the Secret Compass to contend with but the Rising Sun Group."

"What can we do?"

"Get out as fast and as far as we can. I have gathered together fake passports and other papers we can use. I also have airline tickets for both of us for next Thursday but that may not be soon enough."

"And if it isn't?"

Lilith didn't answer Paul's last question. She let it hang in the apartment like a bad smell that wouldn't go away or perhaps the wrong type of sentence – a death sentence. With shaking hand, he pressed a tea towel as firmly as he could against his wound. It had stopped bleeding but he still felt as if, at any moment, he might pass out.

"No more hunting," Lilith whispered to him, her face looking grim and more angular than it ever had before. "I share a victim with you tomorrow night to give you a chance to heal and then we stop. After tomorrow night, we do not feed again until we have left this country. Understood?"

"Yes. Where are we going?"

"To America."

"Where we'll be safe?"

"We'll be safe if we use more common sense than we have here."

"But for how long?"

"I do not know. The Secret Compass and the Rising Sun Group have long memories and many operatives."

"You saw me in trouble. You came to my rescue. Why?"

"I was flying, looking for prey when I saw what I saw. We have a mission, nein? You get the jockettes, the bimbos and the cheerleaders, nein? I get the jocks and the thugs?"

"Yes, I suppose..."

"Until that changes I will need you, I will protect you. Unless you continue to act stupidly, we will continue together. Now rest. Sleep, heal. We go to America. Think on that as you dream. Think on what it will be like to set foot on another part of our world."

It was a struggle but Paul made it to his bed before darkness took him and the sandman provided the best venue for the very necessary healing to commence.

Chapter 11

Redfern, Sydney, Third Friday in November, 1976

There was nothing Paul could do but sleep away all of the day and most of the night. He couldn't leave his bed without re-opening the place where the star knife and spear went in and nearly ended his existence. Feeling to his arm and hand was coming back, assuring him that his shoulder would eventually be all right. Lilith told him there wouldn't even be a scar. He found that difficult to believe. Still he'd had broken bones knit in less than a fistful of days so why not the lack of a scar where there should be one?

With sleep came images from his past. He saw himself as a small boy. His mother, Mary was nursing him through chicken pox. A few years later, it had been pneumonia. Then one day he fell off his push bike, cutting his knee badly. She raced him to the doctor and he received a dozen stitches. There had been a scar. Had there been a scar since his rebirth? He hadn't thought to look. Somehow it had slipped his mind.

He remembered his mother letting him stay up late to watch *Star Trek* and how, when she baked a pie, she would share out the leftover pastry with him and his sisters, Dorothy and Kate. She used to take them all to Ramsgate Baths in summer for a good swim and then for banana fritters and milkshakes afterward. He had gone fishing with her one time when she brought in this flathead almost as big as she was. He recalled her pride in him getting through high school and landing a job in a bank. His higher school certificate scores were enough to get him into college or university, but he wanted to be out in the real world for a while before he decided on further education. Besides, his parents weren't made of money. It was high time he started paying his own way. He was looking at two years in the real world and then furthering his studies. His parents, seeing sense in his plan, were behind him all the way.

His mother was not so pleased with him going to discos because she felt discos were poison for him. He would come home drunk and he would be irritable the next day because of what had gone on in one of them. She wanted him to find a girl but knew he wouldn't have any luck in a place that made people unhappy. Unfortunately, when it came to girls, she wasn't able to advise him where best to look.

How his mother met his father, Robert, would remain a mystery. It had something to do with his father having lots of sisters and brothers. It also had to do with his father's own kindly mother and father and with summer visits to the local beaches. Back then the Great Depression was on. People were just getting over it when the Second World War loomed up in front of them and money continued to be scarce. Still, his parents had found the way to get together. Maybe it had a lot to do with the times in which they lived. His father had told him that a young man had to make his own way and find his own luck no matter what age he was living in. Paul had wanted to do both but was now going to do neither.

Paul had died just as he'd decided to get off the disco roller-coaster ride. It was taking his money and his pride. It was giving nothing back except the occasional headache the next morning from the scotch. He had died with hatred in his heart for a particular type of female who didn't care and thought too much of herself. If he'd passed away elsewhere, under different circumstances, there might have been something else in him for, say, another type of woman. Hence, in death, he hadn't gotten off the disco rollercoaster he had been anxious to disembark from but had inadvertently stayed on when power had been given over to him. The hate was there and wouldn't go away making it a devilish trap.

Make love, not war? Tell it to the victims of disco. Tell it to those high-and-mighty disco bitches who had taken the dream away.

He could recall his mother and his sisters as being good if not noble people. They were not perfect but he could not recall any imperfection that might have led to even mild dislike for them. He was not perfect either, but when alive, he wasn't a monster. Back then the disco women were the monsters. As far as he was concerned, they remained so until somebody did something about them. When he made his big comeback, he decided, with the help of Lilith, to hunt down the human monsters he'd known and make sure they didn't offend anyone else.

He didn't want innocents caught up in his revenge. On the night of his passing, he'd devised a way to sort out the good from the monstrous. Unfortunately, it was becoming obvious he wouldn't always be able to find an evil soul to slake his thirst on despite his best intentions. Already he had failed twice and was likely to fail again.

Sometime past eleven, he woke to the sound of flapping wings. Lilith had returned. She carried with her a flask containing the blood of a soccer player. She'd run across the player at a bar on George Street near the French restaurant. She'd had her fill of the lout and had brought away with her enough of his life essence to satisfy Paul's rapacious appetite. It was fortunate that the soccer player was a big man who bled well.

Paul could see, as she entered his room that the night had not gone without incident. Lilith had a nasty cut above her right eye from a sharpened sword made of hardwood and a blackened left eye from a South American bola that, when she was in bat form, had brought her crashing to earth. Somehow she had avoided being hemmed in and destroyed by the Secret Compass. Somehow she had escaped being finished off by the Rising Sun Group. She even came close to being arrested by the police which would have really ruined her evening.

"Rough out?" asked Paul as she approached him with the flask.

"Drink now," she said. "Already you heal some, nein? Scar on chest almost gone? But nix to hunting, ya?"

"Your eye," said Paul. "And that cut..."

"All better by tomorrow."

"It will be healthier for us in America?"

"It will be...healthier for a while, ya."

"To America, then," said Paul upending the flask and enjoying every drop.

He had to admit at least to himself, though, that Lilith was not like his mother getting him through chicken pox or pneumonia. She was a female creature that might leave him on a whim, never coming back. She might use him to escape the Secret Compass or the Rising Sun Group. With her, good and bad, anything was possible. He trusted her not to turn on him, though he had to wonder how perilous such a trust might turn out to be. Did he base his trust on her hatred of jocks? Was it her willingness to hunt them down and teach them a lesson before they died? What did she have against them anyway? Who were the jocks she hated the most?

Someday he would have to find out more about her past to gain a little more peace of mind. But he would do well to be careful how he went about doing it, for he might find danger in what he discovered. She had been undead a lot longer than he, and was not a person to trifle with if you valued your own skin.

PART II

THE USA AND BEYOND...

Who minds to the dust returning,
Who shrinks from the sable shore,
Where the high and haughty yearning
Of the soul shall be no more?

So stand by your glasses steady,
This world is a world of lies;
A cup to the dead already,
Hurrah! For the next man who dies.

Extract from a British fighter pilot drinking song from World War One

From "Biggles – the Camels are Coming" by Captain W. E. Johns, 1932, Red Fox edition 2003, UK

Chapter 1

Somewhere between Sydney and Hawaii, 4th Thursday in November, 1976

Being undead so far had been a whirlwind of experiences, most of them unpleasant. There had been revenge. There was being on top for once. He'd experienced broken bones and the insertion of a star knife into body parts where star knives don't belong or at least not in the West. He'd gotten back at people he'd been angry with for a long time but other people he didn't even know wanted to track him down and be rid of him forever. There was time spent with the not very talkative Lilith.

Paul was hungry and airline food didn't agree with his dietary requirements, though the stewardess and a number of his fellow passengers would have done nicely, thank you very much. He'd last eaten two nights ago, sharing a neighbor's cat with Lilith. The cat had been scrawny with not much red to spare. Still, it had reminded him of what it was like to once again put his fangs to proper use. Unfortunately, the neighbor who owned the cat was out of bounds since she would have been missed more than the cat.

Paul was feeling desperate and knew that with this feeling came the strong possibility of making one hell of a mistake. Subtlety and starvation did not go well together. Yet to survive anywhere he needed a certain amount of subtlety. To just charge out of the plane when it landed, attacking the first healthy specimen of humanity to come along would, no doubt, get the local authorities off side. It would let his and Lilith's enemies in Australia know where they had ended up. Thousands of feet above the water below, he could do nothing but try to think of other things. The magazines were useless. He didn't even want to try the music. If they served up Hot Chocolate or Tina Turner, he might have gone mad over the sugary sweetness turning the aircraft into a flying morgue. This would upset Hawaiian ground crew and baggage handlers when they finally landed.

He and Lilith wrapped themselves up like mummies to protect themselves from the sun. They wore gloves and dark glasses. Both carried fake certificates from the Concord Repatriation General Hospital burn center in Sydney to get them to the burn center at Alta Bates Medical Center in Berkeley, California. As so-called burn victims going to the USA for expert treatment with the papers to prove it, they could travel without arousing suspicion. If anything, they were objects of pity. The bandages had itched, but the itch was going away. The moist preparation under them meant to keep the burn victim's flesh supple for further treatment helped. Lilith looked funny all wrapped up. He probably looked funny too. To outsiders, they were Mr. and Mrs. Invisible Man taking a flight to the USA. H. G. Wells would be pleased.

It had been some time since Paul had seen his parents and his sisters. Thoughts of them and what they must have gone through since the night of his disappearance, churned in his head but were over-shadowed by his hatred for the disco and the difficulties inherent in unlife. He missed them. He realized that, if he had met more women like his mother and his sisters, there might be one less vampire. Lilith and her ways wouldn't have had so much appeal. It was quite possible that, under those conditions, Lilith wouldn't have given him a second look.

Sleep did not come easy, but Paul was tired and it was daytime. The window blinds pulled down prevented deadly rays from getting to him even through the bandages. A tiny pillow provided a smidgen of comfort.

He was leaving his past behind and he should have been glad. He felt uncertain but that was to be expected. From the first vampire bite he no longer had a family – now it was official.

As with most humans, money continued to be an issue. He no longer ate the regular three square meals a day/night of living humans, but he needed accommodation, clothing, false papers and passports. Lilith had presented him with these necessities this time, but there was no guarantee she would continue to do so. He would eventually have to find his own way.

He knew Lilith took cash from her victims. At first, he was reluctant to follow her lead. But he couldn't work the way he used to, and the money for unliving expenses had to come from somewhere.

Jocks and jockettes, if you caught them early enough in the evening, could provide generous funds. There was a sense of justice in taking what they had and giving death in return. People who had skimmed the cream off the milk of the kindness of society most of their lives should give something back. That thought made robbing them seem less detestable.

Lilith was curled up beside him, her eyes no doubt closed under the dark glasses, her breathing regular. Gone for the moment was the fierceness of the attacker and the defender. Gone was any sign of the self-righteousness they shared. Her features were smoother, less sharp not only from the bandages but from being asleep. Her chin seemed less like a potential weapon.

A steward and a stewardess trundled by with a coffee cart but Paul ignored them. At one time, he would have loved a freshly brewed cup but that time seemed far away and getting further as he continued on his present course. He wondered why he was going with Lilith and whether he really had much choice in the matter. In her own way, she was offering him a future.

As he drifted off to sleep, the last ten years of his existence seemed to melt away. He saw a boy in his room looking over his comic book collection and his model airplanes. It was quite a collection of both he had, though now it seemed far away and unimportant. Still it spoke of neatness and order. Nothing was around to distract the eye from what the boy thought had importance.

The shelf over his bed contained a few classics such as Charles Dickens' *A Christmas Carol*, H. G. Wells' *The Invisible Man*, Norman Lindsay's *The Magic Pudding* and several *Biggles* novels by Captain W. E. Johns. The *Biggles* novels had pride of place. The room had no football or surfing magazines. There was Boy Scout gear in his chest of drawers and a scout uniform in his closet. He kept a dozen photo albums in one of his drawers along with a cheap camera. At this stage, he was a keen photographer but had run out of things to photograph. He wondered what it would be like to develop his own film, enter photography contests, win them and have trips overseas where he could find plenty of new things to capture on film.

Not much evidence existed for an interest in girls. Some eagle-eyed observer might have noted that some of his comic books pointed in that direction. Some of the comic book women were quite voluptuous. They were also honest, brave, and caring. They were super-heroines as the men of this class were superheroes. The young Paul Priestly would like to become one of those superheroes so that those super-heroines would take an interest in him. It would have been keen to have the power of flight. It would be like flying in a Spitfire only without the Spitfire.

A short time ago the local church had given a sex education lecture aimed at people his age. They showed a fuzzy biology film of a few meaningless diagrams of people's insides, and talked about dos and don'ts aimed at embarrassment rather than real understanding. Nothing was said about love, feelings, or what a guy might say to a girl. *This is total bunk*, the young teen Paul had thought. His parents had meant well taking him along but the church should have known better. As a representative of God it should have had some right answers. Instead it had nothing but bleariness and gas.

There was a soccer ball in his closet he didn't use much and a fishing rod he got to handle every time his dad was able to toss in a line with him. A Melvin Star push bike stood at the base of his bed. For exercise he rode this bike around the neighborhood. Sometimes his eldest sister Dorothy would join him but too often he rode alone. She had friends her age in the street. He had no one, except a boy a year younger than Paul. He left the area when his oldest brother got into trouble with the cops and somehow the trouble meant the whole family had to pack up and leave. Paul wondered what had really happened, and so he spent the years before primary school mostly by himself then the years during primary playing catch-up with his new peers. He was learning at an early age what it was like to be an outcast, and the feeling of isolation it engendered had never really left him.

The years ran forward and the room was no longer the room of a boy. It was now the room of a sixteen year old. The comic book collection had grown. One super model of the starship Enterprise replaced the airplanes. There was a coffee mug with the face of *Star Trek's* Captain Kirk on it and a *Star Trek* water pistol. A poster of the Milky Way hung in one corner of his room and one of Uhura on the Enterprise bridge in another corner. Dead centre above his bed was a poster of Emma Peel from *The Avengers* in a slinky, black jump suit that didn't leave much to the imagination.

Paul kept a pile of *National Geographic* magazines under his bed. Five of them contained photos of nude and semi-nude African and Islander women. Deep down he knew his parents, even his sisters understood what the interest in National Geographic was really all about but he kept quiet about it anyway. Those magazines were his business. They were the first objects in which he felt the need for privacy. It was a sign that he was growing up, though maybe not the best of signs.

The soccer ball had long since gone. The push bike and fishing rod remained. He still had a use for them.

Paul now had science fiction works by Isaac Asimov, Robert Silverberg and Ray Bradbury. Also James Bond novels by Ian Fleming and Doc Savage stories that had originally appeared in the old pulps. Except for the Hammer movies he sometimes saw at the local cinema, he had no interest in horror. He tried to get his hands on superhero novels but couldn't find that many around.

In his mind, this Paul could see himself rescuing an attractive girl around his age from a fire or a flood and have her eternally grateful to him. He could imagine her kissing him. He couldn't quite imagine him kissing her but the distinction between the two actions didn't seem to matter. The important thing was to have done something brave and to be rewarded.

There were dances at school he didn't bother attending and one weird science teacher who had a chip on her shoulder the size of a giant redwood. Whatever her problem with men and teenage boys was, it stemmed from her marriage and subsequent divorce. It stemmed from men being lazy and not taking responsibility for their actions. In her eyes, women were doing too much of the hard work and not getting enough of the credit and/or profit.

Sex education under this woman centered on making the girls feel noble and good. Also in giving the guys the guilts. *I haven't done anything wrong yet, so to hell with her*, was Paul's sentiment. Unless he did do something wrong, he felt no teacher had the right to make him, or anyone else, feel bad about what they might do. Fear, loathing and guilt do not instill a sense of responsibility in anyone. They didn't do that for Paul. What noble thoughts and aspirations he had were slowly eroding. No super-heroines in that classroom. Not a single one, the teacher included.

It was around this time Paul tried to get interested in modern music. He had Beatles records and tapes. He also had the Rolling Stones, the Deltones, the Small Faces and the Animals. His eldest sister Dorothy had country music and his youngest sister Kate was yet to form any view on the matter.

There was talk of a new way of life where war, fighting and anger would become obsolete. There would be love, flowers, dancing and goodwill for all. To quote the Beatles, it was all "Lucy in the Sky with Diamonds" sort of stuff but that was okay. Paul couldn't see how it would all come about but certain television episodes of *Star Trek, Ironside* and *The Mod Squad* pointed the way.

Paul's parents were perplexed by the changes the "with-it" generation wanted to make. Though flower power had nice ideals, they thought it silly and unworkable. "People can't think that way for long," his mother had told Paul. "I wish they could but they can't."

"When they get their feet back on the ground and find they have to make a living, things will change," his father had said.

"A beautiful dream," Dorothy had said, "a beautiful hope that should last forever."

"Yes," agreed Kate. "Forever and ever and ever."

The Beatles were part of the hippy movement along with other bands such as The Mommas and the Papas. The chicks wore love beads and psychedelic mini-skirts; the guys went for beards and long hair. Communes were sprouting up everywhere. Even some teachers were trying to be cool.

Underneath the realm of the adorable positive, however, were the seeds of its ultimate destruction. Drugs such as angel dust were coming to the fore resulting in too many kids getting hooked and finding hell in what could have been paradise. Love was one thing but it had to be without chemical aid that blew your mind. Peace shouldn't come from an early grave. The Church tried to sort out the moral issues with the young but Christianity seemed so wrong. Wasn't a vicious, gangland style dictator, for example, put in charge of South Vietnam by the Americans on the grounds that the Americans thought he was a good Catholic?

Paul tried to follow the politics on the news broadcasts on television as best he could but a lot was still beyond him. The hippies spoke a simple language he could understand. When somebody said, "Make love, not war," he could see the sense in that. Who wants to get shot up on some battlefield? Certainly not Paul. On the other hand, who wants to make love to some swinging bird? Here Paul would gladly answer in the affirmative. Of course nothing is as clear cut as a choice between love and war.

The years ran forward once more. The room now belonged to Paul but a week before his style of existence changed forever. The comic book collection had gone and there were now *Star Trek* novels among his books. There was also a copy of George Orwell's *1984* and Aldous Huxley's *Brave New World*. His records and tapes hadn't grown by much and he no longer had a push bike. He was in the process of saving up for a down payment on a car.

In his closet he had three good business suits. He still kept his tried and true fishing rod, reminding him of good times with his father. The *Star Trek* mug remained as did the Enterprise model but the water pistol, which fell apart some time ago, had been thrown away. The posters of Uhura, the Milky Way and Emma Peel could still be seen. Two *Playboys* had replaced the *National Geographic* magazines. There was also a half drunk bottle of Black Douglas scotch.

At this stage, he was feeling cynical because of the disco scene. He was a guy who wanted a gal and the gals he might have wanted seemed to be at such venues. Even though he wasn't loaded with money, he would soon have enough to get some wheels and a place of his own. His job at the bank wasn't exciting but not many people his age had exciting jobs. Taking all into account, he could look in the mirror and see a fine fellow with good prospects staring back at him. Why then, he wanted to know, was it so hard, outside of family, to get the opposite sex to see the same thing?

"You'll be all right," his mother had told him. "You just have to keep at it, that's all."

"It's not easy, I know," his father had said. "What's worthwhile is never easy. You'll get there. Hey! I did!"

Promises had been made by the disco, promises that had not been kept. Instead of being a remnant of the hippy lifestyle it was proving to be something else. At first Paul thought it was him. Then the more he visited various discos the more he came to realize there was a kind of nastiness going on in and around such places. It didn't just have something to do with too much drink and too many drugs. The nastiness had a lot to do with attitude, a new version of not caring for others that had come into existence. It was ingrained in too many of the high schools, spilling over into the world of the young adult. No one could escape or ever understand it.

"Where are the heroes?" Paul asked himself, looking into the full body closet mirror. "Where are the heroines, the women worthy of the heroes? Have they all gone? And where's 'make love, not war?'"

What happened to something as straightforward as good manners? Heroes and heroines have that. It barely existed among young men. It didn't seem to exist at all among young women anymore.

"Wouldn't it be great if someone made them show good manners, or else?" he said to his reflection. "All they have to say is either yes thank you or no thank you. What's so hard about that? Nothing, I say. Wouldn't it be great if they had to pay for not toeing that particular line? Villains and villainesses always pay in the end, don't they?"

Gone were the days when Paul would dream of rescuing some poor damsel. No longer could he imagine there being, outside family, damsels worthy of such care. Now his thoughts had become more sinister, less noble. He still loved his mother and his sisters but those with poor manners or no manners at all had already wounded his sensibilities. Given the chance, he would exact revenge upon them.

Enter Lilith and his change of status from ordinary human to vampire.

"From hero to possibly villain," he told himself. "Mother and father would not be proud but that's life or whatever this is. No going back now, not even if I wanted to. No going back at all."

Then he was not far from *The Blue* putting the bite on Lizzy who seemed to deserve what she got from him. After that he was running from the Secret Compass and the Rising Sun Group. Finally he was tossing and turning on his little pillow in a cramped, air conditioned space as a new night in a new land came upon him.

Paul woke to find the still sleeping Lilith on his shoulder. Her chin was digging into him but he didn't mind. It was contact of a sort though not really human. He felt in need of some kind of reminder that he was indeed still flesh and blood and of this world.

Darkness had come. The plane was about to touch down in the USA. Cold was about to greet most of the passengers as the aircraft came to a halt and the doors opened to the outside. Paul and Lilith would not be affected by any such drop in temperature. They did, however, have other pressing needs. Both were determined to be as discretionary as possible in fulfilling the most outstanding of said needs; otherwise, they might never visit mainland America. It was important to appear as if they were timid burn victims even if it meant suffering from emptiness just a little bit longer.

"We've arrived," said Paul, shaking Lilith awake.

"Good," replied Lilith, yawning and stretching. "Gently does it. Remember that in five hours we fly out of here. Meanwhile we do nothing to delay our flight plans."

"But we sup?"

"We sup, yes, but with care, nein? Follow my lead. We'll share a meal if we have to. That way we'll be less likely to find ourselves in serious trouble."

"There are Secret Compass members here?"

"I don't know. More than likely there are members of the Rising Sun Group. Either way we keep low. We don't remain here any longer than we have to. Agreed?"

"Oh, yes, Lilith."

Both Paul and Lilith could barely control the shakes as they left the plane. They only just got through the check-out. At least one person looking on suspected they should be rushed to the local hospital. They knew they had been lucky that no one had done so. They would not likely make it through check-in without first obtaining sustenance. Something had to be done quickly but with discretion.

The airport staff had to be off limits. So did their fellow passengers. Even the stray ten year old girl who had wandered away from her parents and was calling out for them was too much of a risk. Someone would see them with her and ask questions; they would be delayed and then quite possibly destroyed. Besides, Paul felt the girl far too young to have the question put to her and, without the question, he didn't know if he wanted to go on. It was the only type of moral imperative he had left to him and he was barely holding onto it with his metaphoric fingernails.

Out past the airport's main entrance, they took on bat form and began looking from on high for potential victims. A cool breeze, however, kept everyone inside off the streets and beaches. All they could come up with were two mongrel dogs sheltering between two garbage bins in a dark alley. Still, blood was blood and they could not go on without it much longer. The mongrels protested but their yellowing teeth were nothing compared to the fangs of their attackers. The dogs had neither the speed nor the cunning needed to get away. Red spilled forth from whimpering fur and was eagerly collected. It tasted foul but it was warm. It filled them up. What's more, no one would miss two mongrel dogs. It wasn't the most stylish of ways to remain in existence but it would do.

With some haste they flew back to the airport to catch their next flight. A customs official, who had checked their papers earlier and was checking them again, wondered where their new vitality had come from. Perhaps they had sought medical care in Hawaii during their stopover. His thoughts on the subject were strong enough to be read. A ticket collector also wondered how they were doing and whether they could really be helped at Berkeley. It wasn't often that burn victims from Australia came their way. Paul calmly boarded the plane to San Francisco as did Lilith.

They were shown to their seats and, as the plane got underway, were offered refreshments. The attendants were keen to stress that they had straws they could drink from. Paul and Lilith declined the coffee or tea and asked for pillows instead. Settling down to sleep was easier this time. A young child three rows down wanted to cry, but Lilith took off her glasses for a minute to blast him with her eyes. That stopped him. A teenager was beginning to whistle a tune only to find, thanks to Paul's stare, that neither his lips nor his brain knew how to perform the act anymore. A large man was about to tell a story in a loud, uncouth voice to his young female companion when, according to commands generated by Lilith and Paul, he found he could no longer speak. The glasses went back on and they settled down for a rest. As vampires they had super-human hearing. They could block out some annoying or hurtful sounds when they were awake but not anywhere near as well when they were trying to drift into slumber. Once they had succeeded in drifting off, of course, they were literally dead and very hard to disturb. Getting from the state of wakefulness to slumber was the real issue.

What will San Francisco be like? Paul wondered as he drifted off. It had been a place where flower power had really taken hold. Maybe some of it still remained. Maybe, somewhere out there, heroines still existed and not every second woman was a heartless Lizzy. Still, what could it matter now that he was a vampire? True goodness, true light were beyond his reach and, he suspected, would always be.

Usually Lilith was hard to read unless she wanted to be. As she fell into dreamland, Paul picked up a few scattered sentences and, in his drowsy state tried his best to make sense of them. He made out something about a World War. There was also something about a Nazi devil and his black soul. She talked of revenge and of a growing evil that could only be combated by her darkness. What any of this meant was beyond Paul. He wondered, as he went more deeply into the land of slumber, if it would make more sense in the future and perhaps point the way to how Lilith came to be and what her plans were. He knew she'd been around for a while. Maybe she went back as far as the 2nd World War? It was a possibility. But what's this about Nazis? What was the connection with Nazis? He gathered she was against them but couldn't be sure. She spoke with a Polish accent or what he now took to be a Polish accent but some of her words were German. Were there Nazi vampires around? If there were he wouldn't be too keen on meeting up with one. They had been bad enough as ordinary humans but would be terrifying as members of the undead. Still, if they were around, he would fight them as best he could and maybe, just maybe, that was how he would lose his second life. If so, it would be a noble way to go if nothing else.

Chapter 2

The bowels of Mitchell Library, Sydney, Christmas Eve, 1976

Miles Henry looked over the reports with Long but, try as he might, he couldn't change the overall result. He couldn't get past Long's conclusion.

"You're right," said Miles, putting the papers aside. "They've gone. The question is, where?"

"They could have moved into the country," Long ventured. "Train tickets to Bathurst or Orange are easy enough to come by."

"We should have caught up with their trail by now if they had. We've got operatives posted out there. We also have people down south in Wollongong and people to the north in Newcastle."

"What about going to another state?"

"Nothing so far from any of our men in Victoria, Queensland, Western Australia, Tasmania or the Northern Territory."

"How about overseas?"

"Difficult but not impossible. If so, they would have left within the last three weeks and could be anywhere."

"I'll put the usual feelers out. We could get lucky."

"Yes, it will boil down to luck, won't it?"

"At this stage, it will."

"If only we had coordinated our efforts with the Rising Sun Group. Between us and them we came so close. Together we might have at least brought down the more experienced vampire, leaving junior to fend for himself and so be easily taken down as well."

Miles couldn't help but recall the incident he was referring to. It began with the keen eyes of a stranger to his city. A bola thrown by the son of a South American friend, who was visiting Sydney, had waylaid a larger-than-for-real bat. Her legs had been entangled in the thin rope and one of the balls of the device had clunked her in the eye. She'd hit the roof hard then plummeted to the pavement. Miles and his men had two hundred yards of open park space to traverse to get to her and they were pouring on the juice to do so. Unfortunately, she recovered fast, changed form, untied herself as a human, reverted to bat and was on her way just as a bullet from Miles' gun whizzed past her hairline or what would have been her hairline if she'd remained human.

Further on her flight, a thrown stave, launched by a Rising Sun Group member, had brought her down. Quickly, she became human and was cut on the head while avoiding getting her neck sliced off by a Rising Sun Group swordsman in black who seemed to be out for revenge. She threw the swordsman into a woman in black carrying star knives and gave a large fellow in black, who was approaching her with a spiked club, an upper cut with her palm before, once more, changing and taking to the sky.

Sometime later, she was seen in human form on George Street with a flask presumably containing blood attached to her belt. A police officer, who was also a Secret Compass field agent, called out from his car for her to stop but, by the time he got out and gave chase, she was long gone. This seemed to confirm reports that the vampire who had killed Lizzy had been hurt and needed to recuperate. Nothing of significance was reported after that though there were people everywhere on the lookout.

In the search for the two inhuman fugitives, three vampires who were not connected to Lizzy's murder were found at the Cross by his men and eliminated. Discos such as *The Blue*, which had lost patronage of late, were said to be back up to full strength. The pub where that muscle bound ape had his back shattered and his girlfriend's life taken seemed to be doing better business than it had in a long time. The bar staff were all smiles and there were new customers, more than enough to replace the ones who wouldn't return.

Miles, who played football in high school and college, understood better than most people what had happened. There were idiots who let their prowess on the football field turn them into something most people wanted to avoid. Miles had been headed down that path when a girl he was keen on told him she didn't want to go out with a part time lunatic and a full time thug. Lucky for him he took the hint, looked around to see where he was headed and went in another direction. Too bad he never got to marry her and settle down. The army got in the way and then there was his present occupation.

Above all else, his earlier life and his straightening out had taught him that, wherever it was possible, to have patience and to give others a second chance. He was hoping to be able to shake Lizzy out of her arrogance and self-centeredness because he knew his sister, Patricia. Knowing his sister, he suspected there was a better person inside Lizzy determined, some day, to break out.

Discipline was a consideration. For him it had been the army, the Church as a faithful layman and, finally, the Freemasons. He'd fought as a group captain in Korea with Long as his medic. Then after the police action that looked very much like a war was over, the Secret Compass got in touch with him. He was introduced to another type of police action that looked like a war only it never made the papers as such. If it was waged correctly, the average person need never even know it was going on. He recruited Long, and, after proper training in a place called Knightswood in Scotland, they became a firm part of the most under-cover arm of Freemasonry ever. Considered by those not in the know to be glorified senior librarians, they had been responsible for protecting humanity from numerous supernatural threats and would continue to do so for as long as it was reasonably possible. This game was really for younger men and sometimes he felt it in his bones. Sometimes he saw it in Long's face.

There was a time when Miles might have thought of Lizzy as a future operative in the Secret Compass. When entering her teens, she had been intelligent enough to be real trouble and so, on the positive side, was capable of great things. If only he could have gotten past her willfulness in her later years and gotten her to understand the world more as he knew it. Her lack of self-discipline had formed a wedge between them. No matter how hard he tried; he couldn't win her over to a place of safety. Her parents were having difficulties of their own with her when she died. Miles had wanted to give her, not only a second chance, but as many as she needed to come good but, some things are not to be.

Now, on her behalf, he had to try to outthink the two undead he was after and bring them to justice. So, where would they go? Europe? It was a possibility. He got the impression that the elder of the two he was hunting was East European. Maybe they were headed back to where she had originally come from. If so, they might well elude the Secret Compass forever.

In the Eastern Block counties and in Russia, the Secret Compass had no operatives. The authorities there were against anything that smacked of Western religion and Western beliefs including Freemasonry. The Secret Compass, which was a branch of Freemasonry, and got its funding from main source Freemasons, would have to move cautiously there. Secret Compass sensitives, such as Helen Kiln had long suspected that the communists and socialists had their own methods of dealing with vampirism and they were as effective as those used by the capitalists. Nothing could be proven. Not even the Secret Compass PSI division could break through whatever mind blocks were used much of the time. Occasionally, a word here or a sentence there escaped the forced isolation and gave rise to speculation among Western sensitives. It was believed by the Secret Compass PSI division that their E. S. P was waylaid by sensitives on the other side, preventing flow of information. If this was so then it was more to the advantage of the enemy that both sides shared than to either side's true and genuine benefit. The Secret Compass wasn't interested in state secrets but in fighting the evil they knew most people did not acknowledge. They would have been happy to have worked with the East.

There was also the possibility that the ones Miles was after had fled to England or possibly the USA. Data from the UK suggested that the elder vampire, or one similar to her, had spent some time in London after the Second World War. Would she return? There was no evidence that she'd ever been to America. If this was so, perhaps that would be reason enough for her to go there with her companion. Of course if they went in either direction they would eventually make their whereabouts known and word of where they'd gotten to would get back to Miles and Long. Now all they could do is let the sensitives in the major cities in Great Britain and the USA in on who they were after then wait and, while waiting, get on with other cases.

"When they surface, we'll get them," said Long because Miles had gone quiet and he felt someone should say something.

"Damn right we will," agreed Miles.

There were times when Miles wished he was in some other business where there was less uncertainty and more rewards, where there were fewer life and death decisions to be made and less death. This happened to be one of them.

Chapter 3

San Francisco, February 1977

There was little wonder that the Golden Gate reminded Paul of the Sydney Harbor Bridge. Like the Brooklyn in New York, they were based on the suspension principle and looked like giant, ornate clothes-hangers. They had, however, somewhat different histories and were regarded in different ways by the public.

During the mid-70s, some idiot artist in Sydney had created these paintings of the bridge of bridges in light, airy pastels. For his pains, he got the bad reviews from the critics he so richly deserved. He also got a general thumbs down from the public. The bridge, after all, was mighty not wimpy. It did an important job. It had also been completed during the great depression and had been there as a much needed example of what Australian workers could do given the chance. By simply being mighty, it had given the whole nation hope for a brighter, shinier future. At a time when the world seemed a hopeless place, there it was, as big as life and ruggedly handsome in the way only a bridge can be. There's something about solid stone and elegantly rendered steel that speaks of permanence and strength. Banks may fail but people who can span a great waterway with their guts and their skill cannot long remain in the doldrums. Yes, the bridge indeed radiated and continues to radiate power, a force to be reckoned with, and a can-do attitude. And yes, any artist mad enough to use pastels and thus argue against its magnificence really ought to find another line of work or another city to work in.

Around the same time, in the mids-'70s, there was a San Francisco artist who dared to create a series of paintings of the Golden Gate. He rendered his paintings in every color of the rainbow but keeping the primary colors red and gold. This the people didn't mind. They even praised him for it. The critics applauded the work, saying it joined the staid land mass of one generation with the more "go-go" land mass of the swing set. The unwarranted display of color might have softened the design but that, to the people of San Francisco, was of little concern.

Everybody knew what the bridge really looked like. Everybody knew the bridge was sturdy and that , if you want an exact likeness of it rather than an interpretation, it could be done just as well with a camera as with canvas, brush and pallet. There was also such a thing as freedom of expression which was highly prized even to the point of absurdity.

Besides, no one was actually attacking the integrity of the structure. Even if they were, one artist wasn't going to make it crumble to dust. The worst a painter in this instance could do was create a work that would not sell. As it turned out, the artist, saying something about the times through the bridge, did help himself and his contemporaries.

As he sat atop one of her cables, the Golden Gate spread out before Paul in its entire late night splendor. As he sat in awe of what was before him, he thought of the two artists and their paintings of bridges. He thought of their fate and wondered what other differences he would find between the folks of this San Francisco and the ones he'd left behind in Sydney.

The Golden Gate was slightly longer than its Australian cousin but just as busy. Only past ten at night did the flow of cars and trucks become a trickle. In his bat form, the lights from passing cars bedazzled. The rolling hills making up the bulk of the city by the bay were something strange and new. Why did they build the place here and not on flatter ground? One hill for defense in the days before jets and A-bombs would have been fine, more than one or two or even three seemed somewhat absurd. Still the architecture that climbed and fell, ebbed and flowed was magnificent. And there were the colors of the earth everywhere, competing with ugly, more modern glass and steel and, of all things, actually winning. Such color reminded Paul of the Aboriginal flag and of the Aboriginal reverence for the land. It was a reverence he had once shared with them. It came from the days when he'd go fishing with his father.

Lilith had told him she had her sights set on the strange gyms and the even stranger bodybuilders they produced. Some were of either German or Austrian descent. This, for some reason, was of importance to her. "They're not quite the enemy," she said to him the other day in their two-room loft over the bay. "But they've got plenty of red."

"Good," answered Paul. After that period of going without, they both had the need to do well at the dinner table. They were just getting back to full strength.

Discos were a bit different here. For some of them, it was as if the age of long hair and psychedelic clothing, multi-colored strobe lighting and groovy music hadn't come to an end. Many of the dancers showed a kindness and a politeness toward him that put them off his menu. Of course there was always one every night willing to hang herself with her asp's tongue and he only needed the one. He wasn't a greedy vampire.

As he glided down from the bridge and coasted his way to the mainland, he watched a flight of fruit bats wend their way to a nearby park. There were ships in the harbor including military types. He wondered if the USA was getting ready for yet another war. He didn't think they would so soon after Vietnam but he couldn't put it past them. If the USA did beat the war drums then nations such as Australia would soon follow. Talk of make love, not war was already growing stale. Someday soon it would lose all meaning.

A pleasant smell came his way, drawing him in and down to a small coffee shop that had large, multi-colored pillows instead of chairs and popcorn and peanuts instead of expensive muffins and brownies. The posters that lined the walls were early pop art which dated back to poetry readings and lively bongo playing. There were people smoking weed but what titillated his sensitive vampire nose was the coffee. It was rich and freshly made. Here "instant" was a dirty word along with "establishment" and "pigs." There were men and women, sitting around in jeans and baggy jumpers, talking about women's rights as well as the rights of African-Americans and what might be done to further such causes.

A young woman with large pink glasses framing her high cheek bones and adding to the charming effect of short, brown hair curling-inward saw him at the window. She waved him in. At first he was going to walk away, but her smile and her insistence won him over. There was a little bell over the entrance way that announced him. The shop owner, a middle-aged man with a soft, luxuriant beard, made him feel welcome by offering him a pillow and his choice of coffee. Paul, to be polite, bought a mug of mocha he couldn't possibly drink and settled down to listen to more freedom and rights talk.

There was conversation about equal rights and equal pay. All that was said seemed reasonable. It was a far cry from the Sydney disco scene where the music was too loud and it was all take, take, take without discussion, without reason and never, ever the suggestion of giving something, anything back. Some of the women were angry. Maybe they had a right to be. Maybe there had been women in Sydney who were also angry and had been treated badly or, at any rate, thought they had. Just because the women he had worked with as a bank teller got the same wage he got didn't mean it was universal. He had never been up high enough in the business world to even glimpse this glass ceiling that permitted men to get ahead in the world of the executive but not women. Maybe this ceiling existed and maybe not. Chances were good that he'd never find out for sure.

Cat Stevens was singing "Father and Son" on the radio and it was putting Paul in a thoughtful mood. He was feeling rather mellow. If he had come to this sort of place in Sydney, rather than to *The Blue*, his life might well have worked out better. It not only might have been better, but he would have had a real life rather than the imitation he had been given by Lilith. Being a walking cadaver had its moments, but this wasn't one of them. Here, revenge was far from his thoughts. Here, he wondered about light and goodness and heroes. Here, he wondered if he could return, in spirit, to what he was before the disco betrayed him.

"What do you think of all this?" a redhead wearing an orange beanie asked him. She was young, intelligent looking. He suspected she was fresh from college.

"I don't know what to think," he told her.

"Good. That's a start. You're not from around here, are you?"

"Australia."

"How lovely. Your first visit?"

"Yes. But I suppose there has to be a first time for everything."

"You know you are allowed to participate in the discussions if you want to."

"I'll just listen."

"The Cultural Revolution was all about everyone having their say, you know."

"In Australia it was about getting the vote at eighteen."

"Done much with it?"

"What?"

"The vote."

"Early days, really. Something might be done."

"I hope so. The world's in a mess. Young people, a few years back, thought they could make a difference. Maybe they did in some small ways."

"Yes, but change has to come from within. Maybe no one has anything to offer anyone except promises they'll never keep."

"That's a real downer. You really believe that?"

"Sometimes. Then I meet someone like you and I don't know."

"How sweet. Are you here long?"

"No. I'd better go. I have things to do."

"You are free to come back, you know."

"I'll keep that in mind."

Paul got up and left. He was sorry to go but the night was getting old and he didn't want his victim to come from among people he thought of as decent types. He still had his standards.

At a bar near Fisherman's Wharf, he came upon a middle-aged drunk with a mouth on her like an open sewer. She wasn't perfect but she met his need and his standards. He decided to have her. She didn't squeal much in the alley as if death would be a blessing. He almost felt sorry for her. Unfortunately, her blood turned out to be filthy with alcohol and hallucinogenic drugs of some sort. All at once he did not feel very well and the feeling got worse.

Changing to bat form, he found himself on a trip in which lights were brighter and more engrossing than they needed to be, where sound was muted one moment and horribly loud the next. His stomach did flip-flops as he flew from one rainbow moment of near collision with a streetcar to the next rainbow moment of near collision with a lamp post. *Poisoned!* He thought as he sped on.

Somehow he found his way back to his lodgings, transformed and collapsed on his bed. From the drunk with the drug problem, he managed to get a few dollars before the substance of abuse, whatever it was, hit him. When Lilith came in about an hour later, she had a few hundred dollars plus a couple of expensive looking rings. What's more, her dinner wasn't playing havoc with her body.

"We've made the rent already," she told him. "This city is a gold mine."

"If money's all you care about," Paul mumbled. He was trying valiantly to nod off to sleep and didn't want to hear about someone else's good fortune.

"You're not well," observed Lilith. "We'll talk later, ya?"

"Later," agreed Paul and was permitted to sleep the uneventful sleep of a corpse. No dreams assailed him which he found strange and, at the same time, comforting. It was fortunate that his body healed quickly. The nasty aftereffects of that less than pleasing woman's life essence had dissipated. Still, he would not forget the incident and would be just that bit extra careful concerning where he took his nourishment.

Paul was riding a streetcar one night when he overheard talk about Berkeley and the young people who studied at the colleges and universities there. Apparently, there was a comic book called *Slow Death,* put out by *Last Gasp*, the more radical among them were reading. It illustrated some of the sorriest, saddest moments in American history and warned of the dangers of the continuing arms race. It had nothing to do with the superheroes he grew up with but it had a strong purpose, a strong reason for being as did the people responsible for it. He made further enquires at the coffee shop he'd visited before only to discover that many of the people who were regulars there had once gone to Berkeley. What's more, some of them had copies of *Slow Death* issues and other underground comic books known as comix they could show him.

"Going there's an education in itself," said the girl with the pink glasses he'd met there before. He was inclined to believe her. What's more, he had a yen for some kind of knowledge that went past high school, the bank and his adventures so far with Lilith. He could see a new future at the head of an intellectual vampire army intent on saving mankind from its own tendencies towards self-destruction. He could see a possible way to find someone to share his unlife with besides Lilith who was more like a big sister, or a surrogate mother, than anything else.

Paul dined that night on a barmaid who enjoyed using a lot of four letter words but who was otherwise clean. Then he met up with Lilith. He told her what he planned to do. At first she was taken aback by what he said. Then an approving smile crossed her face.

"Yes," she said after some thought. "We should recruit. We need new followers. And if you want a taste of college and university, I don't see why you should not have a taste."

A week passed in which they gathered the funds together for a bus trip inland plus accommodation for a month when they got there. Of course Lilith could have managed the money in one night but wanted to stretch things out a little in order to do maximum damage to the establishments she wished to destroy before leaving the city behind. Paul understood this and, though he was anxious to get going, didn't make a fuss. It was better to have her in a good mood and keen to go than in the dumps about things she had wanted to do but hadn't given herself the chance to do. Besides, San Francisco wasn't a bad locale to spend more time. Apart from the money, they needed new papers for they were once more to travel as burn victims. The fakes they had which got them to San

Francisco were good but needed updating. According to the new papers, they would still be travelling from the burn center at the Concord Repatriation General Hospital in Sydney to the burn center at Alta Bates Medical Center at Berkeley.

On their final night before wrapping themselves up like mummies with sunglasses and catching the bus, things started to pop. Paul took a wrong turn and swooped into Chinatown. His entrance was met by a dozen star knives that barely missed him, thrown from a two story window. Then there was an arrow that tore into his leathery wing, sending him plummeting off balance toward a cop on a motorcycle. With a great deal of effort, he pulled out in time and, instead, ploughed into a row of garbage cans. Dazed, he struggled to become human and, after succeeding, made his way out of the Asian sector of the city as fast as his legs would carry him. The only reason he didn't get star knives in the back or worse was the fact that the street was crowded. He was able to use his fellow pedestrians for cover. It was only when he had put some distance between himself and the place he was bushwhacked that he transformed once again and took to the sky. Due to a spreading rip, his flight was erratic but it took him to where he needed to go. Even so, he'd been given a nasty fright.

Paul told Lilith of his run-in with the Rising Sun Group San Francisco style and showed her where the arrow had scored a deep wound in his arm. She countered by telling him of her close encounter with an FBI agent posing as a weightlifter. He'd pulled a crucifix out of a rolled up towel and was about to stab her with a stake when some woman screamed at what he was about to do. Startled by the unexpected noise, the FBI man had dropped his guard for a split second, which was time enough for Lilith to knock the crucifix away and then serve him his own stake through the heart. She had his credentials as an FBI agent on her, still soaked in his blood.

"It seems we both need to leave in a hurry," Lilith told Paul.

"Yes," he agreed with some enthusiasm. "We can't afford to be squeezed between the FBI and the Rising Sun Group."

"And then there's the Secret Compass to consider."

"Right! If we stay, it won't be long before they figure out where we are and then we'll have them to contend with as well."

"So many enemies! We need allies, ya?"

"More than ever I'd say."

The bus trip was thankfully uneventful. Both vampires spent much of the journey wanting to scratch their bandages but refraining from doing so. Other passengers left them alone. Paul was glad. The last thing he wanted to do was leave a trail of corpses everywhere they went. He suspected Lilith of feeling the same way.

It was past seven in the evening when they disembarked and went into their motel room. They were grateful to be able to get out of their now dried out coverings and breathe more freely. Breathing wasn't really a necessary act but it was a habit left over from true life that was hard to break.

An hour later, they were on the prowl. They ended up at a nearby drive-in bottle shop. It was there a Hells Angel bike rider and his girlfriend decided to give them a rough time. First it was abusive language and then it was pushing and shoving. It was no trouble at all for either Paul or Lilith to push back which they did with gusto. *Some people ask for trouble*, thought Paul as he sunk his teeth into weather-beaten female flesh. Lilith was delighted with her kill when she discovered a swastika on his arm and the words "Kill them All, Let God Sought Them Out" on his grubby T-shirt. His jacket, of course, had Hells Angels on the back but that was of little concern to her. She told Paul as much.

Berkeley was leafy which added to Paul's exuberance. The following night, he set out to explore the nearest college and to gather in his first convert. He wondered at the rightness of such an activity. Being undead hadn't made him entirely happy. Then again, if there were undead aplenty, it might make a difference to his quality of unlife. Who could know for sure but, with a lot of undead out destroying the sinful and putting things back the way they should be, he might come to truly treasure his own existence. He might even come to fully understand why he was chosen for this unlife.

There was a German linguistics professor giving a late evening lecture. After the lecture, Paul saw Lilith pounce on him. She carved him up with her claws before bothering to bite. It was obvious he was not going to be made into a vampire. What he had said that could possibly have upset her was unknown to Paul. He'd never seen her act more vicious or more willful. The attack took place under the shadow of an elm which was only in shadow because of two dull street lamps. What's more, it must have been observed by half a dozen amazed students who were understandably frightened. Two male youths tried to run interference for the professor but were brushed aside. At the man's death, Lilith scurried off well aware she'd left clear evidence behind of vampiric activity. By then there was little she could do about it.

Paul was tempted to not hunt that night but he had to eat. His target was a bright young computer science student named Lilly Fielding.

She was shy, hard working and had shown distaste for the local college football star. As it turned out, she was easily seduced and brought into vampirism. She didn't want to live in a world where her brains meant less to people than someone else's brawn. He was there to give her a way out. She took it, showing little resistance. She had to squeal as death descended but that was understood. Even so, the sound made Paul uncertain but by then it was too late to save her. It was too late to back out and leave her be. Four days later, the body of one of the local footballers was found in nearby parkland naked, bitten all over and white from unexplained and, to the local sheriff's department, unexplainable blood loss.

Paul felt good about Fielding but she was hardly the companion he was after. She was far too wild. It seemed there had been a lot of pent up fury that exploded once she'd gotten her new start, her new powers. She'd felt helpless for ages. Now she was taking out the bad guys and having the time of her unlife. Unfortunately, telling her to cool it and to be more concerned about how she disposed of her victims' remains did not work. By the end of the month, one college football team was no more and she was definitely responsible. She'd left bodies everywhere, indicating that the fellows didn't simply leave the area, but that they were murdered.

"She's a magnet for vampire slayers," cautioned Lilith the day after Fielding's first slaying. Lilith's recent behavior had left a lot to be desired but Paul didn't buy his way into that argument.

"We're all magnets for the slayers," he said diplomatically.

"She'll draw them to us," Lilith added.

"She'll be fine," Paul lied. He could already see their stay in the neighborhood becoming a short one. He didn't want to have to destroy Fielding. He didn't want Lilith to do so either. But Fielding was out of control.

Paul's next pick happened a week later when he heard a tall blond woman give a talk on saving the Amazon rainforests. Her name was Kate Minsk. She was a post-graduate student in social studies. She was aiming at getting her P.H.D and the hecklers in the audience that night were not helping. Four nights later, the bodies of the hecklers would be found in a nearby reservoir stripped of wallets, watches and rings. Whatever she took from them ended up funding the Save the Rainforests Foundation, which Paul thought was good. If nothing else, at least he could approve of her agenda. Unfortunately, she was on a crusade and had all the zeal and lack of common sense of your average crusader. Next, she went after the people who worked in a nearby factory that polluted the land and the local waterways. Paul urged her to be more subtle about what she was doing and how she was doing it. In the end he had to leave her be.

Lilith had converted two Ancient History professors who did not take the conversion at all well. One murdered a local hockey coach before going out into the sun to commit suicide. It was said he blazed for a good hour though he probably got his second death after only twenty minutes. He had stopped screaming after about fifteen minutes, or so the local paper reported. What happened to him was put down to spontaneous combustion. The other professor robbed the campus clinic of its blood supply then took off for parts unknown. No doubt he took off to contemplate his future. At least the second one wasn't likely to become a spectacle or bring immediate trouble down on them.

"Strange people," said Lilith, concerning her professors. "They seemed to want a new life, a new existence. I gave it to them and this is how they repay me."

"Yes," agreed Paul.

The only explanation Paul could come up with was that the men had been too old to take well to such abrupt change. It was one thing to want something different to happen to you. It was another to get it handed to you with no way of going back if you had a change of heart. Lilith had been the way she was too long to realize this. Paul still had doubts about the unlife he'd been given. Those doubts, he knew, made him more sensitive to the newly undead.

The weeks that followed were busy for Paul and Lilith. More vampires were created but it was becoming obvious that, out of the material they were working with, they were not going to get their dedicated army. What they were getting, at best, were individuals destroying their past tormentors and preventing others from being tormented by them. At worst, they were producing rampaging creatures that had little care, when it came to consequences, and who could not acknowledge a foreseeable future they could become interested in. Also there was the question of how they were being recruited. Paul couldn't help but feel that their blunt approach, followed by their too speedy conversion of chosen candidates, was also to blame for the less than desirable results.

Eventually, with signs that the local law was growing desperate and thus willing to bring in outsiders to help with ongoing investigations, it was time to head back to San Francisco. Whatever they had done at Berkeley, they figured wouldn't last for long. Paul saw it as a noble experiment worth repeating elsewhere with, hopefully, better results.

He saw Lilith as the main reason it had all gone sour. The insane killing of the German professor he considered to be the moment of no return. From there on, insanity seemed to lead to more insanity. The notion of an ordered pack of undead, with discipline and an understanding of a shared destiny was simply lost. He tried to revive the dream but it was impossible. Now he was beginning to wonder how Lilith had managed in Australia to get her own followers and whether she'd be able to do so again.

Lilith understood his misgivings. In way of explanation for her most devastating action, all she could offer was the fact that there was a period, decades past, when some, though not all Germans, had done bad things and that loathing for what they had done sometimes spilled over into her present.

"Sometimes the past compels me to do terrible deeds," she told him candidly. "If you do not understand this already then someday, I am certain, you will."

Paul stayed with Lilith another month after getting back from Berkeley. Then they went their separate ways. He had learnt all he thought he could from her. It was about time he was on his own. Lilith was sad to see him go but understood. Neither of them would stay in San Francisco much longer. The place was getting too hot for them. Lilith had seen members of the Rising Sun Group outside of Chinatown and they were both aware of FBI agents skulking around the waterfront.

Lilith told Paul, upon parting, that they would meet again. He believed her. Where they would meet neither one knew but that was fine. It was something Paul could look forward to and, by then, whatever had made her act the way she had at Berkeley might well have worked its way out of her system. It was something to contemplate as he made his way alone in the world. He also wondered how well he would be able to manage on his own and whether Lilith would now be able to make it on her own.

In Orange County, California, three months later, Paul came upon a hippy commune. It reminded him of the hippy commune he'd visited in the Blue Mountains in Australia when he was a kid. He was very glad to see it. A dozen wooden huts, each housing three or four of the love generation, spread out over a hundred acres of prime fruit growing land. It was one of the last remnants of a beautiful dream that, for a short while, swept the Western world.

Here, love beads were still being made, mostly for the tourists, as well as homemade jams, scones, flapjacks, orange juice, lime and lemon juice. Seasonal fruit picked daily. It was a cut above subsistence farming and the commune did pay its collective tax. Even so, the lifestyle was close to what had been promised by people who couldn't see themselves taking a life and who would rather get out of the country or go to jail instead.

"Make love, not war," Paul whispered almost reverently as he approached the main structure.

"Amen, brother," replied a gaunt, long-haired man behind a counter. "Fancy someone your age knowing that."

"The times they are a' changing," said Paul.

"Bob Dylan first said that," the gaunt man reminisced. "Hell, I was even at one of his concerts back in the day."

"That must have been something."

"Oh, it was, it was. He had a craggy voice not worth spit but he sure could play guitar and he sure could move a whole generation."

"You really are a hippy aren't you?"

"Yeah, that's me. I saw the Mamas and the Papas live and I once went to a Seekers concert. The Seekers...They were Australian weren't they? Just like you. Well, it's getting late and I have to close up shop. Is there something I can interest you in?"

Paul bought a photo of the commune, taken in the early years of the project by a commune member, and then left. On the way out he met a tall woman in her thirties with long blond hair and a charming smile. She was in the photo but as a precocious twenty-something girl with flowers behind her ears and the Egyptian symbol for life painted in black, so it stood out, on her forehead. It was enough like a cross to make Paul feel uneasy about it.

"Did Lem talk your ear off?" she asked him in good humor.

"I think I have his ear somewhere on me," replied Paul in equally good humor.

"We made him the shopkeeper a long time ago because he likes meeting people. When he's not talking up a storm, he can sell a thing or two."

"I bought a photo."

"Let me see...Oh, yes. Good choice. We were so young back then. We actually thought we could stop people fighting and dying. We were so naive and we had such high hopes."

"The wheels keep turning. The world moves on."

"Yes it does. Enjoy your photo. Please come again."

Paul knew he would never return. He would not take the chance of risking their lives with his vampiric appetites. It was something he could never explain to them, it was something they could never understand, but to show his love and approval for their life style, for what they continued to stand for, he had to stay away for good. It was a sad business, but that was where unlife had taken him. He wondered what Lilith would have made of them.

Down the road from the hippies Paul knew there was a community of cottages belonging to the local Indian tribe. Since it was known that the North American Indians, just like the Australian Aborigines, had many arcane secrets unknown to other people and deadly to evil spirits and the walking dead, it was best to avoid contact with them. And so Paul walked briskly past the side road leading off to the Native American village, not daring to look back for fear of whatever looking back might spark.

When he was young, his father had read to him the story of a Lakota medicine man who had invoked the spirit of the wily coyote to deal with a man who had passed away in a hunting accident but had returned to the land of the living for his bride. The man could not understand why, being newly married, he couldn't take his wife with him into the land of the shadows. The coyote showed him his future if he persisted on his chosen path. It involved his wife hating him. He was shown the alternate path in which his wife continued to remember him fondly. The man chose the alternate path.

"It was just a story, nothing more," Paul told himself as he continued, just as briskly, away from the Indians. "Just like Aborigine stories of beautiful women changed into birds by evil magicians and Dreamtime stuff about why the animals and plants and birds came to be the way they are. It's primitive nonsense, nothing more."

Despite his words, there was something in the back of his head that told him it couldn't all be rubbish. How, for example, did a primitive people come upon the idea of conserving natural resources before the great Western powers saw the need? Yes, the Aborigines had to score points on that one and so come off as perhaps more knowing than others believe. The American Indians of Dakota only killed enough buffalo, at any one time, to satisfy their needs. It was the American government, in order to destroy their way of life forever, who promoted, among Americans and visiting Europeans, the wholesale slaughter of the big, black hairy beasts without any thought of what such destruction might do to the land.

Paul didn't know the name of the tribe he was now running from nor did he care. To try to find out might invoke their interest in him and he didn't want that. He didn't relax until he was more than a mile distant from them. Even then he wondered if some medicine man or woman could read him and possibly still do him harm.

Of course he could have traversed the distance a lot faster on the wing rather than walking, or even running, but he felt that transforming himself into a bat might give him away. It would show up as a blip on the natural world and any sensitive close by worth anything would pick up the anomaly. He suspected this was harder to do in cities and large towns where there was a great deal of manmade objects. In places where greenery prevailed, however, it had to be a lot easier. Paul was loath to deal in any way with people whose powers he didn't even understand.

It was said that in the American south, around New Orleans, there were black men and women with extraordinary power. They had a mixture of French and African mysticism capable of sending them on marvelous spirit journeys and furnishing them with abilities beyond the ken of ordinary mortals. Paul was determined to stay away from them too.

A little while later, Paul was walking alongside Vine Street in the Hollywood hills. There, he came upon a blond, blue-eyed twenty-something hitchhiker thumbing for a ride. He went to exchange pleasantries with her but she was rude to him thus opening up other possibilities. He mesmerized her, taking her to a ghost town that one of the major movie and television studios had used as a setting for Westerns and horror flicks. It hadn't been used for some time so it was a perfect locale for him to sleep during the day. It was also a perfect locale for him to drain the hitchhiker of every drop of blood. He did so with relish.

There was no point in making her over into a vampire. She was far from the type he considered worthy. He had never, however, slept with a woman and, in a sense, this was his chance. He could have done it earlier but hadn't wanted to while Lilith was either close by or still fresh in his mind. So, as the sun came up over the old, decrepit town, Paul settled down in bed with her clothed body (he thought it improper, for some reason, to unclothe her) and fell asleep as she went from warm to corpse cold in his embrace. It wasn't as if he could have real human sex with her at any stage because that was impossible for a walking corpse. Still it was nice to even lie with a woman after so long dreaming about it.

The next night he left the ghost town that now had at least one resident ghost. He didn't even look back. He felt a little ashamed of himself but didn't quite know why.

Four months later in Saint Louis, Paul came upon a trendy club that catered for vampire wannabes. The members ranged from kids in their early twenties to adults in their late fifties. All had money and preferred to dress in black. Paul, in scruffy jeans and grotty blue T-shirt, almost didn't get past the doorman. He was allowed in when he showed his credentials by lifting the doorman over his head and then hissing into his face. He thus showed off muscles he shouldn't have and fangs the members would literally die for.

The members all wanted to be made over into the undead. They had all sorts of fanciful notions of what it would be like. They were based on Hammer movies from England, the novel by Bram Stoker and some of his short stories, plus a few Universal cinema classics made back in the '30s and '40s. The women in black silk hoods and black widow dresses looked divine. To most real vampires like Paul they were absurd in their darkness inspired glamour. Even so, he needed a place to rest up and thought the club might be amenable to playing host to one real vampire for a couple of days.

It took some persuading but they talked him into turning five of their women. He said it would take five nights and that was okay with them. They had a special coffin he could use during the daylight hours but he preferred a closed room with a bed instead. He explained that coffins were not necessary and that all a vampire needed to sustain him was blood, native earth somewhere on his person when he slept, and to be kept away from sunlight, torches, sharp wooden objects, garlic and holy water.

Paul chose as carefully as he could the five women. One was a doctor of theology, two were known authors of modern vampire romance and the other two had made their money on the stock market and now no longer had to work. The women were chosen as much for their intelligence and ability to cope with change as for their beauty. Three were in their late thirties but Paul considered this a plus. He figured someone with a P.H.D could arrange her schedule to work at night. He thought people who wrote about vampires probably deserved to find out, firsthand, what it was really like, and he considered that anyone who could make themselves independently wealthy, could do anything with the gifts and the curses he was bestowing on them.

After Paul turned the five, he left wishing them all the best of luck. The theologian told him he could be their leader if he stayed but he begged off. He knew, straight off, he wasn't as smart as a university professor or someone who could make a lot of money figuring out what the stock market's likely to do. They might make him leader but common sense said he wouldn't be leader for long. In gratitude, they gave him two large bottles of AB- to take away with him in a big leather carry-all bag they also gave him.

He knew the five were most likely going to turn more club members and that the club might become one big undead family. He wondered how long such a family could last. He figured it would do better than the young women he'd turned back at Berkeley. He rather fancied the idea of people who should have been horror movie extras actually acting and needing to act like the true undead. If nothing else, it was something he could smile about.

Corinne Kelly was the only one of the five Paul had second thoughts about on his continuing journey to discover his place, if he had one, in America. Was it the fact she was only twenty-five, close in age to Paul when he became undead? She was one of the writers and, of the five; it was the writers he'd taken more of a cavalier approach with. Both had their following of readers but Corinne only had two novels under her belt, a few short stories in a few magazines and a scrawny Bachelor of Arts degree.

One of the reasons he'd gone along with Corinne was her breeziness and almost total lack of understanding of life's bigger picture. She was a short redhead, who wore a black ribbon in her hair, pink John Lennon style glasses, liked New Wave music and had an appreciation for Monty Python style humor. She was the most British American he'd ever met. He wondered how this had impacted on his decision. Bram Stoker, who had little interest in women, would have taken a liking to her and it was possible that Vlad Dracul, the real Dracula, would have taken her for one of his demonic maidens. Vlad, it has to be said, would have enjoyed corrupting her innocence, her naivety. Paul, of course, had no intention of corrupting anyone as fully as the count had a penchant to do but even to corrupt a little is considered a sin.

Mandy Provost, the other writer he'd made-over, was thirty-seven with ten well received books under her belt, short stories in a dozen magazines and had been on two current affairs style television shows presenting her wares. What's more, she was a big, blustering woman with long black hair, a straightforward manner and a love of all things gothic. Her favorite places in the world were Vatican City with its marvelous catacombs, London with its sinister tower, Notre Dame with its cathedral and Boston with its various old churches. Paul made it clear to her that, from now on, places of worship would be out of bounds for her. This did not faze her a bit. She said she was just as drawn to burial sites, places of execution and old, broken down castles. Here Paul was happy to take her at her word. There was a brightness and determination he could see behind the eyes that told him that if any of the five could survive as one of the undead for very long she would be the one.

Paul, to salve his conscience about Corinne and the others, decided to keep tabs on them as best he could. He did this by occasionally walking into a bookshop that was open at night and looking around for titles belonging to either Corrine or Mandy. In the space of the next two years, both writers had managed to get out three bestsellers, each with their surprisingly new approach to vampire fiction. Then they stopped. Paul was in New York at the time with some money on him from a dead executive who preferred cash to MasterCard in her transactions and in her purse. Thus he looked up the vampire club in the Saint Louis telephone directory and made a long distance phone call. At first no one answered. Then a hard male voice asked for his name and where he was phoning from. Paul hung up.

Sure, there had been male members as well as female in the club but, instinctively, he knew the guy he'd spoken to wasn't a member. There was something wrong with the timbre of his voice. He was most likely FBI. If this was so, then the club, the five vampires and the rest were no doubt finished. After two years of making merry with Saint Louis and, no doubt, other places, they'd run afoul of the vampire slayers and that was that. Still, two years can be a long time as a member of the undead community. He would like to think that, in the end, they'd gotten all they could get out of the experience or at least had had one or two thrilling moments with real fangs.

Chapter 4

New York, July, 1980

New Wave and Punk had, to some extent, replaced disco music at discos. More than ever young people were living for the now, not giving a damn about tomorrow. Debbie Harry's voicing of "Die Young, Stay Pretty" from her Blondie days said it all. If it didn't, then any of the British Punk band, "The Sex Pistols" songs was all that was further required. Wall Street insider trading was making life difficult for everyone save a select few investors who knew what was really going on. Trendy restaurants and clothing stores were everywhere, soaking up what they could of outsider money coming into the city. New York was now called the rotten apple and was struggling to stay viable as a great trading center. Inflation had gone through the roof and no one seemed to have any idea what to do about it.

In the Bronx there were kids with boom boxes on their shoulders walking down the streets, annoying anyone they could find over thirty with either Punk or Heavy Metal. They viewed Paul as one of their own not realizing his true age. There were teenage girls with steel spikes in various body parts and women in their twenties with tattoos all over their arms and legs. No one seemed to care about possibly getting lockjaw or something else just as nasty from a contaminated metal decoration or a dirty needle. No one seemed to give a damn about being turned down for a job because of the way they looked.

"I'm in the land of the barbarian," said Paul to himself as he approached a tattoo parlor. Two black leather freaks on Harleys got off their rides to sort him out. They wanted to do this because he looked so neat and tidy in the suit he'd taken from a dead Wall Street speculator. He'd found this speculator laid-out in a morgue. The freaks took him for some greenhorn who'd wandered onto their turf by mistake and whom they would make sure lived to regret it. Such mistakes, they felt, should come with hard lessons attached. Paul sorted them out instead and, since one was female, he supped on her before going on his way. She was a bit on the dumpy side and her blood tasted of amphetamines but it served its purpose. He was glad she wasn't on heroin or something worse.

He'd once seen a vampire strung out on angel dust infected blood rip a man in two then leap out into the light of the rising sun. As she sizzled and died her second death, though, she managed to rip a second man in two. She then saw Paul and wanted to do the same thing to him but, by that time, her bones were turning to powder. All that reached him behind the closed door, where he was hiding, was one finger, with fingernail attached, and one crazed eyeball. Both body parts disintegrated.

Until angel dust sent her mental, this particular member of the undead community had been as thoughtful and considerate with her victims and her kind as it was possible for her to be. She'd even admonished another vampire once for unnecessary cruelty.

Paul saw the ingestion of angel dust in any shape or form, including blood, as not only a terrible way of beating a path to destruction, but also an excellent way of ending up hurting people you don't want to hurt. Both possibilities scared the hell out of him.

Meanwhile, Paul had created a real problem for himself. The tattooist, seeing two brutes outside his shop assaulted by someone who should have been a victim, did something he usually refrained from doing. He phoned the police. Then he got in touch with the FBI agent who had been snooping around. The FBI agent who told people he would pay for information on unusual happenings.

Paul was long gone before any of the authorities arrived. Even so he wasn't out of the area when alarming information flowed to him from a friendly New York vampire. Something odd had happened near the tattooist's establishment and the tattooist had acted in an uncustomary way concerning it. Apparently the information had come from the tattooist's mind. It was picked up as the vampire was walking past the fellow on his way to the train station.

In his dingy Queens apartment, Paul relaxed in front of the television set after a night of minor pleasantries. The freak's woman had been reasonably good value on the hoof and it had been nice tossing her thick-headed boyfriend around. He even made things a little more exciting when he came at Paul with a greased-up trucker's chain. The excitement didn't last long, though. Paul, after all, could move at super-human speed to snatch the chain out of the moron's grasp. Also this particular antagonist's stomach got in his own way when he tried to kick out with one of his workman's boots. It took little effort on Paul's part to simply grab the boot, spin the fellow around and give him a good wallop with his fist. To someone looking on, it might have appeared to be martial arts in action. He might have gotten away with it as such but, when his fangs came out dripping saliva and he fell upon the female's neck, it was all too obvious something else was going on. She screamed a little to make it just that more obvious for the watching tattooist.

"God," cried Paul as he reviewed his actions in his head. "I have been stupid."

Just the other night he'd run across an old San Francisco vampire who'd gotten the hell out of the city by the bay when some mad Aus-tralian vampire hunters had turned up. One of their Sydney sensitives had picked up that their quarry, whoever that might be, was on the West coast of the USA. They'd flown out to get them. The search was further narrowed when a body turned up in San Francisco with tell-tale marks on it. Now the whole bay area was being turned upside down by the FBI and the local Rising Sun Group operatives. The more knowledgeable members of the Catholic and the Protestant churches were also lending a hand. Already half a dozen vampires had been turned to dust with more, no doubt, to follow.

Paul had asked the old San Francisco vampire about Lilith. He was told that the last time she was seen by her own kind was on a plane headed for Miami. This was about a week before things had gone wrong for other bloodsuckers. If she'd been the one the Australians wanted to get so badly then they'd just missed their chance. As things stood, San Francisco was not a place any member of the unliving should venture into for a while unless they were feeling suicidal, wanting maybe to take a few hunters with them.

Paul had been relieved that Lilith had managed to give the Secret Compass and their American allies the slip. Even so, they probably brought at least one of their sensitives along. That sensitive might have pointed toward Berkeley. At Berkeley, Paul had sired half a dozen women over to vampirism. He had also supped and killed a dozen more. He had been quite proud of his actions there and hoped that the Secret Compass would not render to a second death all of his college and university converts. He suspected most of them were gone now thanks to the actions of American vampire slayers. Nothing could be certain. None of them had turned out to be stable enough for long term survival.

From Berkeley, Paul had travelled back to San Francisco and then to Los Angeles. From Los Angeles, he got a plane over to the East coast, thinking it a good bet the Secret Compass wouldn't follow him across such a distance in a hurry. He knew he needed time and room in which to breathe. Room was important. In practical terms, he only breathed because it was a difficult habit to break and it made him look more human. He had to wonder if he would be spending the rest of his unlife on the run.

Paul had only been in New York two weeks and already the pace was driving him mad. On the pavement on some streets, even at night, the human traffic was elbow to elbow. *How can they live like this?* He had to wonder. *How can anyone live like this?* He hadn't come across any unlife threats but he suspected they were on their way. Still, with so many millions of people around in such a small land area, it was easy to stay hidden or so he was coming to think. The noise and the pollution, however, grated on his nerves, making him far too edgy for his own good.

The incident with the freakish couple had helped. Dealing with them had made him feel much better about his own circumstance. If nothing else, he had stopped them from, in the future, picking on someone less capable of defending themselves. Surely the one he'd allowed to live would have to think twice now about getting into a fight with anyone. If this was so, he had indeed achieved something. If that couldn't put a smile on his face then nothing would.

As Paul settled down to rest, he wondered where he could go and not be found by his pursuers. He began to think of countries that were poor and would no doubt always be poor. He thought of countries where there was war or where war erupted every second month. He thought of places where there were terrorists on the loose and bombs going off in the streets.

"Maybe the Middle East or Northern Ireland would be good this time of year," he told himself as he twisted his pillow into a comfy shape.

He wondered how either the Middle East or Northern Ireland would figure into his own views on morality. In the Middle East he couldn't very well put the question to women who didn't understand English and whose culture was very different from his own. In Northern Ireland the conditions people lived under might be traumatic enough to render his question useless as a moralistic measuring stick. Even so, he had to go somewhere he could gather his thoughts and maybe make a proper stand against the ever present jocks and jockettes. He had to go somewhere he could belong for a while and maybe make whatever contribution his kind could make to any society.

That day, he dreamt, for the first time in quite a while, of the family he'd left behind in Sydney. The family he had planned never to see again. He missed them but there was little he could do about it without endangering their lives. He had to remind himself that they were better off thinking he was dead, killed at or near the disco he had frequented once too often. *The Blue*, he figured, deserved whatever bad publicity he could heap on it.

Even so, he wondered what his family was up to and how his life might have gone if he hadn't become one of the undead. Maybe he might have met a girl. Maybe they might have gone out together and eventually married. Then who knows what might have happened after that.

"Love, sex, marriage – the whole damn thing," said Paul to himself, wondering what any of that meant to anyone who had it all.

The very next night, Paul was on the look-out for prey as he always was. He came upon a couple apparently "in love." Both twenty-something, they were coyly holding hands and making goo-goo eyes at each other. For some reason he couldn't fathom, he found this behavior distasteful. They were well dressed and smart looking. He guessed they had good jobs to go to and a life worth living. They were what other people were beginning to call "Yuppies." He couldn't help but hate them for what they had and the things he could never have.

They were on the same train he was on and they were headed for Wall Street. How far they got, he figured, was up to him. It would have been easy to wrest the girl away from her male companion. It would have been simple to remove her from this world. He could, at the same time, deliver the guy a hurt he'd carry around for quite a while. He wanted to do these things and he wanted to do them badly. He spooked them with the obvious loathing in his eyes.

For reasons he couldn't fathom, he wouldn't destroy them. He wouldn't even come close. When they found themselves harassed by three members of some inner-city gang, he came to their rescue. And there he was, saving the fair damsel like some real life superhero. There he was thumping heads together and looking for more heads he could thump. One member of the gang was a female who pulled a knife on him before her thumping. He was tempted to turn the blade on her instead but didn't want to waste her blood that way. When he did taste it, though, it tasted of cheap wine. Still, he had experienced worse.

The couple he saved didn't thank him. They got off at the next stop and bolted for their lives. *Just as well*, Paul thought. He'd beaten the cheap male thugs to death and had taken all of the street woman's life essence. Next he took what money they had on them.

Why the thugs didn't pick on him in the first place rather than the couple was a mystery. He was only one person whereas the couple offered to be double the trouble. Maybe it had to do with the fact he didn't appear to have two pennies to rub together. This time he'd gone out into the darkness in old jeans and T-shirt rather than the nice suit of the other night. Maybe they too were jealous the way he had been of the couple. Maybe they hadn't even noticed him until it was too late for them.

Day came and in his apartment, as he drifted off to sleep, Paul wondered some more about sex, about companionship. Sex was something he'd never really had and never would have since becoming a walking, talking dead guy. He couldn't help but think about it every once in a while. He couldn't help but wonder if it was part of what ultimately made people human and him something else.

Chapter 5

New York, August, 1980

Miles and Long, along with the Secret Compass sensitive Helen Kiln, met midday with the FBI agent in charge of unusual events at a cozy restaurant near Battery Park. Over Italian they discussed what they knew about the two vampires Miles was especially anxious to catch.

It was definite the miscreants had travelled from Sydney to San Francisco, going on from there to cause havoc at Berkeley. From there things got hazy. The vampires probably returned to San Francisco and, for whatever reason, split up. The older female with the East European accent may have stayed longer in San Francisco than the male before moving on. But where had she moved to and where had the male gone? They had reappeared in different boroughs of New York. Helen was certain of this as was the FBI. Were they planning to get back together?

Maybe they'd ended up in the Big Apple because, for decades, it had been a vampire haven. Those nights were long gone but not every vampire in the world was aware of this. Meanwhile, there were some who viewed it as safer than, say, Chicago, where the Pinkertons had their main headquarters, or San Francisco where there'd been a major crackdown.

"The woman known as Lilith was last seen on the Street of the Americas sucking the life out of a small time publisher," said Patrick Lenny, the FBI representative. He was a thin man in a plain brown suit that appeared to be one size too large for him.

"What happened?" asked Miles.

"She knocked down two of my men getting away and broke the necks of two more," replied Lenny. "One's dead and one is still in critical condition in Mercy Hospital."

"Did you manage to wound her?" Long asked hopefully.

"We were aiming to shoot her down and then stab her through the heart but she's fast and deadly," admitted Lenny.

"She's been around long enough to know what she can and can't do," said Miles.

"I'd say she's been around since the Second World War," ventured Helen. "There's a Linda Krakowski in our London office files. Apparently, she was taken from her Polish village and force-fed to a Nazi vampire. Her village had a German and a Polish population before the war. We've been told the Lilith we are looking for speaks with a Polish accent but sometimes uses German words with her English. It all fits."

"Surely being force-fed to a Nazi vampire would have been the end of her," said Lenny.

"Well, she died all right," added Helen. "They'd locked her in with him, but something happened that no one counted on. When she came back, three nights later, she came back with a vengeance. She ripped out his throat and shoved her fist through his heart. Then she took his blood and used his corpse as a battering ram to break out."

"Really?" asked Lenny. "How did London get this information?"

"From closed Nazi files found in Berlin after the war," said Helen. "Linda had been a farmer's daughter and the Nazi who had turned her had been a star athlete with a brain not much bigger than a walnut. In the notes it states that Linda developed a long standing hatred of what she calls jocks. All up, a long term hatred against athletes both male and, it seems, female as well."

"And what were the Nazis after in putting Linda with this brute vampire Nazi?" asked Lenny.

"The usual thing," said Helen. "They wanted to build a master race of night time storm troopers and female agents with super strength they could drop behind enemy lines, or order to fly in under the radar. The first woman they picked to experiment on happened to be the wrong one. She had too much of a mind of her own and didn't like one bit what had been done to her and by whom. Whatever the Nazis did to her, apart from the vampire biting and the sharing of vampire blood, certainly came back to haunt them. She became undead alright, but she also managed to ruin their future plans by destroying their prize vampire. Then she escaped into the night."

"And she's still around?" asked Lenny.

"No report of a second death," said Helen. "She surfaced after the war, first in Munich where she took out a couple of American G.Is. Then she made her way to Berlin. There she went over the wall that was under construction to, no doubt, take out a couple of Russians. The animosity between America and Russia prevented a concerted effort to be launched to catch her. She then turned up in the British sector, killing a few British officers before slipping back into the Russian sector."

"Sounds smart," said Lenny. "And they never laid hands on her?"

"We don't know about the Russians," said Helen. "What we do know is that she came back on our collective radar in the mid-1950s. She was a dancer in some dive in Soho, London. She did that for about a year, living off the toughs in the neighborhood, thinning out the razor gangs. Then she went back to the continent. Next she appeared in the early 1970s during the German Olympic Games where she murdered two German sprinters and three French soccer players."

"And then she turned up in Sydney?" asked Lenny.

"That's right," said Helen. "If we are to believe Linda Krakowski is this Lilith person. A few weeks before the first incident which occurred in *The Blue* disco, a female vampire attacked a young man leaving a gym. The young man was Caucasian but he had Chinese friends. Well, the next night she came back to the gym, waited outside for another victim to emerge, and was set upon by three warriors of the Rising Sun Group. They had butterfly swords and thought they'd do all right against her.

"She proved them wrong by breaking the backs of two of them and snapping the neck of the third. She was simply too fast for them. In parting she said: 'I am Lilith, little men, fear me!' Unbeknown to her, they weren't all dead. The warrior with the neck injury was saved by a passing cop who got him medical aid in time. He's not likely to ever walk again but he's alive. Anyway, she liked calling herself Lilith and so decided to continue to do so. A number of recent spirits I have made contact with have told me about her. They all refer to her by that name."

"It does add up," said Miles.

"We now have motive for her," Long concluded. "But we don't have any clear indication of where she'll go next or what she'll do."

"The spirits are quiet on that one, for now, I'm afraid," said Helen. "They don't know me here and are reluctant to give out much information."

"What about the other one you're after?" Lenny asked. "Do we have anything on him?"

"I don't know his story," said Helen. "The spirits, both here and in Sydney, have been very quiet about him. I don't know why. Sometimes they can be like that for reasons we'll never know or appreciate. They did tell me he was responsible for what happened at some tattooist's parlor, if that's of any use to you. All I sense, when it comes to him, is a lot of confusion, a lot of anger. We don't have any records that I know of dating back past Sydney for him. I believe he's a genuine newcomer."

"His accent is Australian," put in Miles. "Fred Mills, one of our operatives, said so before he died. I'd say she picked him up at that disco and turned him somewhere close by in Sydney."

"And now they're running loose here," said Lenny.

"Yes," agreed Miles. "Those are the facts."

"I'm assigning men to aid you," said Lenny. "But tell me; is there some personal reason for what you are doing? They're away from Australia now, out of your jurisdiction, if a vampire hunter can have jurisdiction."

"We're Secret Compass," Long answered, before Miles could open his mouth. "That's personal enough!"

As the afternoon faded to night, Miles and Long left Lenny at the restaurant. They took a cab back to their hotel where they dropped Helen off. They went a few streets, got out, paid the cab driver and caught the underground to Queens. They were hoping that, by interviewing the tattooist who'd come forward for the FBI, something more might be found out about Lilith's former, possibly future, companion. They armed themselves with guns that had true vampire stopping power. The bullets were hollow points with slivers of wood soaked in holy water at the centre. If one of them hit an undead but failed to destroy the heart it would fester, slowly killing its victim until removed. A regular bullet could be absorbed into the vampire's system after a day or two's rest. If, of course, the new bullet did hit the heart then it would be over for the vampire without any reprieve. Crossbows were great, so were bolas that brought down vampires in their bat form but this was real progress.

"Science marches on," Miles told Long as he patted his .45 in its holster.

"Yes," agreed Long as the train came to a stop and they got off.

It was a three-block walk to their destination. It was across the neighborhood of a vile street gang but they were not worried. After facing mobile cadavers all else seemed tame. Two streets down, Miles and Long should not have been surprised to find their way interfered with by a dozen street thugs wearing black bandanas and sporting lots of hardware. There were baseball bats, flick knives, plumber's pipe and machetes. Each thug had the appearance of a walking arsenal.

"Any vamps you reckon?" asked Miles.

"No," Long said. "They're not that stupid – vamps I mean."

Before any of the thugs could mount a reply, Miles pulled out his gun and fired two shots into the air. At the same time Long got out his weapon and waved it menacingly about.

"Fucking mad!" cried one of the thugs.

"As a cut snake," Long agreed.

When the thug who had spoken turned around to confer with his mates, he found he was alone. It was not a pleasant way to be.

"Time you were off too," said Long and the thug took the hint.

"When next we meet them," cautioned Miles, "they'll probably have more impressive weapons."

"Yes," Long agreed. "When next we meet, if we ever do, we might have to enlist the FBI men who have been tailing us to lend a hand. I mean the ones hidden behind that garbage disposal unit across the street. In the meantime, we have other business."

The tattooist was a brawny individual with lots of tattoos up and down both arms plus one almighty beard. He was in his forties but age hadn't mellowed him. Understandably, he resented anyone taking out his customers or would-be customers. He made this plain to Miles. It was the only reason he was willing to talk to federal agents or friends of federal agents. The shop was dark and two women in the waiting area were in shadow. Long had an uneasy feeling and drew out his crucifix. After Korea and then his time so far in the Secret Compass, he had learned to go with his feelings. The women flinched and hissed at him, proving that not all was as it should be.

"Trap!" Long cried for Miles' benefit and took out a bottle of holy water. He then sprinkled the contents on the two females who were getting to their feet. They began to sizzle and squeal.

Miles threw his crucifix at the tattooist. It landed on the fellow's beard causing it to burst into flame. He then pulled out his .45, emptying the chamber into the tattooist and his females. All went down. Only the tattooist was burnt to ash. Long staked the others just to be sure.

"They could have had us," said Miles. "Without your nose for trouble, we would have had it."

"Something definitely didn't smell right," Long agreed.

It was now obvious that Paul had retraced his steps and had made over the people in the tattoo parlor into vampires just for them.

"He's getting smart," said Miles.

"Yes," Long agreed. "I hate it when they make plans."

"I'll get that bastard yet," said Miles. "For Lizzy, I'll get him."

Long nodded his understanding.

Chapter 6

New York, September, 1980

It was turning out to be a hot and sweaty month. There wasn't much relief from the heat for the humans and this Lilith viewed as a good thing. It made them restless at night and more of them tended to stay out late. It distracted them at times when they ought to be paying attention. It could also slow down their reactions to where she had them at more of a disadvantage than usual.

What's more, sweat didn't bother her or her kind. You needed a fully functioning heart to sweat and it was something she didn't have or even wanted to have. The last occasion, in which she had one in full operation, she was facing a Nazi monster she had no hope of winning against. Once it was stone cold, however, she was able to defeat the Nazi monster, going on to fight and go after other monsters like him.

It was with supreme confidence that Lilith stood atop the Empire State building getting an eyeful of her city. Here she felt almost like Athena looking over Athens. Only, where Athena was kind and just, Lilith was more like a raging Fury. She then recalled from her studies when she was much younger how the goddess Athena had placated in ancient Greece the anger of the Furies with soothing words and the promise they would always be remembered by the Greeks. This had stopped them throwing destructive temper tantrums on the people of Athens. Nothing, however, was going to stop Lilith from showing the New Yorkers any anger she felt. New York, as far as she knew, didn't have a guardian goddess.

"They will know of me!" shouted Lilith to the wind that rose hot from hell. "And they will remember!"

She had ripped a hole in the protective barrier that prevented people from getting too close to the edge and had stepped past it to the very edge. A man who thought only a mad person could have the strength to do such a thing was watching her.

She was in a contemplative mood which was just as well for Phillip Alcibiades, the guard of Greek descent shaking nearby. His job, apart from a multitude of others, was to get potential suicides safely off the building. He didn't want to say or do anything that might make her act any more irrationally than she already was acting. *She's dressed in black evening dress for Christ's sake*, he thought, *and her hair's running wild like nobody's business. She's got expensive jewels on a necklace around her neck and a funny little sack on a chain. She's got brown leather boots that come up to her knees. If she's a jumper then she's high class for one. Could she have just lost a lot of money in pork belly futures? Is that her problem? If it is, I almost know how she feels.*

Phillip knew that a lot of corporate pigs were trying to fly without wings this night over those pork belly futures. He'd only lost what he could afford to on the stock market. Others went the whole hog and ruination was staring them in the face. It had also happened when the airline stocks plummeted then rose, also when certain promising computer software companies went belly up.

The guard thought he'd better say something but thoughts of joining the strange woman in a plunge downwards made him continue to hesitate. He didn't want to shout. Then again he didn't want to get close enough to whisper where she might grab him. He heard that mad people could have great strength and she had already demonstrated she was no weakling. He felt that, in this instance, he owed it to his wife and children not to find out how strong. She was about fifty paces away. In his mind's eye, he could still see her killing them both.

Unbeknown to Phillip, she could smell his spreading fear and his cheap aftershave his wife had given him last year for Christmas. She could sense some of his thoughts and be amused by them. He'd already phoned for the police on his walkie-talkie. That was all he was prepared in the end to do. They didn't pay him enough to do anymore. Besides, he wasn't at all convinced his craggy voice wouldn't be the very sound that sent her over.

Then she fell. It took Philip by surprise even though he was expecting it to happen. She was majestic in her falling, if one can indeed fall in such a manner. If she'd had a pool to splash into, her form would have been excellent. She might have won a gold medal at some swimming carnival.

Madness! Thought Phillip and backed away. Minutes later, he came to the ledge to look down. He didn't want to look but he felt it was the least he could do. What he saw didn't add up. There wasn't a broken body on the pavement, on the road or on one of the parked cars so far below. There was nothing but a lone bat, first circling the building, then heading out toward Elis Island.

Phillip felt some relief but a growing curiosity. Maybe the wind had been so strong that it had taken her out of his range of sight so that she plonked to the asphalt nearby but not as close as he might have expected. Or maybe he was too far up to get a good idea of what went on down at street level. The street lamps weren't all that good and he was forever wiping sweat from his eyes with his handkerchief.

"She jumped," Phillip reported in. He didn't mention the bat and wasn't going to until a pair of FBI detectives brought up the possibility. They came to see him half an hour after he first spoke about the incident. They were hungry for details. He told them about her clothing and about her having a chin that, given martial arts training, could smash concrete blocks. He thought that was enough.

"Why?" he asked them. "What difference does it make if there was a bat hanging around?"

"That's FBI business," said the shorter detective.

"Was it a suicide or something else?" Phillip asked them. "I can't believe you'd bother with a suicide."

"Can't say," said the taller detective and left it at that.

"Yeah, there was a bat," Phillip told them, not wanting to be accused of interfering with an FBI investigation, "but so what?"

"That's all we needed to confirm," said the shorter detective. "Consider it paperwork."

"Yeah, sure," said Phillip. "Want to know how many pigeons in the park I saw today?"

"No," answered the taller detective. "We'll be off. If there's anything else you can remember, give us a phone call."

The taller detective left Phillip his card.

A week later, Paul met up with Lilith in a bar and grill in the village. Both were looking at the menu but not the menu the seated humans were looking at. They were eyeing the other customers to work out what would be good on a sweltering night. There were men and women of all ages to choose from. By invading their thoughts, it was possible to put together a moral profile that would satisfy Lilith's curiosity and Paul's continuing need.

"Good to see you again, Paul," Lilith told him.

"How are you doing these nights?" asked Paul.

"I have a high-priced apartment in Battery Park that puts to shame any of the places we had while we were in Sydney."

"What about keeping a low profile?"

"This is a low profile of sorts. I work for an escort agency. Clients either visit me or I visit them. I am safe so long as I can have three clients a night and don't drain any of them completely. Thus I can continue in an unlife style that is compatible with both my needs and my desires."

"And they're all jocks, these clients of yours?"

"Some are. I have learned to be practical."

"I understand."

"But you don't approve? Better to be well off than dust, nein?"

"I suppose so, but what are you doing here?"

"A night off, a stroll, a hunt...It's in the blood, I suppose."

"I don't enjoy the hunt."

"You don't?"

"What about our mission?"

"We must survive. And if we can do better than mere survival then, why not?"

"You've forgotten..."

"I forget nothing! The jocks pay! The jockettes pay! Is this not so?"

"Yes!"

"Then we are in agreement, nein? Just like old times, ya?"

"Just like old times."

That night Paul and Lilith supped on an out-of-town couple that met Paul's specifications. She was an Olympic class swimmer and he was a football coach. They laid the bodies in a dumpster and piled rubbish on top of them.

"I'm being pursued again," Paul told Lilith as they walked away from the dumpster.

"Do you have any idea by whom?"

"No."

"It could be the FBI or perhaps the Secret Compass. Did you see any ninja weapons?"

"No. I hope it isn't the Rising Sun Group. I still have bad dreams over the last time we tangled."

They strolled down to the docks and looked out at the shipping. There wasn't much to see except a few oil tankers and two cargo vessels. There was the smell of rotting seaweed and a chemical odor Paul couldn't place. It had something to do with factory waste. The surface of the water was greasy, giving the blackness a silvery film in the moonlight that was broken up by tiny surface rainbows.

"If there are fish here," said Lilith, "they wouldn't be fit for the humans to eat. Lead and mercury, I believe, are high here. They could clean it up. They may very well do so some day. They're not beyond cleaning up their own mess, you know. Population-wise, things are getting out of hand. When it comes to these humans, we can help keep their numbers down."

"I used to fish," said Paul, only taking in half of what she'd told him.

He used to do a lot of things back when he was human he didn't do anymore. Some of those things were well worth doing while others he missed on principle. He wondered if there was anywhere one could really fish in America. He remembered San Francisco being a disappointment in that regard. The people living there were already talking about bringing the water back to what it was supposed to be like. There were even politicians in full agreement that something must be done. Maybe the people could clean up the mess, even the mess of generations, if they were the right people.

"I'll remain till the end of this month," said Lilith. "Then I will take passage to England. Perhaps this time I will visit Scotland and Wales. There are wild, forested places in Scotland where one might get lost and never be found. They say there are caves in Wales you can get lost in and never, in a thousand years, find your way out of. What do you think?"

"It sounds good though somewhat purposeless."

"And what will you do that has more purpose?"

"I don't know. Canada seems welcoming. I've been told Canadians are a lot like Australians. I'd like to find out if that's true or not. I'd also like to find out if that's a good thing for me or not. Maybe then I will move onto the countries where there's a lot of killing and little reasoning. Sorting out the jocks and the jockettes there from the rest of the populace would be worthwhile."

"And recruits?"

"Yes. I will look to siring more like ourselves. At Berkeley, I had much of my work undone by vampire slayers, or so the word on the street informs me. Perhaps, elsewhere, they might grow larger in number before they are discovered and that might make all the difference."

"Yes. One can only hope that will be so next time, nein?"

"I'll plan better."

"Yes. And I will plan better too, for when next I try that experiment."

Paul thought about bringing up the things that had gone wrong at Berkeley, also why they had gone wrong. In the end, he decided to leave it alone. So long as he wasn't staying close to Lilith, and there was some evidence in her current behavior that she was no longer as rash in her actions as she had been, there seemed little point in revisiting those particular elements of their shared past.

Paul and Lilith were about to make their farewells to one another and to fly off to their resting places, before dawn could catch up with them, when they both caught a particular scent on the wind. It came from behind a pile of old oil drums. It was human and it somehow made Paul think of Sydney and of the Secret Compass.

"Trap!" cried Lilith, changing to bat form. Paul followed her lead. He couldn't yet see the danger but he knew it was there. Other scents beside the one he'd detected were telling him that there were humans, definitely on the move, and no doubt out to destroy them.

Just as Lilith was getting airborne, a flame-thrower nozzle edged out of some wooden boxes near her. She found herself engulfed in flame. Some human opened up with a hunting rifle. He hit her square in the chest thus bringing her to him as his burning angel of death. He went up, rifle and all. It was, however, the end of Lilith, too. She screamed and cursed her way to oblivion. In the spectacle of her demise, Paul was able to get away.

Alone! He thought as he sadly made his way to his present roost. *All alone!*

It didn't matter in the least that he hadn't spent much time, of late, with her. What mattered was the fact that, if and when he really did need or want her, she would no longer be able to come to him. Lilith wasn't someone most humans or even most vampires would miss. He would miss her, however, and maybe, just maybe that's the only legacy she would ever have.

The flames were a horrific sight. He knew the undead were susceptible to them but never thought they would ever be used that way against his kind. It was a matter of logistics. Things such as flame-throwers, hand grenades and possibly rockets could not be used where the human population was dense but, otherwise, would most emphatically be let loose. Locale-wise, the docks just before dawn just happened to be perfect.

Paul was reminded of the way the American soldiers barbequed Japanese soldiers and civilians during the last months of the 2nd World War. Fire-cleansed was how some people put it. Saying burned alive was more honest. But then, considering what happened to Australian prisoners under the Japanese back then, there was no reason why any Australian should sympathize with the Japanese of that era. Still, an inhumane act is an inhumane act, no matter who it is perpetrated against. It can be recognized as such even by someone inhuman. *Just who are the monsters?* Paul wondered as he replayed in his mind what had just happened to Lilith. *Just who, for God's sake, are the monsters now?*

With the smell of smoke still in his nostrils, Paul went to bed for the day. He had a feeling his dreams would be bad. Maybe it was worse that he didn't dream at all. The next fistful of days he dreamt plenty and woke up a number of times screaming. His eyes would then be wide with the pain he'd seen in Lilith's orbs before they turned to jelly. His mouth would quiver upon remembrance of her prominent jaw collapsing in a flurry of red and yellow flame. The heat, even from a distance of twenty feet, had been frightful and that very frightfulness was bound to stay with him for a long time. He wondered how others survived seeing such horror.

On Elis Island, a short time later, Lilith was seen floating around with the other ghosts that, for various reasons, were earth bound there. Unlike the others, she had a reddish tinge in her blueness and she was naked. The others had on images of clothing that had represented them, in one fashion or another, in life.

There were many ghosts and Lilith didn't think she would spot anyone she knew but she did see Lizzy. She sensed some of her thoughts before she saw her. Her thoughts were pathetic. It was a lot of: "Oh, woe is me!" "Why me?" and "Why at *The Blue* of all places?" If Lilith had a good and proper stomach it would have turned. It would have been her pleasure to vomit all over the stupid blue creature in her mini-skirt and blouse. The fact that she was tall made her whimpering to Lilith seem all the worse.

With anger smoldering in her eyes, Lilith went up to the kneeling and weepy Lizzy, pulled her up by her now tangible hair and gave her an almighty slap across her solid face. Then Lizzy's hair and face went back to being non-solid. This shocked a few spirits. It was, after all, common knowledge among the dead that it was impossible for one ghost to touch another let along do the things Lilith had just done. Why did Lizzy's hair and face, for a moment in time, become corporeal so that the hair could be pulled and the face slapped? How could Lilith's hands become solid enough to do what they did then go back to being vaporous? Lilith was an ex-vampire and that apparently made all the difference.

"Why?" whimpered Lizzy, looking into Lilith's stern face. She had stopped her crying and, if this nasty, naked blue creature with the fading red tinge didn't come up with a good answer or an apology, she was prepared to flit to another place where ghosts congregate. Hopefully there, wherever there might be, she'd never be slapped by anyone ever again. Her wispy face stung a little from when it was abruptly made corporeal. Considering what had happened to her in Sydney to shorten her physical existence, she thought this creature's actions beastly and unfair.

"Fly away from here and, by God, I will find you. I will give you the spanking you should have gotten from one of your parents when you were alive," said Lilith.

"Why?" sobbed Lizzy. "I've done nothing to you. I don't even know you."

"Ah, but you do know a friend of mine," stated Lilith. "His name is Paul Priestly. You were rude to him at *The Blue* and that's why you are here in this form."

"He killed me?" squeaked Lizzy. "And you're his friend?"

"Through being rude to him, you opened the door that needed to be opened so he could take your pitiful life."

"Why? How? I don't understand."

"You are a stupid, stupid girl! You hurt so many young men at *The Blue* and other discos you visited. Did it never occur to you that one might have his revenge upon you?"

"Hurt? I never hurt anyone. I danced, see?"

Lizzy began to flit about Lilith but the ex-vampire would have none of it. She grabbed Lizzy by the arms, something else most ghosts cannot do with each other, and said: "Stop it!"

In a huff, Lizzy stopped and Lilith let go. Then Lilith sat her down on a ghost rock near a real one and took a nearby spirit rock for her own seating.

"I will now tell you about my life in Poland," said Lilith. "I will tell you about growing up on a farm and about the German invasion of my country. I will tell you how I suffered under the cruel hands of Nazi brutes and how I met a Nazi vampire who was stupid enough to allow me to defeat him. He was a jock and he was a Nazi who had foolishly turned me into a vampire like himself, thinking he would still have me under his control. He was wrong and earned his second death because he was wrong.

"I escaped the Nazis and for decades sought my revenge on the type of men who had given me the most grief in my life. In my unlife, as I wandered away from Germany, it came to me that many of the Nazis, the ones like my original tormentor, began as simple-minded thugs, jocks as you will, with simple-minded athletic ambitions on the football field, or elsewhere, and no true heart for their fellow human beings. I not only sought to destroy such jocks but, in fairness, I decided to train at least one young man who had been hurt by the female equivalent of the jock, to also properly seek revenge on his past tormentors. The young man I chose was Paul Priestly. His first female jock, his first female Nazi like victim was you."

"No! I'm not one of them! I'm not a female Nazi or a female jock! Me? That's crazy!"

"It is true and you are dead because you measured up or, perhaps I should say, down."

For an hour, Lizzy listened dumbfounded to Lilith. When next she shed a tear, it wasn't for herself but for all the Liliths and Paul Priestlys who had ever suffered at the hands of jocks and jockettes. It was enough to break the invisible chains holding her and so she began to ascend to the heavens, not to end up with more earthbound spirits somewhere else, but to go blessedly elsewhere. As proof of this, she was no longer blue but golden. Strangely enough, Lilith found she was turning to gold and that she was ascending as well. Other ghosts who had heard Lilith talk tried to ascend but it was no use for them. They would have to find their own way.

Neither Lizzy nor Lilith knew what to expect at journey's end, or even if the journey they were on would end. It was enough that they were away and that something better awaited them elsewhere or, at any rate, the possibility of something better.

Chapter 7

New York, November, 1980

Long looked over the telegram Miles handed him. Its message was plain enough and not at all unexpected. The Secret Compass in Sydney wanted them back. There were other cases to solve. There was a general belief that enough time and resources had been spent by them on what had now become an American problem. Courtesy for overseas vampire slayers could only stretch so far. Already Helen, the sensitive who had accompanied them from Sydney, had been sent home.

"They have reasons for wanting us back," Long said. "Vampires have been terrorizing tourists at the Jenolan Caves. A corpse drained of blood was found in a Piper Cherokee plane that crash-landed in the Georges River, near Bankstown airport. A whole swarm of rats attacked a greengrocer closing up for the night at Greenacre."

"We're not the only people they have as field agents," groused Miles. "Surely they can do without us a little while longer. After all, it's not as if we've been doing nothing while we've been here."

"I suppose we could lose the telegram," Long said. "Better yet, it might take us a week or two to book our flight out of here. You know how the airlines can be this time of year. Hell, it might take even longer."

"Yes. You're right, Long. And you're a good man."

Long handed Miles back the telegram. Miles shoved it into his coat pocket.

It was three o'clock in the afternoon. Night, even in winter, was at least two hours away. They'd already checked their equipment and made their plans for the evening. Now all they had to do was to book late passage back to Australia, answer the telegram and wait.

While Long phoned the airlines, Miles checked over some FBI reports that had come to them that day. There was something about vampire activity in Baltimore but no indication it had anything to do with the vampire he was after. There was vampire activity in Cleveland but the local FBI operative there felt the vampire in question was Irish, not Australian.

So close! Miles thought. He and Long had been there, on the dock, when an FBI agent had opened up with the flame-thrower. What went down then was the worst thing he'd ever seen or been involved in. Lilith or Linda Krakowski or whoever she was had gone up like a Roman candle. She'd taken an FBI agent with her. It was the one who had fired his rifle at her. His hands shook when he thought about it. There were days when he couldn't sleep for fear of seeing blazing death in his dreams. It wasn't his idea to use that damned leftover piece of kit from the 2nd World War. He took some comfort in that. Still, they had failed to get the young Australian male; the work was far from complete.

There was a polite knock on the door followed by a waiter with a covered tray on a cart.

"We didn't order anything," said Long, looking up from a report Miles had handed to him. He'd just gotten off the phone.

The waiter didn't reply. He went for what was sitting on the tray under the covering. Miles saw the glassy stare of the man and so, grabbing his gun out of its holster, ducked behind the sofa. He beckoned Long to do the same but, before his companion could follow him, the waiter had pulled the pins on two live grenades. Long struggled with the waiter to get the pins back into their respective holes but the waiter held him at bay with what amounted to a strength born of madness. Miles wanted to fire at the waiter but knew he could not do so without first hitting his friend. A great explosion followed. Long and the waiter were torn apart as windows shattered and tables and chairs smashed up against the bathroom door. The sofa was ripped apart too but there was enough padding and metal in it to protect Miles from serious injury.

Miles got slowly, painfully to his feet, the gun shaking in his hand. He didn't feel any loss for Long because his death had happened so quickly. What he did feel was a growing numbness. He looked at his gun hand and tried to control the shaking with the other one.

Hotel security came running, saw Miles' gun and rushed away to phone for the police. Miles, however, was regaining presence of mind and was able to phone Lenny of the FBI on the special number Lenny had given him before the police arrived to take charge. He could dial the number fine and wait the few seconds it usually took for the call to be put through, but found he couldn't hear what, if anything, was being said on the other end. He had to hope that by repeating himself six times before hanging up he got his message across. Since it was Lenny's private line, he was hoping it was Lenny and no one else he had been talking to or possibly yelling at. He had no real idea of the volume of his own voice or even if he had gotten through, for he couldn't hear any sound at all. He had never felt so helpless. He picked up the earpiece and dialed again, repeating the exercise just in case.

He hung up and did it all for a third time. Phone calls could be taped, he remembered, and if one of his calls was taped, Lenny or one of the FBI's other operatives might pick up his voice via their electronic equipment. At any rate, if he remained on long enough, they would be able to trace the call. With this in mind, he phoned a forth time and simply yelled "Help, Lenny" and left the receiver off the hook so the call could be traced.

Lenny came in time to show the arriving police his credentials and give them a cover story they could use in their reports. Miles couldn't hear what Lenny was telling them. His ears were bleeding. There was a ringing sensation that would not stop.

Miles was taken to a new room in the hotel where his head was bandaged and he was given a shot of brandy. Then an FBI agent with experience as a medic came in to examine him. He put a call out for an ambulance for Miles.

"I examined his eyes with my flashlight. His pupils are responding which is a very good sign. Naturally the brain has been upset but I can't see anything to worry about," said the medic to Lenny as he finished his examination. "Mind you, he does need a proper examination and the kind of care I can't provide him with on the spot. I'll keep an eye on him for severe headaches, dizzy spells, vomiting and blurred vision but that's about all I can do.

"I have examined his hearing. In each case the blood seems to be from the walls of his ear. If that's the extent of the damage then they'll heal in time. I don't believe the eardrums have blown. He must have put his hands over his ears in time to block out the worst of it. He won't be able to hear for a while; then it will come back in stages. He might experience some fading in and fading out of sound. Then he will hear better in one ear than the other for a while. The nerves have been traumatized. Keep him active until the paramedics get here. Talk to him and get him to answer. It could be very dangerous for him if he were to nod off here, right now."

Miles learned from Lenny via a hastily scribbled note what the FBI medic had to say about his condition. After about another ten minutes, words began to filter into one of his damaged ears. It was Lenny cursing and waving his hands. "Body...*or maybe bloody*....(something)...How glare...*maybe dare*...something...Fod... (probably God) awful ...something ...Gad (maybe bad)...(something)." More time passed and the words began to make more sense and fit into sentences. Lenny talked for maybe another ten minutes before Miles saw fit to answer. He expressed a concern about getting him to a hospital. There was also a concern about moving him to where another assassin might be possibly waiting to spring into action. This meant getting more FBI men to guard all other entrances and exits to the hotel. Miles seemed to be stabilizing which had to be a good sign. The FBI medic thought so.

The ambulance came; the paramedics put Miles on a gurney and took him away. Lenny and the FBI man with the medical background went with them. When they were in the ambulance and speeding toward Mercy, Lenny continued his dialogue with Miles, understanding the importance of keeping the Australian Secret Compass man awake and alert until a qualified doctor could make a more educated judgment.

"The worst of it is we can't even blame the dead waiter," said Lenny to a Miles struggling to comprehend. "The man had obviously been under the spell of some damned vampire. It was a vampire who had gotten it into his or her head to eliminate two genuine overseas slayers."

"They...do this very often?" asked Miles in a shaky voice. He had picked up about half of what Lenny had said but his Secret Compass detective skills were enough to put together the rest. "I mean...Do they do this often in America?"

Miles indicated that Lenny should write his answers on his notepad. Lenny did so but he also spoke his answers out loud, thinking this might help Miles to recover his hearing. He didn't know why he thought that. He just did. Besides, Lenny knew sometimes he could think better mouthing off.

"I've heard about the undead using living humans but haven't come across it myself until now," said Lenny also writing it down. "It doesn't happen very often but it can happen. They hypnotize some poor dope and send him out during the day when we think we're safe from them. Poor guy wouldn't have known what he was doing when he killed your pal and himself. God knows what some devil had made him think he was doing when he did what he did."

"Why do you think they did this? Why here? Why now?"

"I don't know for sure but I imagine it might have something to do with our roasting of that female vampire. Word probably got out and now the vampires are organizing, or at least trying to."

"I doubt the vampire I am after could have thought of this or been able to lay his hands on the grenades to make it happen."

"I tend to agree. It might have been Lilith's doing before we got her. She might have planned it ahead of her second death."

"She might have but I doubt it. This isn't her style."

"You're probably right. Here's the hospital. We'd better get you looked over again. Then we'll try and figure things out."

Miles spent a couple of hours at Mercy being further patched up by doctors and nurses. A specialist told him, via notes and speech, he had ninety percent temporary hearing loss in one ear and ten per cent in the other. A nurse said he had bruises on his right side, including three bruised ribs. The doctors wanted to keep him overnight for observation or at least until the ringing stopped. Miles had other ideas. Three FBI men, including Lenny, however, got him to stay. They knew he wanted to be where the action was in at least the initial search for his partner's killer but it wasn't to be.

After an X-ray came back showing no apparent skull fractures, the doctor okayed a sedative so he could rest. The FBI man with medical know-how was assigned to further look out for Miles. He wouldn't get in the way of proper medical hospital procedures but he could tell if something didn't look right and could act accordingly. There were now painkillers Miles could safely take, and the FBI man would be good company. His plain detective talk and notes wouldn't drive Miles to distraction. This way the Secret Compass operative could be made to feel he was still useful and part of the ongoing investigation. It was the best Lenny could do for the Australian's state of mind.

"I got a call on my walkie-talkie," said Lenny on his way out of Miles' sickroom. "They want me on the road. I have a lift waiting for me in the parking area. I've got to go. You're lucky to be alive. Do me a favor and stay that way. I'll let you know if anything breaks." He also wrote it down and handed the paper to Miles.

"Long's not so lucky," answered Miles sadly. The loss was only beginning to touch him and he knew he needed something to do before it really sunk in, before it made him useless. Yet there was nothing he could do until he healed.

Lenny got into the passenger seat of a black FBI four-wheel-drive. It then came over the radio that other FBI agents had cornered a member of the undead community in an old, condemned bottle factory in the Bronx.

"We'll have to move," said Lenny to the driver. "Lives are at stake."

"Understood," said the driver.

The four-wheel drive took up speed, and before many minutes had passed, they were parked outside the factory, looking at its gray shape against a darker background of developing storm clouds. Three FBI trucks were already there plus an FBI station wagon. The new arrivals were greeted with waves from agents getting into place near and around the factory. No one had moved in yet.

There was the flap of wings as the FBI men drew closer to the factory including the front opening. In the semi-darkness created by a few second-rate streetlamps in key positions, guns were drawn and hand signals given to move. Twenty men and women covering each of the four entrances went forth as silently as ghosts or ninja. No one wanted to be the first to make a sound. At a hand gesture made clear by Lenny breaking up some of the gloom by lighting up his digits with his own flashlight, all the other flashlights came on and everyone looked about for signs of vampire activity.

There were bats in the rafters all right. They squeaked at being disturbed and sought a way out in their hundreds. All avoided contact with the humans. All registered on the heat seeking FBI equipment as being warm and thus alive.

"No go," said an FBI woman over a walkie-talkie. "Someone probably saw a bat and thought it was one of them."

"Yeah, and the place is spooky enough," observed a male companion.

Someone pulled a trip wire with their feet. The result was a bomb going off which blew up the two FBI agents that had been conversing plus wounding three more. It wasn't an explosion large enough to do serious damage to even a dilapidated structure such as the one they were in, but enough to make the ones not blown up or hurt step cautiously on the way out. Lenny helped his driver with one of the wounded.

"They were here," said Lenny. "It was another trap. The undead are getting restless. We'll cordon off the area and send in bomb experts in the morning. For now let's get the hell out of here before something else goes wrong."

"Another trap," repeated the FBI driver. "The undead are getting restless."

"In this burg it was bound to happen," said a female agent. "This used to be a good neighborhood for them. Now they want it back."

"Now they're using their brains to get it back," said Lenny.

Lenny returned to the hospital and Miles' sickroom. He didn't expect Miles to be awake but he wanted to look in on him anyway.

While the incident in the Bronx was happening, Miles tried to convince himself that the ringing in his head was white noise, something to be expected and totally irrelevant. He tried to rest in a way to avoid putting pressure on his sore ribs. Pills given to him by the hospital staff and approved by the FBI man helped. He managed to nod off a few times but couldn't get into sound slumber. Some sixteen or so hours later, the ringing stopped and, despite the ache from the bruising, he was able to get some good sleep. Two days later Lenny made another visit and this time Miles was awake. He informed Miles of what had happened in the bottle factory.

Four weeks later, the FBI decided Miles no longer needed a bodyguard. He was discharged from the hospital and went via cab to a hotel room. The FBI made sure that what was left of his belongings was there in the hotel room before his arrival.

Once settled back in a hotel room, Miles was feeling well enough to test his legs. On the walk he took, Miles visited a small antique store in the Street of the Americas. There he came upon two identical, and highly stylized, Saint Christopher medallions made of silver. They were no bigger than an American quarter but were made in Northern Ireland by a silversmith who knew his business. He had obviously fashioned them for a married couple who were going on a long journey. They dated back to the late 1850s. It was the period of great migration from Ireland to America and Australia, which began much earlier in the 1840s but continued on until well into the 1870s. It was also just before the American Civil War which began in 1861 and went on until 1865.

If a married couple had travelled, say, from County Cork to New York which side would they have been on in the up-and-coming conflict? Miles wondered as he studied the medallions. If they had stayed in New York it would have been the Union. If they had moved south, it might have been the Confederacy. If asked to do so, Miles would have wagered on the Union.

He paid twenty dollars American each for the Saint Christopher medallions and another ten dollars to have silver chains attached to them. One medallion was for his great nephew, Todd. The other was for Long's great niece, Pauline Sharp. Todd would make what he wanted of the present but Miles knew his sister, Patricia would see its significance and love him for it. As for Pauline, it would be something she would remember him by. It could also be his continuing pledge of friendship to Long's family. Legacy who helped out the families of fallen Australian soldiers didn't recognize fallen Secret Compass agents and the loved ones they left behind. Miles, on the other hand, did.

He wondered, for a moment, what would happen if Todd and Pauline ever met. Would they get on? Would they do better than just get on? Would there be cherry blossoms and magnolias and wild banksias in flower, on a good day for a preacher to say words over them in a church?

Miles smiled to himself as he put the two medallions-on-chains, wrapped in tissue paper, into his coat pocket. It was the first time he had done so since Long's death. He felt guilty for doing so; then he thought of Long calling him a sentimental twit. After shedding a tear, he had to smile again.

Three weeks later, Miles went to the airport. There, while waiting for his flight, he bought a copy of Corrine Kelly's best selling vampire novel, *And my Cup Runneth Over...with Blood!* to read on the plane. On the flight, he found it to be less ridiculous than he thought it would be and more accurate than most romances are when it comes to the undead. Could this Corrine Kelly be a vampire or perhaps a vampire hunter? She could, of course, simply be a talented writer who has stumbled onto a few truths. That was most likely the case.

Lenny had once told him about an investigation his supernatural division of the FBI did of some writer by the name of Barbara Custer. They thought she might be one of the undead or maybe one of their operatives, under a different name, relating too much to the public, calling it fiction. It turned out she was just one of those intuitive types, maybe like Helen Kiln but without the PSI training he knew was available through the Secret Compass.

Miles returned to Sydney with less than what he'd wanted to have accomplished in the USA and without Long. The body parts identified as Long had travelled home weeks earlier. Miles was sad he hadn't gone with them.

Miles' sister, Patricia, and her husband, Tom, were there at the airport to greet him. Over coffee he told them of the destruction of the one who had made the creature that had killed Lizzy. There was little more he could say except that the authorities in the USA were still on the case and they would inform him if anything new came up.

"The one we're really after may return to Sydney some day," said Miles. "Then we'll get him for sure."

"Yes," agreed his sister with a half smile. "I'm sure you will."

Before Miles' flight from the USA touched down, the Bankstown vampire had been caught and done away with. The same could be said for the one who'd made the Jenolan caves his home. The rat menace at Greenacre turned out to be of a non-vampiric nature. He would, at least, be returning to a quiet office in the underground complex beneath Mitchell library which was his headquarters.

He was not finished with the undead as he was sure they were not finished with him. It was at his desk, the first day back that he shed a tear or two for Long to go with the two he'd shed in New York. Considering all they had been through together, and all they had managed to accomplish, it was only fitting. If any man said different, he'd get his head punched in.

At ten o'clock, Miles phoned Helen Kiln and would continue to phone her, at the same time every work day, for the next ten years for the latest PSI news on his yet-to-be-caught vampire. Usually, she would have nothing for him. Once she told him the felon was in Boston of all places. Another time she said he was headed for Canada. Then she surprised him, one morning, by saying that the place he wanted to go, where he would spent the most time, is the Middle East.

"Why the Middle East?" asked Miles.

"It's where bodies turn up so often that it's very easy to hide one among the many. And it's easy to keep doing so night after night."

"But that's not everywhere in the Middle East."

"There are enough hot spots to choose from and our friend has yet to make up his mind."

"Let me know when he does."

Miles knew all the psychics, or sensitives as they were sometimes called, including Helen, made a trip to Central Station late at night, at least once a week, to talk to the spirits there. Every now and then, they would speak to the spirits in and around the cathedral near the town hall building. Legend had it that the stone lion's heads on the corners of the town hall make it impossible for the spirits to tell fibs to the living. He knew, however, that the psychics didn't believe this and always double-checked, as best they could, what they were told.

Out of curiosity, Miles had studied the lions and knew each head was an individual in its own right. One was said to have the personality traits of a particularly boisterous 19th Century foreman. *Why had the architect and the sculptors done them this way?* he wondered. *Was it by whim or had it something to do with the realm of the supernatural?* If it had to do with the latter then he might never find out. If it was mystical then the psychics, including Helen, really did know and for some reason weren't telling.

117

Helen did eventually let him know where, in the Middle East, he should look but, no matter how he cajoled the powers above him in the Sydney branch of the Secret Compass, they refused to send him. They mentioned his age and then said it was no longer their business. There were other operatives, living closer to that part of the world, just as capable as he was and who were now affected by that particular vampire's goings-on. So all he could do was wait for further information and get on with other work while others tried to do what he considered to still be his job.

Three months after his return, a report came from the FBI that made Miles' day. Lenny had managed to find the vampires responsible for Long's death and the explosion at the factory. They were three ex-army men who had worked in munitions. It seems that, one night at a bar; they had met a vampire of Lilith's description and were transformed into members of the undead. Lilith must have known what they would do. She probably thought she would leave New York while they went ahead and blew things up. It didn't matter to her that they were jocks. Maybe she thought they would make themselves high visibility targets for the FBI, anyway, so they would eventually be disposed of. By turning them into vampires she had signed their death warrants.

The three vampire explosive experts were caught trying to plant a bomb inside the mayor's podium the night before the mayor was due to give a speech. Two of them were killed outright with special bullets; the third was captured by a group of agents with crucifixes and bottles of holy water. The one remaining vampire told all he knew under bright lights, crucifixes and the threat of a dunking in holy water. He was to be executed but some agents believed he should be kept as an example for new agents coming into the force.

"Hang the new agents," Miles telegraphed back to Lenny. "Execute the bastard or you'll lose him and there will be hell to pay."

Two weeks later, a report from Lenny was received by Miles concerning the third vampire's demise. He'd tried to escape, giving his captors no choice but to execute him. It was done with special bullets and then with a stake to be sure.

"Good," wrote Miles in reply and sent it off to America.

118

Chapter 8

New York, December 1980

In the more well-to-do parts of the city, Christmas carols were being sung. Everywhere Santas were ringing their bells for charity. In Harlem, Paul dropped a few coins into a black Santa's pot and was thanked kindly for his donation. He hadn't been to Harlem much since he arrived in New York. He figured the people living there had more than enough problems without him adding to them. He didn't understand the new music coming out of their streets and he didn't want to try. If it was good for them, then that was fine. If it was a betrayal like disco then they would have to find their own avenger. He wondered what had happened to cool Jazz and Blues.

There was a lot of energy coming out of the village. Some people remembered Bob Dylan's early years as a musician and were playing his songs. Others were listening to old Cat Stevens recordings while still others were caught up in something totally awesome and, since it only dates back to 1971, relatively new.

Paul had to stop by a bar and grill where John Lennon's lifetime masterpiece, *Imagine*, was being played. He could see, in his mind's eye, his mother, Mary falling in love with it. He could also see the glimmer of hope for humanity he hadn't seen in a singer and a song in a very long time. He wondered what the ex-Beatle was thinking when he wrote it. He certainly wasn't thinking of revenge or of making the world a better place by the removal of certain people. It was all back to "make love, not war." The hope of a generation and more generations to come was encapsulated in one song. The very notion took Paul back to before the world dumped on him and before he met Lilith who promised to help him set things right.

Back then there had always been "The Doctor." The number one science fiction show out of England was *Doctor Who*. It spoke of a better way, a more intellectual way of dealing with violence. The idea of out-thinking your enemies was pure *Doctor Who*. The only time he'd tried it of late was at that tattooist's establishment and, according to word on the street, the results had been less than he had hoped. Once more, he had made vampires and they had been destroyed.

The song ended, Paul moved away from the eatery in search of he knew not what. The sight of the occasional Christmas tree in a shop window gladdened him. He missed his family more than he had in months but there was no way he could join them even for the holidays. He was glad he couldn't feel the cold. It would have saddened him even more since, in Australia this time of year, it was anything but cold. People, where he grew up, enjoyed frosty beer and the surf in December, not hot toddies, indoor games and sticky date puddings. It was the other side of the world where he had landed and was trying to make the best of his situation.

Down a dark alley Paul wandered, becoming more and more aware of being followed. There were dark alleys; it seemed, even at Christmas. There were people who felt comfortable using them for less than kind practices. When he turned around, he found himself con-fronted by four gang members in dirty jeans and jackets. As a sign of which gang they belonged to, they had on bright red bandanas. Three of them spoke to each other, for a moment, in a language derived from Spanish. The fourth one was a girl of Anglo-Saxon origins but certainly of gang member status. She appeared to understand what they were saying but did not join in the discussion. When the talking stopped, they looked at Paul in a meaningful way as if they'd been talking about him. One of them shook his head sadly and another smiled the smile of a predator about to pounce.

"What do you want?" asked Paul as if he didn't know.

"Your money, gringo!" said one of them.

"Or your life!" said another.

The girl remained silent, eyes all a sparkle. The same could be said for the fourth bandit.

"Already taken," said Paul, shrugging his shoulders.

"Your money?" asked the one who called him gringo.

"No," corrected Paul, "my life. And you can't have my money."

"We shall see," said the girl.

There was the flick of cutlery, four knives in all. Paul was surprised no one owned a gun of some sort. Maybe they hadn't robbed enough people yet to be able to afford such a luxury.

The three males came at Paul like a pack of savage dogs. He shrugged them aside and grabbed the girl. It took no effort whatsoever to wrest the knife from her grasp and to walk her away from her friends. She was a skinny blond with not much weight to her at all. The males followed and attacked again. This time two ended up face down in the same dumpster. The third tottered off in the opposite direction, carrying the hand he busted when he gave Paul his best Sunday punch.

"You're mine," Paul told the female. Dressed in leather with black make-up on, she still looked too young for what she had been doing. She looked too young for what he was about to do to her but that didn't faze him. By his reckoning, he'd been too young for the sort of things that had happened to him at *The Blue* in Sydney.

"Don't!" she whispered as he put her up against a wall, fangs extending, fangs dripping with saliva. *It would be so easy to feed*, he told himself. *So why am I hesitating? Why don't I give her what she deserves?* There was, however, innocence about her he might only have perceived at Christmas. It wasn't much but it was enough to move him to do something unusual. Of course, it might have been John Lennon's song, *Imagine*, still ringing in his head, imploring him to be a better person if that was possible.

"You're mine," whispered Paul back at her, looking as menacing as he could make himself, "but I'm going to let you go. I am going to give you back your life. Take it. Call it a present from me to you. If you like, call it foolish sentimentality on my part for this time of year. Call it what you will. Know this: If I ever catch you on these streets again, trying to mug people with the help of your friends, you are dead. What's more, there will be no regrets on my part. Do you understand me?"

"Yes sir!"

"Good. Now go and try to stay out of trouble."

When Paul put her down, she bolted into a garbage can and then into a street lamp, but was away before he could stop laughing and garner together second thoughts concerning her fate. He knew he should have pressed his considerable advantage. He knew he should have taken her for every drop of the good red she had.

"I'm getting dumb in my old age," he told himself before taking on bat form. In his head, he heard another vampire chuckle. The voice was that of a male. He knew then that the girl he'd let go was going to be someone else's dinner. *So be it!* He told himself. He'd let her go all right but he wasn't responsible for her. He now felt even more foolish for letting her go in the first place.

As he flew off, he saw the other bat circling, getting ready to go in for the kill. Sometimes, even when you let them go, you couldn't always save them. Paul had never seen two vampires fight, but it would have to be over a better reason than some stray gangland type. She should have been at home with her family rather than gallivanting about, looking for a dishonest way to get some cash.

He might not have let them go if he'd known that the lads he'd knocked about had squealed to two FBI agents who were now after the girl and her attacker. Also, he might have felt a lot better about letting her go if he'd seen the FBI men catch up with the other vampire, just as he was putting the bite on his victim. He did, however, hear the guns with the special ammunition discharge. The acidic smell of cordite drifted his way. He didn't know what to make of the sound and the smell, until he heard the shriek in his head which ended with the other vampire's second death.

Paul wondered at his luck and the girl's. This night they had been entwined. Maybe someone upstairs, or possibly downstairs, wanted them to share the same planet for a while longer. The question was for how much longer. Neither of them, he figured, had great prospects.

Just for the sake of the season, Paul would go to bed hungry and put in an extra effort the following night. He knew his family, back in Australia, if they were aware of what he'd become, would want it that way. He also knew he wanted it that way because some things about being human still had to make sense to him, even if he was never going to ever be completely human again. This had to include forgiveness and charity on certain nights of the year. On this particular occasion, peace and goodwill toward others included miscreants in dirty jeans and jackets.

Before going back to his lodgings, Paul approached an all night bookshop with the intention of providing a gift of sorts to certain members of the undead community. There he bought a copy of Mandy Provost's novel, *Stark White under the Stars*, and Corrine Kelly's short story collection, *Blood on my Lips and other Tales of the Macabre*. He arranged, via mesmerism, for the shopkeeper to order in fifty extra copies of each work the next day. Then, after it was done, to forget about having done so but to have it in the back of his head that it was an important thing to have done.

Two months later, Paul spent some time in Boston. There, two members of the FBI's section for dealing with the supernatural caught up with him and came close to staking him. What went wrong for them was the holy water they splashed him with. It should have burned him, even blinded him for the staking. It did nothing more than make him damp. The crucifixes, which they'd brought with them from New York, had disorientated him when they were first held up. Now that they had been lowered, they could not be raised in time to do any good.

I don't understand, thought one of the FBI men before he was thrown against a wall, *we got the water from a church! It was blessed and everything by a priest.*

"Run!" cried his fellow agent, not bothering to notice that his companion was in no condition to go anywhere.

The second agent did as well getting away as the first. In his panic, he dropped his crucifix and so was left at his adversary's mercy. Paul didn't kill them; he merely damaged their heads against stationary bricks and mortar.

Like the agents, he had no idea at the time why the holy water hadn't worked. Years later, he would read about priests who had, for decades in the Boston area, acted against the best interests of both church and state. That was as good a reason why the water did not do its thing. After all, a priest who was not truly good could not, to any certainty, collect holy water. Oh, he could beseech God to make water holy all right but, since his vessel wasn't clean, the water couldn't remain holy for very long. If, for example, you put soup into a dirty bowl, you end up with spoilt soup. If a priest has done great wrong and hasn't confessed, then whatever he touches must also be spoilt. Hence parts of Boston, at this time, were open grounds for the undead. If Paul had only known, he would have stayed longer instead of heading further up north. By the time he did find out, the clean-up had begun and there was no point in going back.

Chapter 9

Montreal, Canada, Early December 1982

The cold weather had set in, ushering in snow. This affected Paul indirectly, since he didn't feel the changes in temperature. A walking cadaver, he couldn't catch a chill or come down with pneumonia. What he could come down with, however, was a good case of starvation. It was fortunate for him then that people were already spending their evenings Christmas shopping.

Here Santas were on just about every street corner collecting what money they could for charity. Carolers were singing in French and English. Venders were selling roasted nuts and hot potatoes smothered in sour cream and chives. There were shops with sweets the like of which Paul had never seen. It was a great pity he no longer had the stomach for human food. Still, he could become intoxicated with the smell of it all and try it out secondhand through the blood of those he bit.

Paul didn't have anyone to buy for, but he did have certain vampiric acquaintances whose novels he wanted to keep in the public eye. With this in mind, he went to the three largest bookstores and mesmerized the manager in each one to have ten thousand copies of Corrine Kelly's re-printed *Vampire Love* and ten thousand of Mandy Provost's re-printed *Undead among the Flowers* ordered in from the USA. He also put into them the inability, for a month, to cancel the order.

He didn't believe either novelist was around to collect royalties but he wanted to support them anyway just in case. Besides, he thought their novels were good reads since he'd sired them. Now that each of the three bookshops had lots of copies coming their way, they were sure to advertise them in Canada for all they were worth. Since he knew they

124

wouldn't remember being mesmerized, they would have to justify ordering so many to themselves if not to someone in higher authority.

On the way out of the third bookshop, Paul came upon a man with a gun robbing a woman in her late twenties. She had a child of four clinging to her great coat. This angered him and he rushed into action. Before the gunman could react, Paul had him bouncing off the nearest wall and falling onto the sidewalk, unconscious. In the next instant, he returned the stolen purse to the woman and ran off before she could thank him or even acknowledge what had just happened.

It was on his way back to his hotel room, after supping on a less than pleasant cocktail waitress at a bar that it struck Paul why he had been so incensed by the mother's plight. In terms of looks, the woman in her late twenties, whom he had helped out, could have been his youngest sister, Kate grown up with a daughter of her own. Of course the chances of one of his family moving to Montreal and settling there was remote at best but it was still possible. He was glad he had saved her and the child. *Let it be my gift to these Canadians*, he thought.

Paul slept soundly the next day and, when night came around again, he stepped forth, looking for someone to taste. It was snowing heavily and there was a definite crispness in the air that made even the dirtiest of streets smell fresh and new.

He was about to go into a Canadian disco when he felt something tugging at him. He looked down and was startled to see a small round face with big, round eyes looking up at him from a body wrapped in a tiny coat, at least two tiny jumpers and a red pom-pom hat. It was the child from the other night and she was getting his attention by pulling on his coat sleeve.

"Are you a superhero?" she asked with great curiosity.

Slowly, sadly he shook his head. He didn't know what else to do. He was often so grim that children her age were often frightened of him. Then the mother turned up.

"I hope she hasn't been bothering you," she said. "Marielle has such an imagination. I don't know where she gets it from. My husband and I are such practical people.... Say you're sorry, Marielle and we'll be on our way."

"But he is a superhero!" insisted Marielle, stamping her foot and moving away from Paul. "He just won't admit it 'cause he isn't wearing a mask!"

"I don't know what to say," said Paul truthfully.

"Mommy, he saved us last night," said Marielle. "He did it with his super powers!"

"You were the man?" enquired the woman.

"I helped out, that's all," said Paul. "I'm a cop from Australia on holiday in your fair city."

"Superhero!" cried Marielle, pointing up and now across at him.

"All right, yes, you got me little lady, I am a superhero," said Paul with a sudden urge to play along.

"Maybe...a cop from Awstralsiya?" murmured Marielle, uncertain. Apparently, superheroes never admitted they were superheroes even when pushed into it by precocious four year olds.

"Australia, dear," corrected the woman. "My name's Arlette McKenzie. I'm French Canadian. My husband's Scottish Canadian."

"I'm both," put in Marielle.

"I'm Paul Priestly," said Paul, for once seeing no reason to go under an alias. She wasn't likely to check into his background and discover that, not only wasn't he a cop, but he wasn't even supposed to be alive.

The adults shook hands. Marielle wanted to join in but she couldn't figure out how. Her hands were trapped in mittens and they were a lot smaller than everybody else's.

"Can I buy you a hot chocolate?" offered Arlette. "I've never met a police officer from Australia before. Are you all as fast on your feet?"

"We do our best," said Paul. "I'll decline the offer, though. We're not supposed to accept gifts for that sort of thing even if I wasn't on duty."

"Just like our mounties!" beamed Marielle. "Is your uniform red like my hat, too?"

"No. It's blue," said Paul who knew what a New South Welshman's police uniform looked like.

"I think red is prettier!" claimed Marielle. "Yours should be red like ours!"

"Marielle!" cried Arlette with a touch of anger in her voice but only a touch. "Show some manners, please!"

"I suppose blue is all right," conceded Marielle.

"I have to go but it was nice meeting the both of you again," said Paul.

"Joyeux Noel, mon ami," said Arlette in farewell.

"Joyeux Noel, mon ami," echoed Marielle.

"Merry Christmas!" intoned Paul and walked away. A few minutes later his sensitive hearing enabled him to hear Marielle saying: "Australian superhero cop!" and her mother, Arlette replying with: "Oh, Marielle! He was a lovely young man. Can't we just leave him at that?

Let's get some nice, hot chocolate, shall we? Then we have to meet your grandmother at the mall and you can tell her all about your new Australian friend. Won't that be fun?"

Paul skipped the disco and visited a nearby medical centre instead where he mesmerized a nurse into giving him a couple of bags of A+ blood for twenty dollars Canadian. He got her to put his meal into a large brown carryall so that he could walk back to his hotel room with it without raising too much suspicion.

For a week, Paul got his food at the medical centre, paying for it through cash and mesmerism. Then he left Montreal, never to return. The memory of Arlette and Marielle would stay with him forever.

In mid-February, 1983, Paul found himself in Mosinee, Canada where he ran into six members of a Scottish arm of Freemasonry called the Maclean Secret Compass. He was ambushed outside a pub and forced to reveal his true nature when a crucifix was held up in front of him. "Now we know why you wouldn't take a dram of whisky with us," said one of them. A traveler not taking a shot of whisky-on-the-house, obviously, had to be suspect. It was the first time Paul had come up against Scottish pikes and claymores, the traditional Scottish clansman sword. If not for his superhuman speed coupled with his ability to change into a bat and fly away, he would have been a goner. Even so, a pike thrust into the air almost got him.

He was fortunate to find a quiet space under an upturned fishing boat on the beach, to rest up during the following day, before trekking out of the area the following night.

Chapter 10

London, May, 1995

Paul sat atop Big Ben, looking out over the ancient city like some friendly gargoyle. He felt old despite the fact that, in human form, his appearance hadn't changed since Lilith had made him over into one of her own. Theologians say the eyes are the doorway to the soul. As the doorway to such a place, Paul had to wonder if his eyes might have changed of late with all he had been through. He had a tendency to stand up straighter than before he was bitten but that was about it.

Still it was hard to get a glimpse of how he looked. Mirrors, polished metal surfaces and pools of water didn't give him back his reflection. The only way he could see himself was in a dead person's eyes. The image was small and somewhat distorted. He'd heard about female vampires going for bug-eyed victims so they could pretty themselves up. Paul wasn't so vain. He only thought of looks as a way some people had of getting what they wanted while others missed out or worse. Now the mesmeric power of the undead satisfied his needs in that direction and hence most of his desires.

It seemed there had always been a London. There had been a few name changes, of course, over the many, many centuries of its existence. Even before Roman times, there had been a settlement in the area and trade did go on. Over time the city had had its financial ups and downs. The late seventies and early eighties was a down period for not only London but for the whole country. This was the period when young people felt most betrayed by their elders.

Punk music was born. The Sex Pistols raged, especially in London, and a whole generation of unemployed raged with them. Paul had seen some of the spillover in New York. He had seen plenty more in Hamburg and other German cities. Perhaps this had something to do

128

with Germans living regimented lives and maybe their young having the need to rebel before economics and the law forced them to settle down.

Fortunately for London and the rest of England, the present "up" period followed the bad times. There were economists who felt that Maggie Thatcher, the iron maiden Prime Minister, had turned things around with her hard as nails domestic policies and her efforts in finding new markets for British goods. It happened that New York had made a come-back too and probably for similar reasons.

Paul was glad the people of Britain had a change of fortune but it didn't affect him much. The less prosperous areas of London such as Soho were still his best bet for a no-nonsense feed with less possibility of future repercussions from the authorities. After all, this was not Afghanistan or Pakistan where he'd spent much of the mid-eighties to mid-nineties. Here, in the West, women had more behavioral choices and real power for good or ill. Over where he'd been, there was a strict dress code, little in the way of education on offer and they had to, in many instances, marry whoever their fathers wanted them to marry.

In many parts of Afghanistan, thanks to the Taliban, television was seen as an affront to Allah. A free press could not exist and only religious songs could be tolerated. The men weren't as bad off as the women but it was, according to a Western vampire, a crazy way to live. Back there, Paul didn't have the heart to kill any woman for her blood to leave her corpse to rot, so he ended up making lots of them undead. Many of his converts were meek and mild enough when truly alive but, once vampire, they were all for the destruction of the men, for the destruction of the society in general that, for generations, had done them no favors. There were probably caves in Afghanistan and villages in Pakistan where, thanks to him, the living did not dare to venture.

Paul had left that safe haven part of the globe because the abject poverty he saw every night was getting him down. It came with its own stench of hopelessness and longing for something better. Because he was a foreigner, beggars expected him to be able to offer aid. This he did at first until the night he ran out of coins to give anyone. He had to steal from the headquarters of an American textile import company stationed at Sukkur, in Pakistan, in order to get a flight to the West. It wasn't an act to be proud of but it had been necessary for the sake of his sanity. One can only tolerate so much filth and decay before one must scream.

After a couple of stopovers, he made it to England. To get him through the daylight hours of travel he had on him a fake certificate from a Pakistan hospital declaring him a burn victim going to the burn center at Chelsea and Westminster Hospital, London for special treatment. He got it from a Pakistani doctor he'd mesmerized into filling it out for him. Travelling once more in bandages was uncomfortable but necessary. He breathed a sigh of relief when he got through British customs at the airport and made it to a place of safety where he could remove the dark glasses, the clinging coverings on his face and the gloves on hands.

Looking back, Paul could recall his high school studies, when the English had a great many problems with pollution. There were cities and towns in the 19th Century that existed in a continual haze created by giant smoke stacks from industry. It took legislation and a desire for a better way of doing business, but the smoke stacks were tamed and now there was less muck in the air.

According to his studies, there was a time when the Thames stank to an incredible degree in summer; sometimes Parliament had to adjourn early because of the stench. Sometime in the 19th Century government spending on sewage works and better plumbing solved the problem of river pollution. It meant the average Londoner would no longer have to drink water contaminated by his own refuse or possibly be overcome by disease originating from such contamination. Now the Thames had a fresh, crisp smell to it that welcomed rather than repelled.

Back a century or so ago the world was coming to terms with rapid industrialization and its less pleasant consequences. Londoners were learning how to deal with an ever increasing city population. One way was cheap rail travel to ocean resorts and to areas set aside for recreation. In this way, the modern Sunday picnic was born.

Where possible, government or common land was set aside so that the average workman and his family might have areas in which to play and grow during the off-hours that were coming to be known as weekends. The idea spread to places such as the colonies in Australia and to the people of New Zealand. Americans also needed to have land set aside in which to exercise, grow, play and breathe free.

Yellowstone National Park was one of the first sites in the USA developed for the wellbeing of the average person. A place called Royal National Park in NSW and, of course, Centennial Park in Sydney are early Australian examples of local authorities showing some care for the common man and his needs outside of work. Paul could remember some great times hiking with his father in the Royal National Park and bike riding for the fun of it with his whole family in Centennial Park where it cost little to hire out bikes for the day. They were memories that would stick with him forever and a night.

Paul left Big Ben in bat form, falling two hundred feet before being taken up like a leaf by the wind, and moved across the stars. It was wonderful that the clouds that had collected earlier were now gone, giving him more to look at, more to enjoy. It would have been better if the Southern Cross could have been seen in this strictly northern heaven. He wanted to get back to Sydney to see how the place had changed in his absence. More to the point, he wanted to go home.

Paul flew past Parliament. He circled London Bridge, marveling at the second image he could see of a ghost bridge made long ago and packed with shops, residences and people. This shadow bridge bespoke of a great disaster that had happened long ago but which the spirits of the dead still remembered. He was aware they could only be seen by the dead, the undead and not by many of the living. Even so, he found the hairs on the back of his neck rising with what he could fathom and before long he was glad to be leaving the area.

Paul alighted for a while on the Tower of London, scaring the sacred black birds there and disturbing the ancient spirits of the long dead that still hung around in their wispy blue forms. Then he took off, coming to rest on the top deck of a bright red double-decker bus. There he changed to human form and went down the narrow, winding steps to where two passengers were huddled together against the cold. They were old and frail so he didn't bother with them. He still had some standards.

Though there were signs of summer to come during the daylight hours, the nights had a frosty edge. It was good that the frostiness could not bother Paul. Once you were a corpse, the cold could not make a difference except in terms of how many people were out and about.

A ticket collector pestered Paul for some change and he handed over a twenty-pound note.

"Can't change that!" complained the fellow. "Got anything smaller?"

"Keep the rest," said Paul.

"Don't know if I can," muttered the fellow.

"Just do it!" ordered Paul. The fellow shut up and walked away.

"Must be made of money," whispered the old man to his elderly female companion.

In answer to this remark Paul reached into one of his baggy coat pockets and pulled out a wad of twenty pound notes.

"Here!" he said, handing the old man the money. Before the ancient fellow could register his surprise, Paul had jumped off the bus at the next stop. He was going to get off anyway.

The money didn't mean much to Paul. Since he'd discovered automatic teller machines outside banks, he'd been having fun with them. With little effort he was able to rip such machines off their respective walls, pry them open with his fingers and help himself to the contents. No credit card was required, just superhuman strength. Of course he realized that he shouldn't do that too often in case the police and the local vampire hunters got wise. Doing it every now and then would be fine. He'd done it four times so far without being caught.

He was still getting used to the idea of pounds instead of dollars. In Afghanistan and Pakistan he was mostly using the barter system. It worked this way: he would let the person he was facing know that, in order to continue to live, they must be of service to him. If they were not of service to him, he would kill them. Considering some of the characters he ran into, that seemed more than fair. His fangs helped put his case across. Very few people who could be of service had refused him. In his memories, he would have liked to have put the cooperation he had received down to his winning personality but he knew the truth of it.

Paul chuckled when he thought of that old married couple suddenly a hell of a lot richer. Would they tell the police? He didn't think so. They might, however, give the grouchy ticket collector a few notes to shut him up. If they did so, that was fine with him. He felt a little like Ned Kelly on one of the Kelly gang's good nights, minus the armor. There was nothing like being generous with other people's money.

There was word on the street that the Secret Compass in Australia had, some time ago, contacted the Secret Compass branches in various parts of Europe to be on the lookout for him. He wouldn't have been surprised if the Rising Sun Group had done the same thing and had just as long a reach.

As he walked past a Japanese restaurant, a shadow caught Paul's attention for a split second. He knew he was in trouble. Then a dozen men and women in black came out of the night to confront him.

"Rising Sun Group!" cried Paul.

He didn't think they'd be operating in England even though they were an international organization. Still, how did they know he was around? He hadn't tasted an Asian woman since coming to the country. He had avoided doing so because he suspected it would bring all sorts of grief down upon him.

"Just in case you are curious," said the female leader of the warriors he was facing, "we trailed you from your destruction of teller machines. You probably didn't realize they come with cameras. Most of the images of you were blurry, thanks to the damage you wrought, but we have experts who were able to come up with a usable image. This image we circulated. Apparently you were once active in Sydney, Australia. With an image to go by, our people combed London until you, as a bat, were spotted alighting on one of our London buses. The rest you know."

Paul looked around for a way out but they were closing in from all sides. Some of the men and women had butterfly swords. Others had spears tipped with oak. At the moment, the spears worried him the most because they had a longer reach. They could be thrown quite accurately.

When a spear was launched, he managed to ward it off with a flick of his hand. How many times he could sense them coming like that and act was something he preferred not to test. One slip and he would be gone. Meanwhile, some of the females, taking advantage of his interest in the spears, danced closer to him, pulling out handfuls of rice powder from their pouches. They blew the powder into his face to blind him. He got his hands up in time to protect his eyes but it was close.

Four men with butterfly swords tried to take advantage of this minor distraction by lopping his head off. They attacked him from behind but, with his extraordinary hearing, he heard them coming. Before they got close enough to succeed, he had one by the arm and was crashing him into the others.

Star knives came out and Paul grabbed a garbage can lid to protect himself from the menace of their potent bite. A hooked rope came down from a first story window and an attempt was made to pull his arm wide so that another Rising Sun Group operative could get a good shot at his chest. Paul flexed his arm, sending the rope holder soaring out of a window to smash into three spear wielders below who had been preparing to throw their weapons.

If I were human, he told himself, *I'd have build up quite a sweat by now.*

Even with the Rising Sun Group operatives he'd managed to down, Paul could see the odds were still against him. *What now?* He asked himself. He had to find a way out.

Then he heard a rat in the distance gnawing on chicken bones left in the gutter from some slob's visit to a fast food outlet. Someone had obviously eaten the meal while walking to a bus stop, dumping the rest. The rat appreciated this lack of public consciousness on the part of the human. It wasn't as if he could squeak for takeout. Even so, his tiny brain and the tiny brains of other nearby rats could be gotten at by Paul. All it took was a little concentration on his part. This gave him an idea. He'd discovered this ability with such creatures in Pakistan where there were plenty of vermin to practice on but he hadn't used it much. Rats, once you got them on the move, were hard to control. They understood the mental words *food* and *eat* and sometimes *danger* but not much else. Now he was rousing, as best he could, as many as he could with the words *here food* and *good eating*. He hoped they would arrive in large number and in time to save him.

A tall Rising Sun Group man thrust a spear, barely missing Paul's side as he turned away from it. This brought him in line with three star knife wielders who were about to introduce him to a lot of pain, if not death, if he wasn't careful. Before he could act, one of his attackers screamed. There had been strange movement at her feet and, when she looked down, she saw rats aplenty. More screaming followed as the rats leapt onto the Rising Sun Group agents. This allowed Paul to use the distraction they offered to transform into a bat and fly off. Two star knives were thrown in his direction but he outdistanced them. By the time he turned around in the sky to look back at what he'd wrought, the rats were in their thousands – a brown wave of horror for the Rising Sun Group.

Paul watched from on high as smoke bombs were thrown at the toothy hoard by various Rising Sun Group members while others threw fireworks. This was enough to let the rats know there wouldn't be any easy meals. They retreated to where they hoped to find better luck. They invaded the Japanese restaurant, two nearby pubs and several empty ground floor offices. Paul heard them cry out *food* plaintively then *FOOD!* with much more energy and joy when something edible was found. He hoped none of the food turned out to be fallen Rising Sun Group people, though he imagined other Rising Sun Group members would make certain that did not happen.

After circling the area twice out of curiosity, and almost having a thrown spear hit him in the head, Paul flew away from the confusion and horror he had caused. He made his way back to his current place of rest. He was certain that the Rising Sun Group of London were far from finished with him and that to stay in this city much longer would be madness. They were far too well organized and disciplined for his liking.

That day, to get his mind off of rats and ninjas while he slumbered, Paul's thoughts turned to his three months in Ontario, Canada, during the summer of 1981, and his weeks in Montreal in the winter of 1982. Even his time in Mosinee where he met Scottish Secret Compass members for the first time was gone over.

He had left New York, heading north until he found himself at Niagara Falls. He stayed there a few weeks then continued on into the land of the maple leaf and the mounted police. It was beautiful country, Canada. In parts it was much like the Blue Mountains back home in New South Wales only, for the humans living there, colder. There were fishermen throughout who claimed the fishing was excellent and the air, in many areas, had a purity not found any more in most parts of the world.

Ontario turned out to be a modern metropolis with a friendly, open outlook. In point of fact, this friendliness proved to be a problem that drove Paul away. With his moral compass the way it was, it became more and more difficult to find appropriate victims. In these terms, Montreal, with its French charm and frontier spirit, wasn't much better. Mosinee, with its hearty Maclean Secret Compass operatives, was too dangerous. He headed back down into the USA.

From Detroit, he flew to Berlin, Germany. There he encountered pepper spray cans and tazers. The pepper spray certain police and INTERPOL agents used on him stung his eyes, making them water. He found that, instead of having a nice, quiet meal with fangs extended as intended with, say, a female INTERPOL member, he would be so pained, so aggravated he'd rip her throat out with his hands instead. The tazer proved less than ideal for those who used it against him. The shock distributed to him, via launched wires, did not disable the way it might a normal human. Instead, it angered him to the point where he would pummel the person who used it near to death before he destroyed it. After a dozen pepper spray and tazer incidents, Paul left Germany for Cairo, Egypt. There, he hoped such modern and painful technology would not be used against him.

Cairo proved to be enlightening. The museum there, with its mummies and artifacts from the distant past, spoke to him in a way they could not speak to the living. He could smell blood; even ancient blood dried to a very fine powder. He had enough of a sense of it to realize most so-called modern Egyptians he met on the streets were not the descendents of ancient Egyptians. They were descendents of Macedonians or Romans or the last of the conquerors, the Arabs and then the Turks who had brought the faith of Muhammad and had made Egypt a pillar of the Ottoman Empire. Too many of the ones whose blood could be dated, by his nose, back to truly ancient and glorious times were of the Coptic Christian religion that was being persecuted by fanatics and thus, simple-minded followers of Muhammad. Instead of showing proper respect to a people who had created great architectural wonders the like of which they could barely comprehend, they were condemning these people for not being Muslims.

So incensed was Paul by the obvious injustice being done to Coptic Christians, either being beaten until they changed faith or killed outright for their beliefs, that he stopped blood sucking on Coptic Christians altogether. He then showed no mercy whatsoever to anyone he perceived to be of definite Arab or Turkish descent. When he learned of the cruelties inflicted upon the Coptic Christians in some quarters, he would inflict them tenfold upon the followers of Muhammad. They would suffer for making better people suffer.

They would suffer for not having the manners to respect the great achievements of others and be humbled by them. The least the Coptic Christians deserved was the respect of their Muslin brothers and the right to live in peace in their city. Paul wanted to grind into dust the Muslims who did not feel the Coptic Christians deserved to live. Unless, of course, these attackers could create modern day wonders equivalent to the complexities concerning sound and image found in the ancient hieroglyphs or the superb engineering feats that can be discovered in the pyramids, they had no moral case for a defense against his actions. They were simply bully-boys picking on some clever kids just because they weren't as clever and knew they never would be. Paul hated bullies.

While he was there, he read, in a text for English tourists, that Coptic writing was the closest to ancient Egyptian writing and that if the Coptic Church was ever destroyed the last link to what had been truly glorious would be lost. This incensed him so that he arranged for a pig to run through a mosque thus showing his contempt for those who would destroy the last link. He was amazed to find that he couldn't actually enter one of their places of worship because of the presence of God or Allah being there. This was strange. This made him review his own beliefs. Maybe there were good and righteous followers of Muhammad as well as the persecuting scum. Maybe it was time he rethought what he was doing to both the good and the evil among them. After mesmerizing a couple of locals into torching one mosque, which was close to where the fanatics lived and therefore deserved to be torched, Paul decided to stop. He would continue to only prey upon those without true ancient Egyptian blood but would no longer go any further.

Paul, after reading one of Mark Twain's 19th Century accounts of the British in Egypt and the terrible destruction they wrought on mummies in that period, developed contempt for current British visitors. He didn't mind showing his contempt in his actions. The very idea of corpses being used as fuel for trains angered him. Other accounts of corpses and their linen being crushed up to make a powder for dubious medicinal purposes or as a pigment for an artist's pallet infuriated him. Unwrapping had occurred in country homes in England with imported Egyptian mummies for the sole purpose of entertaining, possibly enlightening guests. Paul showed no concern that the British he was preying upon had nothing to do with past desecration. It was enough for him that their ancestors may have been responsible.

While he was in the land of the pharaohs, he felt a great need to be the protector of the ancient dead against the exploiters of the West and the evil perpetrated against their true descendants by certain members of the so-called modern Egyptian state. He didn't know why this need had come over him but he went with it because it gave his unlife purpose beyond dinning on the living.

From the ancient dead of the sand, Paul learned of humanity's quest to live beyond the years allotted to human beings and how the stars may have entered into the belief of a possibility for a kind of immortality among them. He also managed to learn the hieroglyphic alphabet and was able to partially read the hieroglyphs on temple walls, at least enough to know that birds and animals figured into the ancient Egyptian belief that there was, indeed, a way to defeat the specter of death.

Could vampirism have once been an experiment by ancient Egyptian priests to extend life? If this was the case, then it was an experiment that had gone terribly wrong, creating an eternal menace for the living. There was some indication for this in the Valley of the Kings and in the Great Pyramid. He heard whisperings in the great temples and in the museum at Cairo. The Sphinx said nothing, guarding her secrets as she had for more than fifty thousand years. Paul suspected if she could be made to talk, then all would be revealed.

Some scholars said the Sphinx wasn't Egyptian at all but was the stony remains of an even older, perhaps more sophisticated civilization whose wisdom and sophistication had been lost in time. There is what some scholars took to be a watermark on the Sphinx's body, indicating an age forgotten when that part of Egypt was more fertile. Back then, if the watermark happened to be true, there had been more yearly rain to the point of flooding because of it. Such a time is incomprehensibly distant, a part of a history to be reclaimed. Could it ever be reclaimed? Was it written down somewhere in hieroglyphs yet to be discovered in some still buried tomb? Perhaps it is within the Sphinx. There's a story amongst certain Egyptian spirits that the Sphinx is hollow and contains wisdom that will someday be released back into the world. From an article in a magazine he'd read, Paul got the impression that there are modern scientists who had done instrument readings and thought there is something hollow underneath the Sphinx. It could be a cave or a series of caves. It might be man-made tunnels. If such a hollow, indeed, exists then that is where people will most likely find the answers.

Did these forgotten people—the before Egyptians—write? Legend has it they taught the Egyptians how to do so and then, for reasons now unknown, disappeared. It was further said that, at the time of their disappearance, the knowledge of how to write was lost, or perhaps thrown away as too dangerous. For at least two hundred years it could not be found. While some Egyptians were scrambling to get back what they, as a race, had once known, the Mesopotamians and the Sumerians had moved forward with their own versions of the written word. Today Sumerian tablets predate anything Egyptian. According to some ghosts, nothing predates what will someday be found in the heart of the Sphinx. Today some archeologists also believe it to be hollow, containing the mysteries of an as yet unfamiliar age.

Perhaps the before Egyptians were smaller in number than the Egyptians and so were absorbed into the greater Egyptian culture. Perhaps, just on the cusp of greatness, they were destroyed by their own folly. Perhaps they had created the first vampire and were unable to control it. The legendary Lilith, not the one Paul had known but someone or something a great deal older had her origins in the Middle East but with yet another people. Yet that people had known the ancient Egyptians so there could well be a connection.

Paul spent two years in various parts of Egypt, always returning to Cairo, before a British arm of the Secret Compass caught up with him, making things too hot. During the day, they got together with the locals to try to find out where he was sleeping so they could destroy him in his sleep. At night, they had men and women carry holy books and ancient charms against evil about with them. Paul, feeling the squeeze, headed for Afghanistan where, for over three years, he made over many women into vampires. Then he went to Pakistan where, for eight years, he did the same thing.

From Pakistan, Paul journeyed to England where he now rested. Pakistan had been a great place to eat undisturbed but it was aesthetically displeasing. England, he knew, would be more hectic for him but a lot greener and more agreeable to the senses. He wondered if he had made the right decision in coming back to the West.

The next night, Paul took a train to Manchester where he hoped to find peace from the Rising Sun Group. What he found there was a group of local Secret Compass intent on doing him in. He dented the heads of three of them who, outside a plaza complex, were trying to sneak up on him, from behind, with drawn stakes. He threw one of the stakes at a fourth man who was drawing a bead on him from the other side of a newspaper in a nearby coffee shop. The stake hit the fellow in his gun arm, causing him to cry out, bleed a little and drop his firearm. After that Paul made his getaway. He didn't want to stay to see if there were any more Secret Compass guys getting ready to go on the attack. He wondered what these guys did, if anything, when they weren't hunting down his kind.

Paul stayed in Manchester for a week, dodging bullets. Some of them came from high-powered rifles where the shooter was in a strategic position on top of some building overlooking a place that might interest the undead. Others came from handguns where the marksman tried to get in close so he wouldn't miss and run the risk of hitting a civilian.

There was a disco with old-fashioned strobe lighting and actual disco music, played by a live band. Paul had gone into this place one night for supper. He did manage to feed on a foul-mouthed brunette dancer with delusions of someday making it on the catwalk in London but he received a bullet in the shoulder on the way out. The bullet was a hollow point containing a sliver of wood soaked in holy water. He had to have it cut out. It wasn't till the following night that he found a doctor he could mesmerize into doing what had to be done. By then the wound had festered and was hurting him to tears.

The following night, he went back to the disco, not to find another meal, but to locate the gunman. When he did, he broke the gunman's neck, tore out his heart and threw his body on stage. There the fellow could bleed all over the dancers and the band. The heart he tossed at a table of young women he thought might be in need of such a pumping organ. He enjoyed the expressions on their faces as they tried to dodge the splatter and keep their dresses clean. *Too bad they're not that keen on keeping their souls neat and tidy or they wouldn't be here*, Paul told himself as he smiled at their dismay before leaving.

From Manchester Paul headed north until he was in Scotland. He hoped the Scots would know less about vampires and how to deal with them. He wasn't very optimistic. History told him the Scots were great fighters and not likely to go easy on his kind. Besides, he'd already run into Scottish Secret Compass agents in Canada and found them to be quite formidable. Still he had to go somewhere while he decided what to do with the rest of his unlife. Staying in England any longer than he had to was not a good idea.

Chapter 11

Dixon Street, Chinatown, Sydney, June, 1995

Miles Henry was sitting in a restaurant opposite Mr. Lee, an old Chinese gentleman dressed in an Italian business suit. Mr. Lee was having a sirloin steak medium rare with small potatoes and greens. Miles was having sweet and sour pork with a side dish of boiled vegetables and rice. Both were having green tea.

Mr. Lee had instigated this meeting. Miles had gone along hoping something good might come out of it for the Secret Compass. Mr. Lee was the top man of the local branch of the Rising Sun Group and may have been looking to cement better relations between his organization and the one Miles represented.

Miles knew there was a lot to admire about the Rising Sun group. Some people thought of them as just ninjas and samurai but they were far more than that. They took in other disciplines from other parts of Asia and South East Asia to create a unique blend of the martial arts that best suited their overall purpose. They had begun fighting the undead and other terrors of the supernatural about four hundred years ago in Japan and, as vampirism and other terrors of the supernatural spread, so did they. Two hundred years ago Chinese and Korean warriors joined them bringing with them new ways and possibilities for battling the common enemy. As the Asian people migrated to countries such as America and Australia, the Rising Sun Group went with them as their protectors against the forces of darkness.

Miles remembered stories from his dad's childhood about the Chinese and their opium dens at The Rocks and elsewhere in Sydney. He remembered they had and still had medicines strange to the West that added to some people's suspicions about them.

In 1901 the Chinese were considered the yellow peril. By weight of numbers they were going to try to take over Australia and kick the white man back to Great Britain or so many people, living in Australia at the time, feared. The newspapers were full of such stuff and so were the politicians of the day.

Miles knew the Second World War, with its Japanese atrocities against the Chinese and other Asian races saw, for a time, a splitting of the Rising Sun Group. This splitting was later exacerbated by communism as a threat to Japan and the West. In the name of a greater good, such problems and difficulties have been resolved. Stronger than ever, the various parts of the Rising Sun Group was ready to reach out to the Secret Compass for aid and possible inclusion in future joint projects against the undead.

Even so, Miles could not help but recall that in the 1950s, when he was a young man, the Chinese were still, according to many white folks living in Australia, the yellow peril but with a difference. All of a sudden they would not only invade and take over but force communism upon everyone they could. Miles had fought in Korea against that twin threat and now he was on the opposite side of a table to a Chinese who wasn't a communist and had not shown any obvious desire to take over the country. *Were we wrong about most Chinese in the first place?* Miles wondered. Now he considered that possibility.

Miles hated political correctness with a passion because it did not deal with the truth. It did not allow people to sit across from one another, as he was doing with Mr. Lee, nut out their problems, and come up with solutions agreeable to both parties. From the implementation of such solutions friendship was possible. He knew it wouldn't happen in a day or even a week between the local Secret Compass and the local Rising Sun Group but he could see a time when he might even become Mr. Lee's friend. Already he had no discernable dislike for the man. What he did have was impatience caused by the knowledge that people were counting on him to get as much as possible out of a Secret Compass/Rising Sun Group alliance. All up, he was afraid of being yet another superior in the Secret Compass ranks to make a big mistake and so stop young people, who should be united in a common cause, from being thus united.

Damn it! I'm not going to be the villain in this, Miles thought. *If you want a villain, Mr. Lee, you will have to be the villain yourself because, by God and all the blessed saints, I won't allow it to be me.* He had to concede that Mr. Lee probably had similar thoughts.

Miles knew it wasn't simply a whim on Mr. Lee's part that he was having an occidental meal. Miles had ordered first, thinking that Chinese was the way to go in a Chinese restaurant. He didn't imagine Mr. Lee would do the opposite but he was glad that he had. If he read this sign correctly, it meant Mr. Lee was getting ready to negotiate in earnest with him and that he had a good chance of walking away with something in his pocket of value to the Secret Compass.

"My family has been in this country three generations," said Mr. Lee. "What about your family?"

"The same," answered Miles. He suspected Mr. Lee had done his homework so he wasn't about to lie to the man's face. He wondered if he knew about the death of his niece, Lizzy, or about the demise of Lilith in New York. He wouldn't put it past him to know about both events and more. Mr. Lee wouldn't go into any meeting unprepared.

"Yet we are so different," said Mr. Lee.

"Yet so much alike," put in Miles.

"How true and yet how very frustrating," mused Mr. Lee.

"Why frustrating?"

"I remember how the man who had my position in the Rising Sun Group came to your organization with a similar proposition to the one I am prepared to offer to you. He was turned away. It was such a pity, too. He was a good man and wanted the best for us all. "

Miles drank his tea and ate some of his rice. He was hoping Mr. Lee wouldn't bring up the past but to be fair to his own people he had to. Back in colonial times, the Chinese were not popular and when Australia became a Federation there was a period when even the Chinese born in the country were denied proper citizenship. Despite the fact that those days had long gone and amendments had been, to some extent, made there were emotional scars amongst the older generation of Chinese Australians that he knew hadn't healed. Not every head of the Secret Compass had acted in a fair and just manner toward the Rising Sun Group. The discrimination exercised in the past could not be overlooked; it could not be buried and forgotten for fear that it might someday rise again.

"I am not turning you away," said Miles. "I am here, having a meal with you and I am listening. You have my full attention. I am not like one of my predecessors."

"Yes," agreed Mr. Lee. "You are of a different generation who no doubt does not understand such things."

"I learned a healthy respect for Koreans both north and south during the Korean conflict in the '50s," said Miles. "That also goes for Chinese people. It was a matter of survival."

"There are better ways of gaining respect."

"You're right," agreed Miles. "But I think we can leave it to the young to find a better way if we can but make a start for them."

"Yes we can. But I do wonder if we can truly work together."

"We can try," said Miles. "We can share information and, to some extent, resources. We can start small if you like."

"Small, yes," Mr. Lee nodded with agreement.

"We have experimented with smoke bombs containing sawdust that can disorientate the enemy to the point where they cannot safely take flight."

"We have such smoke bombs. We have had them for centuries but only use them sparingly because they only disorientate the enemy. They do not fully incapacitate or destroy."

"Though our men and women are trained to have good if not perfect night vision, we are affixing night sights with laser locking beams to our rifles."

"We could have night vision sights," Mr. Lee allowed, "but we prefer not to bother with them in case our people get lazy over technology and there comes a night when they will no longer be able to target without such devices."

"We are also working on a grenade specially designed for what we do," Miles told him.

"This is of interest. Will it be ready soon?"

"It is being tested as we speak."

"Anything else we need to discuss?" questioned Mr. Lee.

"I know how concerned you are about modern technology taking over and I agree that modern techniques and tools don't have to be the complete answer. I have seen how a South American bola can bring down a vampire in flight. A person I came to know from that part of the world showed me, here in Sydney, how it was not only possible but how it is done. I have seen your butterfly swords and samurai blades in action. Nowadays I am as open as I can be to ideas coming from anywhere. The upshot must be that, if it works, we want to test it, train people in its use, and incorporate it into our overall methodology if that is at all possible. You are not looking at a man who is stubbornly ignorant. The younger agents coming up through the ranks won't allow it."

"Yes, I understand. I too have young people crying out for new methodology and new weapons. It is an ongoing struggle between the need for tradition and discipline and the need to embrace the future."

"I think we can help each other."

"Yes. I believe it is past time we did, don't you?" With that, Mr. Lee reached down to the base of his chair to retrieve a black satchel. He handed the satchel to Miles.

"A gift," said Mr. Lee, "to show my good faith."

Miles opened the satchel and examined the contents. There were files on the Secret Compass in Australia and on a number of vampires at large both agencies were after. There was even a fuller description than the one he had of the vampire he was personally after. Unbeknown to Miles, the photo from London that could have accompanied it had been withheld.

"Much appreciated," said Miles. He shook Mr. Lee's hand.

"One thing though," added Mr. Lee. "I know about your family loss. Do not ask me how I know but I do know. In fairness, I will tell you that my own family has suffered a similar loss. My niece Lotus was murdered by the same young male vampire who murdered your niece."

"We are in competition then?" asked Miles who wasn't expecting this wrinkle.

"We needn't be," said Mr. Lee. "We could work together to destroy him."

"Perhaps," said Miles. He really wanted to get this undead killer by himself or, at worse, through the use of Secret Compass operatives. On this one he didn't want to bring in an outside agency but, at the same time, he didn't want to snub Mr. Lee and have the Secret Compass forever at odds with the Rising Sun Group.

"I can understand your reticence," said Mr. Lee. "I had to think long and hard about it too."

Miles reached into his coat and pulled out a gun. He handed it to Mr. Lee.

"A gift," said Miles, "to show my good faith."

"We can get guns," said Mr. Lee as he reached for the weapon.

"But not the bullets it contains. They are hollow points with slivers of wood soaked in holy water. Something new I can assure you."

"Very good!" Mr. Lee smiled. "It is quite acceptable. I can see we will be able to do business." Mr. Lee put the gun in his coat pocket and Miles put the satchel close to his side on the seat where he sat.

"It might interest you to know that we have heat sensors from Japan that can, in an instant, let us know if a person is living or one of the walking dead," Mr. Lee said after a moment's thought. "We do not have enough for all our field agents but we are getting more."

"They could be useful. The FBI in America has something similar."

"We are getting in devices that radiate light. They are capable of sending an ordinary person blind for a few minutes but the intense radiation is enough to reduce a vampire to dust without the necessity of a heat source capable of harming buildings or doing any permanent damage to the living."

"That's brilliant. How soon could you get them for us? Where are the devices made?"

"One type, the hand held version, is made in Tokyo," Mr. Lee told him. "The throwing device type is made in Singapore. Very soon new supplies will be shipped our way."

"We must have them!"

"We have acceptable areas for future negotiation then?"

"Oh, yes. I believe that we do."

"Good."

Miles and Mr. Lee ate the rest of their meal in peace and, when they finished, they had more tea. Miles left with the satchel. Mr. Lee patted the place where the gun rested in his coat and smiled as Miles closed the entrance door of the restaurant behind him.

"Contact has been made," Miles told his superior over his new mobile phone. "The future with the Rising Sun Group is looking bright."

"Wonderful. You did well," was all his superior had to say, before breaking contact with him.

Miles sensed he was being watched all the way on his walk out of Chinatown but that was fine with him. The Rising Sun Group was acting as his protector, making sure nothing bad happened to him while he was on their patch. It was something he could understand and appreciate. If the meeting had taken place somewhere in Macquarie Street, it would have been members of the Secret Compass standing guard in just as clandestine a way for the leader of the Rising Sun Group. *Yes, we are alike,* thought Miles, *yet quite different. God only knows if we can really work together.*

Chapter 12

Botany Bay, Sydney, August, 1995

Miles looked over the ultra-violet light devices supplied by Mr. Lee. There were five crates in all. Each one contained twenty designed for throwing and thirty meant to be hand-held. Helen Kiln was with him wondering why she'd been summoned down to the company's warehouse. It was small and they shared it with half a dozen commercial businesses connected with Freemasonry as a cover against the general public finding out too much about the Secret Compass.

"One thing you have to say about the leader of the Rising Sun Group," said Miles. "He keeps his word."

"It's been a while since you've had anything bad to say about that particular outfit," Helen replied.

"We sent them boxes of hollow-points they wanted, together with suitable guns and rifles, and they've sent us these weapons like they said they would. Thanks to them, I've been promoted. Now I'm officially in charge of my section. I wish Long had lived long enough to see that happen."

"You want to ask Long something?"

"If I could talk to him again, see him, or learn through you what he thinks of these developments, that would be great."

"I can't help you. I can only contact earthbound spirits, the spirits of the dead that are, for whatever reason, compelled to stick around. He is not like that. He is not earth bound. At the moment after he died, he did go on to a better place. He really did ascend and I am glad for him. I thought I made that clear."

"You did. I didn't bring you here so I could get you to tell me how I can talk things over with my old partner. What I want to know is if you've ever come across Lotus, Mr. Lee's niece. She passed away a short time after we lost Lizzy. We suspect the same vampire killed her. Maybe she's earth bound. Maybe it's possible for you to talk to her or someone in the spirit world who knew her."

"No. Sorry. I've never come across Lotus. Maybe she has moved on too."

"Let me know if you find out anything about her from your spiritual contacts. Anything will help. She may be a window into getting the vampire who killed Lizzy. We think we know why he was attracted to killing my niece but that doesn't explain why Lotus had to die."

"He was new to vampirism at the time. Perhaps it was a case of hunger getting the better of him."

"That's my conclusion for the moment but, any tidbit into the psychology of the one we're after, has got to help us catch him. Agreed?"

"Yes. Of course."

"I have something to show you."

Miles pulled out a sheet of paper from his pocket, unfolded it and handed it to Helen. Now the meeting was beginning to make sense. The talk so far could have been done over the phone.

She suspected he may have wanted to see her because there was an occasion when she knew he wanted to date her. Unfortunately for him, Long had asked her out first and had gone out with her a few times. She knew he considered himself too much of a gentleman to even try to cramp Long's style. Even after Long's death, he had been reticent to cross the moral line he had concerning how he felt about her. She found his attitude sweet, in a bizarre sort of way, and also maddening.

"What's this?" Helen took the sheet. There was writing on it in both Mandarin and English and it was on rice paper.

"It's an invitation to another meeting with Mr. Lee, but I find it suspicious. Why is it in two languages? Mr. Lee knows I don't read Mandarin. He wouldn't rub that in my face, not after supplying us with these goodies you see before you."

"And what is written in English is the same as what is written in Mandarin?"

"Yes. I had it checked out. There's no reason why Mr. Lee would send a letter to me like this, unless it came from someone else who wants me to think it's from the Sydney head of the Rising Sun Group. Even the paper is suspicious. Why use rice paper? Again, it seems to make it look like it came from the Rising Sun Group. Where we are to meet is dubious. Why not at another restaurant during the day? Why not at the same restaurant we met before? Why meet at eleven o'clock at night? It isn't the witching hour but it is rather late for doing so."

"I ...am...picking...up...something." Helen fingered the paper, closing her eyes, and breathing deeply at first between words. "It is not from Mr. Lee or any member of the Rising Sun Group. You are correct in your misgivings. It was addressed to you at your office in the Mitchell Library. It was mailed by Brian Chance, a vampire from Victoria who was once a highwayman. This was during the gold rush last century. He is an old vampire who has been in contact with the spirits of the dead. He believes that a solid alliance with the Secret Compass and the Rising Sun Group here in New South Wales will spread.

"First, he believes, Sydney will become a definite no-go zone for the undead and then Melbourne will follow. This letter is an ambush. You are expected to go alone to this meeting at The Rocks under the pillars of the Sydney harbor bridge. There will be a Chinese vampire dressed like Mr. Lee. From a distance, you are expected to believe it is Mr. Lee. There will be a dozen other vampires, possibly more, including Chance, waiting to swoop down upon you and turn you into one of their own. You will then visit Mr. Lee and, it would be hoped by Chance, turn him into one of the undead. Is that clear?"

"Yes. Thank you, Helen."

She handed the letter back to him and rubbed her temple as if it had given her a migraine.

"He is a nasty piece of work, this Chance," said Helen.

"Are you all right?" asked Miles who sounded concerned.

"I'll be fine. It will just take me a moment to recover. Are you going to this meeting?"

"Yes. I have to go. But now I know what I'll be up against. I'll arrange for five of my top agents to tail me into the meeting. They'll keep a low profile until things start to happen. We'll see if we can't turn the tables on them."

After wishing him luck, Helen walked out of the warehouse. She made her way back to Mitchell Library where she'd been busy trying to catalogue the information sent to the Secret Compass by the Russians and the now former Eastern Bloc countries. It had come via the KGB and the FBI since the fall of the Berlin wall in '89. Even though the translators worked through the lot sent so far, it was a massive task she'd only been given to work on six months ago. She was only halfway there.

Among them, she found a report the Russians had done on Lilith back in the late 1940s. Some days ago, she had copied it and sent it on to

Miles. Since Lilith was gone for good, she didn't believe it would hold much relevance except to point out that the Russians in Germany at the time had been as frustrated with her border hopping as had been the British and the Americans.

Two nights later, Miles was under the pillars of the bridge at The Rocks, waiting for the fake Mr. Lee to materialize. Miles was on time. It was eleven o'clock and the wind was howling. No doubt the intense sound of the wind was meant to confuse, even disorientate his all too human senses. Half an hour later, the Mr. Lee look-alike, in his fine western style suit, came out of the encroaching dark and said: "So we meet again Mr. Henry."

"If you were Mr. Lee, this would be a true enough statement," replied Miles.

"Look closely," said the fake. "I am the leader of the Rising Sun Group. Come meet my followers."

Out of the shadows came a dozen vampires that hadn't even bothered to dress like members of the Rising Sun Group. Out of another patch of night came a dozen true members of the Rising Sun Group. Miles knew the Rising Sun would be around because he invited them but where were his men?

"The real Mr. Lee sends his regrets," commented Miles. "He could not make this meeting. Ah, but he did send his men."

Before the look-alike could answer, Miles threw down a light bomb which exploded, in ultra violet emissions, reducing, with a scream, the look-alike to dust. He wasn't able to cover his eyes in time to keep the emission from hitting them.

For a dangerous minute, Miles could see nothing though he sensed movement around him. He felt in his top pocket and got out his crucifix. He wasn't sure if it would do anything if he couldn't see who he was waving it at but he had to try something.

Then he began to see blurry black and gray blobs. He got the impression that there had been other light bombs going off, for he could make out fireworks.

He was pushed out of the way and some other man took on the vampire meant to claim him. He heard the sound of blades locking and scraping against one another. Did one of the undead have a sword? It was probably Chance, the highwayman. The swords rang and then there was a squishy sound followed by a loud gasp. What followed after that was the smell of rapid decay.

Slowly, Miles' sight returned. When he was able to translate moving shapes into people, the fighting was over. The nine Rising Sun Group warriors stood over the bodies of three vampires and the ashes of nine more. Three of the Rising Sun Group men lay dead. One had his throat ripped out; two had their necks broken.

A Rising Sun Group man with a bloody samurai sword in one hand and a saber in the other approached Miles. He bowed then wiped blood with a handkerchief from the samurai sword. He then squeezed the handkerchief until the blood that was soaking it dripped onto the cutting edge of the saber. After bowing once more he presented Miles with the saber.

"For you to remember this night," said the swordsman. "I present you with the enemy's blood and the blood of our comrades."

Miles bowed, taking the blade. "Relay this message to Mr. Lee: 'The Rising Sun Group and the Secret Compass can work together.'"

In a flash of white smoke, Miles found that his allies had gone no doubt back into the darkness from which they had come. He looked around for the three dead Rising Sun Group members but they too had disappeared. No doubt they had been spirited away by their comrades. Miles put the saber under his pants belt. He knew some of the red would get onto his clothes but he didn't care.

On a jetty a short distance away, Miles noticed a strange collection of odds and ends he couldn't quite make out in the dark. He pulled out his old service revolver he kept in a holster hidden by his coat along with his crucifix. He then went to investigate. He should have phoned for back-up but he was in no mood to do so. Besides, it was likely that the odds and ends had nothing to do with him. What he did come across was the five Secret Compass men assigned as his protectors and whom he thought would lead the way in the attack against the fake Mr. Lee and his minions. They were dead, slain by the vampires no doubt before the so-called meeting had begun. Three had been cut down by a sword, quite possibly Chance's blade. Two had been drowned then laid back on the dock. There were two piles of dust near the corpses indicating that two vampires had received their second death in the encounter. The dust was slowly blowing away in the wind that was coming off the harbor. He would have to phone for a clean-up crew to remove the bodies and then inform the relatives of his men who had died as to what had happened to them. Sometimes being in charge wasn't much fun.

Chapter 13

Macquarie Street, Sydney, September, 1995

Miles Henry was putting the final touches to the diary featuring his various battles with the undead when he collapsed. It happened in his office in the heart of the Mitchell Library underground complex. His colleagues arranged for him to be rushed to Saint Vincent's where he would get the best care. There he made a recovery. It was the first stroke he'd ever had and it had been terrible. It was as if a plug had been pulled on a machine. One minute he saw himself working; the next he saw himself in an ambulance wondering what was happening and why he couldn't recall leaving his office. An hour's worth of memory from the day when the stroke hit would never return. This in itself was frightening. In any event, it scared the hell out of him.

One month and one week later, after spending some of his sick leave in hospital and a week of it at home wondering what to do with himself, Miles returned to his office. He simply had to complete the work on his account of the undead he'd encountered over the last few decades, or so he thought. To his surprise, he discovered it had almost been completed by a writer whose way with a pen matched his own. All that was left to do was to finish off one lousy sentence and scrawl "The End." *Not good,* he told himself. *If a man can't remember his own actions, what good is he?* He still felt a bit unsteady on his feet but he was told that would get better. It was his mind that concerned him the most.

Lucky I'm getting out, he thought bitterly. Retirement hadn't sat well with him. Now he could understand the need for it.

He had commanded men in combat during the Korean conflict. Later on, he had seen to the demise of fifteen members of the unliving community. He would have been prouder of this total if he'd gotten the vampire he'd been after for so long. Now he had strong doubts that would ever happen. He just wasn't up to it anymore. His body - or his mind – was trying to quit on him. Something, in any event, was trying to go AWOL and he didn't like it one bit.

Miles didn't even know his vampire's name. It could have been Paul Priestly who had disappeared and was presumed dead just before Lizzy was murdered. It might have been Mike O'Dea, a drummer with a band, who disappeared weeks before Lizzy's demise. It might have been some young male bloodsucker from Queensland or Victoria who'd come into New South Wales and had hooked up with Lilith. Miles had always considered Paul Priestly to be the prime suspect. From the start he had gone on his instincts in that direction. He'd even introduced himself to Paul's next of kin in order to get to know him better. Mary, the mother, seemed gentle enough. The same could be said for his sisters, Dorothy and Kate, who wanted to help in any way possible to find out what had happened to their brother. His father Robert was very much an old fashioned gentleman. Maybe, Miles had to admit, he'd been on the wrong track and this Paul Priestly was simply another innocent victim of vampirism and had nothing at all to do with Lizzy.

Miles had been too young for military involvement in the Second World War but just old enough for Korea. He'd been smart enough to rise in the ranks during the fighting and so get out of uniform, when it was over, with credit against his name. Now he wondered what that fighting in that part of the world had been about and also why the United Nations couldn't have found a better way of dealing with nations in conflict. He also wondered about the other portion of his life from which the public had benefited but had known nothing about. Had it been worth it? Long had given his all to the Secret Compass, thinking so and Long had been no fool.

It's time to go, Miles told himself, putting his diary in a large plain envelop and, with the lick of his tongue, sealing it against the curious. He had a junior staffer send it by Secret Compass courier to his great nephew, Todd Lawrence care of his mother, Anne. The lad would hopefully become a Freemason some day and then, if luck ran true, a member of the Secret Compass.

One can only hope Todd, my niece's son, can finish what I started, Miles told himself as he left Mitchell library for the last time. He'd already had his farewell party. It was held at a nearby steak house. He'd been given his pension details. It wasn't much money per fortnight but it was about all an old war horse might expect. He wished they could let him continue working instead

Miles had been old for some time with receding hair turning silver and an expanding gut. He hadn't really felt old until now. Being let go from the Secret Compass because of his health and his years plus the stroke had been a wakeup call. He wondered what more he could do with his life. He hadn't married. Maybe it was high time that he did or at least looked into the possibility. It wasn't as if he hadn't had special lady friends in the past. But what female in her right mind would bother with a war horse well past his prime? Maybe go for a female war horse past her prime? He smiled at the idea. Now where was he going to find such a filly?

Miles' sister, Patricia fussed over him nowadays more than she had when they were growing up. It was nice sometimes to know that she was around. It still grated that his work for the Secret Compass couldn't have lent itself to the one thing that would have helped her. He wanted very much to avenge Lizzy but now he didn't have any official power left to act. His only hope was that his notes might someday help young Todd get his aunt's killer.

Two weeks after leaving the Secret Compass, Miles went to Patricia's two-story home at Menai for a meal and a chat. She tried to keep the talk light and comforting but he had a restlessness of the soul that wouldn't quit. He'd given over his gun, holster, bottles of holy water and stake to the ordinance people at Mitchell Library as per regulations before leaving. Now he wanted the lot back. He wanted, once more, to be on the move, on the hunt.

"You're not young anymore," his sister told him over coffee.

"Damn straight I'm not," he conceded. "But HE still is, and not likely to get old, and not likely to ever turn to dust."

"Leave it alone," she told him, resting her hand upon his. "You've done all you could, now it's up to others to carry on the fight. You've always wanted to take up golf, now's your chance. You've wanted to do more fishing; now's your chance for that too."

"It's so damn hard to let go," he told her with a mild touch of anger and self-recrimination in his voice. "It's the hardest damn thing I've ever done."

"Todd's growing up fast," she told him. "My daughter says he'll be as big and tough as you were some day."

"And smarter too I hope," he added. "They get trickier as time passes, you know."

"The undead you mean?" she said. "I suppose they would."

Miles and Patricia toasted Todd and his possible future success over sherry. Then Miles took his leave of her for the final time. It was not a totally sad farewell. Miles had at last come to terms with his life and where it had taken him. He would look for work and maybe find ways of becoming more active in his local community. He would search around for the toughest, meanest golf course and join up. Hell, he was even beginning to enjoy the idea of looking for that old filly and courting her.

Todd, upon receiving the diary, sent his great uncle a thank you note. Helen Kiln, who was still working in the PSI division of the Sydney based Secret Compass, began sending him copies of reports to read concerning certain recent goings on in England involving a vampire with an Australian accent. Apparently, after upsetting the London banking community and having tangled with the Rising Sun Group over there, he'd headed north. He was last seen in Berwick. He was expected to, at any time, cross the border into Scotland. From there it was anyone's guess where he might go. Glasgow would be inviting with its population but, then again, maybe he wasn't looking for a large population base.

Miles read the copies with interest and wrote out some advice on tracking down this particular miscreant. He made it clear that the fiend had to be kept in sight as much as possible and that eventually, as Helen had long predicted, he would return to Australia. Perhaps he wouldn't return in the next decade but he would do so. When he did, the Secret Compass here would have to be ready for him.

Miles based the notion of the monster's return, not on Helen's abilities alone, but on the brand of homesickness he'd seen in other vampires he'd pursued. The fiend would miss his old home and, when he missed it enough, he would come back. Hopefully the Secret Compass would have him.

A month passed in which Todd was too busy to further correspond with his great uncle. This Miles didn't mind. He found a golf course to his liking and played a few rounds. He did a little recent fishing but was yet to latch eyes on that suitable female.

While cooling off after a game of golf at the club house, he suffered a second stroke. This time it proved to be fatal. Death came swiftly. One minute he was watching some silly program on the club's overhead television set about Elizabeth Bathory, which was anything but completely factual; the next he was slumped over the bar, dead.

The funeral took place in a small, white chapel on the outskirts of North Ryde across the bridge from Sydney proper. It was a charming, uncomplicated structure with comfortable pews and not much in the way of adornment besides the obligatory cross. Patricia and her husband Tom attended together with Anne and her son, Todd. There were precious few others who did so. Four senior men from the Secret Compass turned up and there was one FBI agent from New York by the name of Patrick Lenny who flew over to give his last respects.

In his ill-fitting attire he was some sight but at least he was there. Unbeknown to all but one of the other mourners, Lenny had a habit of putting on weight when he was inactive and of buying clothes and doing other things for which he normally didn't have time. He would work out in the gym when not after the bad guys but there would be paperwork to catch up on that tied him to his desk and restricted his physical activity. He had to believe that the best exercise for him was the chase. It was what he lived for. Hence when he did get active again and lost the weight he had gained, he was a happier man. He also ended up with suits he'd purchased when overweight that were no longer right for him. He was loath to tell that to anyone save a few of his buddies in the FBI. Helen Kiln was the only one there at the funeral who knew and that knowledge had come from a naughty surface reading of his thoughts back when they had first met in New York.

Mr. Lee had sent flowers, a mix of Chinese dragon lilies and Australian wattle. Helen knew he also had Rising Sun Group people in hiding outside the chapel just in case there was an attack upon the people inside. She knew because she could sense their presence. Apparently, the leader of Sydney's Rising Sun Group was determined not to let what Miles had helped to start die with him. It was, in itself, a fine tribute.

Red poppies came from the Greek mystics and a selection of orchids from the Melbourne branch of the Secret Compass. Also there were roses sent from Frank Mullion, the man who had taken over from Miles. There was a card of condolence from Sandford Maclean in Scotland who had trained with Miles at Knightswood in Scotland in the late 1950s. With the card there was a large bottle of Black Douglas to be poured and drunk during the wake. It was in remembrance of the drinks Miles and Sandford had shared, not only to celebrate becoming full-fledged Secret Compass operatives, but also to keep the chill of a Scottish winter at bay.

Patricia flipped a switch on a tape-recorder and it played a selection of music including: "Waltzing Matilda," "Advance Australia Fair," "Danny Boy," "Amazing Grace," "Abide with Me," "Moon Shadow," "Stairway to Heaven" and "The Last Dance." When the music ended, Patricia was called upon to talk about her brother, which she did as best she could, and then the preacher said his piece. Only Patricia and her daughter, Anne shed any tears.

Miles' casket was jet black, the way he wanted it to be, to signify his secret legacy to the people still living. There was a crusader shield with a red Knights Templar cross to signify his warrior status which was on a white background to signify the purity of his cause. He was to be cremated to avoid even the slightest of possibilities that he might return as an enemy of those he cared about. This was not standard Catholic practice but it was something most Secret Compass people went in for and it was necessary for Miles' peace of mind in the afterlife.

His will gave half of what money he had and what money was coming to him to his great nephew, Todd for future travel. The rest went to his sister. What books he had of value were to be donated to Mitchell Library for generations to come to prosper by.

There was a wake held at Patricia's home in which toasts were made with good scotch or bourbon. There were sandwiches and other eats to soak up the alcohol.

"I have a special duty now," said Todd, raising a glass with one shot of Sandford Maclean's Black Douglas in it and plenty of coke.

"Yes," agreed Anne, his mother.

"I will get aunt Lizzy's killer for my great uncle," said Todd slowly and with deliberation. "I will get her killer for the family."

"Yes," agreed Anne, "for the family and other families as well. Your great uncle would have wanted that too."

A week later, Frank Mullion moved into the office that had once belonged to Miles Henry. His new desk was tidy save for a great bloodied saber that rested in a corner away from the piles of papers. He picked it up, examined it and said to the nearest paper jockey passing by: "What is this?"

"It's a sword," said the young woman who had stopped to answer him.

"I know that," said Mullion. "What's it doing here?"

"It was a gift from the Rising Sun Group," she replied cautiously.

"Is the Rising sun Group in the habit of handing out soiled swords to senior Secret Compass agents?" asked Mullion pointedly.

"Only if they're soiled with vampire blood," was her reply, "and only to senior Secret Compass agents they like. Shall I get you the report? It might help you decide what to do with it."

"Please do," said Mullion, expecting a fascinating read. He was not disappointed.

An hour after handing him the report, the young woman returned for it and also to learn the fate of the weapon.

"This sword must be removed from my new desk," said Mullion firmly. "It does not belong to me and therefore should not be on the desk assigned to me. Understood?"

"Yes sir," sighed the young woman, clearly not happy with such talk.

"Now as to the fate of this object," ground Mullion, "I want it put in a glass case and the glass case mounted on the wall behind me at a height where it can be seen by anyone entering this room. Understood?"

"Oh, yes!" said the young woman brightening up. "Anything else?"

"There should be a plaque on the case which reads: 'Donated by the Rising Sun Group in honor of Secret Compass senior agent Miles Henry.' I think such an action only fitting, don't you, Miss..?"

"Pauline Sharp," said the young woman. "I am in agreement though I admit to being somewhat prejudiced."

"How so?" asked Mullion.

Pauline showed Mullion the antique Saint Christopher medallion she had on a chain around her neck.

"Miles gave me this to remember my great uncle, Frank Long by," she told him. "I've had it for years. I will be a field agent some day. It's in the blood, you know."

Mullion studied what he had thought to be just another pen pusher. Yes, she was bright and he suspected she did have nerve. There was a crying need for more female field agents. She wasn't all that tall but height didn't always count nor did raw strength. Vampires were super strong and anyone who pitted just their strength against one was soon enough a corpse in their own right.

"You might do," he told her. "Now take this sword and do what I have instructed. Mind you don't touch the bloodstains. I want them to stay just where they are."

"Understood," she told him, picking up the sword and report. If saluting had been in vogue in the Secret Compass, she would have done so before leaving.

Mullion studied Pauline Sharp's file and two days later she was transferred to the training facilities at Newcastle on the north coast.

With some tact, he let it be known to the Rising Sun Group and Miles' family the fate of the bloodied saber. Neither the Rising Sun Group leader nor Miles' family saw fit to send him a reply. It was just as well since he wouldn't have known what he could further say or do about the matter.

He was hoping for further contact with the Rising Sun Group. He was hoping they would make the next move. After three months had passed, he made formal contact with Mr. Lee. At first, the old Chinese gentleman was rather distant and cool toward him but quickly warmed up to the suggestion of further exchanges of anti-vampire goods. Mullion thought he better not mention possible exchanges in personnel and possible joint operations. He felt it was too soon for such considerations. First he would have to win Mr. Lee's trust. *How the devil did Miles do it?* He wondered.

In the meantime, Mullion kept in close contact with Helen Kiln and her psychics. He kept alive the file on the vampire Miles had been so keen on disposing of. *I'm no Miles Henry*, he told himself, *but I'll do my damndest to keep things in order around here and to bring down the undead responsible for this Lizzy person's death.*

Chapter 14

Knightswood, Glasgow, Scotland, January, 1996

Paul had come into the land of rolling hills surrounded by golf courses at a time of year when golf wasn't played. He was now in the most influential Freemason district in the whole of Britain with, attached to it, one of the most powerful local arms of the Secret Compass. If he'd known the latter, he would have kept away and gone elsewhere. Instead he rented a flat with some of the money he'd taken from a bank teller machine in Moffat two months ago. It was situated not far from the single golf course in Knightswood and close to a small shopping centre where he hoped to find sustenance. He knew Glasgow airport was about half a mile away, in case he had to leave the country in a hurry, and there was an old cemetery about the same distance but in the opposite direction. Some town planner must have thought the noise of planes taking off and the necessary quiet of the cemetery didn't mix.

On his first night in Knightswood, a small private hospital less than five blocks away had inadvertently supplied him with enough bags of blood and plasma to, for the present, allow him to avoid taking a human life. He had put two orderlies under a mesmeric spell, instructing them to get the stuff for him. Once it was in his hands, the spell remained and part of it was a total lack of recollection that they had acted any different from normal. When questioned the next day they could say nothing about what had happened to the missing stock.

Paul took what he needed for his survival and went on his way. Plasma, for all its nutritional value, had the body and the taste of what, for a human, would have been diet soup or low cal coca cola. Still it was a good supplement and would do, in place of blood, when the real thing could not be had. He could live on a steady supply of the gunk forever though the blandness of it would eventually drive him back to the food he appreciated. It did, however, have the virtue of being easier on the palate than animal blood, which few vampires touched unless they were in a tight situation without a viable alternative.

Every night for a week, Paul got blood and plasma from the orderlies. He then decided to cool it for a while. Doctors and nurses were beginning to talk in earnest about supplies disappearing. It wouldn't be long before everyone, including the orderlies he was controlling, came under investigation.

Knightswood was the home of a high tech medical research firm which Paul hoped had a supply of blood and plasma. It was ten blocks away but not a great distance for a bat flight. He broke into the place on the second week of his arrival only to be caught by two guards. They had been on patrol inside the complex when they heard Paul snapping the handle of a locked door. They responded to the sound and Paul found himself in what would have been, for anyone else, the awkward position of having loaded guns pointed at him.

"Hands up!" cried one of the guards.

Paul went to comply but instead wrested the gun away from the guard and shot both of them through the heart before either one could stop him from doing so. Superhuman reflex and speed had won out. One of the guards happened to be a woman in her thirties. Instead of having her bleed out and waste all that precious red, Paul made the mistake of planting his fangs into one of her ample bosoms, close to the already emptying hole. He then took what he could of her fading strength and energy. It was a mistake because, in the morning, one of the cleaning staff, and a long time member of the Freemasons, would recognize the provocative bite as a telltale sign of vampire activity. He would then pass his discovery on to the local Secret Compass.

Paul left the high tech medical research facility with a dozen bags of plasma, half a dozen bags of whole blood and the knowledge that some Scottish women who were large breasted tasted rather sweet. He was tempted to pick up and take away the revolver he'd used but didn't bother. He was also tempted to come back the next night for more blood and plasma which he stupidly did.

Three men in Maclean-Duart-Hunting tartans of splendid bottle green with black and white lines and carrying heavy but powerful claymores were waiting for him. As soon as he broke in, via a window, he

160

came within inches of losing his head. Only his speed saved him. It helped him against a second sword attack which lopped off part of his left ear. He knew the damaged portion would grow back but it was disconcerting. The third Maclean Secret Compass man came close to chopping off one of his hands. Paul had flinched in time to avoid catastrophe. He was pretty sure a missing hand would grow back, but he didn't want to test the theory.

Paul was in an office. This meant there were chairs and a table. He used the table to ward off more sword strokes and the chairs to knock down two of his adversaries. He then heaved the table at the third man before it could be split in two and thus be rendered useless for that particular exercise. As the third man went down, he threw a dirk, a Scottish dagger with a long straight blade. It hit hard, dug into and stuck in Paul's shoulder. It was too sharp to hurt much at first. There was more a deadening effect. The injury the blade caused would pain him something awful, though, when he flexed his shoulder muscles. Paul pulled it out easy enough but then he began to bleed from the now open wound, making him think he might have been better off leaving it alone until he got back to his flat. Of course, with a dirk in his shoulder, he wouldn't have found it easy to fly and he wanted, above all, to be able to fly out of the trouble he was in.

Changing into bat form, Paul flew out of the window he'd broken, and was about to clear the grounds of the research centre, when an arrow from a long bow pierced his side with such force it knocked him to the ground. As he was transforming back to human and getting back his footing, three men in Douglas grey tartans and two in Cunningham burgundy came out from behind five large poplars to give him more trouble. They were carrying long spears tipped with hazel. Paul couldn't believe his eyes as they charged toward him yelling like banshees. It was all he could do to outdistance them with his feet and then transform back into a flying, though somewhat damaged, rodent. The arrow in his side did not help him to climb or retain height and it made turns to avoid objects, such as houses and trees, very awkward. A second arrow came close to getting him but, after avoiding it and in doing so almost tail-spinning to earth, he made it the rest of the way unmolested.

Somehow Paul managed to make it back to his flat before dawn. He had one bag of plasma left over from the night before which he dug into. It wasn't much but he was grateful for anything after what he'd just been through. He removed the arrow from his side as cleanly as possible to avoid infection. He then staunched the bleeding in his shoulder and side with linen from the bedroom closet. *Who are these wild men?* he asked himself as he repaired himself as best he could with the tools available. *Lucky I heal fast.* He wondered about the colorful ways in which they dressed and how they had charged at him. *They've fought my kind before,* he concluded. *And if I stick around they'll find a way to do me in. They'll probably see it as their honor to do so. One thing's for sure, I don't want to give some clansman a thrill in killing an Australian vampire. If I stay, that's what is likely to happen.*

Though Paul had seen Secret Compass Scots before, these seemed more savage and anxious for a kill. He could be wrong, his mind being played with by the immediacy of the situation. There had been scary moments with them in Canada. Even so, he thought it would be a happy night when he was to never again clap eyes on a Scottish vampire slayer.

The following night, Paul arranged for passage on a plane out of Scotland and into Northern Ireland where he stayed for five years. During this time, things calmed down between the English, the Protestant Irish and the Irish Catholics to the point where he could no longer use their battles to hide his own blood taking.

During this time, 9/11 happened and Americans talked about preemptive strikes against enemies both real and not so real. Paul saw on Irish television the twin towers destroyed by nonmilitary aircraft used by Muslim madmen and knew the world would never be the same again. "Make love, not war" was out. Tears in New York and other places washed the psychedelic colors out of what hippy shirts remained. The love beads of a mere generation or two ago were either thrown out with the trash or trampled underfoot. A few communes would survive to show how things might have been if the madness had not set in.

America found herself asking the question: *Why doesn't the world love me?* And the only reply, apart from the heartfelt sympathy of people in Australia, New Zealand, Canada and the UK, was the silence of their own mangled dead.

The American comic book industry responded to 9/11, not only to what had happened to the Twin Towers but also the incident in Washington that had taken lives and the deaths of the brave men and women who, on board a doomed plane, would not give in to terrorists. Impressive comics superbly bound featuring the old superheroes Paul had grown up with came to the fore with words of praise for the rescuers, especially the ones who had died during the rescues. They also carried the necessary warning not to hate all foreigners or Americans who were born overseas and had settled in America for what had happened.

The *9-11 September 11th 2001* comic, put out by D.C., was especially poignant in that it featured artists and writers who loved New

York or America in general but were born elsewhere. There was Tom Grummett, a Canadian artist who lived at the time in Canada but cared for New York. There was Michael Moorcock, an English writer who could reflect upon the terrors of the London blitz and how wonderful the emergency services in London at that time had been and New York in the present were. Neil Gaiman, also an English writer of renown, wrote *The Wheel* reflecting upon the wheel of life and the need for courage at times of adversity. Among these heavyweights was a young Australian writer, Chris Sequeira, who wrote *Tall Buildings*, a moving account of the people who had made New York great and would continue to do so.

Marvel also put out a number of tributes to the emergency service people who went into action during the twin towers disaster including *Heroes* which featured a great many of Marvel's best in terms of artists, writers and costumed characters. Also, a group of small, independent comic book companies got together and pooled their resources to mourn with the others and to try to offer reassurance for a better future in their own book.

The profit collected from the sales of these items went to help those put in need by the evil of 9/11. Paul wished he could have done something heroic, written or drawn something that might have helped but it was not in him to do. The best he could come up with was to mesmerize certain comic book shop owners of outlets in Ireland that stayed open late to get in and keep getting in the 9/11 comics for the following three months after they had first gone on sale there. It wasn't much, he had to concede, but it was something.

Paul, as he left Northern Ireland for the South, hoped the Northern Irish had, at last, found some peace with themselves. Peace among humans could be a damned inconvenience for his kind but he could remember back to when he was human and that made a difference. He was happy to exploit other people's violence but not to revel in doing so. Maybe that made him, in the end, better than Lilith, the vampire who had sired him.

Chapter 15

Istanbul, October, 2003

Paul entered the heart, if not the soul, of Turkey in a tailored Italian suit with fine, leather shoes, also Italian. He had on British after-shave and carried a briefcase made in Paris containing British and Irish pound notes valued at five thousand pounds. Thanks to a few wealthy victims, he was able to stay in a fine hotel and appeal to local businesses the way well-off tourists generally do. No one wanted to cause him trouble. Everyone wanted to make his stay as pleasant and as profitable for themselves as possible. The following night of his booking into his hotel, when a body drained of blood turned up three blocks away from where he was staying, no one, not even the police, bothered him about it.

Istanbul is a Muslim city where Jews, Christians and strict non-believers are welcome. It has been a trading hub for over two thousand years and has been fought over many times and has acquired many names. Before the Christian era it was called Byzantium. Then, in the 4th Century, the emperor Constantine renamed it New Rome. It was meant to become the new capital of the Roman Empire, since Old Rome was considered to be too decrepit to remain the capital. Then, over time, the empire collapsed but Christianity remained and so did this city of cities.

New Rome was renamed Constantinople in remembrance of the first emperor of Rome to embrace Christianity. Some would have us believe that Constantine had renamed the city a second time after himself before his death and had, just before the end came, bequeathed the Vatican to the Western Church, but this is not so. It is however part of the intrigue and the strange politics that have been the history of the Vatican and what is now Istanbul.

During the early Crusades, Istanbul, then Constantinople was a place of rest and recuperation for the Crusaders. Then, in 1453, after much struggle and much bloodshed, it fell into the hands of the Turks and has been a Turkish city ever since. It continued to be a trading hub because it would have been foolish of the conquering Turks to have it any other way.

It was said that at the time of the Crusades the smell of drying fish and fish oil could be detected ten miles or more from the city. For some, it was a pleasant odor welcoming them into the city of cities but for others, who were not used to such smells, it was too striking to be an invitation. For centuries now, it had been replaced by the heady aroma of spices from various parts of the orient, tobacco being smoked in the cafes, fresh tobacco leaf yet to be processed, figs, dates and the local coffee.

Nowadays it is said by visitors that the coffee alone could drag a man by the nostril hairs into one of the many bazaars and not let him go until he has sampled the brew. The Turks like their coffee strong.

Paul had tried Turkish coffee after he got out of high school and before he met up with Lilith. It was at a Turkish restaurant in Surry Hills, Sydney where he was dinning with his family. He found the coffee to be bitter but fine with a side dish of baklava to add much needed sweetness. Now, since he couldn't drink coffee or eat sweets, not even sweets laced with honey syrup, it didn't matter. He suspected, though, that if he supped on a woman with Turkish coffee and baklava in her blood, the combination would most likely keep him awake the next day.

Many of the older mosques were formerly churches and, in terms of architecture, magnificent. They radiate an energy Paul found repulsive. The worst offender, and the most beautiful, was the mosque known as Santa Sophia. It was built in the 6th Century as a church and, to Paul's chagrin, has retained its holiness.

Paul found the boats anchored in the bay of particular interest. Some had a design dating back to the days of Helen of Troy or of Xerxes the great. Others were larger, more modern and belonged to rich shipping magnates. The more modern ones sometimes housed female American or British tourists. Paul found it wasn't that difficult to coax such tourists into making themselves amenable to not only his vampire needs but also his code of honor in such matters.

One night he came upon a large, modern yacht loaded with raw opium covered by tobacco leaf. The tobacco leaf was supposed to hide the opium smell but Paul's nose was good enough to tell him what was under the tobacco leaf. The thugs aboard were not happy to see him even fifty feet away from the vessel and so one of them opened up with a pump action shotgun. The blast missed him by inches, scoring hard against a pylon. Paul retaliated by closing the fifty feet in a hurry, getting aboard the vessel, and tossing the shotgun wielder overboard. The other thugs spoiling for a fight went overboard too. He dumped the tobacco and raw opium into the water where it wouldn't bother anyone again.

Two nights later, Paul was wandering down by the docks, looking for a meal, when someone took a shot at him with a rifle. The bullet missed his face by a fraction of an inch but the message was clear. If he remained in Istanbul, the smugglers would find a way to pay him back for lost property and lost future earnings. They probably thought he was an American DEA agent or someone from INTERPOL.

By week's end, Paul had passage on a tourist boat headed for Greece. He had thought to spend some time in Athens but, almost from the moment he landed there, he ran into problems. First it was with Greeks who had the inner vision then it was with special INTERPOL agents skilled at vampire hunting. Finally it was with English members of the Secret Compass who were there on holiday but keen to put their vampire slaying skills to the international test.

For five days and nights, the city of Athena was turned inside out looking for him. Two Athenian vampires were caught and dealt with by the English in Athens and a third undead, who happened to be a visiting German, was taken out by INTERPOL with the aid of two Greek mystics also in Athens.

Paul managed to escape into the hills where he stayed in a cave for three of the five days. Then he hitchhiked to a small town where he took the bus to Sparta and caught a flight to Egypt. There he wished to find better luck. He'd been to Egypt before and it was his hope this go 'round, he wouldn't meet up with any English Secret Compass members.

In the first week of his return to Cairo Paul ran into trouble. It wasn't the English Secret Compass as before but INTERPOL. They tried to ambush him at the airport and then, one fine morning, at his hotel room. It was during his rest that two men with INTERPOL identification on them broke down his front door. They were about to enter his bedroom and stake him when, one of them tripped a wire he'd set up, causing a bolt to fire from a crossbow. The bolt hit one of the men above the left knee, causing him to howl with pain. Paul, smelling the blood and hearing the noise, rushed out of his bedroom to slam the other intruder against the wall and into the furniture. He grabbed the stakes and drove them into the hearts of both men.

Two nights later, Paul left Cairo.

Chapter 16

Alexandria, Egypt, November, 2003

This was Paul's second visit to Egypt but first time in one of the key cities of the country. He wondered why he hadn't gotten around to Alexandria way back in the 1980s. It wasn't that far from Cairo where, for a while, he felt as at home as a walking cadaver can feel.

There was something for everyone in Alexandria, including a perplexed and demoralized Australian vampire. It was a city named after Alexander the Great and ruled over for centuries by the descendants of one of Alexander's most loyal generals, Ptolemy, said to be the great man's half-brother. This meant the place was Macedonian for a long while and had been injected to the gills with Greek culture and Greek love of learning. It had retained much of its ancient Egyptian heritage but, to this day and no doubt beyond, it would be the model of what multiculturalism could be elsewhere.

Paul found the place quirky in comparison with Cairo and Thebes. In private and public gardens throughout, there was Egyptian sculpture dating back to the Macedonian period. There were Greek style terraces. Legends with more than a touch of the Greek about them were everywhere, a continuing delight to the tourists. There had been a fabulous lighthouse, one of the seven wonders of the ancient world that had collapsed into the sea. There had been the most magnificent library that had ever existed, which had been torched by mindless savages and allowed to crumble into the waiting waters. Even though the index scrolls to the library survived into modern times, nothing else did, leaving modern scholars with a fabulous list of books and not much else.

Upon his first night in Alexandria, Paul was amazed by the ghost images of the lighthouse and the library of libraries. He visited the lighthouse but wasn't impressed. It was large and no doubt had once done a wonderful job but it was just a lighthouse. He'd seen lighthouses, even ones built to burn wood and coal for the light, before on his travels. He flew inside it and around it a few times and left.

The library was different. When he went in, he was greeted by a ghost librarian, one of many, who wished to be of service. The fellow wore the ancient robes of his office and, unlike ghosts elsewhere, he glowed gold rather than blue. All the ghosts here shone in gold. Unfortunately, Paul couldn't understand a word of ancient Greek or ancient Egyptian and the librarian had a difficult time trying to figure out modern English. He was, however, rescued by one of the younger staff members who knew the English language intimately.

It just so happened there was a scholar who had died in 1928 while on an archeological dig not far away. He had come to the library after his death and had stayed on to become a cataloguer of new ghost scripts and modern texts. His name was Professor Ernst Stamp and, being British, he found it jolly good to meet, at last, someone from the colonies below the equator. He was lean and yellow-bearded with keen golden eyes that shone with enthusiasm. He had on khaki shorts and shirt.

"Tell me," asked the Professor, "have the Huns been playing up of late? Quite frankly, the treaty of Versailles wasn't worth the paper it was typed on. I doubt if the Huns will honor it. I told them that in 1919. I told them it simply isn't cricket to treat even our enemies that way. Nobody would listen. They thought I was just an old fuddy-duddy with silly notions about what our empire ought to be."

"That was a long time ago," said Paul. "A lot has happened in the world since then."

"What, pray tell, has happened?" enquired the Professor.

"There was a second world war. It ran from 1939 to 1945."

"How did we do?" the Professor asked.

"We won."

"Oh, capital! Simply capital! Oh, I must write this down. Must keep records, you know, can't let the old library fall to ruins."

"No. I suppose not."

Paul found he didn't have the heart to tell his new found companion, or perhaps to remind him, that the library had gone up in flames and then had fallen to ruins a long time ago. He found he couldn't go far beyond the entrance without coming to the edge of a mighty cliff. He could go all the way to the end of the great supernatural edifice but that would mean changing into a bat. He suspected the change would frighten the Professor and many of the other scholars.

The Professor went off to one of the tables, picked up a quill, dipped it in golden ink and marched back to Paul with quill and empty scroll.

"So there have been two great wars," said the Professor evenly. "Sad business that. Now how did you colonials do with the second one? Did you make us proud the way you did in the first scuffle?"

"We did fine." Paul thought of reminding the Professor that Australians hadn't been colonials since 1901 but didn't want to upset him.

"I thought you lot would. Now, on to more important matters: Are we still thrashing you chaps at cricket?"

"I'm afraid not," admitted Paul.

"Standards have fallen. Never mind, let's not stand around in this foyer forever. There's some hot chocolate on the stove somewhere and there's a chap from Damascus due to give a lecture on water clocks in one of our lecture rooms. Can't chat here with you all night, though I would love to catch up with what's been going on back home. We get so few newspapers nowadays. Rather makes it hard to keep up. So, how do hot chocolate and a lecture sound and then you can tell me all about home and, of course, Australia?"

Paul begged off, claiming he was leaving on an important mission and that he had only looked in on the library to see if it was still there.

"Of course it's still here!" cried the Professor. "Where would it go? Look at all these men of science and culture. Where would you have them go? This place is wonderful. Simply wonderful. Oh, and there is so much to learn and so much to do one could spend an eternity here and not have time to do it all.

"Look! There's that Italian chap, I think his name's Galileo, having a pleasant conversation with some Greek astronomer. And over there we have some woman who calls herself Virginia Woolf, having a rather heated discussion with a Jewish fellow by the name of Freud, Sigmund Freud I believe. She's a writer. She apparently wrote a novel called *The Wave*. I tried to read it once some time ago but, quite frankly, I can't make anything out of it. He's in a new branch of the sciences. Oh, dear! She just called him a chauvinist pig whatever that might mean. He doesn't look very happy. He looks confused. See, he's turning a little blue, poor man. Fiery, isn't she? He seems somewhat perplexed by her. I am too when it comes right down to it. Still, all are welcome here and I, for one, would not want to change that policy.

"People come and go but some of us remain because, I suppose, we can't imagine wanting to be anywhere else. The hustle and bustle that goes on here sometimes would make your head spin. Libraries elsewhere may be dull but not this place. I love it here. Must get on, though, hot chocolate, lecture and all that. I've noted down about that second Great War and that unfortunate business with cricket. You must return, though, and tell me more."

Paul did promise and he did return several more times. In the between hours, when he wasn't sleeping in his hotel room, he snacked on tourists from Australia, Canada, England and the USA. There were clubs and bars for the tourists and it was never difficult to find at least one woman who understood English and was more than willing to be unpleasant with him in the language.

Each time Paul did go to the library he was amazed at the goings-on of the spirits there. Freud had come back twice to confront Woolf and, on their third meeting, they kissed and made up. The Professor scribbled down plenty of information concerning the current history he'd missed out on due to his death and, on Paul's last visit, he was introduced to Sir Arthur Conan Doyle, the author of the Sherlock Holmes detective mysteries. Doyle was amused by how well his fictional detective and medical sidekick were still doing and amazed at how far the idea of moving pictures had progressed.

There were Turkish, Greek, Roman and ancient Egyptian scholars Paul would have loved to have talked with, but he didn't have the language skills. Having a translator help out was difficult and tiresome. Paul did note that there was a female poet from Lesbos who had taken a shine to Virginia Woolf and, though he couldn't understand the Greek they were talking in, he suspected it was more than just an intellectual shine.

On the mechanical as well as intellectual scene, a fellow by the name of Caxton was helping a medieval German fellow build a better printing press. Where the parts for the ghost machine came from Paul didn't know but the success of the project seemed to rely on whether the two men could get along and whether they knew what they were doing. Paul had every confidence the machine would be completed but couldn't remain to find out for sure.

Eventually, through a Greek mystic originally from Athens, INTERPOL and a group of British Secret Compass agents, which included three men from the Scottish Maclean branch, began to close in on him. He had to get out of Alexandria. He headed to Damascus where he hoped he'd be safe for a while. Another Greek mystic picked up his scent on the astral plane and so he had to keep moving.

Even though Damascus was far from being a Greek city, it had Greeks and therefore Greek influence. It had born and bred Syrian Arabs who did not countenance foreign blood suckers coming into their country. They were more than willing to work with resident Greeks in getting rid of them. Paul knew he had to get out of the areas of major Greek psychic influence or wind up a casualty of Greek, not to mention Arab, English and Scottish enthusiasm, in dealing with the unliving.

On the jet out of Damascus, Paul wondered if he would run into problems with Greek mystics if and when he ever came back to Australia. Now that they had him tagged in some way he didn't understand, maybe their power, their influence now reached into parts of Sydney and Melbourne it hadn't reached before. Maybe Greek Australian mystics working for ASIO, the Australian government spy agency or even the Secret Compass were better able to track him because of his sojourn in Turkey and Greece. If so then, mystically speaking, he was in for a rough ride no matter where he went in the Western world.

Chapter 17

Menai, New South Wales, January, 2006

While cleaning up the attic, Todd came across a box full of old Zen Buddhist books his aunt had enjoyed reading, together with the photo album of her 18th birthday bash. There were also loose photos of her prancing around as a ballet dancer when she was nine and then ten years old.

Todd had told his mother Anne he would be joining the Secret Compass. She seemed upset about it. He'd been out in the real world now for some time, away from high school and university. He had worked as an accountant's assistant, as a civilian clerk for the Navy and then as a computer researcher for the tax department. The jobs hadn't formed any kind of a pattern except they were indoor jobs and provided him with a living. If anything, they showed a certain restlessness he longed to end. Now he wanted to try job with special meaning.

His father Sam tried to explain to him his mother's mixed feelings. She was proud of her son for wanting to do something about his Aunt Lizzy's premature death, but she was his mother and deathly afraid of losing her son to the forces of darkness. Todd's father couldn't offer much in the way of advice concerning his wife beyond treating her well and listening to her. This sounded weak to Todd but it was something he could go along with.

In another box there was an old soccer ball and some rolled up socks too small to fit him anymore. They were too torn up and filthy to give to anyone. His mother had probably kept them for sentimental reasons. He knew if his father saw them, he'd throw them out fast, assuming that Anne had forgotten they were there.

Todd gave up soccer for martial arts training soon after he was told the real story of how Aunt Lizzy died. His parents had gone along with this, thinking it was good exercise and probably nothing more would come of it. Now that he had a black belt in karate, he wanted to do something for his aunt, his Great-uncle Miles, and his mother. He knew he would need further training but that was fine with him – the Secret Compass would provide it.

He tried to remember the fun times he'd had with his aunt. There were only a fistful of them but they were precious to him and his family. He remembered playing chasings with her on the beach when he was five and, barely a year later, playing Frisbee on another beach with her. Then, during that same summer, they flew kites together on the sand dunes at Corrimal. He remembered that he couldn't get his kite to do much beside flounder around uselessly in the wind until she showed him how it was done. He also recalled an occasion, just before her death, when she was generous with her popcorn at the movies and another occasion, not long after, when she helped him with his math homework.

He was jarred out of his contemplation of the past by his father's footsteps on the stairs. Quickly, he put everything back in the boxes except the socks. They made up one lot of clutter that could easily be discarded. Once she'd seen them, even his mother would find it difficult to come up with a practical reason why they should be kept.

"You know your aunt wasn't an angel," said his father, picking up a photo of Lizzy off the attic floor that Todd had missed in his haste to pack up. It showed Lizzy poking out her tongue at Anne.

"What do you mean?"

"She was a human being who had her faults like anybody else."

"Like what?"

"She wasn't always nice to her older sister, your mother. Sometimes they would argue. Sometimes your mother would call her selfish, or too wrapped up in whatever she wanted to do to care about anybody else. And, in saying this about your aunt, she would more often than not be absolutely right."

"Mom told me she loved her sister."

"Oh, she did but she also knew, as she continues to know, that she wasn't a plaster saint."

"What are you trying to say?"

"I'm just saying it is easy to remember the good that was in her, especially if you didn't know her long. It is also easy to forget the bad, especially when a lot of time has passed. To play fair, we must try to remember the good and the bad."

"Now I'm beginning to understand. You think there should be other reasons to join the Secret Compass beside what happened to Aunt Lizzy."

"Are there other reasons?"

"The work will require travel, I want to travel. I will, no doubt, be with a bunch of good people, including my great-uncle's friend, Helen Kiln, and I'll be doing a job that needs to be done whether most people know it or not."

"And this is really for you? You've made up your mind?"

"We'll find out Monday."

"I suppose we will. Your mother said to fetch you. She's making coffee and has some fresh scones for our afternoon tea."

"Very well then, we better not keep her waiting."

Todd took the photo off of his father, noticed what was on it and how unimpressed with her sister his mother looked in it, and tossed it into one of the boxes. Yes, his aunt hadn't been an angel or a saint but did that mean she wasn't entitled to some justice?

He followed his father down stairs to the lounge room where the coffee and scones were waiting with his mother.

A week later, at a Secret Compass training camp in the Blue Mountains, Todd was wondering why he was learning archery when, an hour after nightfall, a black object larger than a regular bat flew overhead in line with the full moon. He tried to notch an arrow in time to fire at the object but failed. One of the other first year students was faster and had managed to, not only fire in time, but also hit it, bringing it down. The object landed hard and there was a momentary hissing sound that made the hairs on the back of Todd's neck rise. Then someone shouted: "It's a fake! It's mechanical!"

Out from behind some bushes an instructor emerged with a set of controls no doubt for the flying menace. "Congratulations, Abdul," he said to the successful shooter. "Good, solid moves. As for the rest of you, all I can say is that one of you is either dead or on his way to becoming undead by now."

Of all the people to succeed it had to be Abdul, the one person Todd felt didn't belong. He felt this way because of what had happened at Cronulla not so long ago. In a way, war had been declared on his people when the sacred institution of Beach Life Saving had been defiled by a punch to a Life Guard. That punch had come from someone who looked like Abdul. Todd knew only that this Abdul person was, by the fact that he was a Muslim, one of those responsible, someone who shouldn't have been allowed into his country. There were a few other first year Muslims but Abdul stood out and, in standing out, was to Todd the face of the enemy.

"It wasn't a fair test," Todd protested. "We were supposed to be shooting at fixed targets today. No one said anything about other stuff. Besides, we're just getting used to bows and arrows."

"Understood," replied the instructor. "Life in our business, however, can be unfair. What's more, other stuff has a habit of coming up at the most awkward times. Not only must you learn the tools of our trade and learn them well but you must prepare yourselves, as best you can, for the unexpected. Swift, decisive action on your part will save your life. Not every vampire you are likely to come across will call you out like in the old fashioned Westerns on television."

Todd wondered about these Westerns. They must have been made and shown a long time ago because he couldn't remember seeing even one of them. It showed how old the instructor was and how far back his little quips ran.

Two days later, when Todd was about to wrap his bola around a stump as the exercise they were doing called for, he spotted a dark shadow about to descend upon him. Glancing in the right direction, he saw it was a giant bat and so let loose the bola in that direction instead. The South American weapon wrapped itself around the artificial legs of the mechanical beast and the weight of the bola's balls forced it to plummet to earth.

"Very good," said the instructor, the same one who had admonished him before. This time he emerged from behind a large bolder with the set of controls. "You learn fast, Todd. I'll make a note of that. Now you're up there with Abdul. Congratulations."

"The bola has its uses," answered Todd. He didn't like being compared with Abdul and it was glowingly obvious.

"True," replied the instructor. "It was your great-uncle who brought it into service here in Australia, is that not so?"

"Yes, it was my Great-uncle Miles," stated Todd.

"A man of infinite understanding, a man who thought experimentation important," said the instructor. "I met him a few times when I was on patrol in Sydney. I am pleased to say he saw fit to teach me a thing or two about staying alive in our business. It is a real pity he is no longer with us."

The instructor then turned to the whole class: "Please understand this test was made before sundown for a reason. Though it is true that vampires cannot venture out into the daylight, they can get creatures, even humans to do things for them in these hours. Hence you might never be attacked by a vampire while the sun is still shining but it is a mistake to let your guard down when hunting one just because it's day and not night."

The following morning, Todd found himself jogging with the rest of the first year students along a mountain track known to be tough on seasoned hikers, and even most seasoned hikers were sensible people who did their sport in either spring or autumn. It was summer so it was very hot, sticky and thirsty work. Todd kept alert as best he could thinking, at any moment, something would spring out at him or come swooping down from the heavens to carry him away. He noticed the others, including Abdul, were also trying to stay alert in the heat. Nothing untoward did happen. They simply jogged, getting a lot of exercise on the way to becoming fully fledged Secret Compass operatives. The lesson of being prepared for anything, however, had become entrenched in their being which, they could appreciate, was a most powerful and valuable lesson indeed.

Chapter 18

Iraq, September, 2006

Paul was in Baghdad, but he saw no magic flying carpets around or men on camels waving scimitars about. There wasn't a genie, blond or otherwise, to be seen or a temperamental jinn or a thousand and one other things one might associate with *The Tales of a Thousand and One Arabian Nights,* American Sinbad movies or that television show *I Dream of Jeannie.*

More to the point, there was a lot less accommodation available than there used to be. Bombs from American planes had seen to that. Also, the homes and hotels that remained didn't always have running water or electricity. Sometimes it wasn't even safe for an ordinary person to go to the shops. There were jobs to be had, if one wanted to work for the Americans, but that could be a good way of getting yourself killed by those who hate Americans.

Under the guise of being an Australian journalist, Paul had managed to find lodgings for the day. He did not need them to be too fancy. He didn't even need running water though he did like to shower. He had no need for electricity except to watch television or listen to the radio. If need be, he could get his news elsewhere.

The rooms he ended up with in some ancient hotel were basic by Western standards but they offered a bed, a shower, a small television set and a stove with its own gas cylinders. He was quite pleased with it and told the Americans who had found it for him as much.

American soldiers were stationed everywhere. Other towns and cities had British or Australian troops. Paul felt sorry for the Americans on duty that he met. Being a member of an occupying force was not easy.

Being a member of an occupying force that had failed to win the hearts and minds of the locals was even harder.

Things had gone from bad to worse for the occupiers. The Americans, unlike the British and the Australians, had not brought along enough translators to prevent language and cultural problems from getting in their way. Also, not enough body armor had been issued to the soldiers in the first few months, making too many of them vulnerable to attacks. They talked about bringing freedom to the country they were occupying and, at the same time, newspapers that printed anti-American stories were being closed down, by order of the American military. Local reporters who had anything negative to say about the occupation were being arrested and thrown into prison.

There was local talk about Americans using torture on prisoners in the Middle East long before it became known in the West. The previous regime had used torture and the Americans claimed to be better than that. When it became apparent they weren't, those who had welcomed the Americans as heavy-handed liberators developed a bad feeling about the Americans being around at all. Liberators didn't use torture. They don't interrupt weddings while looking for enemy guerrillas, nor burst into people's homes during evening meal time looking for weapons, drugs, or both.

Paul liked Americans. This made him feel sad when they didn't live up to their great potential. Like the British and French before them, they were making mistakes in this region of the world that would follow them around, like so many stray dogs, for decades to come.

Apart from the possibility of being blown out of bed during the day by a missile from a hand held missile launcher, the general chaos created by fear and suspicion made this place perfect for a vampire reluctant to publicize what he had to do to retain his existence. Lots of guns in too many hands, weird religious rivalries within the Muslim faith the American military authorities were struggling to come to terms with, and the occasional shooting also helped. If you'd finished draining someone of their red and wanted to dispose of the body, there were landmines on certain roads that could do the job nicely, if not neatly, for you. It was also possible to dump your victim with a pile of other victims who had died that night hence hiding your crime among those of others.

It might have been the language barrier that made it difficult for Paul to find local women who came down to his standards. With fear often comes politeness and he was loath to turn to a corpse anyone who showed even the inkling of politeness toward him. Even having a woman scream and run away in terror couldn't do the trick. No, the woman had to be genuinely rude in order for him to make supper out of her.

Paul supped mostly on female American, British and Australian army personnel. Among them each night, he could usually find someone with enough arrogance for him to want to work his magic upon them.

One night Paul came across an American armored car that had hit a mine and then been sprayed with enemy fire. Some of the blast got through, killing the passenger who was a captain. The driver was a young female private who called for his aid. She'd been hit in the leg and the chest by shrapnel from the blast and had sustained a bullet wound in the shoulder. When she saw him passing her destroyed conveyance about an hour after the violence had ended, she thought she was saved. She didn't think to ask what a civilian Westerner was doing out so late at night and in a dangerous part of Baghdad. She didn't even ask why when he began to show fangs at the smell of her blood and that of her dead captain.

The doors were stuck, jammed by the exploding mine. Paul should have said he would go for help; instead he reefed one of the doors off its hinges. It came with a squeak and a crunching sound. The driver couldn't believe her eyes. Things seemed to get clearer for her when he found a medical kit and gave her a jab of morphine to kill some of her pain. He could easily have sucked out the rest of her blood and left but, despite having the old urge to do so, he didn't. Perhaps it was because he had recently eaten and didn't need her blood. Instead of attacking her like he might have done, he scooped her up in his arms, as if she weighed half a feather, and headed with her to a more American friendly locale.

"Who are you?" she asked, but he didn't answer.

Down the road, a sniper took a shot at them, hitting him in the back. He winced with the pain but kept on going. Still further along, an old fashioned Molotov cocktail was thrown at them. Even with the woman in his arms, he was able to hear the flaming bottle rushing through the air, gauge where it was going to hit and be able to use his superhuman speed to catch it instead. After having caught it, he took some satisfaction in hurling it back to where it had come from. This resulted in a greater explosion than he had anticipated, indicating that Molotov cocktails weren't that particular attacker's only weapons.

"That was impossible," said the driver, trying to fathom whether what she'd seen him do was real or part of some dream. She knew she was beginning to drift in and out of consciousness.

"Please yourself," he told her and kept on moving.

"Why would I have an illusion of a man and have him talk with an Australian accent?" she asked sleepily.

"Because you like Australians?" he ventured, beginning to enjoy the idea of not being quite real.

"But I don't know any Australians!" she griped in defense of her mental faculties. "I like Mel Gibson but he only grew up there."

"Don't ask me, love," he replied, "I'm your illusion, remember?"

"I guess Australians are nice," she said and drifted off for a few minutes.

She was coming to again by the time they arrived outside the nearest American service personnel club. There was loud Heavy Metal music and some laughter going on inside so Paul had to come close to breaking down the entrance door to get any attention. As it turned out, it was a burly sergeant who opened the door. When he did, he found the wounded private deposited into his arms like so much laundry, the man responsible already speeding away.

"Miss!" he cried then corrected himself and said: "Private! What happened?"

"Australian!" she said, grinned and pointed toward where her rescuer had been then promptly fainted.

The following night, Paul's back wound healed enough for travel and so he left Baghdad. He knew that what he'd done with the driver would make the papers and get on the news services. He couldn't afford the notoriety. *Why did I do it?* He asked himself but couldn't come up with a good enough answer. Maybe those American comics growing up had gotten to him. Maybe remembrance of his sisters or his mother had something to do with it. For all he knew it was the *Star Trek* influence or *The Lone Ranger* since he had an urge to send the lucky private a silver bullet.

Two weeks later, Paul crossed the border into Pakistan and never looked back. He was happy enough to wish the girl he'd saved a long life but that's as far as it went.

Paul was grateful to discover that there was no mention, by the media, of one of the locked and damaged doors of an American armored car being ripped away from the rest of it by someone with incredible strength. What had happened to the door was obviously taken as the result of the original mine going up. There was no mention of a man who can catch tossed Molotov cocktails and send them back where they came from. It was too unlikely an event to see print. What did make it into the papers was a young woman's gratitude for her shy Australian rescuer and one sergeant's dumbfounded awe when he found himself with an armful of wounded but smiling female soldier.

There was word that there were radicals in Pakistan keeping the fighting going in Iraq by supplying anti-American forces with firepower. This did not sit well with Paul and he decided to seek out some of these gun runners and knock their heads together. In his first month back in the country, Paul gave a dozen gun runners severe headaches and transformed a dozen worthy women into vampires.

In his second month back he noticed that his vampire women had consolidated themselves into a combat force. They were prepared to stop a certain area of their native land from being used by future gunrunners. He left them to it. When they ran out of radicals to attack, he knew they would move on. By the time they did so, he hoped the hostilities in Iraq would be over.

Chapter 19

Menai, New South Wales, December, 2006

Todd sat on one of the patio chairs of his parents' home, looking out over glorious bush land in one direction and residential housing in the other. His grandparents lived only three blocks away and he could almost see their double story house. He was enjoying a cup of coffee and a marvelous sunset. He was also thinking about how much he'd grown of late and of how many hard lessons he had learned.

Since joining the Secret Compass, he had gained a new perspective on Muslims, especially the ones living in New South Wales. When he was in his late teens and early twenties he'd gone to parties at the homes of friends living around Menai. It would be him and his mates and girlfriends, on a Friday or a Saturday night, sitting around listening to great music. Maybe drinking because they were of legal age to do so. Then the house they were in would be raided by Arab type thugs bent on bashing in heads and giving people a bad time. Playing music in a residential area after dark and there being lots of young non-Muslims around, were the key factors in attracting their kind of violence. Some kids were patched-up by doctors the next day. One or two of Todd's friends had to be taken to hospital after the fighting during a particularly nasty raid. It was by pure luck that a life wasn't lost.

The reasons for these unwarranted confrontations escaped Todd. If Muslims didn't like teens and twenty-something folk partying of a weekend then they should go back to where the hell they had come from. What right did they have to break up legitimate, harmless partying in other people's homes on legitimate weekends? The police took down details but no one ran down these criminals and punished them for what they were doing.

For a while, every time Todd saw a Muslim type person walking down the street or shopping some place, he felt like delivering them a punch as fast as he could. He dreamed of tossing them around like rag dolls with the martial arts he was learning. According to Todd, they didn't deserve the luxury of being in his country and he resented the crazy political correctness freaks who said they should remain as well as the politicians who liked them because they needed their votes in up-and-coming elections.

When the Muslim gangs began harassing young non-Muslim women for sun baking in bikinis on Australian beaches, things got ugly. Kala, Todd's girlfriend at the time, had been name-called and pushed around by them. This had happened when she was with her girlfriends and he was at martial arts training. He was livid with rage when she told him what had happened. It was fortunate that none of the girls had been hurt. Next time, if they didn't cover up like good Muslim girls did, they were told that just might happen.

Todd got Karla to promise not to go to the beach without him or without the protection of at least one of his mates. It was an awful thing to have to put to her, for he knew how much she valued her own independence, but the Muslims were taking it away, not him.

Todd saw the rights of honest, decent women being trampled upon by unjust scoundrels, who came from elsewhere and he didn't like it. After being pushed too far by some Muslims, he was prepared to brand them all as being bad. He was getting ready with his mates to fight them since, it appeared; the police seemed helpless to do anything. *Justice must win out*; he had told himself at the time. *We must be free!*

When a Muslim youth hit a life guard on a beach at Cronulla, this was the signal for war. It was thus that the Cronulla riot broke out. Anyone who looked even remotely like a Muslim was either chased off the beach by angry gangs of non-Muslims or savagely bashed. There was not, at first, enough police to contain this uprising. Racist groups came in from elsewhere to add to the violence and confusion. They were used to obscure the issues that had created the uprising. When it was over, Muslim gangs went mad in other beach suburbs, causing a lot of damage.

The state premiere at the time, a slimy cane toad of a politician, made the unrest a political correctness exercise, stating that he believed in multiculturalism. He did not come close to addressing what had gone wrong and why it had gone wrong. It left people feeling empty and helpless. This emptiness and sense of helplessness was perfect kindling for a future riot.

Todd's mother, Anne had prevented him from being involved in the Cronulla riot. At the time, he resented her interference. Now he appreciated what she'd done. It wasn't right hurting innocent Muslim Australians just because there were some bad ones around. Inevitably, in such situations, the innocent are harmed along with the guilty. Besides, some of the rioters had gotten drunk before the fight and this added to the tensions and the general sense of self-righteous fury that prevailed.

The news reported that two police officers had to protect a middle-aged Muslim man from being hit by two aggressive attackers. The police officers had to use their bodies and their batons. This particular Muslim had enjoyed going to Cronulla with his family for the last decade and had never been involved in any violence toward anyone.

It wasn't until Todd joined the Secret Compass and came to train with a few Australian Muslims that his views toward Muslims softened. He didn't want to have anything to do with them at first. When he found out that they loathed the party crashers as much as he did and felt that all Australians should have the right to express themselves on their beaches, provided that they didn't interfere with others doing likewise, he came to look upon them as being all right. He got to like them and to appreciate their own personal views of living in New South Wales.

There were a few Muslim clerics and elders who, as a way of keeping their power over the young, saw to it that they were alienated and remained alienated from the rest of Australian society. They did this by taking a hard-nosed approach to what they believed were lax moral standards among the general public. They painted a free and easy society as the devil's own and those who would do harm to such a society as angels for Allah. It had nothing to do with the true nature of the Koran or of proper Muslim practice. Still, these old men with their influence over certain others were ruining things for Muslims who wanted to settle into Australian life and be decent citizens. It took Todd a while to realize this and to pass the information on to his mates but, when he did, he felt much better. He would still have to protect his women on the beach and at parties but at least he knew he didn't have to hate all Muslims.

By this time Kala had had enough of Todd telling her what to do and who to be with. He kept informing her he didn't want to, but she would always bring it around to the fact he was doing it anyway.

"Someday we'll get our freedom back," he told her in way of compensation, "and then we can do whatever we want on our own beaches."

"I need my freedom alright!" she cried. "I need it from you!"

"But it's not me. It's them. Don't you understand? Don't you see? You need my protection!"

"All I see is someone bossing me around who isn't my dad and I don't like it. You and your mates have good intentions, but I want a boy-friend, not a fulltime bodyguard. Sorry, Todd, but it's not working out."

"We're breaking up?"

"We both have some growing up to do and we can't do it and be together at the same time. I'm sorry Todd, I really am."

Todd felt bad. It took him a while to work out what he had done wrong and not to entirely blame others for his own actions. There had to have been a better way to handle the situation, to keep all of the women in his life safe without annoying the hell out of any of them. Maybe when he found that way he could once more be with Kala.

Soon after the Cronulla riot, the life guards there decided to try to make peace with the Muslims coming onto their beaches of a weekend by recruiting a couple of them as trainee life guards. It was a gesture that did not go unnoticed or unappreciated. Todd came to think of it as a move that was likely to bring real peace to the area.

It turned out that there was an excellent reason to bring Muslims into the Secret Compass. There were now Muslim vampires running around and, though they were susceptible to holy water and stakes through the heart, they did not react to the use of the crucifix. They could more readily be affected by passages said out loud from the Koran.

Many of these new vampires were female, having been converted in countries such as Afghanistan and Pakistan by a Western member of the undead community. The word was out that the Western vampire was either an Australian or a Canadian. Could he be the vampire who killed Aunt Lizzy? Todd thought it was possible.

What was certain was that the new style vampires hated Muslim men and sometimes this hatred spilled over to include all males. Why they should feel this way, Todd could only guess. What he did find out when he went along on a day time raid on a storage shed facility near his home in Menai, was that they could be quick, strong and incredibly dangerous.

He was at the end of his first year with the Secret Compass. A friend of his great-uncle, Miles Henry, thought it was time he got a taste of what vampire hunting was all about. In this spirit, Helen Kiln talked to Mullion who assigned Todd to what Helen called a milk run.

Armed with holy water, stakes, a garlic-soaked net plus five seas-oned field agents, including two who could read out passages from the

Koran in Arabic, and five trainees including Todd, they drove in two four-wheel vehicles to the site. They got the keys off the owner of the place, who was a member in good standing of the Freemasons, and began to open the storage sheds one after the other.

There were twenty-five sheds. Twenty-four of them were filled with the usual junk such as someone's old sports car or furniture. The last one housed a surprise that came leaping out at them as soon as they opened the door.

She had long black hair, a short black dress, olive skin, dark brown eyes, fangs, and very long fingernails that went for the first man she spotted. He went down and it took a supreme effort on the part of three men to pull her off him. She was already beginning to smoke from exposure to the sun but this did not stop her from wanting to take one last male to hell with her.

Placing the net over her head calmed her enough for Todd to get the stake into place and to smash it home with a hammer he'd brought. She cried out in pain and hissed at him before giving a great sigh. After that, she collapsed into a near lifeless heap.

Todd was taken away from her by two of the seasoned hunters as the smoke became flame and she was eaten up by it. Where there had been a beautiful, though crazed, female creature, within a matter of twenty minutes there was nothing but ash. A combination of sun, stake and garlic had done her in. The sun alone would have been enough. Todd was amazed by what he had seen. He had an idea of what to expect but the reality of it managed to hit him hard.

Among the effects found in the vampire's shed were a street directory of the local area, a bag of earth from her home country, several dresses, a fake passport, and the two-day-old corpse of a male Muslim no more than thirty years old. There was evidence that the male had been badly knocked about before he died. Todd, recognizing the fellow as a former party crasher, could not fully sympathize with what had happened to him. To some extent, he had gotten what he richly deserved. It was hard to feel sorry for a bully that has been bullied to death.

An hour later, Todd sat in a pub in the heart of Menai killing schooners of Guinness and wondering if even Aunt Lizzy would have approved of his career choice and where it was taking him.

"Cheer up," said Abdul, one of his fellow trainees who seemed to prefer straight orange juice to alcohol. "You're alive and that's good value in anyone's book."

"Yes," agreed Todd, still feeling stunned. "I'm alive."

Todd took heart in knowing that the other trainees, including Abdul, looked as taken aback as he felt. When he talked to his great-uncle's friend, Helen Kiln over the phone after supper that night she laughed. She told him that, after she'd slain her first vampire and was thoroughly covered in its blood, she threw up all over her supervisor's new shoes. "She wasn't impressed," Helen informed him.

This story, true or not, made Todd feel better about how he did on his first case. The business wasn't easy but he was not about to give it up. He knew he had a job to do that few people even knew about. He had slain a vampire for real and he could do it again.

Todd finished his coffee. The sun had set at Menai and it was growing dark. In the final glow of the sun, a black cockatoo flitted past. It was joined by a dozen of its mates. Todd watched the birds for a few minutes then went inside the house to join his parents for the evening news on the television. He wondered what Abdul was doing and came to the conclusion he was doing much the same thing.

Chapter 20

Sydney, Friday 11th of July, 2008

Helen Kiln was conferring with Aspasia Eneas, a Greek Australian mystic and an invaluable member of her team of psychic investigators for the Secret Compass. Since her recent promotion to head of the PSI branch, she'd been trying hard to work out just how these Greek mystics operated. Obviously, they had psychic powers similar to the ones she possessed, but their powers were, for the big stuff, only able to function when they were linked in their minds to other mystics. It was this chain, this sisterhood they had going for them, she didn't understand. She thought it important that she try but Aspasia was having a tough time explaining the intricacies of joining and of what could be found there. It was like one little computer chip being asked to explain how the whole computer goes about doing what it does. This mental networking didn't always happen and didn't last for long but, when it did, lots of messages were sent and received. Every once in a while a message came through that had something to do with Sydney, Australia.

The phone rang and Helen and Aspasia thought it a blessing. "We'll talk later," said Helen, dismissing Aspasia. "I don't know why you lot have become more active since our main quarry's visit to Athens but I am determined to find out. Oh, and I don't believe in Athena or her owls, understood?"

"Yes Ms Kiln," said Aspasia, walking off. "But it would go a lot easier on both of us; believe me, if you did."

Helen didn't know how to take that remark. Was Aspasia being tongue-in-cheek? Helen wouldn't put it past her. *A case of ask a silly question and get Greek fables and tales of great and glorious goddesses thrown at you? Why not? We're all good Christians here. Sometimes there was the need to lighten up. Get too grim and things might start falling apart.*

On the fifth ring, Helen picked up the phone. On the other end was a field agent who hadn't been with the Secret Compass long. He'd convinced himself he'd seen a bunch of wild vampires in broad daylight swimming in the surf at Bulli on the south coast. He wanted some sort of psychic confirmation before he informed his superiors. Helen rolled her eyes, something she was glad this young operative couldn't see.

"Now let me get this straight," she said, "they're out there in the surf and you think they're vampires?"

"Do you have any idea how cold it is here?" he asked with some passion. "It's winter. It's bloody well freezing. I'm wrapped up in a coat and I'm cold. They're wearing swimming trunks and bikinis. It's a known fact that vampires don't feel the cold."

"They don't go out in the sun often either," said Helen coolly.

"Ah, but it's a cloudy day," ventured the agent who'd thought this out as best he could. "They're saved from the full impact of the sun. It might even rain at any moment."

"Tell me, is there a white flag with a red cross not far from where they are?" asked Helen.

"Let me look. Yes, it's about fifty yards from them," answered the field agent. "Do you think they've build up some sort of immunity against the crucifix then?"

"No," replied Helen, exasperated. "They're tourists from Switzerland, here for International Youth Week and the Pope's visit. Our winter is like their spring. My advice to you is to go down there, wave your crucifix about and make some friends. Oh, and keep in mind that vampires don't even like cloudy days and are not likely to congregate anywhere near a flag with a great big cross on it."

Helen hung up. A smile crossed her face. Now that she was off the phone she could allow the humor of the situation to hit her. She wondered if he would take her advice but didn't really care. She was glad she didn't get his name. She didn't want to make trouble for him over something so petty and ridiculous. Besides, next time he wanted to phone it might be a real vampire threat and she didn't want to put him off from doing so.

Aspasia came back with coffee and donuts. They were the freshly made cinnamon donuts that Helen enjoyed. There were enough for two.

When trying to be nice to someone and thus being the one to get the coffee and treat, none of the Greek mystics had to ask the other person or persons little things like how they liked their coffee or what treat it should be. They already knew. Still, Helen thought it would be nice of them to ask a non-Greek mystic anyway.

"Still mad at me?" asked Aspasia.

"I was never really mad at you," said Helen. "I'm frustrated that's all. You've tried to introduce me to this network of yours, this sisterhood, but it didn't work out. Maybe we should try again. The more I understand what you do the more we can co-ordinate our efforts and be more productive."

Aspasia handed Helen a hot mug of the creamy Vienna style brew both women enjoyed with a couple of choice donuts. The brew smelled sweet in a come-hither sort of way and the treat looked light and tasty. There was no point asking Aspasia where she got the food. It would have come from the corner shop Helen frequented this time of day. No flies on these Greek mystics when it came to reading people's desires. They had to be told at times that such readings could be considered an intrusion on other people's privacy.

"We could try again," Aspasia agreed. "But we're likely to get the same results. You're an individual and you always have been. It's where you draw your strength. It's something I don't like to intrude into and you are doing a good job keeping the department together."

"Yes, well, thank you for saying so," said Helen. "But, I do look for ways to improve our efficiency."

"And they've been thinking of cutting us from the budget," said Aspasia.

"They've been thinking of that for the last thirty years," said Helen.

Aspasia left Helen to her thoughts. It was ten o'clock and she was tempted to make a phone call. There was a time when she would always receive a phone call at ten o'clock. Now, the other party couldn't reach her that way or be reached in such a fashion. *I must visit North Ryde tonight*, she told herself. *He'll be waiting for me*.

Helen couldn't help but think of Long and Miles as the last of the true gentlemen. Way back in 1980, Long had been taken from her by one of the undead. She was glad he didn't stay but went to his just rewards. Miles had died more recently. He still had unfinished business among the living and tended to flit from Central to Town Hall, to North Ryde and, when he wanted to be close to his relatives who lived at Menai, the cemetery at Sutherland. Tonight she knew he would be at a private Secret

Compass crematorium at North Ryde because that's where they had arranged to meet. If nothing else, Miles was a ghost of his word.

Long, Helen reflected, hadn't been her first love but he had meant a great deal to her. He was quiet, hard working and loyal. He was intelligent and kind. He had thrived on being a field agent. Perhaps it was just as well he hadn't lived long enough to outgrow that role. He would have been miserable if he had to spend his time behind a desk. He had destroyed fewer vampires than Miles had but he'd been instrumental in many of the ones Miles had destroyed. Only the higher-ups kept count. Long and Miles knew they were good as a team and left it at that.

Miles was more boisterous than Long but Long had asked her out. Miles had decided not to do so out of friendship to both of them. Even after Long's death, Miles couldn't bring himself to cross some ethical line in her favor. He was, in some ways, too much old school.

She knew that women spooked him, especially the ones he found attractive. He'd once been given a nasty turn by a Greek mystic, Claire Euboea over him asking her out. What the mystic forced into Miles' mind, using his anxieties against him, Helen had never found out in great detail nor had she asked. A brief description was enough. She gathered from what the other mystics had said that it had to do with being alone on a battlefield and seeing in the distance loved ones, including Helen, die horribly and not being able to do anything about it. It had to do with being a helpless failure and being mocked by Lizzy, his niece, for not coming to her rescue. Arms like jelly and people needing him were at the heart of it. He had the triple fears of being alone, of being helpless, and of being needed when it was impossible for him to respond. He had prayed they would never be realized. Not only had this mind blast been visual but it had engaged all his other senses. It had blocked him from reality and for a short time created the worst kind of world around him. His scream of rage and pain had been awful. It had been embarrassing when he came out of it and discovered it was nothing more than an awful mind trick. It had taken him years to recover from this hellish attack, before he could even think of asking someone else out.

Claire Euboea had been dismissed from service by the then head of the PSI department for harming a Secret Compass operative. Before she cleared her desk out, Helen had given her hell over what she'd done. Other psychics working for the Secret Compass followed suit. What had made matters even worse for Claire was that the sisterhood broke her off from the chain for unethical behavior. They put blocks in her mind to prevent her from future access to her own powers. She would continue to have these abilities but not know how to tap into them. When she left, she had no psychic abilities to speak of and was last seen working in a coffee shop as a waitress.

Every once in a while, Helen or one of the others from the PSI division visited the coffee shop to remind Claire that what she had done to Miles was not forgotten. On those occasions this terrible creature would have to pay for breaking a lot of cups and mugs as well as using less than appropriate language in front of paying customers. It was a wonder she got to keep her job.

Unfortunately, none of this concern for Miles and his feelings had filtered across to him even when he was alive. Punishing wickedness in the PSI department was deemed to be strictly PSI business.

One psychic did ask Miles out. He was so polite in his refusal revealing, more than anything else, how he had been wounded and, worst of all, confused. He found the woman pretty, but it was a case of once bitten, twice very shy prevailed.

Helen thought that, before visiting Miles that night, she would go to the coffee shop and plant a nightmare in Claire's mind. When Claire slept, it would come to life and there would be snakes and spiders of the mind for her to contend with. Even after the decade or so that had passed, she deserved nothing less. At first Helen wondered why, in all this time, Claire hadn't left Sydney. The answer was obvious. The members of the sisterhood who were still vindictive toward her could find her anywhere. Whether she climbed the highest mountain or went into the heart of the thickest jungle she could still be found and her mind touched, even twisted till she screamed. The breaking of the chain only went one way. She could never again access it but they could forever access her.

Aspasia got back to Helen in the afternoon with word from the sisterhood that the person who had killed Miles' niece would not be making a visit to Australia this year but quite possibly next year. Among other things, the pope's visit had him worried. This was understandable. No vampire in his right mind wants to get back home only to find the place overrun with do-gooders and would-be saints.

"Thanks for your confirmation," said Helen. "I'll make a note of it to pass on to Frank Mullion."

At her meeting with Miles, she learnt that he too was optimistic about the return of Lizzy's killer. He was normally blue but, this night; there was a touch of gold about him. It was as if he were getting ready to ascend.

"How's my great nephew, Todd doing?" asked Miles.

"Fine. There's every sign he'll make a great agent. He has strength and integrity. He's a little too cocky but that comes with youth. At weapons training he's considered the best in his class. He now has two vampires under his belt.

"There's the one I told you about, the Muslim woman. There's also this fellow who attacked a woman on a train coming into Cronulla station one night. In the first instance, he used a stake and others held her down. In the second, he put a hole in the head of his quarry and then emptied the revolver into the fiend's heart. He told me how little there was of the heart after that to stake."

"Takes after me," beamed Miles.

"I'm afraid so," agreed Helen. "He lost one girlfriend by getting overly protective. He's not likely to make the same mistake again."

"Yes," sighed Miles. "Fortune may favor him in that direction. I hope it does."

"It will," said Helen. "I'll look after him."

"I'm sure you will," agreed Miles. "I can't find Lizzy. Is she here or elsewhere?"

"Elsewhere," said Helen. "I've told you this before. There's no point in your looking for her here. Believe me, she was around but now she's gone. I can't say where exactly but she's no longer on earth."

"Good. When her murderer is brought to justice, will I get to go somewhere else too?"

"I hope so; I really do."

Four days later, despite an Australian cardinal's ill-received statement that, in an overpopulated world, possibly dying from pollution caused in part by overpopulation, there should be more children born in the West, the Pope's visit was going well.

"Why not less children per couple born elsewhere?" one man cried out in a crowd of thousands. His voice was drowned by the others but his disbelief and anger resonated. It was picked up by a number of psychics at the docks in Sydney and broadcast to Helen who was at their Mitchell Library headquarters. *Yes*, she thought, *once more this particular cardinal has a lot to answer for. Perhaps I should send him my copy of "Soylent Green" or "Population Bomb" or perhaps a certain episode of the original "Star Trek" in which the subject is examined?*

Helen was afraid the cardinal's statement about the producing of more children would filter down to the countries where overpopulation had already led to starvation, breakdowns in government and a sense of hopelessness for the future.

"The man who has gone too easy on pedophiles wants there to be more children?" argued Helen out loud, who wanted to stay a good Catholic but was finding it difficult when cardinals couldn't understand that most couples in Australia could not afford more than three children, that Australia had been in drought a long time, or that there was the strong probability of future migration from many countries affected by drought and overpopulation.

It had occurred to Helen that maybe the vampires were needed to keep the population in check. They could never have the sort of numbers to do more than that but perhaps that would be enough. In the past, war and pestilence helped out.

There was a time when an expanding population would meet another expanding population, they'd fight and the result would be a double reduction in terms of people on the face of the planet. But modern weapons are so destructive that the damage they cause to the land negates any possible benefit to the reduction in populace. Even going back as far as the Vietnam War, the slaughter was negated by chemicals, such as agent Orange, which polluted too much of the land for decades after the fighting was over. As for disease, most epidemics nowadays are stopped so early in their existence by advanced medicine they can barely be called epidemics.

Yes, vampires were possibly the only hope the world had for a brighter, better future. Unfortunately for most people, including Helen, they came with a price tag too high to pay. There would always have to be victims and no one with a conscience, not even Helen, wanted to be judge over who would live and who would die. *In the book of a lot of people,* Helen told herself, *someone like Lizzy would be a write-off. Yet the rest of her family aren't write-offs and have been affected by her death. So where then do you draw the line?* The answer to her question was the answer she always came up with. You don't draw the line at all. You save everyone you can from the undead, even people like that cardinal.

The new pope seems a sensible man, thought Helen. *Perhaps there's hope in that direction.*

"A penny for your thoughts," said Aspasia as she entered Helen's office. "I promise I won't try to steal them."

"The crowds are good for the Pontiff's visit," answered Helen. "There are Catholics from all over the world in Sydney today. It's quite an occasion."

"Here are the latest reports from our field agents," said Aspasia, handing over a dozen sheets of computer typed paper. "Nothing major is happening on the undead front. This would be the perfect time to go on holidays for a couple of weeks. It will take at least that long for vampire activity to get back to normal."

"I'll think about it," said Helen.

"Crete is nice this time of year," said Aspasia. "I've already put in for leave."

"Yes," agreed Helen, "Crete would be lovely."

Hot days in any part of Greece would be better than the winter chills of Sydney, thought Helen, *But why Crete?* Then she remembered that Crete was where Aspasia's family had lived. She probably had relatives still there and part of her vacation would include visiting them.

"So you'll forward your papers for two weeks off?" asked Aspasia.

"Sure," said Helen. "But Crete is out of the question. I wouldn't get a return airline ticket on such short notice or, for that matter, accommodation."

"Your passport in good order?" asked Aspasia.

"Yes," said Helen. "Of course it is. That's part of Secret Compass regulations."

"Then here," said Aspasia, putting a return airline ticket on Helen's desk. "Also, here's a reservation for your stay at a hotel in Athens for a night, Crete for a week at a fine Inn, and Pyrgos for about a week."

Helen looked at the ticket and the sheet with her itinerary. *Was I radiating that much of a need for a break?* She wondered.

"Thank you," she said to Aspasia who was walking away. Some day she'd get used to working with these Greek mystics but not today.

Two days later, Helen was winging her way to Greece. She had been surprised her leave had been approved so quickly only to discover it had been put in weeks before and there was only the requirement of her signature to make it all official. She felt somewhat railroaded but in a nice sort of way. People were looking after her and that was a good thing. Besides, she needed to get away from Miles and his continuing struggle to bring Lizzy's killer to justice. She had to recharge her own batteries.

Will I meet more of the sisterhood in my travels? She wondered. There was a possibility. She wanted time to herself to unwind and relax. Now she was determined to get it. Helen was surprised Aspasia wasn't on the same plane. Maybe that was indicative she would be mostly left on her own. If this was the case then that suited her just fine.

Chapter 21

Wollongong, South Coast of NSW, January, 2009

On a particularly bright, moonlit night Miles was walking along the main beach, kicking spirit sand into the air when he heard a voice from above calling to him. It was Lizzy. He recognized the tone from long ago. In his mind's eye he could make out her face.

"Time to go," she said. "Todd will do what he can. Whether he succeeds or fails is up to him. There's nothing more for you to do here."

"Really?" asked Miles.

"Yes," said the voice of Lizzy. "Your duty to your family here is done. Don't you want to see your Dad and your Mom? They're waiting for you. There's your old mate Long. He had a new girl friend he would like you to meet. Oh, and some day, I can't tell you when, there'll be Helen. So, what are you waiting for? Just push off with your feet. There, that's the way. The stars await and beyond the stars....I simply can't tell you. There are no words to describe what is out there."

"I did well?" asked Miles.

"Yes. You did well. Now, old man, it is time to rest, to explore, to simply be."

Miles liked the sound of all that. He liked it even more when, in his drifting upward, he broke through the sky and was in outer space. The Southern Cross smiled at him as if he were an old friend. The Milky Way was truly milky this high up. Yet there was something beyond the stars that defied the very logic of existence. He wondered what it could be and why it would be interested, even concerned about him.

"Good soldier," a male voice with a Scottish accent came down at him. "If you'd had a clan you would have done them proud!"

"What is this?" Miles asked. "God can't be a Scotsman."

"And why not?' groused the voice.

"You're not God," concluded Miles. "I know you. It was years ago when I was training in the highlands of Scotland. You're a Maclean. Sure, and I think I know which one. You were my training instructor!"

"Ah, ye remember your old mate, Henry Maclean, aye? And it's about ruddy time an' all!"

"But you're...I mean you've been..."

"I'm past my expiration date? Ha! So I am, Laddie! Now listen carefully and I'll guide you in."

"Will I like what I'll find?"

"I can't say. It's different for everybody."

"Will I meet loved ones?"

"Oh, for certain."

"I can hardly wait."

"Aye you've been a patient one."

"Too patient?"

"I don't think it really matters, do you?"

"No. I suppose not."

As something bright and wonderful opened up before him, Miles thought of his years in the Secret Compass and his time before that in the Australian army. Now it was time to be young again. It was time to enjoy youth once more. He would no longer grow old, his spirit would be renewed and that, as he entered the crossover point, with the faint sound of bagpipes getting louder, more boisterous, was all he needed to know.

The following night, Helen dreamt of Miles' ascendancy and knew that it was more than just a dream. She would no longer meet him anywhere while she still lived. She was happy for him and, at the same time, not so happy for herself. They would meet again and that would have to be enough for the time being.

The next morning at work, she conferred with Aspasia and other psychics about what had happened to her when she was asleep. They were glad to reinforce her belief that, from now on, Miles would be all right. She could not get any impression as to what was going to be Todd's fate. Not even the Greek mystics could help her there.

She remembered her trip to Greece where she met an old blind woman in Crete who claimed to be one of the keys of the sisterhood. Her inner sight made up for, in some way, the lack of normal vision. She didn't speak English but they could communicate with each other via the language of the mind which is universal.

You have male psychics in your Secret Compass? asked the old woman.

Yes, replied Helen. *Some of them are very good.*

I know. I have reports concerning their skill, but they can never be part of the chain of the sisterhood. They are part of everything but in a different way to my charges.

I work with them, said Helen. *I would never dismiss anyone on grounds of gender, never!*

And you must continue to work with these male psychics for they can be very good. We of the sisterhood cannot do so. Therefore you must hold the balance. Do you understand?

I am beginning to, said Helen.

In order to be the balance you can never become part of the sisterhood. Instead you are our link to others who are psychic. Do you now understand?

I think I do, said Helen. *The Secret Compass would like to know why there has been an increase in your activities of late.*

It only appears to be an increase to outsiders, the old woman said kindly. *We are spread rather thin across the globe and do what we can. We have come to concentrate more on your one particular walking cadaver since he touched upon Greek soil and a key in Athens felt his presence. We are, however, losing our interest in him.*

Why?

He does not plan to ever visit Greece again. His plans are no longer as grandiose as they once were. Besides, we have faith in you, your male psychics and the members of the sisterhood under your care to handle things in Australia when he comes home. Now go. I am exhausted. I must rest.

Helen hoped to get more out of her companion but that was all the time the old one could give her. It was enough to confirm her suspicions. She would go easier on the Greek mystics working for the Secret Compass. It was all good what she, they and others who explored the mystic realm in order to aid humanity were up to. She understood that it was folly to even try to fit everyone into a single basket, so long as the field agents got the information and the backup when they needed it.

Just before lunch, Helen got a sharp image in her mind of not just their quarry heading south from Sydney toward Wollongong, sometime in the near future, but of there being a dozen or more vampires awaiting Todd and three other Secret Compass operatives. There would be some members of the Rising Sun Group around but she wasn't sure how many. She forwarded her premonition to Todd's superior, Frank Mullion, and then noted it down in her personal diary. By mid-afternoon, three male psychics and two Greek mystics on Helen's staff had confirmed her premonition with premonitions of their own.

PART III

THE RETURN...

I have heard tales of men, who in the night
Saw paths of stars let down to earth from heaven,
Who follow'd them until they reach'd the light
Wherein they dwell, whose sins are all forgiven...

Extract from "Rapunzel" (1858) by William Morris (Page 62)
Early Romances in Prose and Poetry by William Morris, J. M. Dent and Sons
Pty LTD, 1973, London

Chapter 1

Sydney, February, 2009

Paul's plane touched down and glided to a stop not far from the terminal. A bus was sent out to meet the plane and to take the passengers to where they would officially enter the country. Paul had changed his passport a number of times since Lilith had given him his first fake. Now, he was a computer software salesman who'd spent the last five years in the UK. He was heading home because he had been caught up in an electrical fire that had badly scarred him. He was wrapped up in bandages and had a fake paper stating that he was a burn victim on his way from the burn center at Chelsea and Westminster Hospital, London to the one at Concord Repatriation General Hospital, Sydney.

The airport security had tightened since last he was there. 9/11, followed by the Bali bombing, had done that. Bush had insisted there was an Axis of Evil. Everyone who sided with the USA sided with the angels; everyone who didn't had to be suspect. Even though this could be considered true, it had the power to alienate countries that otherwise would choose to be either lukewarmly favorable to the West or neutral. Big dramatic gestures in the world of politics don't always garner the best results. Conflicts, especially the moralistic kind, are often gray in nature rather than black and white. The world was breathing a sigh of relief that Bush was finished, and Obama was in. America might soon get over its self-absorption and paranoia.

There was talk of American misuse of military authority in Afghanistan and Iraq, clandestine torture used by Americans to, not only break down terrorists, but those they suspected of terrorist acts. The English were struggling to get over their understandable paranoia due to terrorist acts in London. Unlike the Americans, they had been there before with terrorist bombings of London by the IRA in the '70s.

Australia was still having continuing problems with Indonesia. It seemed that, no matter how much money the Australian government ploughed into the Indonesian government, not much of it filtered down to the common people and there was always a demand for more. There were Muslim terrorists still to be caught and brought to justice.

On the lighter side of politics, Paul had learned from the mind of a young man, as he passed an airport newsagents, that a Protestant Christian right wing politician wanted to, not only ban topless bathing from Australian beaches but impose fines on women who failed to comply by covering up. *What a joke*, Paul thought. *As if anyone would take such a proposal seriously.* He suspected that a lot of Australian police officers would not want to try to enforce such a restriction. If it was taken up and made law it might lead to the banning of the bikini. Paul, for one, would be against that. He wanted his mother and his sisters to have the freedom they wanted and deserved. Even when he was alive he was loath to press his own ideas on what they should wear upon them. He knew he didn't have that right and didn't want it. Now that he was undead, he was just as loath to have someone else do it in his stead.

The good thing about some Protestant Christian right wing politicians was that they made Christianity look dumb and that had to be a plus for your average vampire. The fewer humans who believed or were likely to do so the safer unlife was for the undead.

The airport was a vast complex in which getting one's bags and making it through customs took a lot of leg work and patience. Paul was glad it was night when his strength was at its peak. Still, he was hungry and waiting in line for over an hour to be stamped and sent on his way was not much fun. The itching of the bandages he wore did not help. It had been worse in London where it had taken almost two hours getting out. He did not want to know how much time it would be at most American airports.

Once away from the airport, Paul hailed a cab and had the driver take him to the small, grubby hotel near Central he'd booked before his flight. It was a place with an antique and unreliable lift no one ever used. A set of stairs going up to the first and then the second floor creaked with every step but at least did the job it was designed to do. What had drawn him to this hotel was its cheapness for he was low on funds. He didn't plan on being in Sydney for long. With a sigh of relief he removed the bandages.

Paul wondered why he had returned. He didn't expect his family to be where he'd left them, in a house on the outer suburb of Riverwood. They would have moved on long ago. His parents, Mary and Robert Priestly, would have retired. His sisters, Dorothy and Kate, would have married. Besides, he was adamant about never seeing them again. It would be too hard on him and on them. There would be little purpose in stirring up hope for a reunion that could never be. Even so, he had come back to his own country. Maybe that was something the undead needed to do every once in a while.

The small bag of earth Paul had on a chain around his neck probably needed replenishing. He had had it since the night he'd come back from the dead. According to Lilith, it kept him safe and well during the day. She also said it had to be native earth and he was born in Australia.

On the second night of his stay in Sydney, he exchanged new earth for old. He took it from a rose garden in Rose Bay. He took a prostitute's life while he was at it. She claimed to be a keen tennis player and he was famished. The waters of the bay made a good dumping area.

"I've gone a long way simply to come back home," he said to himself on the journey back to his hotel room. Sure, he had traveled but where had it got him? The chase was on. Every time he turned around, either the Rising Sun Group or the Secret Compass was behind him closing fast. His only real respite was in Afghanistan and Pakistan. They were not countries he'd care to spend the rest of eternity. New York had its moments until the Secret Compass and the FBI caught up with him. The same could be said for his short period in Northern and Southern Ireland. His time in Wales had been enjoyable. As it turned out, the caves in that part of Britain were genuine treasures. They had served him well.

Paul had long since realized there was a dedicated force after him and that, for whatever reason, it was personal. But why? Was it about one of his victims? If so, which one? There had been so many. He detested the idea of even attempting to keep track of them all. Then there was the one he remembered most vividly. Her name was Lizzy. Apart from being tall, young, blond and foolish he didn't know much about her. It was enough that she had been rude to him. He didn't delve into her mind in any great detail before he feasted because he didn't want to know too much about her. She had made herself food for him and there seemed little point in getting her entire life story before he took his meal. Even so, her slaying may have started something that might end soon. He knew he was where it could come to some sort of conclusion.

The following night, Paul knew he'd been spotted outside the large theatre complex on George Street by a Secret Compass man. Some hours later, flying over Centennial Park, he was spotted by two Secret Compass field agents who were posing as boyfriend and girlfriend. In both instances, it might have been his own brand of paranoia showing but the George Street fellow looked too keen-eyed to be your average civilian and the Centennial Park couple had a pair of night vision binoculars that made him suspicious of them. Perhaps there was owl watching at the park but somehow Paul doubted it.

Between George Street and Centennial Park, he managed to waylay an attractive twenty-something redhead. It was inside a pub on Pitt Street, not far from the Woolworth's building. She was drunk and being abusive to everyone, including the barman. It took little effort to mesmerize her into a corner where he took her blood. She didn't struggle much and passersby thought they were only kissing. No one said much when he walked away. No one showed any concern when she slid down the wall she had been resting against to collapse on the floor. Drunks did collapse and companions were known to leave them to it. Not until morning did the cleaner come upon her and, finding her ice cold to the touch, phoned the police.

By the time any fuss was made over his latest victim, Paul was fast asleep in his rented room. He was dreaming of what his existence might have been like if he'd walked past Lizzy the night she was at *The Blue* instead of attempting to engage in conversation with her. The funny thing was he could barely remember the words she had uttered which had made her a prime target.

Two nights later, Paul was in a train heading to Riverwood when he saw two teenage guys spray painting nonsense on the exit doors of his carriage. He asked them to stop because the stink of what they were doing was getting up his nose. They continued but with one of them giving him the finger. Less than a minute later, the lads had discovered the horrors involved in taking spray can paint orally. Paul left them gasping for breath with some indication, from the blueness of their faces and their moving about like beached dolphins, that they might not be long for this world. Would anyone with a mobile phone tell the police of their plight or would the other passengers let them die? He hoped the answer would be the latter rather than the former. Paul got off at the next stop. Instead of going on to Riverwood, he travelled back on another train into the inner city.

The following night, Paul visited the shopping centre at River-wood but did not go as far as the three blocks past the station to his old family home. He was heading back to Sydney proper on the train when he met two fresh faced girls. They were in their late teens and they were scratching graffiti onto a train window via the use of a razor blade. When he told them to stop, they threw profanities at him which was just the invitation to dinner he needed. They proved to be succulent. One was plump and tender, the other somewhat lean but with buoyancy in her red that was charming. He enjoyed draining both unto death, and then propping them up in their seats as if one was continuing with her alterations to railway property and the other was nearby, giving her advice. He wondered, as he left the train at Central, how long it would be before someone living discovered that they were no longer living. Already there were ghosts talking to the specters of his recent victims, telling them they were dead. They were gathering information from them as to how it had happened.

Over the news that morning, Paul learned about how the police were now intent on finding some vigilante who had poisoned two paint-can graffiti juveniles with their own paint and had made anemic unto death two razor blade graffiti juveniles. Local high school kids and parents were interviewed as to what they thought of the vigilante and what he was doing. None of them had a kind word. A couple of railway workers interviewed hoped the vigilante might scare other kids away from future vandalism. Some psychologist tried to make out that the vigilante was as bad as his victims while a middle aged man, who had been travelling to work on a train at the time of being questioned by reporters, thought the vigilante's methods a little extreme but somewhat justified in an age when teenagers don't listen to their elders or take responsibility for their actions.

Paul was amused at having done something people would talk about. He couldn't agree with the dumb parents or their hyperactive children. He did agree with the long suffering commuter and the railway workers. As he turned off the television set and settled into bed for the day, he dreamt of there being more so-called vigilantes on the trains, only human rather than inhuman. If that happened, then maybe teenagers would look at what they were saying and doing before they spoke and acted. If that happened, it might herald in a new age in which teenagers showed respect for the other fellow as well as the environment and the creatures that shared the environment with them. It was, of course, too much to hope for. It was good, though, that there happened to be four teenagers who would never create ugliness ever again or take a reckless disregard for anyone else's health.

Two nights later, Paul tried to visit *The Blue*, but it was no longer a disco. Since the early 1980s, it had gone through many changes. At one time it was a cabaret venue, then an Italian restaurant and finally a health club. Throughout all this, it kept its name if nothing else. By the time Paul returned, it was a health club in which he had little interest. *Times do change after all*, he told himself as he walked away from the latest version of *The Blue*. If it had remained a disco he would have loved to have used it the way he had when he first became one of the undead. It would have been like coming home.

As he wandered up Elizabeth Street past Wynyard and toward the Town Hall area, he became aware that two men were following him. He then became aware of two men in front of him. "Now," someone shouted. A net laced with garlic juice was thrown down at him from the top of a nearby building. It missed touching him by mere inches but the stench of the thing began to weaken him. He moved away from it before the two men who had picked it up off the pavement could hurl it over his head. One of the guys behind him had a stake and thought it time he used it. Paul grabbed the stake wielding hand of the fellow, just as he was making his play, and used his momentum to dump him into the two guys with the net, knocking them to the ground. He took out the fourth guy with a sound punch to the abdomen which winded him and thus prevented him from using the gun he'd taken out of its holster.

Paul looked around and, deciding the fight was over, changed form and flew past his adversaries back in the direction of The Rocks, where there were still a few old pubs that might provide him with an easy victim. He found what he was looking for at Circular Quay near a fish and chip shop. She was a woman in her mid-forties who told him where to go in no uncertain terms and he took her there instead. The place, of course, was hell.

On the flight back to Central in his bat form, he passed by Dixon Street and almost got clipped by a speeding star knife. He would have gone back for the person who had thrown it, and dealt with them harshly, but for the sun about to rise. Being home in his room before the sun could turn him to ash he took to be more important. *The Rising Sun Group are still around*, he said to himself as he flew into his window, changed into a man and pulled the curtains closed against the day. Since he hadn't seen any sign of them in Sydney since his return, he had hoped they might have gone away. They had done no such thing.

At Surry Hills, not far from Central, someone had started up a disco called *The Blue* in remembrance of the disco that had once been at

The Rocks. Paul went along one night to see what it was like and was surprised that it was far cleaner and better organized than the original had ever been. The music being played was old disco with New Wave thrown in to spice things up. Some of the people who went along were from the disco era but there were a lot of young people as well. Instead of a glistening ball there was now music clips being shown against three of the main interior walls. Instead of one bar there were three.

One thing they did keep from the original was the food supply. It was easy for Paul to get a meal and leave his leftovers on a chair, facing the disc jockey; as if she was so keen on the music she couldn't possibly tear herself away from the person arranging it all. Sooner or later, someone would work out that she was in fact dead but Paul would be long gone when that happened.

He thought of going back for a second meal but the name of the place had too many bad memories attached to it. The fact that others obviously didn't feel the same way surprised him. Were their memories faulty? Were they all sadists and masochists? It was a strange conclusion for him to arrive at, but some of the people who had visited discos when he had first done so must have had more good experiences than he had. Not all of them had to be rotten to the core; some though few, might even have been decent people.

There was a woman approaching fifty standing on the street outside the reincarnation of *The Blue*. She seemed to be fascinated by the music as if she was remembering better days or perhaps better nights. She wasn't dressed to go in. She had on a simple cotton frock and functional shoes.

It took a moment or two for Paul to see past the wrinkles, sun spots and graying of red hair but he came to the conclusion she was Betty Sail. The last time he saw her was during his second undead appearance at the original disco, *The Blue*. He was taken aback not only by her appearance but by the fact that she was still alive. If anyone needed to "Die Young, Stay Pretty," as the Blondie song sung by Debbie Harry goes, it was this woman.

Paul had gone to the same high school as Betty. To say they had gone together would have been incorrect. Betty was stuck-up, a social butterfly. He was a moth. Paul was one of the guys she wouldn't speak to even to pass the time of day but she would talk in his presence as if that made a difference.

It was no secret that Betty's mother was on every local community project there was and had even created one or two as a further power base. Betty's father was hardly ever mentioned and there was scuttlebutt floating around that he drank which Betty denied. He was just busy with the insurance business, she'd said. He left the running of local affairs to the two major women in his life. Paul tended to think that he did drink because of these femme fatales but, since he had been instrumental in the creation of Betty, it was hard to feel completely sorry for him. It was the judgment of a teenager who had to put up with all sorts of dumb things to try to get a formal education. Paul, many years later, could now have more pity for the fellow, realizing that there are all sorts of reasons why men buy their way into personal hell and find they are trapped there for a very, very long time.

Betty was never especially pretty but she had beautiful hair she wore long in various ways. It was a wholesome red, full and not brittle like red hair tends to be. It flowed like a gentle stream of crimson rather than being choppy or eternally uneven. She put on as much jewelry as the school allowed, and a little light make-up which she wasn't supposed to do but did anyway. She gossiped in class but never enough to get thrown out or have a letter sent home to her parents. In her last two years in high school, she dated the local football star and never looked back. How she managed to see the last two years out Paul would never know. She scored very low in the higher school certificate and left knowing her future would not be an academic one since no place of higher learning would touch her without putting on antiseptic gloves and a face mask.

After high school, Paul had seen Betty a couple of times at the original disco, *The Blue,* with her Sherman tank of a boyfriend and her retinue of female admirers. He was not surprised to learn, a week or two before his transformation into his current state that she'd married the bruiser whose only hope of getting anywhere was on the football field. Considering Betty's current looks and dress, Paul could wager he hadn't made it or his success had been short lived.

When Betty left the new version of *The Blue*, Paul followed. He thought of her meanness to him and a lot of other people, including teachers who deserved better. He wondered how he could best punish her before taking her life. Torture hadn't been something he'd contemplated using except during his rebirth. For her, he was willing to stretch himself in that regard.

Paul followed her to a grubby part of Surry Hills and to a decrepit flat. He made sure she didn't see him. He used his extraordinary sense of hearing and touch to walk quieter than a mouse on slippers. There were plenty of dark spots along the way to hide in if she were to turn around. Even so, Betty bowed her head low much of the way as if she were carrying a great weight on her shoulders. *Is this old age creeping in?* He wondered. He knew by now that he'd never experience it. Even so, he thought he might find it fascinating, seeing it in others who were not so fortunate.

Betty used a worn key to enter her flat and closed the door and locked it with a series of locks. Paul smiled at the ineffectiveness of such methodology in keeping someone like him out. Locks meant nothing when you had his kind of superhuman strength. He suspected there wouldn't be enough psychic energy to prevent him from gaining entry.

For the present, Paul was content to stand on the stoop and look through the window at his intended prey. He'd already fed so he wasn't anxious for her blood. He just wanted to find out more about her current state before taking action against her. He still had a fistful of hours before dawn called him once more into necessary seclusion.

Betty put the keys and a little white purse Paul hadn't noticed her carrying on a small table in the cramped hallway before entering the kitchen. There she was greeted by two lively red-haired girls, one was around twelve and the other was in her early twenties. They were dressed in hand-me-downs that looked like they came from the Salvation Army store. They were emphatic about the fact that they were hungry and something ought to be done about it.

Being undead, Paul had a great sense of smell and was able to smell past the glass in front of him. What he picked up was the odor of cheap wine, beer and packet noodles made up with hot water, half eaten and left to dry and set like cement in various bowls in the sink. As the noise from the youngsters rose, a bulky man with a beer gut entered the room. He came from what Paul surmised must be the lounge area. He asked where she'd been and if she'd brought any beer home. She said that she hadn't and he seemed crestfallen. The girls yelled for food again and the man told them to shut up. Then Betty looked in the pantry and the fridge, sighed, and began making cheese on toast sandwiches for everyone including herself.

Twenty minutes of seeing this part of Betty's life was enough to give Paul second thoughts about avenging himself upon her. His feeling of self-righteousness in getting back at her had deflated to where it was all gone. He felt empty and a little heartsick even if his heart, for all intents and purposes, was a non-functioning lump in his chest.

Walking away, Paul decided she had been punished and was being punished for her misdeeds and her foolishness. He no longer wanted to make her life more difficult than it was and no doubt would become. By the time he got back to where he could sleep for the day, he was even prepared to do something for Betty he thought he'd never do, he was prepared to wish her good luck for the future.

The following night, Paul mesmerized a grocery clerk working at an all night grocery establishment to deliver a boxful of good food to Betty's residence. He had the clerk tell her she'd won it as a promotional prize and that her flat number had come up in the lucky draw. He would deliver boxes of food once a week for an entire month and, when the month elapsed, forget all about having done so. There would be a note explaining the deliveries as being genuine deliveries and Paul would give enough money to the clerk the night the mesmerism first took hold, to pay for what was delivered. No one would be out of pocket save the dead woman Paul had gotten the money from and no one would be the wiser. Mesmerism, being what it was, meant that Paul could not press the clerk to do more. He wondered why he had done what he did but couldn't come up with an answer beyond a sense of regaining some of his lost humanity. It was ironic that he would do it through someone like Betty.

A week later, Paul was on a train heading south. He'd booked a room at a motel in Wollongong. He was looking forward to seeing some clean, unspoiled beaches. Wollongong was a place where one or two were still in existence. He was looking forward to getting away from the pressures of inner city living, or perhaps unliving in his case. But the pressures that most concerned him had decided to tag along.

It was only a couple of hours between Central and Wollongong. In the first hour, just as the train was pulling away from Sutherland, he heard a sound only a person with extraordinary hearing might hear. *Pok!* It was a sudden release of air a distance away followed by *Thak!* A projectile had hit his head rest. It had hit a fraction of a millimeter away from his shoulder. This was close enough to his heart to serve as a warning.

A shot! Paul cried in his head. *But from where?* He looked about for clues. He spotted a small hole in the roof of the carriage from which a gun barrel, with a silencer attached, poked through. No mortal would have seen it. If he hadn't had some idea of what he should be looking for, he wouldn't have noticed it, either. Certainly he wouldn't have noticed it in time to avoid the second bullet.

He launched himself out of his seat and to the carriage doors which he forced open. The train was moving at a speed of about fifty miles an hour along a mountainous track. Jumping would mean rolling down a sharp incline sure to break any human jumper's neck, but Paul's reflexes were more acute than those of a normal human. When he did leave the train for open space and hit the ground at a roll, he was able to leave behind at least one gun totting attacker.

Paul wandered in the bush, eventually surfacing at Austinmer Station, where he managed to break into the ticket office. There he could wait out the early hours of the morning, make a phone call, and then, under cover of a heavy Railcorp all-weather coat, grab a cab to the nearest motel.

Who was shooting at me? Paul wondered. He didn't know but he suspected it was a Rising Sun Group member with ninja claws to grab hold of the train carriage roof and a modern weapon or two for good measure. Was this evidence that the Rising Sun Group had collaborated with the Secret Compass? It made sense that both agencies would work together to develop better strategies for dealing with his kind.

The following night, Paul made it into Corinth, near Coledale, where he found an old shed not far from the station he could break into and spend the day. When the darkness came again he found this south coast suburb to be a strange and bewildering place. It was made aesthetically so by the tips of its huge smokestacks, poking out of the coke works, and glowing red like the ends of Lucifer's pitchfork. There was a gloom punctuated by the sounds of naughty children with no sense of curfew and of angry people in their mid to late twenties planning to do things they would, no doubt, regret having done if they were to live so long.

Gangs roamed the area with noisy and destructive desperation. Mailboxes were damaged and garbage bins turned over on garbage collection night. Graffiti was written on shop walls and cut into the windows. Discipline didn't mean much after the sun went down on these wild streets. Anyone respectable was indoors, either watching television, sleeping or praying for the good light of morning to come.

When darkness fell, Paul left the shed and was walking along a footpath near the railway, when a push bike sped past, missing him by inches. Using his speed and vampire strength, he caught up with the bike and its rider and took what he felt was appropriate action. The miscreant, who was slight enough to be in his mid teens, had tried to scare him by coming close to striking him. Paul, in retaliation, threw bike and rider onto the centre of the road where a car almost whacked into them. The bike was more damaged than the rider. Still the rider was bruised along the left side of his body and got the kind of shock that would make him think twice when it came to menacing pedestrians.

Thinking about what he'd done, Paul didn't care that the lad he'd punished wasn't killed outright. It was a school night and the boy should have been at home, not wandering the neighborhood annoying people. Perhaps now his parents would see to it that, after dark, he would stick closer to home where he'd be safe.

Two nights later, Paul came across two more lads playing the same game of chicken with pedestrians. As one raced past him he held out his arm as a barrier to the fellow's progress. The bike stopped but the rider went flying into the side of a corner shop. Against a brick wall, the boy's head came out second best with a concussion and a large lump likely to become two very black eyes. The second rider, who had been getting ready to copy his mate, decided to make a getaway but Paul wouldn't let him. When rider and bike landed in the middle of the road, they were hit hard by a truck. The driver stopped in time to save the dumb kid's life but the idiot was likely to be in traction for six months or more with a busted up arm and leg. *By the time he gets out of hospital,* thought Paul, grinning as he walked away from the "accident," *the son-of-a bitch may have learned to read and write. Hell, he might even have learned some manners.*

Paul blamed the problems he saw with modern youth in this neighborhood on the fact that their mothers were once disco queens lording it over others and, eventually, raising their sons and daughters to do the same thing. It was a case of ignorant, arrogant and stupid people giving birth to the ignorant, the arrogant and the stupid. No doubt the fathers were just as bad. As thick as a double brick wall with insulation, no doubt they could only teach their children how to fight dirty and how best to swear at people for maximum effect.

Then there were the drugs. There was a definite drug culture in the '60s that grew like some hideous creeper in the '70s. Now it was taking over like the plants did in that Science Fiction novel *The Day of the Triffids* or like in an old episode of *Lost in Space*.

Drug deals went down during the sleeping hours of most honest men so Paul made the decision to only sup on arrogant females in their late teens and early twenties hoping this would make a difference in protecting his stomach from momentary abuse. It was a slim hope that it would. He knew there were drug addicts strung out on heroin as young as fourteen and fifteen. He'd seen them wandering around at night after a fix. Apparently drug dealers were not too worried about age or I.D. so long as the money they were handed was the real deal.

Paul saw drugs as part of the disco legacy and hated it when a supply of blood he was consuming turned out to be tainted by such filth.

In the end it didn't matter because his body could absorb and destroy the effects of any drug or poison, except something containing wood, garlic or holy water, in a day or two. Still it wasn't pleasant having a giddy digestive system for even a day because of someone else's lack of interest in their own well being. Though it wasn't a killer, he avoided the situation as best he could and cursed whenever he was caught by it.

One night, sometime after Paul had risen and left the shed, a white Laser drove by. It blared out loud, obnoxious Acid House music from four or more speakers, turned up as high as they were able to go. Paul retaliated at this unwarranted disturbance to his thoughts by picking up a nearby green bin and, with one hand, hurling it through the air, into the offending car's windscreen. The results were dramatic. The passenger in the front seat had his head almost cut in two by a large shard of glass acting as a guillotine, pressed home by the weight of the bin. At the same time, the driver lost an eye because of the shower of glass and had the nerves in his right hand so badly damaged he lost the proper use of that hand. There was a tingling sensation when he put it to the wheel indicating there were some nerves still there trying to do their job. It was no good for steering but he could use it for balance. He used his other hand to guide the car.

The distraction of the bin, the introduction of a lot of pain and being blinded in one eye caused the man to drive erratically. He swerved across the road and into a telegraph pole. Unlike in the movies, the car didn't burst into flame. In the back seat two women in their late teens groaned from whiplash and bruising to their chests and thighs. Paul, after noticing them in the back, ripped open a back door and helped himself to their youth. They proved to be drug free and delicious.

"You are arrogant and stupid," Paul told the driver before departing. "Do you really think the world wants to listen to your music?"

"Help me! Please!" the driver cried in a beseeching tone.

"You're lucky I let you live," answered Paul as he closed the car door and walked away. He knew the driver hadn't yet realized the young women in his care were dead or that their deaths were not on account of the crash. He was in too much agony to think of much more than the dead guy next to him and his own considerable suffering. Paul wondered if the driver would even care when he found out. Were the young women important to him? There came the sound of an ambulance. Soon, at least, one life would be saved. It was a life that would, from now on, be marked by horror.

Paul decided to leave the shed and make his way to Wollongong proper. He took off and flew to Scarborough, a town that reminded him of the novel, *Wuthering Heights*. It was close to the sea. Great gusts of wind would come up and then diminish, just to come up again. The waves crashed against the rocks; a dog barked in the distance. There was the fresh smell of salt in the air. He found it a perfect place to practice his flying, not that he needed it. It was not a good place to eat because there was not a single person to be seen even from on high so he moved on.

At Otford station, Paul came to rest for a few minutes on one of the seats. He was almost rocked off it as a coal train rumbled by. The sheer volume of high pitched noise it created offended his sensitive ears and he thought that, if it had been longer, his ears might well have bled. He got out of there in a hurry just in case another one was due.

Eventually he made it to Corrimal where he booked into the pub up the road. After a day's rest, Paul ventured out. He found that the coke works near the station remained a hive of activity, going into the dark hours, best left alone for someone trying to keep a low profile. The nearby park was well kept and the same could be said for the local gardens, giving the place a mellow atmosphere. Unfortunately for Paul, the local leagues club proved to be far too friendly to offer the kind of food he craved. The local school had some farm animals he could siphon foul tasting blood from but that was about it. Still, blood was blood when you're starving and on the run. Since he didn't take enough from any one beast to do it any lasting harm, he thought his actions were not likely to be detected.

One night later, Paul got to Wollongong. It was much like he had remembered it from the days of his childhood only a little sadder, a little less shiny. Still it held more promise for him than Scarborough, Otford and Corrimal combined.

Wollongong was a big country town which had become a city during the days of high steel production at nearby Port Kembla. Those days were now over and, though there was steel being made in the area, it wasn't enough to justify Wollongong's existence outside of being a big country town. Slowly the city was turning back into what it had once been. Paul had known it as a place of surf and sun. This was all very well in summer but the tourist trade was not enough to provide work for all the locals during autumn and winter. Wollongong University was established to provide employment opportunities but it wasn't sufficient to stop the economic rot. Paul wondered what would do so and if it would ever be found.

The streets were wide. There was a plaza complex in the middle, with all sorts of shops, mostly catering to young people and to potential visitors from Sydney and elsewhere. There were lots of job agencies giving the place a sense, work-wise, of quiet desperation. It was a great locale in which to live but not a place where many people could work. Unemployment in the region was too high, leading to drug use among teenagers or at least contributing to it. Teenagers had a sense of living for the moment and not some future that was not likely to be an improvement on the present.

Paul made his presence known at the motel he'd booked and then he went out to dine. He went to one of the local pubs where he knew he was sure to meet some woman lacking in good manners but full of reasonably good blood. It took him less than twenty minutes to find her. It took even less time to spirit her away to the back of a closed dress shop where he could sink his teeth into her overly-freckled skin. *I'm doing her a favor,* he told himself as he drew away her life energy and made it his own. *Of course she'll never know it and that's just as well too.*

He was ready to dump the body behind some piles of rotting newspaper when he heard a whizzing sound. A bolt fired from a crossbow missed his left ear by a fraction of an inch and a fraction of a second. Instantly, he was on the alert, eyes focused on the direction from which the missile had come. Four men in black came out of the darkness, made more so by two broken street lights they had probably broken that day. They had shot guns no doubt containing ammunition dipped in holy water. Paul took up bundles of newspaper then swiftly hurled them at his adversaries. A second bolt was fired and it hit him in the left leg. He cried out with the pain but was able to hold himself together long enough to avoid a third bolt and then a fourth. He threw the last two newspaper bundles in the direction of his tormentor, striking her hard, causing her to fall off the roof she had been perched on with her ancient weapon.

With great effort, Paul pulled the bolt out of his bone and then examined the fallen woman in black. She was of medium height and Asian. Her neck was broken but she was not yet dead. The men he'd knocked about were coming to. He thought of rushing the lot while they were so vulnerable and ending their lives, but decided not to. If the woman could be saved, he would leave her comrades the task. If she could not be helped, that was too bad but he still had a savagely aching leg as the result of her actions so he couldn't sympathize with her plight.

With a practiced flourish, Paul went from human to bat and flew away. He did not go directly back to his motel but took a circuitous route to avoid being followed. One thing he didn't want was to be destroyed in his own motel room during the day. *So much for the south coast*, thought Paul as he settled down to sleep away the hours when most humans make their living or, at least, wish to do so.

The following night, Paul visited a pub in which two young women were having an argument. He didn't think much of their talk until one of them broke her wine glass and used the sharp glass to cut the face of the other one. This sort of thing he'd never seen before and he was taken aback by it. He took the young woman who had done the damage – a tall brunette – out of the place and, in a secluded corner of the plaza, proceeded to drain her blood. He thought, perhaps, he should do something nasty to her before killing her but couldn't think of anything he felt was appropriate.

The girl with the cut face – a tall redhead – had been taken by car to where she could be patched up. Paul went back to the pub and, through the use of mesmerism, was able to find out the location of the hospital. He then headed back to his motel. When the sun went down again, he set off to the hospital where she was and had the desk clerk, under mesmerism, tell him her room number. Then he had her walk out of the place. Nurses and doctors tried to object but he used his hypnotism on them as well, playing with their minds, convincing them that the authorization papers for her release, which were uppermost in their thoughts, had been signed and that her condition no longer warranted further stay at their facility.

Once he got her back to his motel room, he made her over into a member of the undead community. He thought it was the best he could do for her. He knew that, once she got over her first death, her face would be restored. She would no longer have the life she had but, at least, she would have her beauty. He wondered if what he gave her compensated for what he had taken. Was not having a scarred up appearance that important to her, or did she prefer true life even if it came with hideous disfigurement?

Paul spent another three nights in Wollongong so that, when she came into her second existence, someone would be there to explain to her what had happened and then to give her advice on how to handle being undead. When he did leave Wollongong, he left for Nowra, a town famous for its blow-hole, its fine surf and a nearby aircraft museum. After being delayed by his own sense of duty at Wollongong, he had expected further attacks there by the Rising Sun Group, attacks which did not eventuate. He expected to be attacked, at any moment, on the train. He looked about the carriage he was travelling in to get him to Nowra for clues as to when that would happen. When it didn't eventuate, it left him feeling despondent. Just what was the Rising Sun Group up to?

At a motel room at Nowra, he examined his injured leg. It was healing nicely and would be all better in another day or two. The wood, both going in and coming out, hadn't splintered as he feared it might. There was no sign of infection, and the bolt hadn't been treated with holy water which might also have resulted in inflammation. He felt lucky but, as he had countless times before, he wondered just how long such luck could last.

"If they're going to get me," he whispered to his pillow. "Let it be soon. They'd better be prepared, though, because I'm not going to make it easy for them."

Chapter 2

On a Train Heading South from Sydney, March, 2009

Todd had made plans with his great-uncle's money to fly off to England on his vacation from the Secret Compass in order to bring to ground the menace that had plagued his family for decades. He had cancelled those plans and had taken the train he was on when word reached him that his family's nemesis had been seen in Sydney and then in Wollongong.

"We'll get him now," he told the three Secret Compass operatives travelling with him.

One, Pauline Sharp, was the grand niece of his great-uncle's old friend, Frank Long. She was half a year his junior. She was a compact redhead with a pretty face and a black belt in judo and karate. The other two, Michael Dunning and Fred Bateman, were experienced agents from Melbourne with no vested interest in the enterprise they were on except in seeing a member of the undead community bite the proverbial dust. They had come along to keep Todd and Pauline from doing something stupid and getting themselves and others killed. Todd resented the implication that he might, at any moment, turn into a loose cannon but otherwise welcomed the company. He knew he could use their expertise and their cool headedness. They talked in a kind of monotone he found amusing. They had five vampire kills each to their credit and, in the Secret Compass, that wasn't insignificant. They had managed to get their undead without risking members of the general public and without getting too banged up themselves in the process.

When the train got to Hurstville, an operative got on to hand them the latest report. Apparently, their perpetrator had moved further south from Wollongong but couldn't be too far ahead. The Rising Sun Group had claims on wounding him in Wollongong and had plans to head further south to finish what they'd started.

"A popular fellow," said Todd.

"They get popular like that with age," added Bateman. "Just be sure you're ready for him."

"I'll be ready," said Todd.

"We'll all be ready," corrected Pauline and they nodded in agreement.

It has to be a team effort, thought Todd. *Miles always had Long. When they were in America, Miles and Long also had the FBI. The Rising Sun Group operate under similar circumstance and, love 'em or hate 'em, they do pretty well against the undead.*

Todd got out his stake and his pocket knife. He began putting more of an edge on his wood. Pauline got out her revolver and gave a thorough cleaning. This, however, made some of the non-Secret Compass passengers nervous. Dunning told her to put it away in case a ticket inspector tried to take it from her or someone with a mobile phone got in touch with the police. With a hint of annoyance in her eyes, she put it back in her bag.

At Wollongong, an operative came on the train with a report that their perpetrator had been seen at Nowra where he'd run into three Rising Sun Group agents. Outside a fish and chip shop, he snapped the necks of two of the men in black who had confronted him with wooden butterfly swords. He had choked the third one to death with but the use of one hand.

"Nasty," said Pauline.

"More so than what had happened to the Rising Sun Group people in Wollongong," muttered Todd. "It seems our perpetrator's mood has gotten darker since Wollongong. They say injuring a beast can make it more dangerous. The same must be true for the undead."

"No messing about with him then," said Bateman. "We strike and we strike hard."

"Hard and fast," put in Todd, his mouth dry.

He wondered if his great-uncle had had any feelings at all before going into a fight. The idea of taking on someone who could hear and see better than he could was daunting enough. Vampires also had super-human strength and could change their shape at will. Lots of new weaponry helped but there was always the human factor. A gun wasn't much good if someone couldn't pull the trigger in time or if it wasn't aimed in the right direction. A crucifix that had a neon light so it shone powerful in the dark was fine so long as the person wielding it did have faith.

Todd was nervous and he was afraid he'd give away this apprehension. He looked to Dunning and Bateman who were now playing cards together. It was said that Samurai used to make animals and things out of paper – they called it origami – before a battle as a way of coping with the tension of the wait that preceded going into action. Maybe cards did it for Dunning and Bateman. If that was the case, it made sense. Working on his stake was helping him some. Pauline was now trying to read a silly romance novel she pulled out of her bag. It had to do with vampires and it was by some American author by the name of Corrine Kelly.

As the train rumbled toward Helensburgh, there was a slight impact followed by the squeal of breaks. Over the speaker system came the announcement the train had hit a car. Apparently it had been a blue Suzuki which wasn't built strong enough to save its driver's life. Two ambulances, three police cars and a fire-truck crowded around the stationary train. Before long there were men in various uniforms everywhere. Some were calming train passengers, others were picking up bits of metal while still others had the more grizzly task of finding the various body parts of the dead man. Flashlights came out and the wheels of the train were searched. Some two hundred yards away from the train, the bulk of what remained of the car resided, looking like a used tissue only made out of metal.

"Do you think our undead friend could be responsible for this?" asked Todd of Denning and Bateman.

"No," answered Denning. "But be on guard just in case."

"Vampires are not necessary for this sort of thing to happen," agreed Bateman. "But we must be careful."

"Just some idiot on the train tracks," ventured Pauline.

"Just someone committing suicide," said Todd.

"Just someone committing suicide in such a way he'll get noticed," ventured Pauline.

"But what a thing to be noticed over," said Denning. "Damn inconvenient if you ask me."

Todd spied a drunken teen arguing with a cop. The cop was holding his temper in check. He was big enough to punch to the floor the troublemaker but he wasn't about to do so unless he didn't have an alternative. As cops went, Todd could think of him as one of the good guys. Still, was this incident what it appeared to be or a diversion before a major vampire attack? As it turned out, it was as it appeared to be. Some dumb, inebriated kid was spouting off because he'd be late to his next port of call at getting further drunk and he might sober up too much in the meantime. It was some police officer acting like an immovable mountain whose patience won out, resulting in the kid calming down and taking a seat.

"Nothing sinister about some drunken fool spoiling for a fight and not getting it," said Denning. None of them wanted to stake some teen for vampirism but they would if they had to.

An hour later, the passengers, including the members of the Secret Compass, were taken from the train and loaded on a bus heading south. No one, except Todd, looked in the direction of the impact site as he boarded. He thought he saw a lone eyeball on one of the tracks. It put him in mind of the old singing group, The Beatles and their one time song reference to custard and a dead dog. Was it really an eyeball or something else? He found he didn't want to know for sure and that meant he didn't want to pursue the matter any further. If it was an eyeball, the cops or the ambulance people would find it and that was fine with him. Blood and dismemberment didn't give him the jitters but something about eyeballs where they didn't belong did.

Yes, thought Todd as he headed further south via bus with his team, people don't need undead to bring themselves undone. They don't need the undead at all. Just a car across some railroad tracks will do the trick.

Todd and his group spent much of the next day at a hotel in Nowra either sleeping or going over what they knew about their adversary. On the midday news, the announcer told the story of a man in his twenties who, after graduating from high school bottom of his class, had drifted from one dead-end job to another until there were no more dead-end jobs he could take. He had then left his parents a note on his home computer and ended it all on the train tracks in his secondhand car.

"Nothing supernatural about that," said Pauline, "and in a way I'm glad."

"Why?" asked Todd.

"It's good to be reminded that not all bad things come from the unliving," said Pauline.

"Yes," agreed Bateman. "But enough bad things do come from there to keep us busy."

"Too busy at times," agreed Denning.

Chapter 3

North Wollongong, NSW, March, 2009

For two weeks, Paul had been siring intellectual females from the student body of Wollongong University, as well as the lecturers and P.H.D holders, in preparation for what was to come. Some deserted his enterprise after being dead three nights and then having an hour's worth of explanation. It was to his satisfaction that most stayed. It was funny but back when he was in America he had a similar opportunity. It had been an earlier chance at turning and then leading a group of people smarter than he was. For some reason he couldn't recall he had declined from doing so. Now he wondered why.

He had found a janitor's room he could block off from the rest of the world during the day and, after dark, use as a staging ground for raids on the university and the nearby suburb of North Wollongong. There appeared to be more than enough food in the first week to go around. The university had various facilities used by various sporting types. Then there were the pubs and clubs. By the time there were a dozen undead in his service, raids had to be made on medical centers and the local hospital. Two vampires even went as far afield as Sutherland hospital for supplies necessary to sustain unlife.

Paul was contemplating an incursion upon a pub in Bellambi when word came about three Rising Sun Group agents taking out one of his Wollongong vampires near Woonona. It had happened while the undead woman was getting her bearings, flying in bat form over some bushland. Spinning out from behind a tree, a star knife had come, knocking her to earth. Then, the vampire who had witnessed it all saw three figures in black with short spears approach the fallen undead. The points of the spears were sharp hazel and the stabbing was over before the distressed vampire had any chance to get back on her feet, let alone retake human form. She did, however, become human again after her second death.

An hour later, Paul got word of the arrival of a contingent of Secret Compass operatives at North Wollongong station. They were marked as Secret Compass by the way they dispatched two young vampires upon leaving the train. Some of Paul's gathering forces had taken to pillaging trains as soon as they pulled into a station. In this instance, such actions had proven to be disastrous. They were taken out via three bullets from one of the special vampire slayer guns. A third vampire was wounded in the left wing by the third shot and just managed to get back to tell the tale.

"They're gathering," he told the undead around him, "but we're more than a match for them."

Unbeknown to Paul, there were a dozen Rising Sun Group operatives coming up from Melbourne and they were all equipped with rifles and revolvers that carried the deadly-to-vampires hollow-points. There was also another eight Secret Compass agents due down from Canberra and likely to arrive any day. They had brand new weapons on them. Helen Kiln, head of the Sydney based Secret Compass PSI division, had warned the head of the field agents that there would be more than one vampire to contend with in the Wollongong area and that their base was likely to be in the heart of some local place of higher learning. Then, when other sensitives from other branches got the same impression, it was decided that it would be prudent to send more agents.

When it came to his own situation, Paul was elated. At last he had his own corps, his own power base of the unliving. Yet, despite the numbers he had, there was the feeling that he was heading for a fight he wasn't destined to win. He reminded himself of General McClellan during the American Civil War who once retreated from an enemy he had convinced himself had vastly more men when, in reality, they had a quarter or less of the men he had. He reminded himself of General George Armstrong Custer who once rode into what he thought was the tail end of an Indian camp only to discover it was the centre of a great Indian uprising. Where McClellan could have won the American Civil War if he'd only had the gumption, Custer lost his life, and those of his troopers, at Little Big Horn, because he had too much gumption. Paul wondered which was worse and, after wondering a while, decided to go with Custer. At least no one would ever say that man didn't have the guts to lead. They might say he didn't have what it took to lead well but that was a different matter.

Paul didn't see himself as being as flashy or as big-headed as Custer, who liked to have his picture taken, but he was through being cautious. In fact, he may well have been too cautious when he was fully human. Certainly he had spent a lot of money on drinks at *The Blue* and was getting nowhere when Lilith came along and changed everything. Now she was gone and, though he'd never look it because of his vampiric condition, he was getting old, at least in spirit, and the notion of one last stand was looking mighty good.

He didn't have a saber to wave about and he wished he had one. He doubted he would be able to find such an article anywhere on the south coast of New South Wales. A century or so ago it would have been easy enough to come across such an item but not now. He didn't know where the museums were and, even if he did, he thought it absolute foolishness to go on such a hunt for what might turn out to be a useless antique from a bygone age. He might have to content himself with taking a butterfly or samurai sword off a dead Rising Sun Group member and waving that.

One night later, Paul caught up with a brilliant young computer student who was working late in the main building's computer lab. He mesmerized the fellow into hacking into the university library computer and had the library computer order in a hundred copies of Corrine Kelly's famous work on vampires, *A Journey to Dust*, already in its third reprint, and also a hundred copies of Mandy Provost's book, *Darkness Please Show me the Way*, also in its third reprint. Then he had the computer student put a glitch into the system so that, if anyone made the attempt to cancel either order, the result would be a doubling of each order and then a crash. By the time the crash was resolved, the orders or perhaps the double orders, would have been sent. Just to be sure, Paul put it into the computer student's head to, a month later, also order in another hundred copies of each for the university. This way, Paul felt he was doing something for at least two of the vampires he'd sired in America way back before the '80s kicked in. He hoped that, if by some miracle, they were still around and getting royalties, they'd appreciate the gesture even if they might never figure out where it came from.

Two nights passed without much happening. Then, on the football green of the university, there was a clash between six men and women of the Rising Sun Group and five of Paul's undead. Somehow the Rising Sun Group had found his lair and had followed the five as they left on their nightly quest for blood. It was while the vampires were crossing the green that the Rising Sun Group members struck. A bolt from a crossbow slammed into a vampire, killing her outright. The archer then was dispatched by another vampire who used her teeth and claws to rip apart her adversary. In the ensuing melee it became difficult to establish who started what action. It was enough that the undead were trying to keep hold of their unlife and the Rising Sun Group people were trying to take it away.

Metallic butterfly swords with wooden tips sparked against claws with the inexperienced, though somewhat stronger vampires coming out of it second best with either fingers or hands missing. Close quarter fighting meant that archers shouldered their bows as best they could and drew out their wooden knives. There was an axe man making short work of a vampire's head. A spear wielder, after he stabbed a vampire through the heart, got his neck snapped by the creature before her second death.

Paul watched from a short distance. In a matter of minutes, once the battle had begun, there were only three Rising Sun Group operatives standing and one vampire who had one missing finger. It was then he sent in his second wave of seven undead to eliminate the remaining Rising Sun Group people, to gorge themselves on all the blood that had been spilled and to bring back the weapons littering the green. *Next time we fight back with bows and bolts and swords and whatever else we can find*, he thought. *Let's just see how they feel about being stuck with bolts and chopped into pieces with sharpened wood and steel.*

One of the remaining Rising Sun Group operatives managed to get away. He was the axe wielder and he cut down a second vampire in making his escape. Once he was out of sight the undead, to Paul's annoyance, were so taken with the lush smell of the red life essence about them that they forgot about him. He had killed two of their comrades and the feast still took precedence. Why chase after food, especially dangerous food, when there was already plenty to go around? *What has happened to my fine intellectuals and their power of reason?* Paul wondered. The answer, of course, was that he had happened to them.

The bloodlust was stronger among new undead than those that had been around for a while. It was easy for Paul to forget what it had been like when he first broke another's skin with his teeth and tasted the nectar of the pulsating vein. The act still had a sensuality, even a sexuality for him but he was more in control. His vampires, being so fresh, didn't have the same knack of seeing beyond the red and, he could predict, they never would. He had to cajole them into bringing the weapons back to their nest. Some resented him doing so while others could see his reasoning and grudgingly obeyed.

Once they came back, Paul quickly sent out two vampires to make more of the undead but knew the exercise had come too late. It would take three nights for the sleeping dead to become the undead. As far as he knew, the process could not be rushed. He suspected, and quite rightly, that he didn't have three nights before the next attack.

Nine o'clock in the morning the following day, Paul and his undead were awoken. There were three police officers who had been called in because of the recent commotion on campus and because someone had been playing games with a janitor's room. There was a key but there was a barrier of some sort behind the door, preventing entry. The police had been given permission to use a battering ram which they proceeded to do. Upon the door being bashed in and the propped up wooden beams being knocked aside, there was an almighty scream as one of the vampires was burnt on the hand by the invading daylight. All, however, were able to find dark places to scurry into and wait for the men in uniform to fully appear.

The police officers thought they were investigating a university student prank. At worst, they were expecting to find a university professor tied up for some reason and covered in pig's blood from some nearby farm. Perhaps they might find fake human body parts from some science lab. No one expected real body parts, bloody swords, crossbows with lethal looking bolts and other items that belonged in some 17th Century Asian conflict. They were also ill-prepared to be pounced upon by strangely attractive but inhumanly strong females who didn't see the necessity to explain their actions to anyone. The police, taken by surprise, were dealt with and bled dry, their guns adding to the tally of available weaponry. Paul took one gun for himself. The bullets would only be regular ones but they would be effective on the next lot of encroaching humans.

Amongst the junk in the janitor's room there happened to be a large tarpaulin that could cover Paul plus his remaining undead. So, after he had his vampires load themselves up with weapons, Paul had them put the tarpaulin over their heads. With the tarpaulin as their protection, they scurried out into the day. They were headed for the underground maintenance area of the main building. There they would hopefully be safe till darkness came. It was only two hundred yards away but it was a crucial two hundred yards. Would they be seen? How could they not be? Would the sight of them under their protective wrap be registered as more sports freak misbehavior that tended to go on or something more sinister? Would there be Rising Sun Group or Secret Compass spies watching and then relating what they'd seen? Would a bunch of jocks none of the vampires as yet had made meals out of come along and pull away their cover, exposing them to the sun's awful effects? One thing was certain and that was they couldn't remain where they were anymore even for the rest of the day. Dead police officers tended to attract live police and dead police officers, together with human body parts were, at best, hard to explain away to anyone.

Somehow they made the two hundred yards to the entrance door to building maintenance on the main building without coming across anyone and without attracting, as far as they could know, anyone's attention. For Paul it was a minor triumph.

When the moon rose again it was full and bursting with arcane energy. Paul felt like basking in it. Before he did, he loaded himself up with star knives taken from one of the Rising Sun Group dead. They were star knives that hadn't been used. Apparently, this particular Rising Sun Group warrior had not been able to get to them in time before she died. This was fine with Paul. He would put them to use. There were ten and they were very sharp. He patted the gun he had on a policeman's holster under his coat. He would put that to good use too. Gone was any notion of picking up a butterfly sword so he could have something to wave about. Maybe he wasn't that much like Custer after all.

There were twelve Secret Compass agents and fourteen of the Rising Sun Group waiting for Paul and his vampires on the university green. *This is it*, thought Paul. He only had seven vampires and they had no real idea of what either the Rising Sun Group or the Secret Compass could do. *This is going to be a massacre*, he thought as he sent his people out to deal with the enemy. He knew they had enjoyed themselves the night before and had the up-and-coming blood feast on their minds and not the battle. They were not likely to win.

Paul noticed that the Rising Sun Group men and women had rifles and hand guns this go round just like the Secret Compass operatives. He also noticed that the Rising Sun and the Secret Compass forces allowed his vampires to get within fifty feet of them before taking action. In the meantime, a vampire with a crossbow had managed to take down two members of the Rising Sun Group while advancing. Two vampires with guns had shot and killed two members of the Secret Compass.

At fifty feet, two grenades containing slivers of wood and bits of metal were thrown. The first one to explode took out only one of the undead. The second one took out two more. The debris from the explosions sent the rest into coughing spasms. They turned and ran for their "unlives." After that happened, the riot shields that had given some protection from gun shots and bolts were thrown down and the combination of Rising Sun and Secret Compass people advanced for the final cleanup.

Two retreating vampires with nothing but swords in their hands were shot down. Even the last two, who transformed into bats and took to the air, could not save themselves. Rifle fire brought them to earth. Once they too were down, the vampire slayers turned to staking the lot to be sure.

Paul thought to be in this fight but decided not to at the last minute. While his enemies cleaned up on his recent confederates, he made a dash for the main lobby entrance of the university. He didn't know what he would find there but he sensed there was something or someone he had to see or know before the end. For some reason, he hadn't reached into the holster and pulled out his gun while he was on the move.

"Paul Priestly," called out a male voice as he approached the deserted information counter.

Paul turned around. He found himself confronted by a stocky man in his thirties with a gun in one hand and a stake in the other. He was dressed in a gray suit like he belonged to the Secret Compass. Paul cursed himself for a fool. He was now caught out. If he did reach for his gun, he would be shot, possibly to a second death, before he could come close to getting his hand on it. Superhuman speed, he knew, could only compensate so much for plain, unadulterated stupidly.

"You know me?" asked Paul. No one he hadn't introduced himself to had used his name in ages. He knew it would make a good talking point.

"So my great-uncle was right," the fellow beamed. "You are Paul Priestly."

"Who's your great-uncle?"

"Miles Henry. He was part of the old school of Secret Compass men. He hunted you for years. Oh, he also went after others of your ilk but he wanted to be the one to catch you. A pity he never lived to see this night."

"Why?"

"Why was he after you? He was keen on getting you because of Lizzy."

"Lizzy?'

"Yes, Lizzy. *The Blue* disco, 1976, you do remember, don't you?"

"Ah, Lizzy! If she'd been worthy I might have made her over but she was not."

"She was my aunt. I know of her from a few personal memories, some old photographs and family stories."

"Just as well. If you'd have really known her, you would have felt differently about her."

"And you knew her?"

"Briefly. In one instant, I tasted her soul and found it to be less wholesome than her blood. And you are...?"

"I'm Todd Lawrence and now I will kill you!"

"For your family?"

"For my family, for the Secret Compass and for humanity."

Paul smiled the smile of the cornered fox. He'd taken a star knife from one of his pockets and, while the young man was getting all self-righteous in his talk, he'd positioned it in his hand for throwing. He was about to throw it with some force when a woman's voice cried out: "Watch it, Todd! He's armed!"

It was at this prompting Todd glimpsed the star knife in Paul's grip and fired. He fired until the chamber was empty then he used his stake on what was left of Paul's heart.

"It's over!" cried Todd, standing up and moving away from the dying undead. "Thank God you were here, Pauline."

"I don't know why I followed you. Maybe I thought you were up to something important, leaving the green the way you did."

"Don't ask me how but I sensed his presence. I knew he was here and I knew what I had to do."

"Maybe you're a sensitive. Maybe you should talk to Helen and go work for our PSI division."

"Maybe you're right. I don't think so. Probably this was just a one off thing to do with my family."

Pauline put her arms around him and gave him a hug. She then led him by the hand out of the building to the other men and women who had seen combat that night and would live to tell about it.

Todd knew that his mother Anne would be pleased with what he'd done. His great-uncle Miles, if he had lived, would also have been happy for his success and, at the same time, wishing it was his own.

He didn't know why, but Todd felt empty and, at the same time, tired. He was hungry and thirsty. He wanted to tackle a pizza with lots of mushrooms, anchovies, pepperoni and cheese and consume a schooner or two of Guinness. Before the battle, he thought he might want to swap war stories with his mates in the Secret Compass and his newer comrades in the Rising Sun Group once it was over. He was surprised he felt like doing no such thing. He just wanted the pizza, the brew and, strangely enough, to be with Pauline. He knew he liked to hold hands with her and therein lay certain possibilities for the future that almost put a smile on his rugged face. He remembered his Saint Christopher which he kept around his neck and showed it to Pauline.

"Miles gave it to me years ago when I was a kid," said Todd. "I was told it would keep me safe and see me home."

Pauline looked at it, surprise registering on her pretty face. She then showed him her identical Saint Christopher.

"Miles gave it to me and he told my parents it was in memory of my great-uncle and his good friend, Frank Long," said Pauline. "I thought it was unique. I didn't know there were two of them. They have such beautiful workmanship. It's as if they were meant to be together."

"My thoughts exactly," said Todd. "I thought mine was unique, and no one has ever told me different. Miles must have bought them on the same day in New York and no doubt from the same dealer. I wonder what he had in mind when he did."

"Perhaps we'll never know."

Most of the unliving lying about the field would deteriorate by a week or two. The bodies would have to be taken away and disposed of in the furnace the Secret Compass had for such a purpose in a mortuary establishment not far from Rookwood. Paul would present less of a challenge. He'd been undead long enough to break down and become ash. What there was of him could be tossed to the waves at a nearby beach. The beach chosen was the main strip of sand and surf at Wollongong.

Paul's thoughts came in snippets as his body collapsed in on itself. He remembered Lizzy sharper and clearer than he had in decades. He also saw Lotus, a young Chinese waitress he'd killed which had made the Rising Sun Group take an interest in him. Then there was Lilith who was his mentor and who had gone out in a blaze. There were hundreds and hundreds of others. Would he meet up with them?

What could he say to Lizzy if he now came across her as a non-corporeal being? He couldn't say he was sorry because that wasn't true. He might now feel sorry for himself but that was as far as it could go. He was sorry for what he'd done to the Chinese waitress but too few others. He'd stuck to his code as best he could and that was the best he felt he could have done.

The bullets had hurt a lot going in like so many wasp stings but there was no pain when it came to the stake just as there was no pain as

Paul drifted away from his remains. Where he would go now, he didn't know. Maybe he would follow his ashes out to sea or journey to Central Station or to Town Hall to visit the blue spirits there and perhaps become one of them. There were earthbound spirits he could join in England at the Tower of London or where the old broken London Bridge shadowed the new, unbroken bridge. He might journey to Agincourt, in France which is the site of the great medieval victory of the English over the French or travel to the great library at Alexandria and spend a pleasant eternity cataloguing for some higher power.

There had to be places in the USA where the earthbound congregated and had even made a home for themselves. He might end up swapping yarns with Davy Crockett who died at the Alamo or playing checkers with Stonewall Jackson who made a name for himself at what he would call the battle of Manassas or challenging to a game or two of poker, George Armstrong Custer who overreached himself at Little Big Horn. There was even Alcatraz to consider. Now that would be a gloomy place to end up and the spirit company there would have to be questionable.

Will I pay for my crimes? he wondered as he drifted away from Wollongong University. *Have Lizzy and the rest already paid?* Was he an instrument in bringing them to justice or a fiend that had to be stopped by so many bullets and then have a stake driven deep to be sure? He thought maybe he'd been both and much more.

As he left the clouds behind for open space, he wondered at the majesty of creation and the old hippy words, "Make love, not war" came to him. They gave him hope. Where he was going, maybe he could exist by those words at last. Maybe, where he was going, he could find all the manifestations there are of love and there would be no Lizzy types or Rising Sun Group members or FBI or Secret Compass folk about to louse things up for him.

As he left the earth, Paul felt the oneness of the universe as an embrace warm and comforting. Maybe he hadn't been so bad after all or he had been forgiven. Then again, when his starry sojourn was over, maybe he was due back on his native planet to start over again and maybe do things right. "God is love," he remembered an Anglican minister once saying to a young and disbelieving Paul Priestly. If this was true then everything and everyone everywhere had to work out all right in the end whenever and wherever that might be. It was hope, at any rate, and hope was what he found he needed most of all.

Epilogue

At Katoomba in the Blue Mountains of New South Wales on the 16th of May, 2010, Todd faced the moment of truth as calmly as he had been trained to do. If he messed it up, chances were his moment would never come again. If he succeeded he was sure to be lucky for the rest of his life. He looked at Pauline and found that she too was nervous. She too was facing her own moment of truth. Then the words came upon them and, when the words had gone, they became man and wife. It was expected but still a revelation.

A short distance away stood Abdul Akram, a fellow Secret Compass operative, Todd's best friend and the best man. A month later, Todd would return the favor and be best man at Abdul's wedding. Even now he couldn't believe he'd started out hating the fellow over what others had done. Being there when he killed his first vampire was one thing but earlier on Abdul had taken an enormous step toward true friendship by turning a few Muslim kids around and arguing for the clerics who wanted to have friendships blossom between Muslim and non-Muslim communities. He also argued against those who did not.

Some of what he did made the news and so impressed Todd. Abdul the peace-monger was something to behold. To an extent, Abdul managed to make the beaches at Cronulla safer and more enjoyable for everyone. This enabled Todd to calm feelings among his own non-Muslim friends toward Muslim visitors at the beaches, ensuring that Muslims got a fair go. All up, they made a good team. It didn't matter who you were or what your religion was; you could get as much surf and sun as you wanted without running into trouble. This was important to Todd though not as much as being wed to Pauline or having people he could count on, such as Abdul, in the Secret Compass.

Todd and Pauline took out their Saint Christopher medallions, allowing them to clink together. It was something they wanted to do in memory of Miles and Long. Then they kissed each other. Among the tearful was Helen Kiln who understood the gesture of the medallions before the kiss and appreciated it more than she could say. It was rare for two field agents to get married to each other. They were lucky no one had thought to make it against Secret Compass policy. They had talked it over and both would continue as field agents.

Among the wedding guests was Mr. Lee looking dapper in a pinstriped Italian suit and three of his best Rising Sun Group operatives, also dressed well. Todd's parents, Sam and Anne Lawrence, and his grandparents, Patricia and Tom Sully were in light gray. On the other side there were Pauline's parents, Fred and Tina Sharp, also in light gray.

Frank Mullion had been invited but had to decline because of a vampire threat at Hurstville he had to check out. A Rising Sun Group operative would have the fiend slain by the time he got there but he wasn't to know this beforehand. He promised himself to have words with Mr. Lee to make sure this never happened again. We must co-ordinate our efforts, he would tell the man.

Three of the Greek mystics, including Aspasia, had turned up in flowing, cloudy blue along with several field agents, including Dunning and Bateman, in black.

The after wedding celebration was at a large house on the edge of town which had windows facing The Three Sisters, three magnificent rock formations. The place smelled of native flowers in bloom. Food tables groaned with the weight placed upon them. Drinks, especially Guinness and Black Douglas, were plentiful.

The wedding gifts included a superb vase from Mr. Lee, a handy microwave from Frank Mullion and a DVD player from Helen Kiln.

Todd and Pauline honeymooned for three weeks in New Zealand where they went horseback riding, hiking and sightseeing. What happened behind closed doors during this time can remain there.

Two months later, Helen retired from the Secret Compass and four months after that she had a massive heart attack and went to join Miles. It was at this stage in time that the Greek mystics decided to leave their fallen sister, Claire Euboea, alone for good. They figured that by now she had suffered enough for her arrogance and betrayal. A further torment would be the fact that they would never tell her they had decided to leave her alone.

Aspasia came to be the new head of the PSI division of the Secret Compass. It meant limiting her connection to the sisterhood in order to deal fairly with the male psychics but it was something she was prepared to do for the greater good. She would do it to honor Helen's time with the division. She had liked having Helen in charge and would miss her even more than when she had left her work place.

Vampires continued to come into existence and, in Sydney, were now dealt with, thanks in part to Mullion's insistence, by the coordinated efforts of Secret Compass and Rising Sun Group operatives. Mullion and Mr. Lee could not have been more pleased with the way things were working out between their organizations.

In places such as Pakistan and Afghanistan, vampires sired by Paul Priestly continue to hunt, claiming victims and causing havoc. The writings of American novelists Corrine Kelly and Mandy Provost continue to do well in bookstores and on the internet.

In some cities, including Sydney, the sickness that was part of the disco scene continues to infect the young with its vileness but in more sophisticated venues known as "Raves" and "Clubs." "Make love, not war" is a dream long past.

Somewhere this night, in Sydney or Melbourne, London or New York, an undead creature like Paul Priestly had been awaits resurrection and a chance for revenge on those who have wronged him.

About the Contributors

Rod Marsden:

Rod Marsden was born in Sydney but did most of his growing up while on holidays in the northern NSW fishing village of Iluka where his mom, May, and dad, Chic (short for Charles), taught him how to fish. It was on these fishing trips he discovered through his mom, he actually did like to read and wanted, one day, to be a writer.

Way back in the '70s, Rod visited the USA but never got to meet his heroes Ray Bradbury, Robert Silverberg, Leonard Nimoy, Jimmy Doohan, George Takei, and the lovely Nichelle Nichols. He also never got to meet his all time favorite members of the Marvel Comics bullpen Stan Lee, Jack Kirby and Gene Colan.

It can be said that USA artist Gene Colan's renderings of the sexy, slinky Black Widow made him wonder about becoming an artist.

Rod was first attracted to vampires (femme fatales of course) by the British Hammer series of horror movies, which included *Vampire Lovers* and *To Love a Vampire*, and by certain early Universal films such as the original Bela Lugosi version of *Dracula*.

Rod has a BA in Liberal Studies, a Graduate Diploma in Education and a Master of Arts in Professional Writing.

Rod's short stories have been published in Australia (*Small Suburban Crimes* anthology), New Zealand (*Australian Animals are Smarter than Jack 2* anthology), England (*Voyage* magazine), Russia (*Fellow Traveler* magazine) and the USA (*Cats Do it Better than People* anthology, *Night to Dawn* magazine, *Detective Mystery Stories* magazine). Then there is the more recent NTD book, *Undead Reb Down Under Tales*.

He lives on the south coast of NSW, Australia.

Marge Simon:

Marge Ballif Simon free lances as a writer-poet-illustrator for genre and mainstream publications such as *Strange Horizons, Flashquake, Sniplits, Vestal Review, Flash Me Magazine, The Pedestal Magazine, Dreams & Nightmares, Tales of the Unanticipated, The Magazine of Speculative Poetry,* and the anthologies, *High Fantastic and Nebula Anthology 32.* She edits a column for the HWA Newsletter, "Blood & Spades: Poets of the Dark Side. She is the editor of *Star*Line,* Digest of the SF Poetry Association.

Her illustrated poetry collections include *Eonian Variations,* Dark Regions Press, 1995; *Night Smoke,* with Bruce Boston, *Miniature Sun Press,* 2002 and *Artist of Antithesis,* Miniature Sun Press, 2003. Publications in 2008: *Legends of the Fallen Sky,* with Malcolm Deeley, Sam's Dot Publishing; *Dragon Soup,* with Mary Turzillo, Van Zeno Press, and *Christina's World,* Sam's Dot. Her dark poetry collection, *Vectors: A Week in the Death of a Planet,* with Charlee Jacob, Dark Regions Press, won a Bram Stoker award in 2008.

Along with her solo work, Marge collaborates with her husband, writer-poet Bruce Boston. Their poems and stories have appeared or are forthcoming in *Strange Horizons, Dark Regions, Dreams & Nightmares, Star*Line,* and *Fantasy Commentator.* Website: www.margesimon.com

www.ingramcontent.com/pod-product-compliance
Lightning Source LLC
Chambersburg PA
CBHW050513260626
47157CB00004B/1303